INVINCIBLE WARRIOR

e mail-clad giant appeared from behind the ranks
his men and stalked forward into full view. The
rriors moved back to give the combatants room.

Finn struck swiftly, swinging his sword up beneath Donn's ax-wielding arm toward his ribs. But the
blade rebounded, as if it had struck some unseen,
resilient surface.

Finn staggered back, stunned, as the huge
warrior swung his blade around, the edge sweeping
in toward Finn's neck. . . .

STORM SHIELD
KENNETH C. FLINT

BANTAM BOOKS
TORONTO · NEW YORK · LONDON · SYDNEY · AUCKLAND

STORM SHIELD
A Bantam Spectra Book / December 1986

ISBN 0-553-26191-6

Published simultaneously in the United States and Canada

Bantam Books are published by Bantam Books, Inc. Its trade-
mark, consisting of the words ''Bantam Books'' and the por-
trayal of a rooster, is Registered in U.S. Patent and Trademark
Office and in other countries. Marca Registrada. Bantam
Books, Inc., 666 Fifth Avenue, New York, New York 10103.

PRINTED IN THE UNITED STATES OF AMERICA

KR   0 9 8 7 6 5 4 3

To my son, Gavin,
and my mother,
Ruth Bruhn Flint.

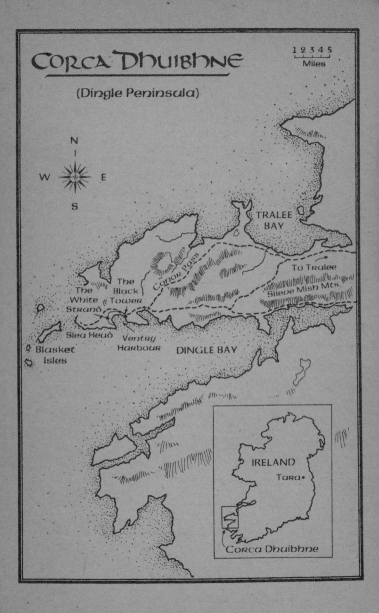

BOOK ONE
THE INVASION

CHAPTER ONE

CAPTIVES

The dragon ships took the little sailing vessel by surprise, sweeping like monstrous sea creatures from the thick fog to strike their prey. Their long, sleek hulls slid up on either side of it, trapping it between. Their serpentine figureheads, eyes baleful, teeth bared in ferocious snarls, loomed high above its tiny deck.

From behind bulwarks lined with brightly painted shields, warriors leapt across onto their victim, shrieking their battle cries. They were burly men clad in coats of mail and pointed, iron caps. Some carried massive broadswords. Others wielded axes with wide, curved blades.

On the deck of the entrapped ship, a much smaller company of warriors prepared to challenge them. These men were taller, but more lean of build. They were elegantly dressed in fine cloaks of bright-dyed wool and silken tunics edged in golden trim. They were helmetless, sporting long and elaborately dressed hair. They set themselves to fight with slim-bladed swords and slender javelins as their attackers swarmed upon them from two sides.

The boarding warriors struck with ferocity. But, amazingly, the small band of defenders was not overwhelmed. For all their delicate look, they fought with skill and savagery, falling back into a tight ring and holding their snarling foes at bay. Bodies began to form a mound about them. Hot blood, steaming in the coolness of the fog, poured across the deck.

Then a new figure appeared amongst the attackers. He pushed through his warriors, a wide, powerfully formed man who towered nearly a head above them. But it was his dress that made his aspect the most terrible. His body was clothed in shimmering coat and trousers of silver mail. His head was fully hidden by a gleaming helmet of several skillfully joined pieces. A cap with golden crest covered the skull; a wide, flaring piece guarded the back of his neck; and hinged side-flaps shielded cheeks, ears, and jaws. The face itself was protected by a mask that had fierce human features. Above a stern mouth curled a mustache extravagantly worked in gold, while a long, sharp jut of nose ran upward to meet arching eyebrows crafted in bronze. Beneath these brows were the dark caverns of eyeholes from which shone glinting eyes that seemed like polished iron.

With no hesitation, he drove into the knot of defenders alone, sweeping around him with a great war ax. Its haft was the thickness of a man's forearm, its blade a broad fan of iron, wider than a man's waist at its cutting edge.

He slashed down the first to face him with a single, sweeping cut and pressed on into the others. One of his adversaries wheeled to strike at him as he passed, swinging down a sword in a hard blow against his exposed shoulder. The blade hit the mail, then turned and slid away as if it had struck solid iron. It left no mark. The astonished warrior was still staring at the useless weapon in his hand when the ax swept back to slash away his head.

The other defenders were helpless against this force. Their formation was ripped open. The rest of their foes rushed in to surround them and they had no more chance to fight.

They expected to be killed. Instead they were only disarmed, their hands bound behind them. Muscular warriors lifted them and slung them across to their fellows in the larger of the two dragon ships. They were herded together in an open spot in the center of the wide deck. Here the helmeted giant moved out from his warriors to stand before them.

He handed his gore-clotted ax to a nearby warrior. With great care he pulled huge, mailed gloves from his massive hands and passed them over too. The curious gazes of the captives were fixed upon him as he raised his hands to the helmet and slowly, slowly lifted it from his head.

The features he revealed were swarthy and crudely handsome. A wide mouth, broad nostrils, and a strong chin, deeply cleft. Prominent cheekbones and wideset eyes beneath heavy, dark brows. A high forehead emphasized by shiny, black hair cut short and combed straight back over a large, high-domed head.

He tossed the helmet to the waiting man and stepped closer to the prisoners. His expression was one of arrogance, of command, of ruthlessness. The cold eyes moved from man to man, their sharp gaze probing, evaluating each. At one man they paused. Clearly this one was older than the rest, his spare face marked by lines about the eyes and mouth, gray strands salting his dark blond hair. The mailed giant studied him for a time, then nodded, a smile tugging up just the corners of his mouth.

"Very good," he announced in a slow, deep voice of satisfaction. "You are what I have sought."

The older prisoner strode forward to confront his captor boldly, his tones angry and indignant.

"You pirates must be mad! It's a great mistake you've made in stopping us." He drew himself up proudly. "I am an emissary of the high king of Ireland, returning from a mission to Alban!"

"I know very well who you are, Glas MacDremen," the other said softly but quite distinctly, each word savored as if he enjoyed the dramatic sound of his own voice. "It is precisely for that reason we have followed you since you left Alban, waiting for just such a chance as this fog to come upon you by surprise. You see—"he smiled again—"I wanted you alive!"

MacDremen's anger had changed to astonishment at these words.

"Alive?" he repeated. "Why? For ransom?"

The warrior gave a low chuckle of amusement. "No, my friend. What I seek is very much greater than that. It is for the conquering of Ireland that I need your help."

Now it was Glas who laughed, but scoffingly.

"Conquer Ireland! Now I'm certain you're mad. What, you and this lot of brigands?"

The man before him abruptly ceased to smile. The mouth drew taut and cruel. The voice took on a chilling note.

"I have forged an army of the finest warriors in all the lands of the world," he said, lifting a hand and clenching it into a massive fist. "Already we have conquered more territories than could be filled by a score of your Irelands."

"By the gods!" one of the younger captives exclaimed in a voice that trembled with his sudden dread. "He must be Daire Donn!"

This seemed to please the tall man. Once more the smile returned.

"Well! I am pleased to discover that my fame has already spread so far! Yes, my friend, I am Daire Donn, High King of the Great World!"

Glas remained unimpressed.

"That is a title you have given to yourself," he said reprovingly. "You are the ruler of no lands. You have taken them only to plunder and destroy. You and your band are nothing more than common raiders!"

"And you think yourself better?" Donn hammered out, his voice rising nearly to a shout. "You, with your ancient lineage and your fine manners and your rich dress?" He leaned down close to Glas, the muscles of his face so tense he seemed almost to vibrate with barely controlled rage. "Well, I have ancestors too," he went on, now in a throaty rasp, "far more ancient than your own, and with a heritage so great you could not begin to conceive of it." He lifted a hand to lay heavily upon the shoulder of Glas. His voice grew more deliberate, more menacing. "So, hear me, my friend: I have long waited to take Ireland, and I mean to do so. I will allow nothing to hinder my success. My invasion will be a complete surprise to your countrymen. But, for it to be so, I must have a place where my warriors can land safely and unknown. It would take a man who has traveled widely, who knows his land well, to tell me of such a place. That man, Glas MacDremen, is you."

Undaunted by the big man's intimidating manner, Glas angrily pushed away the hand.

"Do you really expect me to help you invade my own land? You can't believe me such a fool!"

"Not a fool, Emissary," Donn said with earnestness, "but perhaps a man of some humanity. I think that there is a way you might be persuaded to help." He turned toward the warriors behind him, calling out, "Caisel! Come forward!"

A man moved out from the others, gliding toward Donn with a serpentine suppleness. He had a lean and wiry build, like that of a ferret, with a long body and very short limbs. His face, too, was more a ferret's than a man's. Tiny, reddish eyes were set close to a long, pointed nose. He was nearly hairless, save for a matted fringe about the top of a peaked, bony skull. His mouth was tiny, bowed, open in an avaricious leer that showed small, jagged, and very yellow teeth.

Unlike the others, he wore no helmet or chain mail. His only armament was a small, round shield upon his left arm. It was of a dull gray metal, and was unadorned except for a knob protruding from the center of its front. Set in the knob's end was what appeared to be a gem of blue-white with a smooth and rounded surface.

He stepped up beside Donn, drawing himself to stiff attention.

"Yes, my king?" he asked in a brisk, eager tone. "I am ready to serve you!"

Donn looked back to Glas again.

"This man is Caisel," he explained, "a chieftain of the Lochlann warriors in my army."

Caisel gave a short, sharp bow in acknowledgment.

"He is one of my most loyal and most valuable captains," Donn went on. "Perhaps his greatest value you will see for yourself." He turned to his captain. "Caisel, you know what must be done to convince our emissary to change his mind. Would you show him what I mean?"

"A pleasure, my king," the man said. His tiny mouth stretched in a smile of anticipation as he looked over the captives. He was like a starving man seeing a banquet. "Which one, my king?"

Donn eyed the men of Ireland evaluatingly. His gaze came to rest on a fair and youthful-looking warrior with a braid of flame-red hair.

"That one," he said, pointing.

"What do you mean to do?" Glas demanded in alarm as the chieftain stepped toward the lad and lifted his small shield.

Inside the back of the shield, the hand of Caisel tightened upon its metal grip. A hinged lever set into it was depressed. As it clicked closed, the blue-white stone leapt suddenly to life. A light rose within it and glowed out coldly, like sun reflecting from the ice. In an instant the glow rose to a blinding intensity. Then a beam of white light shot outward from it, streaking across the deck to explode against the young man's chest.

The bolt came so swiftly that the youth had not even time to scream. He was only able to open his mouth before the light burst against him like a gushing jet of water, spreading and enveloping him, playing over his body in waves. He writhed as the strange energy wrapped him. It flickered across his flesh, making a halo about him. It seemed to deflate him, sucking the essence, the substance, the very life, from him. He wasted away, his limbs shriveling, his skin growing withered. The vitality in his eyes was replaced by the cold glow of the blue-white light.

Then, abruptly, the light vanished. Released from its grip, his lifeless body crumpled to the deck, a wasted pile of sagging skin and bones and clothing, no longer even recognizable as a man. The air was scented with the pungent odor of decay and also with that of electricity, as before a thunderstorm on a warm fall day.

Despite their courage, the captives were unable to conceal their terror. Even Glas, taken off guard by this sudden, horrible destruction, stared in open shock.

The killer pivoted smartly back toward his king, beaming in delight at his act.

"Thank you, Caisel," Donn told him, then looked to Glas. "As you see, Emissary, it is not pleasant and, I assure you, it is as painful as it looks. The fate of this poor lad will be that of all the others, one by one, unless you choose to aid us."

The older man had now recovered himself. He faced the mailed warrior with an expression of determination.

"I have never seen greater cruelty or greater lack of a warrior's honor in any man," he told Donn icily. "Nothing—no torture you could inflict on these brave men of Ireland or on me—could bring me to help such a monster as yourself enter our country."

"You sound very noble," Donn answered lightly. "But we'll see how long nobility lasts when your warriors are pleading with you for their lives." He lifted a hand to signal his captain. "Caisel, you may go on."

Again Caisel stepped forward, the shield slowly rising. The captives stiffened, awaiting the beam. The captain's hand began to tighten on the grip.

But, before the weapon could be fired again, there was an interruption.

The sounds of a struggle arose upon the captured Irish ship. The attention of all aboard Donn's vessel went toward it. Soon, a group of the king's mail-clad warriors appeared at the smaller ship's side, two of them carrying a madly struggling figure between them.

It was a very small, very slim figure in contrast to their bulk, yet they still seemed barely able to keep a grip upon it. With great difficulty they got their burden across the bulwarks into Donn's ship and carried it to the waiting king.

As they approached, the figure was seen to be that of a young woman. She was dressed in an elaborately embroidered gown of silk that clung to her, revealing a lithe and slender form. A thick mane of red-brown hair, shaken from its braiding by her struggles, swung wildly about her.

"Look . . . what we discovered . . . below decks . . . my king," one of the warriors got out, finding it difficult to hold on to her and speak at the same time. "We was searchin' for goods and we found her hidden there. A real she-wolf she is!"

Finally exhausted by her hard fight, she now ceased struggling and hung limply, panting, between the men. Donn approached her. The rust-colored hair had been thrown forward across her face, forming a heavy screen that hid her features. He slipped his huge hand beneath her chin and lifted her head. The hair fell aside, revealing a youthful face.

It was boldly featured, more boyish than feminine, with strong jaw and long, straight nose. Not a beautiful face, but clean-lined and definitely pleasing, even twisted as it now was by anger.

Large eyes of a warm brown color lifted to fix on the man who stood over her. No fear showed in them, only the smoldering fire of her rage.

"Animal!" she spat out, and shook her head violently to force his hand away. "Don't you be touching me!"

But Donn kept his grip upon her, voicing a deep roll of laughter.

"Well, a she-wolf she certainly is!" he agreed. "But a comely enough one."

His powerful hand tightened on her chin, holding her head immobile in its vise while he examined her face more closely. As he did, his smile slipped away, replaced by a frown of concentration.

"This face is more than comely," he at last said thoughtfully. "It is . . . familiar!" He turned his head and cast his gaze toward Glas. "It is like your own, Emissary!"

The face of Glas had been frozen into an expressionless mask since the girl had been brought aboard. At these ominous words, however, there came a flicker of fear.

"Ah. I see I'm right," said Donn with satisfaction. "You meant to hide her. You mean to protect her now. She *is* of your own blood. Your daughter?"

Glas did not reply, returning only a stony glare.

"Never mind," Donn said easily. "I see that I am right." He signaled to her guards. "Put the girl down!"

The warriors lowered her onto the deck. She pulled away

from them and stood stiffly, proudly, sweeping a contemptuous eye about at her captors.

Donn moved back across the deck, stopping close to Caisel.

"She will be next," he told the chieftain flatly.

Caisel stepped toward her. But so did Glas.

"Wait!" he said.

Donn fixed him with a hard look.

"You have decided to help me, then?" he demanded sharply. "Speak quickly!"

The eyes of the emissary went from Donn to the face of the girl. She grasped quickly what was happening.

"No, Father!" she protested. "Don't give in to them! It doesn't matter what they do to me!"

"I'm sorry, Cuillen," he told her sadly, his proud spirit seemingly broken, his body sagging in defeat. "I cannot see my only child die." He turned to Donn. "All right. I will show you where your warriors may land."

Donn nodded, his wide mouth stretching this time into a broad grin.

"I thought that might be so," he said, his voice thick with the sweet pleasure of his victory.

The gloating tone returned a certain defiance to Glas. He pulled himself back erect, his own voice taking on a challenging note.

"Don't be thinking that my showing you a place to invade my country will make you its conqueror! You will still have to defeat the Fianna to become that!"

"The Fianna?" Donn repeated in puzzlement. "And what is that?"

"I have heard something of them, my king," offered Caisel. "They are bands of professional warriors. For a fee they have pledged to fight the battles of the lords of Ireland."

"Mercenaries?" Donn said with scorn. "They are the instruments of a people grown too soft and too weak to defend themselves. Ireland is truly ripe. It needs only my hand to pluck it!"

"You are wrong!" Glas countered heatedly. "It is your match that you'll be facing now, Donn. In all the world there are no better fighting men that those of the Fianna, and there is no fiercer leader than their captain, Finn MacCumhal!"

CHAPTER TWO
A DESPERATE MOVE

Finn MacCumhal, the fierce captain of the Fianna of Ireland, lay on his back in the soft grass of the hilltop, humming a pleasant little air and contemplating the shifting patterns in the clouds.

He looked like a very young and very harmless fellow lying there. His bright-green spring cloak and his sword had been laid aside on this warm day. He lay in only his short, white-linen tunic, his lean and muscular body open to the glorious rays of the rare Irish sun. His relaxed features were smooth, the high cheeks and firm chin unbearded, the fair skin unmarked by age or wear. By far the most striking feature of the resting man was the long braid of fine hair, so pale gold that it shone nearly silver in the sunlight.

Close-by on the hill sat another young man, this one wearing both his cloak and his sword harness. The weapon itself was in his hand. He hacked at a log with it in short, sharp strokes that indicated a certain restlessness. Tall, slim, and strong-bodied like his companion, his looks were quite contrasting otherwise. His face was wider, darker, with thick, black brows and a heavy shadow of beard on his square jaws that no shaving could erase. His hair was dark too, a coarse mass of glowing black loosely twisted into a thick plait.

He gave the wood another, harder whack and sighed, looking toward the resting Finn.

"This doing nothing is maddening to me," he said aloud.

Without lifting his head, the fair warrior replied in a slow, easy, and most relaxed tone:

"Be easy, Caoilte. To be alive isn't to be always *at*

something, always moving. We were meant to use all of our senses. Rest easy for a while. Feel the sun. Smell the air." As if to demonstrate, he took a deep breath himself. "Ah, it's scented with the wildflowers of spring. Now, what could bring more pleasure than the likes of that?"

"I've none of your poet's spirit in me," the other replied with a certain disgust, giving the log another chop. "It's a warrior I am, and nothing more. And I'll make no apologies for that! I'm weary of this sitting!" He lifted the sword higher and gave the wood a powerful hack that cut it in two. "I need a good fight to get the winter stiffness from my limbs."

"How can you say that?" asked Finn. "One of the most peaceful springs Ireland has had, and here you are complaining of it. The high king's made no demands on us, and we're free as those drifting clouds to enjoy ourselves."

"It's too cursed peaceful for the likes of me," Caoilte shot back. "Maybe it's time I was seeking some place where they still have need of fighting men."

Finn shook his head regretfully. "It's too full of fire you are, my friend. Why don't you take a lesson from the lads?"

He nodded to one side of the hill where two enormous wolfhounds lay sprawled, soundly asleep. Caoilte looked toward them. They seemed more like great lumps of shaggy, brown fur than animals. Only the slow, rhythmic rise and fall of their bodies showed them to be breathing.

"They look dead, so they do," he responded sharply, "and that I may be myself if there's nothing to rouse me soon."

"We'll be having the wedding of Cael at Almhuin in a few days' time," Finn reminded him. "There'll be some excitement for you then. Lovely women, the finest music, dancing . . ."

"An evening's amusement," Caoilte said, snorting derisively. "And all to celebrate the loss of one more good warrior!" He climbed to his feet and slipped his sword into its sheath. "It's not something that will pleasure me."

"You're too hard, man!" protested Finn. "Marriage is not the end of a warrior's life. And Credhe is a fine girl!"

"A woman is a soggy woolen cloak upon a man's back," the dark warrior said bluntly. "She steals his energy like those clouds dull the sun's heat." He lifted his arms and stretched himself. "That's something I'll never—"

He froze in mid-stretch, listening. The sound of baying hounds and shouting men could be heard, drifting up to them from the thick woods below the hill. The sounds were faint but growing swiftly louder.

"The hunt's turned back this way," he said with some reviving eagerness. "Come on, Finn. Let's be joining it again."

"But we've gone hunting every day since Beltainne," Finn replied in a bored way, still not stirring.

It was true. Since that sacred day, which marked the beginning of the warm half of the year and the emergence of the Fian clans from their winter quarters, they had done little else. Hunting, next to war, was the Fian warrior's greatest passion. But not for Finn on such a splendid day.

Suddenly a large-antlered buck burst from the woods into the open ground below the hill. It dashed around the slope and vanished again into the woods on the far side. As it did, a pack of hounds in full cry, more than fifty, came from the woods in pursuit. Not far behind them came as many warriors, running afoot, their hunting spears swinging, shouting their shrill hunting cries.

Caoilte watched them circuit the hill below and disappear. Again he turned to Finn, his voice now pleading.

"Come on, Finn. It's a magnificent buck, and a good run he's giving them." He was nearly dancing in his fervid need to move. "Look! Even Bran and Sceolan want to go!"

At last Finn lifted his head enough to glance toward the dogs. They were both up, their huge, sinewy bodies taut, their great heads raised, their teeth bared in their obvious desire to run. Still, their loyalty to their master kept them rooted, looking toward Finn with a longing that equaled Caoilte's.

Finn laughed.

"Take them and go," he said, waving them off.

They did not hesitate for a moment. The three sprang down the hill together, reaching the woods at a full run, side by side. Finn watched them out of sight, shook his head in pity for them, and lay back with a sigh of contentment.

"Ah, well, let them have their own pleasure," he said to himself. "I have mine."

He closed his eyes against the golden glare of the spring sun. In the lazy afternoon quiet that now descended, he let himself drift softly away, like the clouds sailing above, into a gentle, peaceful darkness.

From the darkness lying upon the sea, there appeared a line of ships becoming slowly visible with the rising of the sun.

From the thick black, the squares of glowing white sail first winked into being, and then the shapes of the vessels below. All were dragon ships, each with its lean, sleek hull, curling stern tail, and fearsome serpent head. As they moved forward into the spreading sunlight, more came into view to left and right until the gliding vessels seemed to fill the whole curve of horizon. More than three hundred ships, carrying the invasion force of Daire Donn, moved toward the glowing dawn, slipping toward the coast of Ireland in a wide fan.

At the foremost point of this fan sailed the ship of the high king of the Great World himself. He stood in the prow, Caisel close beside him. On the deck behind, surrounded by a ring of guards, were the Irish captives, looking very forlorn and ragged after their days at sea. Ahead, the rising sun threw into sharp silhouette a ragged coastline that seemed to be lifting slowly from the waves. The emissary pointed toward it.

"There!" he said unhappily. "The land you're seeking. You'll find a safe landing for your army there."

Donn peered toward it suspiciously.

"It seems a very rugged coast. High cliffs and no low shores." He glanced sharply around to Glas. "You haven't been fool enough to try some trick?"

"No, no," the man assured him hastily. "Beyond that point of land ahead there lies a great harbor, sheltered from the sea winds. Within it you'll find a broad, level shore called the White Strand. It's a landing place that's been used by raiders and smugglers of goods for many years."

"Is that so?" said Donn, scrutinizing the shore more critically. "And what is this part of your country called?"

"Corca Dhuibhne. A wild place it is, far from the Hill of Tara. Even the power of the high king of all Ireland doesn't reach here."

"Excellent," Donn told him, "—if you speak the truth." He turned to Caisel. "Signal the other ships," he ordered. "Have them heave to here, out of the sight of land. We will sail in alone and see if this place is as our Irish friend has promised us."

Caisel passed the orders and the ship was soon slowing, allowing those just behind to slide up close on either side. He hailed the captains of each vessel, informing them of the plans of their commander. These captains obeyed at once, turning their ships parallel to the coast and slacking sail. The others of the vast fleet followed their lead, and as they slowed, the single vessel of Donn swept quickly ahead, running in under full sail toward the coast.

Donn and his chieftain remained in the prow, surveying the shore they approached with great interest. For the moment ignored, Glas moved closer to his daughter.

"Cuillen, we must talk," he told her softly.

"Father, what is it you've done?" she whispered in return. "I didn't believe that you would really show them a safe landing place."

He glanced about to make certain none of Donn's warriors were paying heed to them. Then he replied:

"I haven't, Daughter. I knew they would invade Ireland with or without my help. Here there may be a chance to warn our countrymen in time to keep these marauders from ravaging far inland. This is the territory ruled by Mogh Nuadat!"

"I know, Father," she said, still confused, "and he has long let brigands use his territory to hide from the law. He even defies the power of our high king!"

"But he still loves Ireland," responded Glas, "and he is married to the mother of Finn MacCumhal. If Nuadat learns this army is coming to conquer Ireland, he will seek help. Perhaps, if a force of warriors can be hosted soon enough—"

He broke off abruptly as Caisel cried out, "Look there!" and lifted a stubby arm to point ahead.

They had passed a headland of sheer, black cliffs. Beyond, a great bay was now opening up. The mountainous lands that thrust out on either side of it seemed to part like the jaws of some enormous beast as they sailed boldly on into its mouth. Once past the tips of these jaws, the whole sweep of the bay was visible. And along its innermost curve, where the steep hills swooped gracefully down close to the sea, the sands of a wide beach glowed softly silver in the dawn sunlight.

"We are very near to shore now," Glas whispered to his daughter. "When we are as near as Donn will take us, we must try to escape. It is our only chance."

She nodded. "I understand. He will never set us free."

"I have spoken with the others," he said, glancing around at the other prisoners. "They know what they must do. But it will not be easy." His tone became more urgent and grave. "So listen, Daughter! If it is only you who can make it, you must go swiftly to Mogh Nuadat. Make him understand how great a danger this army is! Make him send for the Fianna at once!"

"Father, don't speak that way," she said emphatically. "Both of us will make it."

"You are far too sensible a girl to be certain of that," he said, and took hold of her hand. "If something does happen, I want you to know that I love you, my daughter, my only child. I am as proud of you as I would be of any son. I—"

"MacDremen!" came the voice of Daire Donn.

The two looked about to see the mailed warrior turning toward them, beaming in contentment.

"So, my friend, it is as you said," Donn boomed jovially. "A safe place to shelter my fleet, a fine beach to land my men upon, and no one about to challenge us. Excellent!"

"When will we begin the landing, my king," Caisel asked eagerly.

"Do not be so hasty," Donn cautioned. "This invasion must be most carefully done. There must be no mistakes. No man of my army will touch that shore until all are ready, every weapon honed, every plan made." He looked back to the coast, now so close, his face glowing with expectation, his voice throaty with his desire. "Then—*then* we will sweep into this bay, and we will take this Ireland!"

"My . . . king?" Caisel began hesitantly, clearly reluctant to interrupt his leader's reverie. "Ah . . . should we be coming so near to the shore?"

Donn instantly returned to present realities.

"You are right, Caisel," he said briskly. "We cannot risk even some herdsman raising an alarm yet. Have the ship brought about, and smartly, now! We'll return to the fleet."

During this, Glas had been exchanging glances with each of his men. Now, as Caisel passed the orders to bear about, the emissary grasped his daughter's shoulders.

"All right, men!" he shouted to the other captives. "At them!"

The courageous warriors, though unarmed, obeyed their chieftain without hesitation, leaping upon the guards. For a moment they took the mailed warriors by surprise, throwing them back, opening an avenue to one side of the ship.

Quickly Glas rushed his daughter along this avenue to the bulwark.

"Over the side!" he exhorted her.

"No!" she protested. "Not without you!"

Behind them, the guards had recovered and were ruthlessly cutting down the stoutly resisting prisoners. Donn and Caisel were running toward them from the prow.

"You've only a moment," Glas said to Cuillen. "Don't waste the chance I've given you."

"No!" she said again. "I'll die with you!"

The Irish warriors were all down now, their lives sacrificed in this desperate plan. Donn was himself charging in toward the two at the side, his great ax sweeping up.

"You must save Ireland!" Glas told his daughter, and shoved her over the bulwark just as the wide blade descended.

She had a brief glimpse of the ax striking into her father's body as she fell, crying out in her agony as she crashed into the sea.

"The girl's overboard!" roared Donn, wrenching his blade from the dead Glas. "Get her! Kill her! Caisel, use the shield!"

Caisel ran to the side, shouting to the helmsman to put about. The dragon ship answered smartly, pulling into a tight circle. The eyes of the warriors scanned the water's surface intently.

"There! There she is!" shouted one.

The head of the girl was visible not far away, hair streaming out across the surface behind her as she stroked powerfully toward the shore.

The deadly shield lifted. The firing hand of Caisel moved to grip the lever that released the power. The blue stone flared. The beam of light flashed out across the wave tops. It knifed into the sea beside her and the water exploded. The head seemed engulfed in a burst of spray. It slid beneath the surface and was gone.

The dragon ship swept around and over the spot. Warriors lining both sides of the ship scoured the water's surface but found nothing. The ship turned slowly to cut a wide circle in the sea where she had vanished. The scores of gazes searched far about for any sign. But the girl did not reappear.

"She is finished," Donn announced. "We can take no more time circling within this bay. We'll not risk attracting notice. Head out to sea!"

The ship turned away, pointing its fierce head back toward open water, sailing out of the sheltering bay.

But Daire Donn had not acted quickly enough. Already curious eyes on shore had taken notice of the strange actions of the alien dragon boat.

* * *

The tower on the clifftop was a stark, four-storied rectangle of dark stone that seemed almost a part of the sheer, black cliff beneath it.

It sat on the very point of a promontory jutting sharply out to sea. Its landward side was defended by a series of three curving walls of stone, each taller and wider than the height of a man. The tower's seaward face rose right from the edge of the precipice. Far below its base, the ocean's waves crashed and shattered in great starbursts of spray that glowed white against the blackness of the rock.

It was growing dark. The sun's final rays struck a golden hue from the smooth face of the cliff and threw the tower's inner face into deep shadow. Inside the tower's main hall, a servant was lighting the last of the evening torches to keep at least some of the shadows at bay.

The hall was high, square, and of black stone, and might have seemed quite oppressive without its bright and cheerful decor. Brilliantly colored tapestries with intricate designs hung upon the walls. Polished wood furniture and ornaments in gold and bronze glowed with a warm light.

In the center of the room there burned a fire, hemmed in by a circular hearth of stone. Its smoke escaped through a roofhole in the high ceiling. At a long table of planks sat a man and a woman at their meal. A gray-haired steward and a young servingwoman hovered nearby to attend their needs.

The diners were a curiously ill-mated pair. The man was broad and stumpy of body. His face was wide and squat, the eyes narrow and slanting, the nostrils widely flared, the lips both wide and thick. His near lack of chin and his low forehead gave him a toadlike appearance. The woman was slender almost to frailness, with a fragile beauty and fairness like that of a spring's full, pale moon. Her white-blond hair, unbound, was like a flow of molten silver even in the faint torchlight.

The woman was eyeing her dinner companion with an expression of concern. He was not eating, but was instead staring over his food with a distinctly brooding air. It drew his heavy brows and wide mouth downward, only making him look all the more toadlike.

"What troubles you tonight, my husband?" she finally asked.

He shrugged as if throwing a weight from his shoulders and smiled at her. For all his ugliness, it was a pleasant smile filled with a great warmth.

"I'm sorry, Muirne," he said. "I was only thinking about a report that came to me. One of my warriors patrolling the White Strand saw a dragon ship in the bay."

"But the Lochlanner ships often use the strand for their landings," she said.

"This one was acting most peculiarly," he said. "And peculiar things worry me."

"Everything worries you, my husband," his wife reminded him.

"Surely it does!" he agreed. "And how do you think I've survived so long? But this . . . this was something more. This ship was acting quite mad. It was running in circles as if it was searching frantically for something. And the one who saw it swears that there was some great confusion on board."

"You know what a hot-tempered lot the Lochlanners are," she pointed out in a reasoning way. "It might only have been a brawl amongst them over some loot."

"Perhaps," he said, but without certainty.

Their meal continued. A harper and a player of the tiompan arrived to entertain, and their playing returned a more joyful mood to the dining pair. But the music was soon interrupted by the rather abrupt entrance of a guard.

"My chieftain," he said, his look one of puzzlement, "there is a young woman here demanding to see you."

"I'll be disturbed by no one at my meals," Mogh said irritably. "Tell her to return tomorrow to seek an audience, as is proper!"

"But . . . she's very insistent, my chieftain," said the guard. "And she is also very wet! She says that she swam here from a dragon ship."

"Swam?" said the chieftain, exchanging a knowing glance with his wife. "Quickly, bring her in!"

The guard exited, and immediately returned leading the dripping figure of a girl wrapped in a sodden wool cloak, her long hair plastered about a pale face that was nearly blue with cold.

On seeing the two at the table, she moved forward.

"Are you Mogh Nuadat?" she gasped out. She was clearly near to exhaustion, shuddering with her chill. She stumbled but caught herself, pulling her body back erect with great effort.

The couple rose quickly from their table and moved across the room toward her.

"Oh, you poor girl," said Muirne, grasping the girl's arm in support. "You must be frozen. Come to the fire and rest."

"It's hard to believe she's even alive if she swam in from that ship," said her husband. He gestured to the steward. "Get her some wine!"

"No!" Cuillen protested, turning to him. "There's no time . . . no time to rest! You must listen to me! Ireland is in great danger!"

"Danger?" he repeated in disbelief. "It can't be so bad as that, girl."

"My father died to send me here," she said. "There are three hundred ships filled with the men of Daire Donn just beyond the western sea rim!"

Nuadat was stricken. He stepped closer to her, his eyes fixing upon hers, his look intent now.

"Tell me!" he demanded in a growl.

CHAPTER THREE
THE FIANNA HOSTS

As the messenger came into sight of the fortress of Almhuin, he sat back on his speeding horse to gaze in awe at the structure.

The young captain of all the Fian clans of Ireland had only recently completed construction of this grand home. It was situated atop a large, natural mound in the territory where his clan, the Baiscne, held their sway. It was an imposing dun, even rivaling the high king's fortress of Tara. The mound was surrounded by a deep, circular ditch. Atop it was a high wall of upright logs, sharpened at the tips. A wooden causeway led across the ditch and through large timber gates.

Crowning the mound was the main hall itself, an oval-sided structure of wattle smoothly covered in stucco, rising up nearly three stories to the peak of its wood-shingled roof. The whole was washed in lime to a dazzling whiteness. And now, in the low evening sun slanting across the meadows, it glowed a warm gold that made it seem like some palace from a realm of fantasy.

But even such an imposing sight could not slow the determined rider. His mission was far too urgent. He kept his mount moving ahead at a full run, and it soon reached the outer ditch, thudding across the causeway. He only reined it to a stop when he reached the gates, where a brace of warriors barred his way.

"Hello, mate!" one of them greeted pleasantly enough. "It's a great hurry you're in! But, no worry. You've not missed all of it. The wedding ceremony's nearly over, but there's still the drinking to come, and the—"

"I'm here to see Finn MacCumhal," the rider said, breaking in impatiently. "I've a message for him. Very urgent!"

"Easy, lad," the guard said soothingly. "It can't be so bad as that! Not so bad as to be interrupting Finn in the midst of the celebration."

"It is!" the rider countered. "Ireland's to be invaded! I must see him quickly!"

"Invaded?" the guard echoed in shock. His joking manner vanished. "By all the gods, lad! Get in there with you, then!"

He and his companion moved aside and the rider urged his mount ahead. The horse raced up the mound to the level yard and the man dismounted before the huge main hall. As he started toward its open entrance, the sound of a great and joyous cry welled out to him from within.

He stepped through the threshold and into the structure's main room. It was lit brightly with scores of torches set in the roof pillars that ringed the circular space. He paused just within the doorway, looking out across the scene.

The hall was a colorful place, glinting with the polished weapons festooning its beams and rafters, festive with the painted shields and the banners of the Fian clans hung on the timber walls. Hundreds of people jammed its vast floor, a seething, raucous group, raising mugs in toast to the ceremony just completed and the couple just wed. They talked and laughed heartily, filled with the spirits of such an occasion. They crowded especially around the large central fire, where a company of stewards filled mugs from giant pitchers and as many cooks tended the feast being readied there.

The newcomer could see the young bride and groom themselves, on a raised platform beyond the fire. They were dressed richly in glowing green robes trimmed in gold brocade. Beside them stood the white-robed druid who had just performed the wedding ritual. Around them clustered well-wishing friends and clansmen, vying to offer best wishes and congratulations. The messenger scanned this group, finally spotting a tall warrior moving toward the couple through the press. His shining, white-blond hair identified him.

On seeing him, the messenger started forward at once, pushing with some difficulty through the close-packed crowd.

Finn MacCumhal, in the meantime, finally made his way to the couple, with Caoilte and others of his court close behind him. He beamed happily upon them, then raised his tankard, leading his fellows in a toast.

"I celebrate you both. I've seen no finer couple in all my days!"

The newlyweds were, indeed, a handsome and a winsome pair, but were so youthful in looks they seemed more like two children at their first fair than just-married adults. She—small, pert, and sparkling—seemed charged with inexhaustible vivacity, her waves of chestnut hair rippling about her shoulders as she moved. He—tall and spare and with a boyish attractiveness—was more reserved of manner, shy, rather uncomfortable at this attention.

"I am proud of you, Cael," Finn told the young man, placing a fatherly hand upon his shoulder. "This woman you have found is a great treasure. It makes me wish that I could find such a partner for myself!"

As Cael colored with pleasure and embarrassment, Finn turned to the young woman.

"And Credhe! You have been blessed by Danu herself to have wed such a fine, strong warrior as Cael. Though he has been a fighting man of our Fian only a year, he has done us great honor, and I know he'll bring the same to yourself as well."

Behind Finn, unnoticed, Caoilte made a face that expressed his vast distaste for these gushing words.

Finn lifted his mug once more.

"Again, I toast you both," he said, and the others, including a reluctant Caoilte, followed his lead. "May you have all the success and joy that you deserve. All of us wish you that." He turned to look toward the dark warrior, smiling mischievously. "That's right, isn't it, Caoilte?"

"Aye. Aye," the warrior muttered in a grudging way.

"Now, don't you be worrying, Caoilte," the girl assured him with a broad grin. "I'll see to him well. You'll not be losing him."

"What about a song?" Finn said. "We need a fine song to celebrate." He looked about him at the densely packed crowd and called out: "Cnu Dereoil! My Little Nut! Where are you?"

"I'm right here!" said a rather exasperated voice from just below. A hand tugged at Finn's tunic.

He looked down. A man of the size and build of a ten-year-old boy stood there, looking up with an expression of irritation on his tiny, sharp-featured face.

"I've been nearly trampled upon in this," he complained. "It's like pushing through a great, stupid herd of cows!"

"Oh, sorry!" Finn said, not able to repress a grin. "I forgot that you might have trouble. Here." He seized the little man under the arms and swept him up, setting him atop a nearby table.

"A bit undignified for Ireland's finest harper," Cnu Dereoil said, "but it is much better." And he grinned in return.

"Give us a tune then, Finest Harper," Finn asked. "And make it a merry one!"

From a leather bag slung over his shoulder, the little man pulled an exquisite harp, a graceful bow of red yew intricately carved with entwining birds and richly decorated with inlay of bronze and bright enameling. He struck its strings lightly and a fine, high, silvery sound came from them. Though faint, it carried across the entire room, and its note immediately silenced all the talk. As a man, those in the crowd turned toward the harper, listening raptly as he began to strum a lively air. Its spirit appeared to infect them rapidly, for all were soon tapping feet, swaying bodies, or clapping hands to its rhythm. Where space allowed, some even broke out into a spontaneous, abandoned jig.

Through this, the determined messenger made his way, his urgent mission making him immune to the enchantment of the tune. Finally he found his way to the side of Finn.

"My captain," he said to the listening man.

"Not now," Finn hissed sharply without looking around. "The song!"

"But this cannot wait!" the messenger insisted. "My captain, I've come from Mogh Nuadat! Ireland is being invaded!"

This final word broke the spell cast by the tune. Finn swung around to look at the man in astonishment.

"Tell me, quickly," he said in a brisk voice. "But softly. Don't interrupt the music."

The man explained, his ear close to Finn's so as not to be overheard by those around. When he had finished, Finn moved from him to the side of Caoilte, murmuring to him:

"Caoilte, please fetch for me the Dord Fionn. And no questions now, my friend."

The dark warrior was puzzled by the odd request and by Finn's grave expression. But the urgency in Finn's voice sent him off at once, without any argument.

Finn remained, listening to the music, striking a pose of unconcern. But the carefree light had vanished from his face. Now his eyes moved across the many young faces of his gathered warriors and stopped as they reached the pair just wed. They stood close together, arms intertwined, looking up toward the little harper with expressions that radiated their pleasure, their innocence, and their buoyant life. Finn shook his head in regreat at what he must do now.

Caoilte returned to him just as the tune was ending. He handed Finn a large curved horn made of thinly hammered bronze, incised all about with a complex pattern of whorls. Taking this in his hands, Finn climbed onto the table beside the Little Nut.

With the completion of the harper's playing, the attention of much of the crowd had turned away, the rumble of their talk swelling again. But Finn brought their attention back to him with a single blast on the Dord Fionn. For its deep, emphatic note meant to every Fian warrior a call to arms.

"Hear me, my warriors," Finn called out to them. "A painful thing it is to me that I must so violate this occasion of joy and peace, but I have received word from Mogh Nuadat: A vast army of men from many lands has come to invade our country and conquer it. They may already have landed in Corca Dhuibhne!"

A collective gasp of consternation swept through the gathering like a chilling gust of fall wind.

"Yes, men of Fianna," he continued. "And if the story I've been brought is true, there never has come on Ireland a danger to match what is coming against her now. It is great tribute and service we have gotten from the lords of our country, and it is now our time to defend them in return!"

"We will not go back one step from the defense of Ireland, Finn!" one clan chieftain shouted up to him. And his cry was echoed by the other warriors, their voices joining in a single, defiant roar.

"Then, we must prepare to move quickly," Finn told them. "Every man—go now, gather your equipment, host your clans, spread word to everyone. At dawn we must be ready to march!"

At once the gathering dissolved, the warriors and their families streaming out of the great hall with a loud clattering of excited talk. Finn climbed down from the table, calling out to a thick-bodied man with curling hair and flaring mustaches so brilliant red as to seem like flames licking about his face.

"Fergus of the True Lips!" Finn hailed.

The man moved instantly to his side.

"Aye, my good captain?"

"You are my most trusted messenger. You must see that word of the hosting reaches all the Fian clans. Send your best companions to those in Leinster and Munster. But carry the word into Connacht yourself. I must be certain that Goll MacMorna knows of this swiftly."

"I will see to it, my captain," Fergus assured him, and bustled away, clearly already eager to be on the road.

Finn now turned his attention to the newlyweds.

"It's truly sorry I am that this has come now," he told them with regret.

"Don't think of it, my captain," Cael returned, striking a properly heroic pose, speaking with great boldness and determination. "If war has come, I am ready to go. It is our greatest duty, after all!"

"Good lad!" Finn said, repressing a grin at Cael's boyish zeal. Then he glanced at Credhe and added hurriedly, "Well, I'll leave you to your lady now. I'm afraid our time—and yours—is very short."

He moved away, Caoilte and the others of his retinue close about him, already engaged in a heated discussion of what preparations must be made. For the moment the young couple was left alone in the quickly emptying vastness of the room. Awkwardly, Cael turned to his bride.

"I . . . I do have to go, Credhe," he said. "You understand that, don't you?"

"Of course I do," she told him, smiling reassuringly. "You are a warrior and you must fight with the Fian. It was your strength and your honor and your bravery that brought me to marry you!"

"Oh, I am glad," he said, smiling in relief. "I only thought that . . . well, we've only just been wed. We've had no time together, and now I must be leaving you. . . ."

"Oh, that!" she said lightly. "Well, we'll have our time. I've no intention of our being parted now. I'm coming with you!"

"Coming with us?" he echoed in astonishment. "But, Credhe, you can't!"

"I can," she countered firmly. "Many of the clansmen take their families with them on the long campaigns."

"That doesn't matter. I will not let you go. It's a very hard life, and it can be dangerous." He put a hand upon her shoulder lovingly, his voice filling with concern. "Credhe, I don't want to risk you."

"Nonsense," she said briskly. "I can see to myself quite well, and I've been trained in the healing arts. I'll be very useful." She put her hand caressingly upon his arm, her earnest gaze meeting his. Her tones now grew both tender and stubborn. "My love, please understand me! Nothing will keep me from going with you. Not even the Battle Raven, Morrigan herself, will part us now."

He looked down into her deep green eyes, seeing the determination sparkling in them. Finally, he nodded.

"All right," he agreed reluctantly. Then he grinned. "After all, it was for your own spirit and strength and will that *I* married *you!*"

"What? Not my beauty?" she said in mock dismay.

"Only the greatest beauty in all of Ireland," he told her and, with a laugh, swept her up in his arms.

There, in the center of that vast, now-empty hall, the two hugged one another closely. They turned slowly, as if dancing to a music of their own, for that fleeting moment together, as one being.

A force of men moved across the green countryside. Several thousand warriors formed an enormous wedge, a living quilt whose patches were the colors of the many Fian clans. At the head of each band of warriors was its chief, on horseback. His fighting men largely moved on foot, but kept on at a steady and rapid pace, without sign of weariness.

At the point of this wedge rode Finn MacCumhal himself, with the greatest champions of the Fian clans close on either side. Caoilte rode at Finn's left knee, and young Cael at his right. Just before him, their massive heads reaching as high as the horses' muzzles, trotted the two Irish wolfhounds, Bran and Sceolan.

Behind this van there moved a long train of vehicles, largely four-wheeled carts, that strung out for some way, creating a spear-pole for the striking point formed by the warriors. In one of the carts, Credhe rode with other women of the clans, now clad in a plain and serviceable gown of brown wool. Not far away on either side of her, large herds of cattle could be seen, driven ahead by scores of herdsmen. They would supply the meat and milk for a marching force that no longer had leisure time to hunt for game.

So this army, like some enormous, single creature, marched swiftly forward, across a valley thick with spring grass and up a smooth hillside onto a high crest that allowed a view of the countryside for a great distance.

"There!" proclaimed Caoilte, pointing ahead to where a ragged line of blue-gray peaks was visible. "The mountains of Slieve Mish."

"Good," Finn pronounced. "We'll need a day to skirt them, and then one more onto the peninsula."

"My captain," said Cael, pointing to the northwest of the mountains, "—look there!"

Finn and his warriors turned their attention that way. A large, moving object had just come into view, crossing a hilltop and starting down its slope. It was traveling swiftly to the south and west and would clearly come into their path soon. And it took no guessing to know that this other shifting patchwork of bright colors was an army like their own.

"Could it be the invaders come inland so soon?" Cael asked with some alarm.

"I don't think so," said Finn, staring searchingly toward them. "They're coming from the wrong direction for that. They're coming from Connacht, not off the peninsula."

"How could it be the Fianna of Connacht?" Caoilte said in a skeptical tone. "They couldn't be here so soon."

"We'll take no chances," Finn said. "Cael, pass word to our chieftains to be ready to form battle lines at the sounding of the Dord Fionn."

Cael went swiftly about his task, and soon the army was moving forward with a bit more caution, fighting men gripping their weapons a bit more tightly in readiness.

It was clear now that the other host was aware of them as well. For as it came into the path of Finn's army, it slowed to a halt and waited for their approach.

For what seemed long moments, the tension mounted as the two forces came closer and closer together. Then it was Caoilte who first made an exclamation of relief and joy:

"It is the Connacht Fians, surely," he cried. "I see the Clan na Morna colors at the front."

"You're right," Finn confirmed, peering toward the men in the green and black patterned cloaks. "Goll MacMorna must have hosted them with amazing speed!"

Even as he spoke, a mounted group of the MacMorna warriors started forward, riding to meet them. Finn passed orders for his force to halt, and trotted forward with his own clansmen.

The one riding at the head of the Morna clan was an impressive man. He held a broad, rock-hard body proudly erect upon his horse. His face was large-featured, craggy like a worn cliff-face. A deep scar cut like a rivulet down across his left forehead, halving his thick brow, disappearing beneath a leather patch strapped across his eye, reappearing upon the high cheek below. The remaining eye—a glittering dark bronze—was as clear and sharp as that of a bird of prey.

Beside him rode another, much like him in general feature, but much thicker, with a swelling belly and a softer, rounder face. Thick mustaches hung in flamboyant waves about his mouth, but only a few, lonely strands, combed carefully as if they could cover the vast, naked expanse, clung to the top of his skull.

"Goll MacMorna, welcome!" Finn greeted the one-eyed man as he reached them. "It is hard to believe that you could host so quickly."

The leader of the Connacht Fianna shrugged.

"You told us we must hurry, and we did," he answered matter-of-factly.

"My brother had us rousted from our beds, he did!" grumbled the stout warrior. "It was too bloody early!"

"It's always too early for you, Conan," Caoilte noted sarcastically.

"Watch your words, Firbolg," Conan darkly returned.

"My brother's mood is bad," Goll put in dryly. "His stomach suffers greatly on these long marches. He isn't able to eat often enough."

Conan scowled at this rebuke, but made no reply.

"We are all hosted, then," Finn said, looking over the force that had accompanied Goll. "I have all the clans of the Leinster and Munster Fianna with me."

"Then, if this risk is so great as you've said, we should be delaying here no longer," Goll said. "These enemies of Ireland may be already on our shores."

*   *   *

Goll MacMorna was right.

Even as they spoke, sleek dragon ships were grounding on the White Strand, and the hordes of Daire Donn were pouring from them onto the smooth, clean beach.

CHAPTER FOUR

FIRST CLASH

All up and down the curving line of shore moved the thousands of invading warriors. They were thick, covering the white sands like vermin swarming upon the pale flesh of a corpse.

Daire Donn, his helmet carried by an attendant who moved close behind him, jumped down from his own ship into the surf and waded in. Caisel, already overseeing things on shore, met him as he strode up onto the strand.

"Things are progressing well, my king," the faithful lieutenant announced. "Our companies are nearly all ashore and the encampment has been established."

"Have we been discovered yet?" Donn asked.

"The coast about the bay seems completely deserted. We have posted sentries on the hills above the strand, but they have seen no one. Shall we send patrols inland?"

"No!" Donn said sharply. "If we are still unnoticed here, so much the better. Why raise an alarm any sooner than we must? Every extra moment we have to prepare makes our task the simpler. Are the forges set up?"

"Nearly, my king. The smiths will be at work by dusk."

"See that they are. And be certain every fighting man is well supplied with stores. We must have food and extra weapons in sufficient quantities to sustain us on a long campaign. There'll be no stopping for forage or plunder this time, and no time to waste having our armorers shape or repair weapons once we begin to move. No, we'll stop for nothing until all Ireland is at my feet and every one of her fine warriors is dead!"

"Yes, my king," said Caisel, even he looking a bit surprised by the extent of Donn's ruthlessness. "But . . . the men . . ."

"Will do as I command," Donn finished brusquely, fixing his lieutenant with a chill look. "They know that I will give them their riches. Just see that every one of them is ready, fed, rested, and well armed, Caisel. I plan to march from here in no more than two days!"

"Yes, my king," Caisel replied obediently. "And where are we going, my king?"

A slow, cruel smile lifted the corners of Donn's mouth. He looked to the east, his gaze fixing on the hills.

"To the very soul of Ireland," he said slowly, tasting every word. "To Tara!"

The combined forces of the Fian clans moved briskly ahead.

They skirted the wide range of Slieve Mish and entered more rugged lands beyond. A narrow roadway took them across a rocky gap, their forces strung out, snaking up the steep hillside until they crossed the high point and were looking out across the entire tip of the peninsula. The land swooped down and outward to the west, a great shoe of Ireland thrusting out into a blue-gray haze of sea.

The column wound down from the pass onto the smoother lowlands. There the van reformed, and moved swiftly on. They traveled close to the sea's edge now, on their left the steep black cliffs, on their right the emphatic swells of meadows studded thickly with gray, weather-scoured rock. Except for some grazing sheep—dirty white fluff-balls scattered across the stony fields—the land seemed deserted of life.

"No sign of invaders yet," commented young Cael thankfully.

"If there ever were any!" growled Conan. "If we weren't roused from our beds for nothing!"

Now, ahead, a fortress came into view. First just the square black tower thrusting up starkly from the edge of the cliffs, then the triple curves of its defending walls.

"It's the fortress of Mogh Nuadat," Finn told his companions. "We'll learn more now."

As the army approached the small peninsula on which the fortress sat, the gate in its outermost wall opened. Several horsemen emerged, galloping out toward them. At the head of a small troop of his warriors rode the squat chieftain. Beside him, her unbound auburn hair flying behind her, rode Cuillen.

"It's Mogh himself," said Caoilte.

"And a young woman," Cael added. "Is it your mother, Finn?"

"No!" said the Fianna captain, examining the approaching girl with curiosity.

Nuadat's band soon reached the army, falling in beside Finn's company. Nuadat wasted no time on the niceties of greeting.

"Thank all the gods you've come so quickly," he said. "It may be there's yet time to stop this invasion before it's begun!"

"Where is this force, Mogh?" Finn asked.

The chieftain pointed westward, up the coast.

"They began their landing several days ago, on the White Strand," he explained. "They had a slow time of it, for the weather's been bad—praise Manannan for that! But now my scouts are reporting that they're all ashore and making preparations to move. They could be heading inland at any time."

"Then we must move to the attack now," Finn said with determination. "We must push them back into the sea before they can come off the strand."

"Their forces outnumber yours by quite a bit," Nuadat offered. "From the reports, I estimate them to be three times your own."

"The Fianna have faced greater odds before and won," Finn told him with confidence.

"Well, you won't find Daire Donn so easily defeated!" the girl said sharply.

Finn's attention turned to her. Her young face was set and grim. He looked to Nuadat.

"And who is this girl?" he asked.

Nuadat opened his mouth to reply. But before he could, she urged her horse forward, pushing past him, closer to Finn.

"I am Cuillen, daughter to Glas MacDremen," she answered in a grand manner. "And you may address yourself to me!"

"Very well, Daughter of Glas," Finn said, eyeing this audacious woman with some wonder. "Just what part is it that you have in this?"

"It was I who brought word of these invaders to Mogh

Nuadat," she told him, drawing herself up proudly. "It was I who caused you to be summoned here!"

"Summoned!" Finn repeated, clearly disliking this choice of words.

"What she says is true enough," Mogh hastened to put in. "She was a captive of the invaders. She escaped and swam in from their ship to warn us. She is a very brave and—"he paused to glance at her—"and a very determined woman, so she is."

"That I can believe," said Finn, giving the slender girl a more searching look. "Well, it seems we owe you much. But right now we must be moving ahead, and quickly. Every moment gives our enemy a greater advantage."

He started to turn away, but she pressed her horse in even closer.

"Wait!" she said in a commanding tone. "You can't mean that you intend to attack them without knowing anything about them? Without any plan?"

His expression revealing a growing exasperation, Finn exchanged a glance with his comrades. Young Cael shrugged. Goll raised a disapproving eyebrow. Caoilte grinned quite openly at his captain's discomfiture. None rushed to assist him.

"The fighting men of the Fianna are well trained for battle," he told her, a bit more sharpness in his tone. "Please believe me, we are well able to handle this."

"Oh, are you?" she said with obvious disbelief. "Well, I mean to go with you, just to see!"

At this, the last of Finn's patience quickly ebbed.

"That you will not!" he told her brusquely. "You will return to the fortress!"

"You cannot order me!" she shot back, striking a haughty pose. "I am the daughter of Glas Mac—"

"I've no care who you are," Finn said, cutting her off. "We have no time for this. Mogh, *take* her back to the fortress. We're going on."

He turned away and spurred his mount ahead, away from Nuadat's group.

"Wait!" she shouted, starting after him. But, at a signal from Nuadat, two of his own warriors rode up on either side of her, grabbing her horse's reins.

"You can't do this!" she raged, growing red-faced, but the warriors ignored her, turning her horse away as the force moved on past, the clanking of their arms drowning out her indignant screams.

Finally she subsided, staring after the departing Finn in helpless frustration.

"I am sorry," Nuadat told her, "but this is for the best."

"By great Danu," she said, "I have never met a man with such an impossible conceit!"

"I've found that Finn MacCumhal can usually accomplish what he says he will," Nuadat assured her.

"Can he?" she said. "Well, I can only hope he doesn't lose all Ireland trying to prove so this time!"

An iron spearhead thunked down into the soft sand of the beach, joining a cluster of others embedded there. The muscled, sweating armorer who had just completed it at once seized up another metal point, still hot from forging, and fitted a wooden shaft into its socket.

Around him in the huge forge area, scores of other smiths labored feverishly, their massive forms moving eerily in the smoke and steam of their fires, their constantly working tools creating a great, clanging din, the light of the fire and the streaming sparks casting a bloody glow upon the deadly objects of their skill as they added to the store.

The inventory of extra weapons was already vast, the swords and spears and axes and shields filling racks and forming huge, bristling mounds around the armorers. Daire Donn looked over the work and nodded in satisfaction.

"Enough," he announced to the collection of company leaders with him. "But we'll leave them at it until we depart. No battle will be lost for the lack of one sword more!"

He turned away and started up the beach, his captains close behind. They moved through stalls set up to dole out bread and dried meat and vegetables to lines of warriors, past companies of men drilling to hone their fighting skills, around mounds of more equipment and supplies still being unloaded from the ships.

Already the sands of the White Strand—so long pure, so long undisturbed by other than a crab or a seabird—had been defiled by the invading horde. The garbage and human waste of the thousands stained the beaches, filling the air with their stench. The trampling feet had destroyed the smooth white-ness, crushed its fragile life. Hundreds of fires left scorched, black pits, like open wounds.

"Things are proceeding well," Donn grudgingly admitted to his underlings. He stopped at the center of the encampment, by a pavilion erected as his headquarters. He turned slowly, casting his eye about him at the bustling force. Then his hard gaze moved to the captains and his voice grew sharper. "But it must go even faster. I'll wait no longer to strike into Ireland!"

"But, my king," Caisel said pleadingly, "the weather . . ."

"No more excuses!" Donn boomed. "I will march now! Every man be prepared to leave at dawn even if the blizzards of winter come upon us! Bring me the map!"

An attendant bustled into the pavilion and quickly emerged bearing a long, tubelike object. This Donn took and carefully, lovingly unrolled, laying it out upon a nearby trestle table. The company leaders gathered around, looking at the object with curiosity and awe. It was of a material so thin as to be translucent, smooth and of a yellow-white darkening to a golden brown about the edges. It was square, each side as long as a man's arm. Across its surface was a complex diagram in blacks and browns and greens.

"I've never seen the like," one captain said softly.

"What kind of a strange parchment is this?" another ventured. He put out a hand to feel, but drew it back swiftly at a sharp glance from Donn.

"This is an ancient chart, created by my ancestors centuries ago," the high king proclaimed grandly. "It is very precious to me, and very fragile. It was my intent to have our late emissary, Glas MacDremen, guide us to Tara. Now we must rely upon this." One hand moved across the surface of the chart. "Here we have all of Ireland laid out—its every stream, every hill, every wood. And here—"a thick finger jabbed down onto a spot near the eastern coastline—"here is Tara." He lifted his head to turn a determined glare upon the others. "With this chart's help, my captains, we will find the easiest route to our dreams!"

The group at once fell to a discussion of the most practical ways to move. Donn pointed out the features of the land and his officers argued over problems of march, risks of ambush, best encampments.

But their gloating talk of the best means of ravaging a submissive Ireland was interrupted by a distant cry. And soon after it came another sound: a rumbling, rushing sound like the roar of an angry surf, swiftly increasing in volume.

The men about the chart looked up. One of the captains pointed toward the rim of the hills above the bay.

"My king, look!" he shouted excitedly.

Donn's gaze lifted to the spot. A dark mass, like a liquid spilling over the edge of a cauldron, was now pouring toward the White Strand. As he watched, it flowed swiftly downward, spreading as it descended. Now the flood was recognizable as thousands of running men, sunlight glinting on their weapons. And the roaring could be identified as the rumble of their feet, the clank of arms, and the combined sound of their shrill battle shouts.

"So," Donn said tightly, "they have come against us sooner than I thought. But that only means that their destruction will also come all the sooner." He held out a hand. "My helmet!"

The attendant holding it leapt to his side, presenting the gleaming object to him. He pulled it carefully on, dropping the fearsome mask down across his face. He took up his massive battle-ax, gripping it in both gauntleted hands.

"Pass the word," he ordered his captains. "Host our companies at once! We will go to meet our visitors with a gift of iron!"

The officers rushed away to muster their warriors. But alerting the army was hardly necessary. Already most of the others had seen the advancing force. The alarm had been raised through the entire camp, and the men had thrown down their burdens, abandoned their tasks, and taken up their weapons, quickly forming into their companies. In moments the enormous mass of fighting men was moving across the strand like a tide surging up the sandy beach, rolling to meet the other great wave cascading down.

The two forces roared toward one another, warriors all at the run now, eager to be ahead, to be first to strike their foes, brandishing weapons, faces bright with battle-light, shouting their individual war cries. The Fianna reached the edge of the wide beach first, pouring down from the rocky hillside onto the sand, spreading left and right to form a line matching Donn's army in width.

Finn and his chieftains, all afoot now, moved at the front of their clans. But Donn followed his warriors in, trudging slowly forward in his mail suit, shouting orders and exhortations, watching the movements of both forces with a keen, evaluating eye.

The two armies closed. They were like two great thunderstorms meeting head-on, charging the air with the energy about to be released.

They struck. And it was with a single, sharp, lightning stroke of sound, a crash of thousands of spears, shields, axes, swords, and armored bodies slamming together. Following this came a less deafening but continuing din of rattling arms punctuated by shouts and cries of agony.

The battlefront quickly became a confused tangle of men as warriors sought opponents to challenge in single combat. Finn himself worked his way steadily forward, using his great fighting skills to hew a path deep into the forest of enemies with his blade. Behind him moved a wedge of his clansmen, forcing the cut wider. And on either side, other clans followed their captains' leads, pressing forward.

Both the ferocity and the tremendous battle prowess evident in the Fian attack were a surprise to the invaders. Though greatly outnumbering their attackers, they began to fall back slowly toward the sea.

On one flank of the battle, Caisel kept back the Fian men with energy blasts from his shield. But they refused to retreat before him, bravely diving in at him despite his fearsome weapon. Finally, his triggering of its power produced no effect; no beam flashed from the blue stone. So, as the next Fian warrior charged in, he swiftly retreated, leaving his warriors to be driven back as he made his way out of the press and ran to Daire Donn.

"My king," he gasped, "this is impossible! There are so few, yet they are pushing our men back. They have no fear!"

"Use your shield against them," Donn said. "Blast through their ranks!"

"My king, I have tried!" he whined. "But you know the power of it is limited. The energy has been drained. I must wait for the ancient Fomor magic within it to restore its strength!"

Donn now turned and swept his gaze across the forces battling before him. His scanning eye identified the strongest point of the Fian attack to be near the center of the line, where a spearhead of Irish warriors had thrust deep into the body of his army.

"These fighting men are indeed a challenge," he said. "It

will only make their destruction all the sweeter. And I will see
to it myself!"

With that he moved forward, plunging into the middle of
his ranks, pushing through the massed troops toward the fight.
His warriors, seeing their leader himself joining in, took new
heart. They ceased their retreat, following him forward.

Now the warriors ahead realized that Donn was coming,
saw the gleaming helmet moving above the mass of heads.
They pulled back, leaving the way clear for him to reach the
Fian men.

Finn MacCumhal, slashing his way forward, was surprised to suddenly find himself without opponents to challenge. He gazed around in puzzlement at the invading
warriors as they drew back.

"What's happening?" he asked aloud.

And then he saw.

The mailed giant appeared from behind the last rank of
his men and stalked forward into full view. The Fian warriors
around Finn exchanged astonished looks, and in the faces of
some showed the first sign of fear. Even Finn swallowed hard
at the sight of the huge, glittering figure.

But the young captain did not hesitate in challenging this
foe, lifting sword and shield and moving to attack. His own
warriors, like Donn's, moved back to give the combatants
plenty of room, clearly content to let their leader deal with this
menace.

Finn struck first and swiftly. In a bold move he dove in,
swinging his sword in a hard blow that would have been
enough to sever Donn's right arm, had it struck home.

But the big man reacted with a startling speed for one
who appeared so ponderous. He swung a gauntleted hand up
to simply slap the sword away, at the same time swinging the
ax in his other hand around in a hard, return blow.

Finn threw his shield up and out against it, shoving the
heavy blade aside. Even so, the ax struck with a power that
jarred Finn's whole frame and rattled his teeth. He staggered
back, nearly losing his balance. Then he recovered, doggedly
moving in again, but more cautiously this time.

He feinted to his left, drawing the mailed giant that way.
Then he leapt back to the right, swinging his sword up beneath
Donn's ax-wielding arm, toward his ribs.

This time Donn made no move to protect himself,
allowing the blade to land in a slashing blow across his side.

Finn expected to see his sword cut through the thin links of the chain mail and into the flesh beneath. Instead, the blade rebounded, as if it had struck some unseen, resilient surface covering the mail. The keen edge of the blade never touched Donn, made no mark on the metal rings.

Finn stared at the spot, his expression startled. Though it was only for an instant, his hesitation almost cost him his life. For the huge warrior swung his blade around, parallel to the ground, the edge sweeping in toward Finn's neck.

Finn barely ducked away in time. But as the speeding weapon *whoomped* over his head, he drove his sword, point forward, right for the hollow of Donn's chest.

The weapon slammed home, all of the power of the muscled young captain behind it. But it didn't penetrate! Again it seemed to strike some invisible layer that turned it away. The blade slid sideways, passing harmlessly along Donn's ribs. Finn stumbled forward, dangerously off balance.

Then Donn struck again, this time bringing down his ax in an overhead blow meant to cleave Finn in twain. Desperately Finn threw up his stout, iron shield to deflect the blow. The ax struck the very center of the metal circle, but was not turned aside. The edge slashed through the plate as if it were only thin leather, barely missing Finn's arm behind it.

Donn yanked back, jerking the impaled metal circle from the Irishman's arm. As the shield came free, its iron rim slammed hard against Finn's temple. Stunned by the blow, Finn staggered backward and fell heavily to the ground.

With a sharp flick of his ax, Donn tossed the shield away. Then he stalked toward the fallen warrior, a towering figure, his gleaming mail ablaze with the afternoon sun against his back. He loomed above Finn, the great war ax lifting for its final blow.

CHAPTER FIVE

A NEW STRATEGY

Seeing the plight of their captain, the Fian warriors now charged in, regardless of the danger, blocking the mailed giant's advance. He struck out at them as they closed in around him. His own warriors rushed in to join him, and a melee erupted.

Behind it, other clansmen of Finn seized the fallen man and carried him back out of the press, up onto the higher ground just above the beach. Caoilte and young Cael, seeing their comrade's limp body being removed from the fight, moved swiftly to him.

"Is he dead?" Cael asked anxiously as the dark warrior bent over Finn, examining him closely.

"No real wounds," Caoilte announced. "Just a good knocking about."

Below them, the tide had turned against the Fianna. The loss of their leader had drawn much spirit from the Irishmen, while the entry of Daire Donn into the fight had galvanized his own men to a greater effort. It was now the invaders who were pushing forward, forcing the Fianna to retreat slowly, step by step, back up the strand.

Finn groaned. His eyes opened and he sat up, looking about in a puzzled, disoriented way. He shook his head as if to clear its fuzziness and looked around again, more sharply now, taking in the scene below and his two comrades.

"Caoilte, what—what's happened?"

"You were down. Our clansmen pulled you out."

"I've got to rejoin them!" Finn said urgently and climbed

to his feet. He staggered badly as his head lifted and would have fallen had not Caoilte grabbed him in support.

"You can't go back in there now, Finn," he said. "You're not recovered yet!"

"But, our warriors . . ." Finn began to protest.

"Just let them see that you're alive!"

Caoilte and Cael helped Finn to clamber onto a rocky ledge thrusting up from the ridge above the beach. He stood upright, waving his sword above his head.

"Clan na Baiscne!" he called out.

Below, his clansmen looked up to see their captain still living. A shout went up from them, spreading quickly to the other clans along the front. At once their efforts redoubled. They struck back savagely, countering the strength of the invaders with their own. On the left flank, Goll MacMorna heard the cries.

"The clans of Leinster have not lost heart!" he called to his men. "Clan na Morna, rally to me! We will retreat no farther!"

His warriors formed up around him, stabilizing their end of the line. The whole army of the Fianna dug in, stubbornly refusing to back up another step. The advance of Donn's men stalled against such resistance.

Even the powerful Donn himself was blocked. He tried to press forward, his ax slashing warrior after warrior from his way while the weapons of the Fianna showered upon him like rain—and with as little effect. Still, his efforts could no longer move him forward. His courageous opponents kept always in his way, each one struck down replaced by others, forming a solid, unyielding front.

From above, Finn spotted Donn, pointed him out to his comrades.

"There! There is that armored monster," he said emphatically. "He's got to be stopped!"

Before Caoilte or Cael could prevent him, he turned and jumped down from the rock. But his balance was still impaired and his strength not restored. He landed awkwardly, his legs nearly giving way. Caoilte leapt down beside him, taking an arm again, both to steady and to restrain the rash warrior.

"And do you think you're going to stop him?" Caoilte asked Finn. "You're barely able to walk!"

"Somebody has to try!" Finn told him. "Did you see the slaughter he's doing on our warriors?"

"Finn, you couldn't defeat him when you had your full

strength and your full wit about you. If you go against him now it'll only be to die, like the rest. Finn, listen: He can't be killed! There's some magic protecting him. And we need you alive!"

"We can't just watch him," Finn said in anguish.

"I'll not let you do anything else until you've recovered," Caoilte said, his eye meeting Finn's with a determined light.

"Caoilte," Finn began in an angry tone, "you are my closest friend, but—"

"Never mind!" came the voice of Cael. The young warrior was still atop the rock, now pointing excitedly toward the beach below. "Look there! He's left the fight!"

The two clambered up to join him again. They could easily pick out the gleaming figure of the enormous man as he moved back from the battle line.

Donn had been approached again by Caisel and other officers, who had forced him to leave the fight and listen to their pleas.

"What is it!" he demanded angrily. "I must keep on!"

"It's useless, my king," Caisel said, shouting to be heard above the battle-din. "We're no longer winning! They will not retreat! Our men are nearly exhausted! We must withdraw!"

"No!" Donn snarled fiercely, shaking his bloody ax. "We must finish them!"

"We cannot do it today!" the other boldly argued. "Look, my king, it is nearly sunset now!"

Donn glanced about. The sun was indeed low, its rays just beginning to redden the clouds rimming the sea's horizon.

"The Fianna are badly hurt," Caisel went on persistently. "Let us regain our strength and regroup our companies. Then we can finish them! Otherwise we will only waste more men!"

This cold wave of logic finally seemed to quench the flames of Donn's battle-fury. The helmeted head nodded.

"Very well," he growled reluctantly. "Order the withdrawal. But we must show no weakness. It must be done slowly, as a single force. And the man who shows his heels to these Irishmen will answer to me!"

The officers emphatically expressed their understanding and departed to alert the companies, leaving only Caisel behind.

"That one there," said Donn, using the ax to point out the trio on the rocks above. "It was that green-cloaked one who rallied them."

Caisel peered up toward the white-haired youth.

"That must be their leader," he guessed, "—the one called Finn MacCumhal."

"He is the one they saved from me," Donn said in measured tones. "Next time, I'll be very certain to finish him."

Soon a horn sounded within the invaders' ranks, quickly echoed by many others all up and down the front.

On the rocks above, Caoilte turned to the object of Donn's hatred with an exultant look.

"They're ordering a withdrawal!" he said.

"Should we pursue them?" Cael asked his captain eagerly.

"No," Finn said quickly. "We've stopped them. It's all we can hope to do for today. Pass the word to the clans to let them go."

Cael was off at once, bounding deerlike from the rocks onto the beach. Even as he rushed along the line to spread Finn's word, the invaders were beginning their withdrawal, their warriors disentangling themselves from the melees, breaking off their combats, backing slowly away to rejoin their fellows in solid ranks, finally separating entirely from the Fianna line.

The hard-pressed fighting men of Ireland, themselves nearly exhausted by their battle, watched their foes depart with a certain relief. Between the opposing forces, a strip of beach now opened, widening slowly as Donn's men drew back toward their encampment. The sand there was no longer white, but was stained by a rust-brown swath of blood, littered with the bodies of dead and wounded men.

A vast silence descended upon the grim scene of battle, making the groans of the hurt clearly audible. The sun, now well down within the horizon's clouds, washed all the scene in an appropriate blood-red.

Finn looked down upon the carnage and shook his head sadly.

"This may not be so easy as we thought," said Caoilte.

"I tried to warn you," Cuillen said with heat, leaning over the table to thrust her face closer to Finn's. "What's happened is your own fault!"

She pulled erect again and stalked away, leaving the young captain to stare after her, momentarily nonplussed by her attack.

The others gathered in the hall of Mogh Nuadat's tower

seemed shocked by the outburst as well. The chieftains and druids of Finn's army filled a score of tables ringing the central fire. They sat speechless or exchanged looks of perplexity. But an outraged Caoilte moved quickly to his captain's defense. He rose from his seat beside Finn, his voice threatening.

"Now, look here, girl, whoever you are! We've kept these invaders from leaving the strand—"

"Only that?" she interrupted, wheeling upon him. Her defiant stance and her sarcastic tone made it clear she had no fear of him. "But I thought the great Fianna were planning to drive them into the sea! A simple task, to hear your so-mighty captain speak of it."

Caoilte stalked around the table and toward her, face tightening with his anger.

"No one has the right to be attacking Finn MacCumhal this way!" he told her.

"No, Caoilte," Finn said, raising a hand in a restraining gesture. "She is right."

The dark warrior swung back toward him, expression now surprised.

"Right? What do you mean?"

"I did underestimate their strength, and badly," he admitted regretfully. "Because of me, many warriors died uselessly today. And many more will die before we've won this time."

"But you couldn't know," Caoilte reasoned in a defensive way. "The Fianna have often faced greater odds. Our oath forbids us to fall back before odds less than nine to one, and that oath we have always kept."

"Against ordinary warriors, maybe," put in the girl. "But not against warriors like those of Daire Donn."

Caoilte looked around to her in exasperation.

"Just who was it who invited you here?" he asked.

"I did," came the quiet but clear voice of Finn's mother, Muirne. She and her husband, Mogh Nuadat, sat at the table reserved to the tower's lord, who was hosting this meeting.

"It is as much her right to be here as your own," the fair-haired woman went on. "Her bravery and her father's death have earned it for her."

This reminder was delivered gently, but the rebuke was clear in it. Caoilte, flushing in irritation and chagrin, subsided, resuming his seat.

"All right, then," Finn said. "Young woman, I am sorry. I

should have listened to you. Now, will you tell us what you
know about this Daire Donn?"

Somewhat mollified by this apology, the girl moved to the
center of the circle, near the fire, and swept an evaluating gaze
about at the ring of grim faces. Apparently assured by this that
she had everyone's fullest attention, she began:

"Very well. While my father and I were captives on the
ship of Donn, we learned much from his men. It was not
difficult. They bragged often to us about their great conquests
and their invincible leader, Daire Donn.

"The warriors who have joined him are the hardest and
the most skilled that he could gather from all the lands of the
great world. They are cruel, ruthless men, brought to him by
the promise of great wealth. But there is more. There is also
the belief that with Donn, they can never be defeated."

"Why?" asked Finn.

"They said there was an aura of power, of command, about
him that seemed to cast an enchantment upon them. They felt
that they could do anything. And the proof of his power to
them was in the fact that he could not be beaten."

"You saw Donn yourself," Finn said. "Did you feel this
aura?"

She considered, then responded carefully.

"I felt . . . something. It may be strength, but it may be
madness too. He's surely obsessed to a near-madness by his
desire to conquer Ireland. But, madness or strength, his spirit
does infect them all. Each one would die for him, with great
happiness. I am convinced that so long as he leads them, you'll
not defeat them unless you destroy them utterly."

Finn looked to the stalwart and impassive face of Goll
MacMorna.

"You are my greatest chieftain and my finest strategist,"
he said. "What do you think of this young woman's words?"

"I feel that I must agree with them, my captain," Goll
responded in his even, matter-of-fact tone. "I have never seen
warriors fight with the courage and the strength of these. And
it was most certainly this Donn who rallied them to push us
back by simply entering the fight himself." He allowed himself
the indulgence of a faint smile. "It would seem, my captain,
that his talent for inspiring men is as great as your own."

"Thank you for that, my friend," Finn said. "But just how
strong is his force? Can we still defeat them?"

"I would say no," Goll answered bluntly. "If their spirit

stays as it is, we can do no better than hold them here, and not indefinitely at that. They will slowly wear us down. And with their greater numbers, they will eventually break through us. It is only a matter of time."

"Do you others agree?" Finn asked, looking around the circle of tables.

There were reluctant nods and voices of assent from the others in the assemblage.

"It comes back to Daire Donn, I'd say," put in Mogh Nuadat. "If he could be killed, both the reason for and the spirit of his army would collapse."

"Then he must be challenged," Finn said with determination. "And I must be the one to do it."

"If you fight him, you will die!" Caoilte said bluntly.

"But if there is even a chance to kill him," Finn reasoned, "if there is any chance to save the lives of our fighting men, it must be taken. And you know the risk must be only my own!"

"I know that if anyone could defeat him, it would be you," Caoilte agreed. "But there is no chance. No one can win against that monster."

"In that, he is right," the girl emphatically agreed. "Donn is protected. His warriors bragged of that as well. They said the aura generated by his strength makes him invulnerable."

"There is clearly more than brag in their words," commented Goll. "The experience of Finn and the others who challenged Donn would seem to prove that he cannot be harmed. And his war ax has properties beyond the normal, as well."

"Magic?" asked Finn, and looked to his druids.

"It could be so," responded a gray-haired man in robes trimmed with rich silver brocade. "Such a thing is not unknown to us."

"And what about a way to counter it?"

The man's expression grew uncomfortable. He exchanged glum looks with the other white-robed druids at his table before replying unhappily:

"That, I'm afraid, we do *not* know. We have conferred, but none of us has any notion of what the magic could be, or what kind of spell might counter it."

Finn looked around the ring of tables at the other leaders of his clans. Their faces expressed their own dismay and sense of helplessness.

Taken by frustration, Finn slammed a fist angrily upon the table.

"I will not accept that, my friends! I will not! We cannot just keep on an uneven battle, watching our warriors die, waiting for them to wear away our strength. There must be something—some way to deal with this Daire Donn!"

"Perhaps there is," came the voice of Muirne.

The eyes of the gathering turned toward her.

"What do you mean, Mother?" Finn asked.

"The knowledge of your own druids might not be of help to you, but there is one druid whose knowledge might just be great enough."

Finn's eyes widened in surprise. His voice came sharply.

"Mother, you're not meaning—"

"Your own grandfather," she finished. "Yes, my son, I'm afraid that I do."

"Not Tadg!" protested Caoilte. "That bloody sorcerer's done everything he could to destroy us!"

"Are you speaking of the chief druid to the high king?" said Cuillen. "But he disappeared from Tara over two years ago."

"He chose to . . . ah . . . retire from public life," Muirne said with a faint smile. "He lives in seclusion now, but I know where he can be found."

"He would surely be the one to help us, if anyone could," said the gray-haired druid. "He had magic powers like no other in Ireland. It was said he even had the secrets of the Tuatha de Danaan themselves."

"But he'll not use his magic to our good!" argued Caoilte. "He has nothing but hatred for the Fianna!"

"Perhaps," agreed Muirne. "But it is all Ireland that is at stake in this, and he has a love of Ireland, as we all do. It may be that he can be convinced to help." She looked to Finn, her voice growing more earnest. "However, my son, it must be you and I who go to him. He'll see no others, and no others have any chance of making him listen. Do you understand?"

"I do," Finn said. "But the Fianna are engaged here. How can I leave them?"

"Your presence here will make small difference in your eventual defeat," she pointed out. "Your visit to Tadg could be your only chance for victory."

"It would seem the most reasonable way, my captain," Goll put in. "We can hold them here for a time, and perhaps a long one. But I believe that your best possibility for saving lives would be for you to seek help from Tadg as swiftly as you can. I agreed that you should leave at once."

"But our warriors . . ." began Finn.

"They will be most heartened by the knowledge that you are seeking a way to give them victory," came Goll's simple, logical reply.

"Well, I like none of this myself," said Caoilte darkly, "but MacMorna does make sense, Finn. Finding a way to challenge Donn fairly will be the most useful thing for the Fianna and for Ireland."

Against the force of so many arguments, Finn was forced to give in.

"Very well," he said. "It looks as if I'll be the one to go."

"But not alone, Finn," Caoilte hastened to add. "I say it must be done, but I've no trust for Tadg. You and your mother will be needing some escort."

"We can't be taking a troop of warriors away from the fight to escort us," Finn said.

"No troop," his comrade responded with a grin. "Only one man will be enough. And that's myself."

"Two, perhaps," Goll put in. "It would seem more reasonable to send a man of the Clan na Morna as well as one of the Baiscne. One more good fighter should be a fair escort."

"And who have you in mind?" Caoilte asked.

"My brother, Conan, is among the best of our skilled fighting men."

They all looked toward that warrior. The balding man had sunk into a heavy doze, quite undisturbed by the discussion in the hall, his stout body sagging down into his seat.

Caoilte gave a sardonic laugh and turned to Goll.

"Now," he asked, "are you certain that you can spare him?"

CHAPTER SIX
THE JOURNEY BEGINS

"It will be for you to lead the Fianna now," Finn said to Goll MacMorna. "And there's no better man to do it."

He finished stuffing the last of his spare cloak into his leather traveling bag and turned to face the dour chieftain. The two were alone in the living quarters of the tower while Finn completed his preparations for the trip.

"I understand, my captain," Goll told him gravely. "I will, of course, do all I can to hold the invaders on the strand."

"More warriors is what you'll need the most. I'm sending Fergus True-Lips to Tara to ask the high king to send us any help he can."

Goll raised an eyebrow to register his disapproval.

"You know my feelings about that, my captain," he told Finn. "It is our duty to defend the people of Ireland. It is our honor that says we must do it alone. To ask for help . . ."

"I know, Goll," Finn said regretfully. "It hurts me to do this, as well." He fixed the other with a determined look. "But this is the fate of all Ireland we're speaking about. Her defense is more important than the honor of the Fians. You do see that."

Goll returned his look with one of stubborn pride. Then, finally, he nodded.

"Yes, my captain," he said in a resigned way. "It is the only reasonable course. But there will be few enough with the courage or the fighting skills to join us."

"Every man will give us a bit more time," Finn said. He pulled closed his bag and slung it over his shoulder. "Well, let's go down."

They went down the narrow stairs from the living quarters and through the now-empty main hall to the doorway that opened into the courtyard. This area was faintly lighted by the first rays of the dawn sun. It was the scene of much activity.

Grooms readied horses for the travelers, loading them with supplies. Caoilte and Conan carefully examined their weapons, strapping shields and extra lances upon their saddles. Muirne stood at one side, in deep conversation with Mogh Nuadat. By the tower's main door sat the two great hounds of Finn, one on either side, stiffly erect, heads up, looking like two statues of gray stone there. But as their master stepped into the yard, they came to life, falling in close behind him.

Goll left Finn to approach his brother and engage him in talk. Finn went to his own horse and began to fasten his bag upon its back. As he was finishing this, he noted the girl Cuillen leading a horse from the stables. He turned to watch her as she stopped the mount and began to strap a leather traveling pouch like his own onto its saddle. He left his horse and strode up behind her.

"Just what is it you're doing?" he demanded.

"I'm going with you," she said flatly, not looking around from her work.

"That you are not!" Finn retorted hotly. "If anything, you will leave Corca Dhuibhne altogether. Go back to your own fortress or your courts, where it is safe."

"I have no intention of doing such a thing," she said firmly, going right on with her fastening.

"It's too dangerous," he said.

"Your own mother is going," she pointed out.

"My mother has to go. You don't."

"That I do," she countered. "Someone who represents the will of the high king must see that the protecting of Ireland is properly carried out."

"Are you saying that you don't trust me to do that?" he asked in astonishment.

Her bag securely tied, she now turned to face him, hands on hips, expression proclaiming both challenge and stubbornness.

"No, Finn MacCumhal," she said bluntly, "I do not trust you! I've heard about you in the high king's court. I know how you've flaunted the high king's rules and laughed at the laws of Ireland. I know how you've tried to steal away Conn's power by making your Fianna the strongest force and demanding great riches for your fighting skills. I know that what you want most is for your own good, not that of the high king. Oh, yes, Finn MacCumhal, I've heard all about you. I didn't believe all the tales could be true. But now that I've met you and seen your towering arrogance, I do believe."

As Finn endured this harsh tongue-lashing, his face reflected his growing indignation at her charges. Now he retorted angrily:

"There is no love lost between myself and the king. I've made no secret of that. But this has nothing to do with Conn. It is Ireland that I have given my oath to protect, and no man is more loyal to that oath than Finn MacCumhal."

"You tell me so," she said, clearly unconvinced, "but someone of the court of the high king must see to the truth of it. It would have been the duty of my father. Now it is mine. There is no one else here of unquestionable faithfulness."

The volume of their discussion had risen with its heat. Now the others in the courtyard had stopped their own talk to shamelessly eavesdrop.

"I don't know who you think you are," Finn told her in a voice filled with the tension of his outrage, "but you've gone too far in questioning the honor of all the Fianna. I am the leader here, not you, and it is my order that you do not go!"

She threw her head back haughtily. Her voice was ice.

"You have nothing to say about it. I am the daughter of an emissary of the high king. I have assumed his power. It is with the authority of Conn himself that I speak. If you are so loyal as you claim, you must obey. You are his servant."

"I'm servant to no man," Finn thundered now, all his patience swept away by this last affront. "And certainly to no impudent girl. If you mean to force me to it, I'll have Mogh Nuadat keep you here by force—lock you away if he has to! And you know well enough that I'll make my threat good!"

Her manner changed at this, the proud look slipping into one of dismay, the voice taking on a desperate note.

"No!" she said. "You can't! My father's last words to me were that it was my duty to save Ireland. I must fulfill his duty for the king. I must go!"

The tone of great emotion in her words seemed to act powerfully upon Finn. He looked into the eyes glowing brightly with their intensity. His own expression softened, the anger in it fading.

"I understand," he said more gently. "All right. You can go."

"Finn!" Caoilte began in protest.

"No, Caoilte," Finn told him flatly, cutting him off. "No arguments. She's earned the right to come with us if she chooses, and there's an end to it!"

He wheeled away from her, strode back toward his own horse, and noted his mother watching him. She gave him a smile and a nod, clearly approving of his decision. But as he passed by Caoilte, the dark warrior murmured:

"That, my friend, was a very great mistake!"

Behind him, the girl stood staring after him, clearly nonplussed by his sudden agreement. Then, as if to cover any momentary lapsing of her poise, she briskly resumed the checking of her horse's gear.

Soon, all the horses were ready, all arrangements completed. Finn's party prepared to depart. They made their final good-byes, Mogh Nuadat giving his wife a hearty but gentle hug of affection and admonishing Finn in stern tones:

"Take very good care of this woman now, my lad. She means a very great deal to me." He looked upon her with a vast tenderness. "My whole life, in fact."

"She means the same to me," Finn assured him.

She laughed, kissing Mogh lightly upon the cheek.

"Have no fears, my love," she told him. "How could I be in danger in the company of Ireland's finest warriors? And of these magnificent hounds as well." She stepped forward, placing a hand on each of the massive heads.

The two looked up toward her, mouths stretching in what unmistakably seemed grins of pleasure, as if they understood her words of praise.

With all the farewells said, the five mounted.

"If good fortune rides with us, we'll be returning to you in a few days' time," Finn said to Goll. "And bringing some means to stop Daire Donn."

"We will hold until then," Goll assured him in a firm way that meant that Fianna would die to the final man before one invader stepped off the strand.

The company started away, riding out through the gates of the triple wall and down the promontory away from the fortress. Finn and Caoilte were in the lead, the two hounds trotting beside them. Behind them rode Muirne and Cuillen, and following them, bring up the rear alone, rode a sullen and withdrawn Conan.

The little band moved at a good pace, crossing the peninsula, pushing their strong mounts up the narrow way that crossed the high Conor Pass. The rocky mountaintop was fogbound, the thick gray-white masking the steep hillsides above and filling the depths below so that the riders seemed to glide eerily along, suspended in space on a narrow segment of road. But as they crossed the top of the pass and dropped down again, the fog was left behind—a white, solid-looking mass impaled upon the sharp peak.

Now they entered a country where the line of riders became tiny figures, almost lost beneath the immense waves of land rolling up on either side of the roadway that wound its way through the trough between. Smooth, grassy hillsides swept upward dramatically, so vast that the shadows of entire clouds—sharply defined by a bright, spring sun—were visible creeping across their faces like vast creatures bent on devouring them.

By evening, these hills had diminished in size to something not so overwhelming, with softer ridges thickly covered by forests and brightened by the colors of spring-blooming flowers. It was a more comfortable land, less awe-inspiring than the rugged coasts and mountains of the peninsula, but no less beautiful in its own way.

They made a first camp on the shore of a lake tucked into an arm of the hills that gently enfolded it. The light of a nearly full moon shivered upon a dark surface softly caressed by a faint, warm breeze. Behind the camp, the trunks of pines soared up, forming a natural palisade, making the little band of travelers seem quite secure.

They sat by the fire grouped as they had traveled: Finn and Caoilte at one side with the dogs lying nearby, Muirne and Cuillen opposite, and, forming the third point of the triangle alone, the always-grumpy Conan. So rotund was the balding warrior that he might have been a boulder dropped by the fireside if not for the fact that he was eating with enthusiasm and a great deal of noise. It was not a pleasant sight.

"It's a good distance we've come today," Caoilte said to Finn. "If we can keep up the speed, we should reach this place your mother described in three days more."

Finn didn't reply, and Caoilte noted that his comrade wasn't listening. His gaze was fixed thoughtfully on the girl sitting across the fire. She was absorbed in a game of fidchell—a board game of strategy using pieces of silver and gold. Her head was down, her eyes glowing, a curl of her luxuriant hair, burnished to copper by the red firelight, brushing the fair, smooth cheek.

Muirne looked up from the game and also noted the direction of his gaze. With great casualness, she stood and, leaving Cuillen to ponder her next move, stepped to fetch a cup of fresh water from the leather pitcher beside the fire. She knelt down close beside her son as she did so, murmuring so softly the younger woman could not hear:

"You might try being friendly to her, you know."

Finn's gaze shifted from Cuillen to his mother.

"She's made her feelings about me clear enough," he said.

"You could still talk to her," she persisted. "Anyone can be changed."

Finn looked to Caoilte. The dark warrior shook his head.

"I wouldn't waste any more time on her," he advised.

"She's been through a great deal," Muirne pointed out in a more scolding way. "And you, my son, are being childish."

"I am?" Finn said in an offended tone. "And what about her?"

"Is this the great Finn, the wise and generous leader of the Fianna, speaking now?" she asked. "Well, I'll say not one more word about it. But you know what I think!"

With this motherly jab, she left him, moving back to the girl.

"Good work," Caoilte murmured supportively to his friend. "We've got to be certain this female whelp knows her true place."

Finn nodded, but his gaze still strayed back across the fire again, fixing on the pleasant lines of the girl's face.

Sunrise fell upon a party already well under way. They moved into lands that became smoother and flatter as they progressed. Forests gave way to broad meadows. Herds appeared, the fat cows grazing peacefully, drifting upon the seas of lush, spring grass.

They rode as before, with Finn and Caoilte at the front. But often Finn glanced back toward the girl riding at Muirne's side. She appeared to have fallen into a mood of depression, not speaking, barely even glancing around at the passing countryside.

Finn's mother grew aware of his glances and caught his eye. She emphatically mouthed the words "Talk to her!" and jerked her head sideways at the girl.

Finn gave a sigh of resignation. He moved to rein his horse around. But Caoilte, seeing his move, put a hand upon his arm.

"Don't!" he warned.

"What do you mean?" asked Finn.

"I know you. I can see what you're thinking in your eyes. It'll only cause trouble. You know how you are."

"How I am?" repeated Finn, at a loss.

"About women."

"And just how is that?" Finn demanded.

"Oh, come on now, Finn," Caoilte said impatiently. "You know what they do to you as well as I. A pretty face, big eyes of green or brown or blue—it doesn't matter. You're quite done!"

"I can see to myself well enough," Finn told him with irritation and yanked the reins around, turning his horse back toward the women.

Caoilte rode on, looking after his comrade and shaking his head.

When Muirne saw Finn starting back toward them, she urged her own mount ahead and pulled away from one side of the girl as Finn pulled in at the other. Though obviously aware of this maneuvering, the girl rode stolidly on, not even glancing over at him.

"How are you?" he ventured as a start.

"Why do you ask?" she responded coolly. "I don't see you asking after the others' welfare."

"Look, I'm not really so bad," he said persuasively. "And we are on the same side in this."

"Are we indeed?" she said, clearly still skeptical. "I've told you I heard the tales of you. You are a hard and ruthless man who hates the king."

"Just how well do you know our good King Conn?" Finn asked.

"I've grown up in his court at Tara. My father was a valued adviser and always spoke well of him."

"People aren't always as they seem," Finn said. "It may be he was a good man to your father and to you, but he has not been kind to us."

She looked at him in astonishment at that.

"Kind to you?" she said disdainfully. "And why should he

have to be so? It is your task to do his will. He needn't waste his time in kindness to those who serve him!"

Once more her abrasive manner swept away Finn's attempt to master his irritation.

"Our task, is it?" he shot back. "There you've shown your true self again. You're like every other pampered aristocrat, treating us as if we were your slaves. Well, we are not! Can't you see that?"

"I can see that all you're to be concerned with is your obedience to the high king and your duty to save Ireland," she said brusquely, unmoved by his words. "Now, you can just get on with it. And don't waste any more of our precious time in your foolish attempt to be friendly to me!"

"You've no worry about that!" he roared.

He spurred his horse ahead, rejoining Caoilte, who now rode with Finn's mother. Muirne looked at his anger-reddened face with concern, while the dark warrior grinned broadly.

"Wipe off that smile," Finn barked at him. "And as for you, Mother," he said, turning to her, "if you truly love me, next time ask me to wrestle a mad boar weaponless instead."

CHAPTER SEVEN
IN THE DRUID'S LAIR

The little band left the sunbathed meadows of the open land, entering a thick and mysterious wood.

The trees seemed to creep about them stealthily as they plunged into its depths, growing ever thicker until they were swallowed up by the shadows. Great trees arched above, their twining branches so thick with growth that they shut out the sunlight, creating a strange twilight at noon.

Within this realm, the outside world seemed distant, its normal sights and sounds shut off. Here the night creatures ruled. Stalking beasts crept through the underbrush. Owls and bats swept through the trees above. Their howls and shrieks echoed hollowly in the woods.

And as the riders forged ahead, there were other things.

Ever-stranger creatures—creatures with peculiar, unnatural shapes impossible to really identify, so quickly did they move through the confusing interlace of light and dark—slunk or whisked or fluttered through the shadows. And the wood itself became ever more desolate, ever more ominous.

Areas of marshy land edged the narrow pathway the band followed. Here, dead and rotting trees thrust up like bony hands, and fallen logs lay in the festering black ooze like reptiles waiting for their prey to come too close.

"Keep to the roadway," Muirne warned. "There are places treacherous here. One could quite easily . . . disappear."

This warning was carefully heeded by everyone, even the unsociable Conan, who now rode a great deal nearer to the rest, a hand on his sword hilt, his head turning constantly from side to side.

From behind a rotting stump, a figure almost humanlike but covered in long fur shot up. Its strange, elastic face—a grotesque parody of a man's—stretched as it voiced a high-pitched gibbering. Then it was gone again.

"What in . . . ?" Caoilte began.

"Look there!" said Finn, pointing ahead.

An enormous object, like a ball of unwashed wool shorn from a dozen sheep, was rolling down the path toward them, as if blown along by some nonexistent wind. But their presence seemed to startle it, for it turned abruptly and bounced into the trees.

From somewhere close, there arose a long, undulating, and very mournful howl, drifting and dying away.

Cuillen rode her horse closer to that of the older woman. Looking around her with clear repugnance for the ghastly wood, she asked:

"Is this really the place where your father lives?"

"It's very near," Muirne replied. "I know it's not a pleasant place, but it's well suited to its purpose."

"Its purpose?"

"To discourage visitors."

A shadowy something that had to be extremely large suddenly *whoomped* over them, just above their heads. All of them ducked.

"Well, I can certainly see how it might do that!" Caoilte remarked dryly.

"It is most surely a . . . strange place for a druid of such renown to live," Cuillen wondered aloud. "Why would he leave the court of Tara to come here?"

"It was not really done by his own choice," Muirne told the girl with a little smile. "Father had some difficulties. Others thought it best that he . . . retire from the world for a little time."

"But what difficulty was it?" the girl asked, openly curious now. "There were no stories of it in the court. He simply vanished."

Caoilte twisted about in his saddle to face the women.

"Tell her the truth of it, Muirne," he urged. "Tell her how Tadg conspired with Conn to keep Finn from his rightful place as leader of the Fianna. How he abused his magic powers trying to destroy his own grandson for the high king."

"You are a liar!" the girl shouted. "How dare you make such a hateful charge against such a fine man, you traitorous hound! The king could never act in such a way. And if he did feel Finn should not head the Fianna—something I have never heard the slightest rumor about—it would only be because he felt Finn not worthy!"

"So, the high king is always the perfect one, is he?" Caoilte fired back. "Well, just let me tell you—"

"No more, Caoilte," Finn told his companion. He shot a chill glance at the girl. "We'll not be accused of slandering the king any further."

"But—" Caoilte began.

"Just let it go!" Finn said more sharply.

Caoilte gave a sigh to vent his frustration and subsided. The girl, nodding as if she'd won another battle, turned back to Muirne.

"Even if your father did abuse his powers," she said, clearly still curious about Tadg, "he was a high druid. Who could make a man of such great powers give up his position and come here?"

"Even great druids must answer to someone," came Muirne's vague reply.

The darkness had been increasing for some time. Now there was a canopy of black above them, and the shadows seemed to crowd in on either side. But lights flared and flickered in the dark. And ghostly tendrils, like illuminated whisps of smoke, drifted up amidst the menacing shadows of the trees.

The girl violently brushed away something long and soft and damp that brushed across her face, giving a little shriek of disgust.

"This is a terrible place," she said, her voice betraying her apprehension. Then, realizing she had revealed weakness, she pulled herself stiffly upright on the horse, adding with great force, "It could certainly be quite frightening . . . to some."

Muirne placed a reassuring hand on the girl's arm.

"My dear girl, just ignore it!" she said lightly. "Most of it is only illusion anyway—effects created by magic to frighten away idle travelers who might venture too close. Nothing of any real substance. After all, most magic, even the most powerful, is only trickery and show. Just fog and smoke that a puff can blow away."

She looked ahead carefully. Then her voice took on a warning tone.

"But some magic can still be dangerous. Listen to me

now, all of you. We're very close. From here on, I must lead you in. You must stay near to me and watch me constantly. If you lose sight of me, even for an instant, you might go Astray."

"What's 'Astray'?" Cuillen asked.

"Another bit of magic to protect Father's home. One moment you might be headed directly for it, and the next you would find yourself heading in another direction, very far away and quite lost."

All the others, including Conan and the dogs, pulled into a tight group behind Muirne, watching her intently. They moved on through a corridor of enormous trees, like columns on either side, branches arching up to form a vaulted ceiling high above. Then the way ahead opened up, and they rode out of the corridor into a small clearing.

It was circular, ringed by a high and solid wall of trees that cast the enclosed area in deep, gloomy shadow. In the very center of the clearing rose a mound of earth, barren and rocky. It rose up little more than twice a man's height and was perhaps thirty yards in circumference. Despite its rugged exterior, its symmetrically rounded shape made it seem unnatural.

"We are here," Muirne proclaimed. "You can dismount. There's no need to worry about going Astray now."

They climbed from their horses just before the mound and stood looking at it.

"Is this it?" asked the girl, her tone reflecting some disappointment. "Is this where he lives?"

"It's not very impressive for a high druid, is it?" agreed Muirne.

"Better than that old scoundrel deserves," said Finn.

"Hush now, Son," his mother scolded. "Remember, we are here for his help."

Caoilte had by now made a circuit of the mound and returned to the others, looking much puzzled.

"How can this be a dwelling?" he said. "There's no way to get into it."

"I will show you," Muirne told him.

She walked to the side of the mound where a boulder larger than herself thrust out from the earth. She laid her hand upon a knob of black stone in its center. Instantly it began a shuddering, and a hairline split, running vertically through the stone, began to widen. With a groaning sound, the boulder parted, each half swinging sideways and back, revealing a passageway leading into the mound's shadowy depths.

"I should have guessed," said Caoilte.

"All right then, everyone," Muirne said brightly, "shall we go inside?"

The others moved forward, but Conan stood rooted, staring at the passage with open uncertainty.

"This is more than strange enough," he said slowly.

They stopped to look back at him.

"Well, the bear speaks!" said Caoilte in surprise. "Don't be saying that the great champion of the Morna clan finds a cave threatening?"

"I'm saying no such thing," Conan growled back. "I . . . I only think that someone should stay with the horses in such a place."

"And I think that you are right," Finn said in an understanding way. "Conan, would you be the one to stay here on guard?"

"That I would," the big warrior answered, clearly relieved.

"You'll be safe enough alone," Muirne told him. "We're close to the mound. Its defenses will protect you as well now."

So, leaving Conan, they passed through the opening in the great stone and entered the tunnel beyond. Conan watched them as they disappeared, one by one, into the darkness. When the last was gone from view, the entrance groaned closed, swallowing his companions. He moved toward the boulder, lifting a hand to gingerly touch the smooth face of the stone. The crack had completely disappeared. He looked around him at the ominous black circle of the trees and gulped loudly. Then, despite Muirne's assurances, he drew out his sword. Gathering up the reins of all the horses, he stood, on guard, gazing around him suspiciously at the woods.

Meanwhile, inside the mound, the others were traveling down a narrow passageway hewn through the living rock. A faint light from far ahead shone along it, the glow reflecting from smooth, stone walls shiny with moisture.

"We've been walking so long!" the girl said after a time, her voice echoing along the tunnel. "We should have gone through the entire mound by now!"

"So we should," said Muirne.

"But that's not possible, is it?" Cuillen asked in wonder.

"So it is not," Muirne agreed.

"I understand," the girl said. "More magic."

Muirne only smiled in reply.

Abruptly the tunnel widened out, its ceiling rising steeply as well. As the little band came into this larger space, they stopped quite quickly. For the way ahead was blocked.

A creature filled the entire passageway, its body scraping the walls on either side, its head reaching up nearly to the ceiling. It was a most-peculiar-looking beast, like the parts from a dozen animals ridiculously mismatched. Its enormous body was bloated, covered with a thick, gray, and very wrinkled hide. This was rather inadequately upheld by thin, scaled, and clawed feet, like those of a bird. And tiny feathered wings, clearly incapable of lifting such a hulk, fluttered upon its back. A long, reptilian tail curled about its feet, lashing nervously. A long, slim neck rose to a tiny head that supported a muzzle far too big for it. Small red eyes peered over the length of nose, and long tusks curled out sideways from a wide, drooping mouth, looking more like a flamboyant mustache than dangerous weapons.

"I'm not certain whether to fight or laugh," commented Caoilte, staring in amazement at the preposterous thing.

The head suddenly swooped down toward them on the flexible neck. The big mouth opened and it voiced a high-pitched shriek of irritation.

"Fight, I think," said Finn. "Dogs, defend!"

He and Caoilte drew swords, stepping out before the women. Bran and Sceolan crouched down on either side, snarling.

"There's no need for that," Muirne told them. And before the men could stop her, she had pushed between them and was striding fearlessly toward the beast.

"Labran!" she called to it in a scolding way. "It's Muirne. Give this over, and quickly, now!"

Like a being of snow beneath a blazing sun, the creature began to shrink away. It lost shape, collapsing into a mound that dwindled, evaporating into the air. In moments, nothing of it remained. Where it had stood, there was now revealed the figure of a man.

He was slender and narrow shouldered, clad in a long tunic brightly striped in green and yellow topped by a baggy cloak of severely clashing green-and-purple plaid. His looks were pleasant and open, if somewhat foolish in expression, his face lean and long of feature, with pronounced nose and pointed chin. His coloring was fair, his hair long and fine and very light.

He pushed back a lock of it that had fallen across his high forehead and shuffled his feet, saying in a rather sheepish way:

"I never could fool you, Muirne. How did you know it was me?"

"And who else would create such an absurd beast?" she said, laughing. She went to the young man and gave him a hug which he returned, now smiling warmly himself.

"Sorry, Sister," he told her earnestly. "You are surely welcome here."

Muirne turned, an arm about him, to present him to the rest.

"This is my brother, Labran," she said. "He's a . . . a companion to my father here."

"Ah, say the truth of it, Muirne," he said good-naturedly. "I'm the old man's caretaker, is what I am. And it's a very lonely life, I can tell you. So, I gladly welcome any company."

His eyes fell upon Finn, and he moved forward eagerly.

"Why, you must be my nephew, young Finn," he said with delight. "You've Muirne's hair exactly, so you have. I've heard much good about you." He took the warrior's hand, clasping it heartily. "It's very glad I am to meet you at last."

"And I to meet you," responded Finn. "It's little enough I know about my mother's family."

"Just as well," Labran said with a broad grin. "For we're a most peculiar lot, that we are."

"This is Caoilte," said Muirne, introducing the others, "and this is Cuillen, both good friends of mine."

Labran nodded at the dark warrior, his main attention going to the girl.

"Well, hello!" he said to her. He went to her, taking both her hands in his own, holding them gently, smiling down into her eyes. "Do you know, you are an absolute vision to me," he said with such intensity that she blushed. "It's been a very long time since I've seen a woman so fair." He shrugged and looked toward his sister, adding, "Or any woman at all, for that matter." He sighed, dropping Cuillen's hands and moving back to face them all. "Oh well. I suppose that it's my father you've come to see, not myself."

"We have," said Muirne. "It's something urgent that only he might be able to help us with."

Labran shook his head doubtfully.

"You can try. However, I warn you, he's very hard to speak to about anything. He's always had a somewhat-irascible nature, as you well know. And living here has only made it worse. But, come along. I'll take you in to him."

He led the way along the corridor.

"Why is it you're here if you dislike it so much?" Finn asked his uncle.

Labran moved closer to him, speaking in a confidential way:

"The old man thinks I'm here for company, but, between us, I'm here to keep an eye on him. They—the Great Ones, you know—thought he could use a bit of looking after."

"I understand," said Finn.

"So, as I've always been rather a loss at everything else, I thought I'd offer my services in this. I can be of some use, anyway."

"Oh, come now," said his sister in a bolstering way. "You're not useless at all!"

"Thank you for that," he said with a smile, "though a terrible lie it is. Well, here we are!"

He stepped to one side and raised an arm, ushering them by, out of the tunnel, into an enormous space beyond.

"By all the gods of Ireland!" breathed Cuillen in open awe as she stared ahead of her.

CHAPTER EIGHT
THE SECRET OF DONN

The floor of the cavern into which they now passed was several acres in area. The walls rose up steeply, forming a rough cone whose inner surface was of crudely hewn rock, as if the inside of a mountain had been hollowed out. The walls were very moist, dripping in some places, running down as rivulets in others. Pools dotted the uneven stone floor of the cave.

The very peak of the cavern was obscured by thick, gray haze through which a white light shone palely, like sun through a heavy overcast, imparting a dim and watery illumination to the grim space.

"It certainly is rather larger than it seems it could be from outside," Cuillen remarked.

Labran opened his mouth to reply, but she raised a hand to stop him.

"Never mind," she said. "I know. It's just magic!"

He smiled and turned to lead them on across the cavern floor. They skirted pools large enough to sail upon, and passed strangely shaped boulders twice their height. At last, ahead, they saw a fire burning at the edge of a tiny lake, and by it, on a stool, the figure of a man.

He made a decidedly forlorn picture there, alone, in the center of that immense, lifeless space, slumped forward in an attitude of complete dejection. He seemed quite small and quite harmless.

Labran stopped to whisper to them in a conspiratorial tone.

"There he is. But be careful. It's not very likely he'll be happy to see you here. And remember: though he has lost his

66

place, he has managed to retain at least some of his powers. Only a fraction of what he had, of course, but enough to seem quite vast to you. Naturally, he doesn't want anyone to know that"—he paused and grinned slyly—"but he couldn't keep it a secret from me, being so close. Now, come on, before he wonders what we're whispering about here."

They approached the figure slowly, the details of him and his surrounding becoming more clear. Around him, on the shore of the little pond, were scattered a sparse and crude collection of furniture—some plank tables, simple stools, sleeping pallets of straw, and threadbare rugs. The man himself was small-boned and spare of frame, his features delicate but sharply defined by a gauntness of the face that hollowed the cheeks and made sunken caverns of the eyes. Indeed, the whole look of the man was so wasted as to make him seem more wraith than living being.

The little band stopped near the fire. The brooding man had so far made no move, appearing not to notice them.

"Father," ventured Labran in a cheerful tone, "look here! We have visitors!"

Tadg didn't stir. He continued to stare into the fire.

Muirne stepped forward and made her own try.

"Father, it is me, your daughter, and your grandson, Finn. We've come to talk to you."

Still there was no response.

She exchanged a worried glance with Finn and then stepped closer. Her voice took on a more emphatic note.

"Father, you must speak to us! It is very urgent. We need your help!"

Finally, he stirred. Slowly, very slowly, his head turned. The eyes, glinting dully deep within the dark hollows of the sockets, shifted from the fire to her. His voice came, brittle, precise, and chill.

"My help?" He gave a sharp, derisive laugh. "You expect to get my help after what you've done?"

"What *we* have done?" Muirne repeated in astonishment.

"You have stripped me of my position," he said with great intensity, his words as frigid as a scouring winter wind. "You've caused me to be driven away to live in this horrible, barren, dripping cave! Look about you!" He lifted his skinny arms to gesture around him. "Tadg, the most powerful druid in all of Ireland, reduced to living here! With no one but this incompetent, vacuous son of mine to give me any comfort in my loneliness."

"Dear Father!" said Labran in dismay. "I do as well as I can!"

Now Finn, clearly irritated by the old man's offensive manner, moved forward aggressively.

"Look here, Grandfather," he said in a brusque way, "we did nothing to you. You did it to yourself. When you used your powers against me, you brought dishonor upon yourself. You betrayed the trust of everyone. It's your own, foolish hatreds that have brought you here."

"Yes, Father," Muirne agreed, but in more cajoling tones. "It is time to make amends. Help us now. Perhaps you can redeem yourself."

"*Phaugh!*" he spat out. "I'd rot away here gladly before I'd help you. Go away! At least let me live in peace!"

"Help Ireland, then," Muirne pleaded. "It is her own existence that's threatened here."

"Oh?" he responded with more interest. A stronger glimmer of life returned to his eyes. "And what do you mean?"

"Ireland has been invaded," Finn explained. "A force of warriors led by a man called Daire Donn has landed on the point of Corca Dhuibhne."

"He calls himself 'High King of the Great World,'" put in Muirne. "But he and his men are really nothing more than raiders. Savage men who seek to plunder Ireland."

"But he has powers," added Finn. "We think he has a magic that makes him invincible and his army strong."

Tadg fixed the young captain with an eye that glowed now with more than interest.

"Strong enough even to destroy the mighty Fianna?" he asked hopefully.

"Yes, Grandfather," Finn reluctantly admitted. "The Fian clans are holding Donn for now, but in the end we will lose unless we find some help. And then all Ireland will be prey to this voracious animal. He means to devastate her utterly."

The old man's gaze returned to the fire and he again fell silent. But this time his brows were knit in concentration. The others stood, shifting nervously as they waited, exchanging looks that silently asked the question, Would Tadg condescend to help?

At last, the druid nodded and looked back at them. A

smile bowed his small mouth. His face already seemed fuller, pinker, as if his decision had filled him with new vitality.

"Very well," he said with more-resonant tones. "Your arguments are sound ones. I will help, not for you, but for the good of Ireland."

"Then, you can help us to deal with Daire Donn?" Finn asked with elation.

"I believe I can," Tadg said. "I will admit that I have heard more than a little about this Daire Donn before." He sat back, smiling more widely and in a cunning way. His whole manner was quickly becoming easier, smoother, more authoritative. "I understand the problem that you face. It is true that Donn has a great power that protects him. It is a power he had obtained from his people. But he is also a madman, obsessed with the desire to possess Ireland. This madness comes from his race as well. You see, he is of the Fomor blood."

"Who are the Fomor?" asked Cuillen, curiousity prompting her to speak for the first time.

The sharp gaze of the old druid went to her.

"I know you, do I not?" he asked after a moment's consideration. "I've seen you in the high king's court. Your father is one of Conn's most trusted aides."

"I am surprised you remember me," she said, sounding impressed. "I was rarely at court then. Of course, I remember you, so magnificent in your feather robes, glowing so many colors and—" She stopped, looking embarrassed, clearly aware of the painful comparison she was raising with her memories.

"Rather different now," he said with a rueful smile, lifting the edge of the plain wool tunic he wore. "But, never mind, girl. Such golden recollections of the court sustain me here. And how is your father?"

"He is dead, High Druid," she said tightly. "Killed by Daire Donn. And I've come to see that his duty and the will of his high king are carried out."

"I am sorry," said Tadg, shaking his head regretfully. "He was a valiant and loyal man. I perceive that you are the same. Sadly ignorant, however, of your country's history. The Fomor were a race of monstrous beings who held the other peoples of Ireland in bondage long, long ago. It was the courage of the champion Lugh Lamfada and the Tuatha de Danaan that destroyed the Fomor power, scattering their remnants throughout the earth.

"Many of their descendants have kept up their raiding

life, blending their destinies and blood with that of the Lochlanners, who ravage the eastern lands. Donn himself is of the pure Fomor blood—and of its ruling class, from what I've heard, for only the highest ranks were free of the terrible deformations that cursed the others."

"Grandfather," said Finn, "you said that you can help. Have you some magic to counter that of Donn?"

"That I have not," Tadg replied. "For it's not magic that protects him. It's the skills of the ancient Fomor craftsmen. Far back in time, thousands of years, they were so advanced that they produced devices, engines, weapons, that we could never understand. Donn has somehow found or recreated some of these marvels. He has used them to gain and secure his power. But my magic is as useless against them as puffs of air against a wall of stone. It must be a real, solid force—not one of illusion—that counters them."

"Then, how can you help us?" asked Muirne.

"Because I know that just such a real force as you need may very well exist. And I know where it can be found." He smiled in a smug way at this, as if reveling in the hold he now had upon them.

"Father, please don't be playing your games with us," his daughter told him impatiently. "Tell us what this force is!"

Tadg shot her an irritated look, but then, grudgingly, complied.

"Very well. The armor that protects your Daire Donn is of a special material, as is his ax. They are the product of the ancient Fomor smiths, and are of a quality unlike any we can produce. But, long ago, some of the Fomor metal came into the hands of the Tuatha de Danaan."

The old druid sat forward on his chair, caught up in his tale now, aglow with the zest of spinning it out, holding his tiny audience enthralled.

"You see," he continued, "all those ages ago, at the final battle between the de Danaans and the Fomor, their leader, Balor of the Evil Eye, was destroyed. He was a giant being, made of a strange black metal. The de Danaans thought him invulnerable, but a spear of power sent by Queen Danu herself pierced the giant's single eye, and he was killed.

"The great Tower of Glass in which the Fomor lived was destroyed in the battle, burying the giant's body. But after the battle, de Danaan warriors searched through the wreckage of the shattered stronghold and discovered the blasted remains of

Balor's head. For a time it was a trophy of their victory. Then Goibnu—the chief smith of the de Danaans—suggested that more appropriate symbols might be made of it. He argued that the metal was stronger than any even their magic could create. He convinced them that it should be formed into weapons like none ever seen in Ireland.

"It took the combined efforts of the de Danaans' greatest druids and craftsmen to reshape the strange metal of the head. Goibnu, the chief smith, was in charge of the labors. He demanded incredible powers, all that could be generated by de Danaan skills, for the reforging. For many days the scores of men toiled in the heat of the forges, the workers themselves glowing from the energies playing about them, sweating with their efforts, all of Ireland shaking from the impact of their hammers, its people nearly deafened by the thundering din, as if a thousand storms at once had come upon them.

"But, finally, it was done. The head had been reshaped into weapons of a strength not known before. A sword that no other metal could stop, and a shield that no sword, ax, or spear in Ireland could penetrate. So unique were these weapons that they were given names. The sword became Son of the Waves, and the great circle of black iron, whose voice boomed out like thunder when it was struck, was named the Storm Shield."

His tale concluded, the druid sat back, smiling, clearly self-satisfied at having so spellbound his audience. He waited, now in control, letting them ask the questions that now would have to come. Finn's was the first.

"Then you believe these weapons can destroy Daire Donn?" he asked.

"If anything can," replied Tadg. "Hopefully, they would at least give their bearer an even fighting chance with him."

"That is all I ask," Finn said grimly.

"But where are these weapons, Father?" said Muirne. "I have never heard of them."

"It was decided that they were far too dangerous to be wielded by anyone," he said, "for they would make the bearer unconquerable, and thus nearly omnipotent, in Ireland. This was too great a temptation. So, the de Danaan leaders decreed that until a champion could be found who would use the weapons honorably and unselfishly, they would be put into safekeeping."

Again he paused, obviously to heighten further the dramatic effect. But Muirne grew quickly impatient.

"I know you love making a great show of this, Father," she said in a parental, scolding tone, "but we haven't the time. Just tell us where they are, if you mean to, please!"

"Very well," he replied, scowling at her for spoiling his fun. "The weapons were put into the care of the king of the Country of the Fair Men. He is a man known for his honor and is trusted by all the Tuatha de Danaan. There is nothing that would make him break his oath to guard the weapons."

"Then, will he give them to us?" asked Finn.

Tadg gave a little assuring laugh.

"Why, of course! It will be clear to him, as it was to myself, that you must have them to save Ireland." He leaned toward Finn, his voice becoming more serious, more earnest. "But, mark this, Grandson: It must be you, yourself, who asks him for their use. He'll not give them into the keeping of any mortal man of Ireland. You understand?"

"I do, Grandfather," Finn replied.

"Good!" said Tadg with satisfaction. "Then all that is left is for you to journey to the Country of the Fair Men. It is a long journey, and it is perilous, but I am sure one so courageous and determined as you are will succeed. However," he added in a more cautioning tone, "the location of the country itself will be all but impossible for you to find. It is one of the most secret of the Sid, and is protected by great magic. Of course, I could lead you there and take you within its boundaries safely, but I am forced to stay here, unable to use my own powers." He sighed with tremendous regret. "And I know of no one else."

"Father," spoke up Labran eagerly, "I know the way to the country. I could take them and get them within the Sid!"

"Why of course, my son!" said Tadg, brightening. "I should have thought of that myself!" Then a shadow of despair crossed his features, making him look very old again. "But, that means you would be leaving me alone in this dank, terrible place. My son, you're all that I have left to comfort me. I can't lose you!"

"I . . . I'm sorry for that, Father," Labran said, cowed by Tadg's plea.

"Don't be doing that, Father," Muirne told him. "We must have Labran's help, and he'll not be gone from you for long. Don't keep him from going."

Encouraged by his sister's defense, Labran pulled himself up, striking a determined pose.

"Yes, Father. This is for the safety of all Ireland, after all. And it is my chance to be truly useful for once. I must go!"

Tadg sighed, then nodded.

"I understand," he said, appearing to accept the situation. "You are right. For the good of Ireland I must forget myself."

"Take heart, Father," Muirne told him cheeringly. "Perhaps your help to us will see you released from your exile the sooner."

This notion seemed to revive some of his spirit. He smiled again.

"I do have that hope, don't I?" he agreed.

"Grandfather," Finn put in, "we are grateful to you. But we must be going now. Every day we take means more lives lost."

Labran hurriedly gathered a few belongings into a travel-pouch and fetched a horse from a stable chamber in the outer wall of the cavern. It was a peculiar-looking nag, lank in the neck and legs, scrawny of body, with oversized hooves and enormous, liquid brown eyes.

"Your horse seems a bit wretched to me," said Finn, eyeing it doubtfully. "Are you certain it can manage a long journey?"

"She's much stronger than she looks," Labran assured him brightly.

"I hope so," the young warrior replied.

Making their good-byes to the old druid, the party made its way back across the huge floor and entered the tunnel again.

"This means I'll be having to let the Fianna fight on without me for even longer now," Finn remarked as they started the long trek to the mound's outer portal.

"And what other choice have you?" asked Muirne. "The words of your grandfather make it all the more certain that only your finding of a way to destroy Donn will save Ireland. You must go on, Finn."

"You're right," he agreed. "But you and Cuillen will be going no farther. I want you to go back to Corca Dhuibhne. Tell Goll what has happened. Tell him help will come."

"I will not go back!" the girl flared. "If you go on, I must go on as well. Until I see your task complete, until Donn and his army are destroyed, nothing will keep me from my duty!"

"You will be in the way," Finn told her bluntly. "We'll

waste precious energies protecting you from dangers instead of ourselves."

"That you will not. I was my father's only child. He trained me in the fighting skills as he would have a son. I'm well able to see to myself. The only safety you'll have to see to is your own, Finn MacCumhal."

He looked to Caoilte for support. But that dark warrior, burned far too often in his attempts to help his friend, now only strode on, staring ahead, clearly refusing to be involved this time. Finn looked back to the girl, his expression hard.

"Are you meaning to try defying me again?" he asked in a threatening voice.

"That I am," she answered curtly. "And you can do nothing to stop me. There is no Mogh Nuadat to keep me by force this time. So you can just give over your poor attempt to bully me!"

Finn sighed, looking this time to his mother for help. She gave him none.

"The girl is right, my dear," she told him, smiling. "She is as much a part of this as yourself, and has as much right to choose her dangers. But be comforted. You may need every bit of help that you can get."

They reached the end of the tunnel at last. It seemed a solid rock wall, but a mere touch by Labran on a nearby stone caused it to part again, swinging in. They passed out into the gloom of the clearing.

When Conan saw them, a look of great relief brightened his dour face. Then this passed into an expression of puzzlement as he saw the new member of the band.

"Who is this?" he demanded. "What's happened?"

"We'll tell you as we go," Finn said, taking the reins of his horse from the portly warrior. "But let's be after getting ourselves out of this shoeguy wood before night falls."

They all mounted and started away from the mound. Labran looked around eagerly, clearly elated by the promise of adventure.

"This is going to be truly delightful!" he exclaimed with a beaming grin.

Conan looked at him as if he were viewing a raving lunatic.

As they neared the avenue of trees leading out of the clearing, Labran glanced back for a final view of his mound.

"Oh, look!" he said. "There's Father!"

They all looked back. A tiny figure was visible atop the barren pile, looking very lonely in that gloomy setting. Tadg lifted a hand in farewell, and Labran waved in reply.

"Poor Father," he said pityingly. "The old spirit is so much gone from him. I hope he'll be all right."

Caoilte, who had gone through the whole visit with Tadg in stony-faced silence, now spoke up.

"I still don't trust the man," he said in a harsh way. "I didn't want to be risking anything by speaking up before, but now that we're safely away, I can say what I think. That old druid is a vicious, bloody rogue who's played us nothing but foul tricks before—no offense to you, Muirne, or to your brother." He turned to Labran. "But, aren't you supposed to be his watchdog here? Can he be safely left alone?"

"It would go hard with him if he were caught outside this place," Labran told him in an assured way. "And if he does leave, he does so stripped of nearly all his powers. He'd be quite harmless."

Behind them, atop the mound, Tadg watched the little band disappear into the shadowed corridor of trees. His pale, delicately featured face was lit by a curious glow of triumph, and his small mouth was bowed upward by a cruel and cunning smile.

CHAPTER NINE

TREACHERY

"My king, it is Fergus True-Lips, messenger of the Fianna!" announced the keeper at the door.

The red-mustached Fergus strode into the great hall of Tara na Rie, paused to glance around him, then started across the floor.

He had entered a room that gave clear evidence of the power that resided there, both in its size and in its trappings of enormous wealth. The oaken walls of Tara encircled a vast space that was richly decorated, brightly lit, warm, and comfortable even in the chill spring storm that howled about its peaked roof.

Scores of long tables formed a ring about the central fire, and the hundreds of seats were filled with the members of the high king's court, now at their evening feast. Their dress presented another bright array of colors and textures. To one side were the learned men—ollamhs and bards and druids—their official robes were of red or white or green, as befitted rank, all edged and embroidered with gold and silver threads, while about their throats gleamed the golden torcs of their offices. Opposite them were the tables of the territorial lords and chieftains, who were dressed in the fine silk tunics and the patterned cloaks of many clans, glinting with jeweled bracelets and enameled brooches and fine glass beads woven into the elaborate plaits of their long hair.

But Fergus showed not the slightest sign of interest in this grand show. He strode boldly on, around the fire pit and toward the raised platform beyond it where the two curves of tables met. At another table atop this dais there dined a group whose even-more-elaborate dress marked them clearly as of higher rank than those below. Again the learned men and nobles were divided, filling opposite ends. But it was the man between, at the table's center, who Fergus approached. The messenger stopped before him, struck a pose of stiff attention, and spoke in clear and ringing tones:

"My king, I have brought an urgent message to you from Finn MacCumhal!"

The man he addressed lifted his gaze from his plate to fix it sharply on the man below. Conn of the Hundred Battles, high king of all Ireland, was a tall, lean man made gaunt by age. His features, once elegantly handsome, were now honed by the years to a painful sharpness. The long nose had become beaklike. Sunken cheeks had emphasized a pointed chin and high cheekbones. And thinning, gray hair, drawn back tightly over the top of his head, sharply delineated the shape of his skull, making him look all the more cadaverous.

"Well, well," he cawed, thrusting his head forward on the scrawny neck and giving himself, in this gesture, the appearance of a gray-necked crow. "What is it that brings you here disturbing us?"

"It is very important, I assure you, my high king!" Fergus replied, taken somewhat aback by the hostile tone of Conn's greeting. "I've come from Corca Dhuibhne. Ireland is in grave danger! There is—"

"Yes, yes," Conn said, breaking in, in an impatient tone. "The rumor of this so-called invasion has already reached us. You needn't have wasted your time bringing word here."

"But . . . I haven't come to simply give you the news of it," said Fergus, his face now reflecting his astonishment at the high king's apparent indifference to such calamitous news. "I've come here to ask you for your help."

"Our help?" Conn said with surprise. "What, to aid the mighty Fianna in putting down some raid by Lochlanner scavengers?"

He gave a cackling laugh, as if the thought of something so preposterous was immensely funny. He looked around him at his courtiers, and they quickly and obediently joined in.

"No! It is much more!" cried Fergus, his earnest voice rising above the laughter, silencing it. "It is an immense force of warriors that has landed. They are well-trained, seasoned fighting men from many lands, and are led by the notorious

Daire Donn himself! Their numbers are three times that of the Fianna!"

"And what does that mean to the great warriors of Finn MacCumhal?" the high king responded with a careless wave. "How often have we all heard their brag that not less than nine times their number could ever force them to retreat?"

"Please, my high king, you must listen," Fergus implored. "These are no ordinary warriors we face. They are empowered with an incredible fighting spirit by Daire Donn. The man has some kind of magic, some aura of energy that feeds them, drives them on! The Fianna cannot defeat them alone."

"It is not our task to protect Ireland's shores," Conn pointed out. "It is theirs. And I believe we pay them quite well for it." He looked down the table toward the learned men. "Just how much do we pay the Fians, Chief Brehon?"

"It is quite substantial," piped up a silver-headed man in the green-and-gold dress of Ireland's supreme justices. "They receive a townland in each district, the fostering of a pup in every house from Samhain to Beltainne, free food and shelter in every dun throughout the wintertime, and one quarter of all the gold taken in war or collected in taxes for yourself, High King."

"And for this," said Conn, "they in turn pledge themselves to carry out the will of Ireland's rulers, for the good of its people—isn't that true, Fergus True-Lips?" He fixed a glittering eye on the messenger, his voice growing more strident as he fired each point home like an arrow to its mark. "*They* are to uphold Ireland's laws. *They* are to put down injustices on the part of its chieftains and kings. And—mark this well, Fergus—*they* are to guard the harbors from foreign invaders." He sat back, casting his gaze about him on his assembled court. "We have done our part, have we not? Now it is time that they do theirs!"

There were nods and sounds of agreement from many in the hall, but others remained silent, their expressions troubled.

"Please, my high king," Fergus said, now with desperation in his tone, "you must believe how serious it is! I would not have come to you for help if it were not. You must know that! The pride of the Fianna would never allow it. Many of them even argued against my coming here. They preferred to die fighting rather than be dishonored by admitting their weakness. But it is the fate of all of Ireland that's at stake. If the Fianna are destroyed, all the country will lie open to Donn's army, and he will show our people no mercy. You're risking everything if you refuse to help. You have to understand!"

Conn leaned forward in his seat, glaring down upon the pleading messenger. His reply was an angry one.

"No, Fergus. It is yourself who must understand. We have endured for too long the arrogance of the Fianna and of their leader, Finn MacCumhal. We have been forced to accept their demands for more wealth and power and dignity. Dignity! For our paid servants!" His voice rose in pitch as he went on, becoming quite shrill now. His thin body trembled with his outpouring of rage. "We have been humiliated, weakened, deprived of the rule of our own land. But now . . . now the Fianna must pay. They will do as their oath decrees—alone! They will defend Ireland if the blood of every warrior must spill upon her sod. That is the message you will take to Finn MacCumhal, messenger. It is all that he will have from us!"

Red-faced from his own suppressed anger at the high king's brutal words, Fergus turned on his heel and marched from the hall without a word of reply.

Conn watched him go, and a cruel smile of satisfaction stretched his thin lips into a ghastly, death's-head grin.

"It is well," he said, "—Finn to be in such a strait after what he has done to us. Now maybe he will learn some humility. And if the Fianna are weakened in this, it will be to our own good."

But at the end of his own table, from amongst the chieftains and nobles, a man leaped to his feet. He was quite young, with smooth, beardless features and curling golden hair. Blue-black eyes glowed now with the same fury that blazed in his words.

"Father, you risk the safety of all Ireland to have your own revenge upon Finn MacCumhal!"

"How dare you to speak so, Art!" the old man retorted indignantly. "Is there any man in Ireland who dares to claim a salmon or deer or pig as his own for fear of the Fianna? Is there any who is not in dread to go from one place to another without leave from the Fianna?"

"Your age has made you think this, Father," said the young man. "No others fear or hate the Fianna as you do. In

your need to be rid of Finn MacCumhal, you've become blind
to the dangers!"

"Take care, Art!" Conn threatened. "Though you are my
firstborn son, you dare much to be challenging me!"

Art drew himself up defiantly.

"You'll not keep me from speaking out," he said. "By your
action, you have made cowards of us all. That I cannot let you
do. I am a warrior of Ireland, and I will defend her."

"You will do as I say!" stormed Conn. "I will tolerate
nothing else."

"Will you not?" said Art, smiling scornfully. "Father, there
is nothing you can do to stop me. Once, you were the victor in
a hundred battles. Now you have grown too weak to even
defend yourself. Well, you can cower here in your grand hall
with your fat, simpering lot. I mean to fight!"

He turned from the table and stalked from the hall,
leaving his father, speechless in his now-apoplectic fury,
staring after him.

Horns sounded and the army of the Great World broke off
its attack, falling back toward its camp.

The mailed figure of Daire Donn moved down from the
battle line, pushing through a confusion of retreating men,
skirting litter-bearers fetching wounded men and carts rolling
up to carry off the dead. Close behind him moved an
entourage of his officers.

Evidence of the savagery of the fight was clear on Donn.
His bright suit of mail was spotted with rust-brown drops of
blood sprayed across him from his victims. His ax dripped with
still-wet gore that also reddened his arms to the elbows. Even
his legs were splattered to the knees from his wading in near-
streams of it. As he reached the edge of the camp and stopped
to look back toward the battlefield, he was an image of death
itself.

"Those stubborn, stubborn fools!" he raged. "I've never
seen men so hard to kill or so willing to die. They come into
my way, challenging me—*me!*—even though they must know
now that they cannot win!" He looked at his captains in
amazement at such audacity. "I kill them and kill them. My
own arm aches from it. Still they will not fall back!"

"Yes, my king," agreed Caisel. "Even my shield cannot
cut a way through them. They keep coming against me until its
energies are drained. They are madmen!"

"'They are desperate men," said Donn. "But they must be broken! Reform the companies. We will attack again.'"

"Our own warriors need time to rest, my king," bravely pointed out another captain whose long face and tiny eyes gave him a doglike appearance. "They must have food, new weapons, a chance to tend their wounds. They cannot be expected to carry on sustained attacks every day . . .'"

"Unless you would like your company to carry out the next attack alone, Comor Crooked-Sword, you will spread no more of the disease of your own weakness with this cowardly talk!" Donn threatened.

The man's lip curled in an angry snarl, revealing sharply pointed teeth. But he dropped his eyes in instant submission, falling back.

"No one will falter, do you all understand?" Donn told them, sweeping his burning gaze across the group. "I've not faced an enemy so worthy of my battle skills before. I will have none of my warriors letting them see that our own strength and courage is not a match for theirs. Prepare for a new attack!"

He turned away from them and, as they scattered to their companies, moved on toward his pavilion with Caisel at his heels. Donn pushed through the flaps of its door first, throwing his ax down on a tabletop, lifting his hands to pull off the massive helmet.

"The Fianna cannot sustain such enormous losses for much longer, my king," Caisel told him in a placating way. "I am certain they are already weakening. And, in time . . .'"

"In time!" Donn roared, pulling the helmet free and wheeling to face his captain. "There *is* no time! I want my victory now!"

"It may be for you that the time is running out, Daire Donn," said a voice behind him.

He whirled about. Both he and Caisel peered into the back of the tent. After the brightness outside, the shadows there seemed very dark. Still, the outlines of a figure could just be discerned.

"Who is it?" Donn demanded. "Come forward!"

The figure moved from the shadows into the glow of sunlight slanting in through the door flaps. Donn saw a stranger, a slender, harmless man of almost-effeminate looks clad in a brilliantly white robe richly embroidered in shimmering silver thread. Still, Donn's eyes narrowed in suspicion, and one hand moved to grip the handle of his ax again.

"Stop there!" he ordered. "Tell me who you are!"

"My name is Tadg," the other answered in a soft, sweet, and very amicable voice. "I have come here as a friend."

"A friend?" repeated Donn. "You are of Ireland, and you wear the dress of a high druid. How did you get here?"

"I have ways," said Tadg with a little, cunning smile.

"I am sure you have," said Donn. "I should dispatch you now, before you try your sorcery on us!"

"Yes, my king," Caisel quickly agreed, staring apprehensively at Tadg. "I have heard these Irish druids are full of trickery."

"I will try nothing," Tadg said assuringly. "I wish only to help you. You see, your enemies are my own."

"What do you mean?" asked Donn.

"That I seek the destruction of the Fianna and their leader, Finn MacCumhal, as much as you do. Perhaps more."

"And what reason do I have to believe you?"

"Because I would not have risked myself to face you here otherwise," the druid answered. "You had better listen to me, Daire Donn. It may be all that can save your army and your own life."

Donn stared thoughtfully into the face before him. He saw there none of the wasted, spiritless look Finn had seen so recently. Now Tadg was fully revitalized, fresh and full and glowing of face, as if his new hope for revenge had restored his youth. And in his large, bright silver eyes there shone the hard light of his hatred, so startling in contrast to the delicate features.

Donn's gaze met Tadg's and they locked. Some strange energy seemed to flow between the two. Then Donn nodded.

"Yes, I see the truth in you. I feel the desire raging in you almost as I feel it within myself. All right, Druid, I will listen. What is this great danger?"

"Finn MacCumhal no longer leads the warriors you face here," Tadg said. "He has gone on a quest—a quest to fetch the weapons that can destroy you."

Donn gave a derisive snort of laughter.

"There are no such weapons," he told the druid.

"These were forged of the black metal that once formed the head of Balor, leader of the Fomor race," Tadg replied.

"Balor!" the mailed giant breathed, clearly awed by the very name.

"Yes, Donn," continued Tadg. "I'm certain you know of the properties of his metal, perhaps better than I. So, tell me now, are you so confident that weapons created from it cannot turn aside your own and pierce the armor that protects your body?"

Donn's gaze went to the helmet he still held in one gauntleted hand, then to the ax on the table beside him. A shadow of doubt flickered across his features. Tadg saw it and nodded.

"I thought as much," he said with satisfaction. "With such weapons, Finn might well be your equal—or more. For, believe my words, he has fighting skills like no other man I have ever known."

"He is right, my king," Caisel put in helpfully. "There are many tales of Finn's deeds against giant men and monstrous creatures that—"

"Silence!" Donn snapped at him, then blustered on in arrogant tones: "No warrior in the world is a match for me, armored or not!" He paused, considered, then said more thoughtfully, "Of course, I'd be a fool to ignore the threat here." He looked back to the druid. "So, tell me more of why you have come to me with this warning. How do you mean to help?"

"I can show you how to stop Finn. More, I can help you to destroy him. Think of that! Without Finn, you will not only remain invulnerable, but the Fianna will also lose their leader, their greatest champion! I assure you, once they know he is dead, their spirit will leave them. You will be able to sweep them from your path. The way will be open to the rich heartlands of Ireland. She would be yours to possess."

The druid's words were coaxing, tempting, teasing with the golden image of victory. They seemed to hold Donn, and he stared away as if the glowing hill of Tara itself was before him. Then he shook his head, throwing off the druid's spell, his expression hardening with suspicion again.

"I wonder why you come to me, Druid," he said. "If you have such hatred of Finn, why not use your own powers to destroy him?"

"I cannot," Tadg said angrily. "Because I have acted against him before, I have been stripped of nearly all my powers and made a captive." Then he smiled slyly. "But I have managed to free myself of my guard—my poor fool of a son—and come here. My time, however, is very brief. If I am discovered outside my prison, my life is forfeit. Still, it is worth the risk to tell you where Finn is going and how he may be intercepted. All I ask in exchange for my small service is that you supply me with proof of his destruction." He gave a short, harsh laugh. "I think his head will be enough."

"You make me an offer I cannot refuse to take," said Donn.

"But you must send a powerful force against him," Tadg cautioned. "Finn is a very difficult man to kill, and he is not alone."

"For such a task as this, I'll see that there is no mistake," Donn assured him. "I will send a troop of my best warriors, and with them my most deadly weapon." He looked toward his captain. "Caisel, my good right hand, you will see to the extermination of this Finn for me, won't you?"

Caisel stepped forward, his expression lighting with his zeal.

"I will, my king, I swear it!" he vowed eagerly. He gave his power-shield a loving pat. "He'll never see this strand again."

Donn nodded in satisfaction and turned back to the druid with a cruel smile.

"All Finn's skills will be of no use to him against my captain's power," he bragged. "He won't live to come within a spear's throw of Caisel's shield."

"Take no chances," Tadg admonished. "Many have died underestimating Finn MacCumhal."

"Let us be concerned with that," Donn answered curtly. "A ship will be readied to depart by daybreak. All we need now are the directions to intercept Finn's route."

"I will explain them to you," offered Tadg.

"Do better. Show them to me," said Donn. He went to a heavy wooden chest bound in iron and removed from it the rolled chart. Carefully he unrolled it upon a tabletop.

"A map of Ireland!" said Tadg, clearly impressed. He moved forward to examine its elaborate drawing with interest. "So, you have unearthed more of the Fomor knowledge than even I had guessed."

"This scroll is my own, passed to me by my ancestors," said Donn with great pride. "I am directly descended from the high officers of the Glass Tower, purest of the Fomor race."

"Really," said Tadg, sounding little impressed, his interest all upon the map. "Well, this is excellent. Really excellent. I can easily trace out the way Finn must go on this. Their way lies to the far north, through rough terrain. Your people can be days ahead of them by ship, simply by sailing along the coast, then moving inland to cut them off. Let me show you."

He put forward a slender hand to point out Finn's route. But Donn suddenly engulfed it in the grip of an enormous, gauntleted fist.

"Wait!" he said urgently. "There is something I must know first!"

Tadg's eyes lifted to meet Donn's gaze unflinchingly.

"Ask it!" he said.

"To see Finn dead, you will sacrifice your own country to me," Donn said in puzzlement. "What could cause you to do that?"

"He has dishonored me," Tadg answered in chill tones. "He has taken my dignity, my position, my power—all that I have. If I must destroy all Ireland to have my revenge, I will do so!"

Donn held the druid's hate-filled gaze for a long moment, then smiled in satisfaction, releasing the hand.

"I know what you feel, my friend," he said. "Your heart is truly as my own. We are joined by a common need to repay past wrongs to us, no matter what the cost. And soon, my friend, very soon, we will both have what we desire."

BOOK TWO

IN THE ENCHANTED LAND

CHAPTER TEN

THE TALE OF
BRAN AND SCEOLAN

The longsword drove through the mailed warrior's shoulder as he clambered onto the rain-slicked rock. He grunted in pain, dropping his ax and falling back. His body tumbled down onto his fellows struggling upward from the beach. Some of them were knocked from their feet, sliding back down onto the wet sands. But they recovered and doggedly began the climb again, struggling up through the driving rain and the streams of runoff pouring over the edge of the embankment from the grassy hillsides above.

All along the White Strand it was the same, although the full scope of the great battle was obscured by the gray shroud of the downpour. The men of Donn's army fought their way up the steep rise that cut off the beach. Atop it, the Fianna now had formed their battle line, using the natural defensive rampart of the drop-off to counter the greater numbers of their enemies.

This day's battle had been clearly a long-fought and costly one already. Bodies of dead and wounded men lay draped across the rocks and formed a grotesque wall along the foot of the embankment. The living men fought wearily, but with undaunted courage, throwing themselves against one another with now-hoarse battle cries, wrestling together, hammering away with sword and ax and shield, neither side willing to give quarter.

But the bravery and sacrifice produced no victor. When the horns of Donn's companies sounded the withdrawal, and his warriors pulled back, they revealed a still-unbroken Fian line. They also revealed the tremendous price paid for another day of failure. Hundreds of casualties littered the field between the two forces, their blood mingling with the rain, flowing away in pink streams toward the sea. Scores of their fellows from both armies, under truce, searched amongst the fallen with great care, for the rain, the blood, and the coating of wet sand made identification difficult. The dead were tossed upon the carts in heaps. The less severely wounded were lifted more gently onto litters to be carried to medical help. And those whose damage was too great for hope of recovery were humanely dispatched.

On the hill above, Goll MacMorna stood, unmindful of the stinging rain, and watched the grim procedure with a face of stone. Young Cael of the Clan na Baiscne moved up beside him, his normally innocent face lit by a savage battle-glow.

"We won the day again, Chieftain!" he trumpeted with great pride. "We drove those cursed invaders back! I did for five of them myself!"

"We lost many, many warriors," Goll said darkly, pointing with his weapon to the carnage below. "We held them today, but not for many days longer with our strength being drained away like this."

Cael looked upon the dead and his expression grew sober as well.

"I am sorry, Chieftain. I had not thought of our situation here, but only my own glory." He considered gravely, and then he cheered. "But we'll have more help soon, won't we? The high king will be sending—"

"Nothing," Goll finished tersely. "The high king will be giving no help to us. Fergus returned with Conn's message only today."

"No help?" said Cael, stricken. "But why not? Is he mad?"

Goll turned to him, his face stern, his voice coldly admonishing:

"Warrior, please remember that Conn is our high king and that we are bound by our oaths of loyalty to him. If he has refused to aid us, it was his right. It is our task to defend Ireland, after all. Our asking him for help wasn't honorable to begin with."

"Yes, Chieftain," Cael returned in a properly chastened way. "But without help, we can only hope that Finn returns quickly."

"I don't believe that hope will be realized," Goll replied frankly. "From what Finn's mother has told us, the journey he must make to this Country of the Fair Men will take some days, and she had no idea what he'd be having to overcome to make these weapons his own."

"He'll succeed," said Cael with bright, boyish confidence. "I know nothing can stop Finn."

"I am not so blindly optimistic as yourself, warrior," Goll said in his brisk, matter-of-fact tones. "Still, knowing our captain, I would say that you are likely correct. However, it might well be that he'll return too late to be of any help to us."

"How can you be so unfeeling about this?" Cael asked, clearly amazed by the chieftain's terse response. "Our whole land is threatened! We must do something!"

"You have a great deal to learn, young warrior," Goll said, still in that even voice. "Emotion leads to rashness. The warrior who wishes to survive must learn to think. I have considered the possibilities left to us. It's clear we must increase our ability to hold them back. This rain has served that purpose for us, but it cannot last. And this embankment has aided us greatly, but it is not enough."

"I think I understand," said Cael. "We must build some kind of a defensive wall."

"Yes, though it is something I greatly dislike to do. It violates the warrior's right to an open fight and fair, single combat." He paused, his gaze fixed upon the dead below. Then he went on, now with resignation in his voice. "But with such odds against us, there is no other choice. Barricades must make up for men. Honor must give way to practicality. Tonight we will begin the work." His eyes lifted from the beach and he turned to look off toward the north. "After that, we can only pray to Danu that Finn succeeds as quickly as possible."

Finn MacCumhal was gazing toward the north as well. Periodically he lifted a hand to wipe away the rain that lashed into his face. Beside him, afoot as he was, stood Labran, peering intently in the same direction. Conan, Cuillen, and Caoilte, still mounted, waited behind them with the dogs.

All of them were soaked through by the heavy, penetrating rain that the chill wind drove upon them. Their woolen cloaks hung about them in dripping folds. The long hair of all, save the balding Conan, was plastered about their heads, while the rain-matted coats of the dogs made them seem gaunt.

The land before them was open, rolling, and very sodden, the meadows a dark gray-green, the view of their extent far shortened by the screen of rain. After a long period of staring through the storm, Labran lifted a hand and pointed to another hill, barely visible in the distance as a blue shadow.

"There," he said in a vague manner. "That way, I think."

"You think?" snapped Conan with some irritation.

"I've not been there in some time," Labran said apologetically. "I want to be certain of my directions." He lifted a hand to shield his eyes from rain, peered off again, then nodded. "Yes," he said with more conviction. "I'm certain that's it. Right past that hill, and north."

"How long?" asked Finn.

"Five days, perhaps," Labran told him.

They mounted and the party moved on, pushing forward through rain blasting against them from the north as if some force was bent upon throwing up a wall of water before them. Toward nightfall, they came upon the ruins of a tiny ringfort, its gates missing, sections of its rock wall collapsed. They rode into the yard and looked about. Most of the half-dozen round buildings were fallen, but one stone-walled oval appeared intact and still supported a plank roof. Finn dismounted and went inside, returning in moments.

"This one's all right," he told the others. "Even dry in spots. We'll shelter here tonight."

All climbed down wearily and removed their gear from the saddles. While Conan found a place for the horses in a half-tumbled shed, the others went inside and managed to kindle a fire. Soon, except for the dripping places in the roof, the house was made relatively cozy, the cloaks hung up to dry, and the band enjoying a hot meal.

Their dinner over and their clothes dried sufficiently, Caoilte, Conan, and Labran sought out places between the puddles to stretch out and were soon asleep. But Finn noticed that the girl stayed seated by the fire, wrapped in her cloak, staring gloomily into the flames.

He looked at the forlorn figure for a long time, thoughtfully. Then he gave that now-common sigh of resignation and moved to sit at her side.

"And what is it you're wanting this time?" she asked him softly, so as not to disturb the others.

"You seemed unhappy. I thought that you might not turn away some company. You are far from home and among strangers."

"That's nothing to do with you," she said curtly.

"Why not? We are in this thing together. We should at least try to be civil."

"We are too different," she said. "There is too much between us."

"Look here," he said patiently, "I really want you to believe I'm not your enemy. I did let you come along with us, didn't I? You know I could have had Mogh keep you back by force."

This seemed to have an effect on her. She turned her head toward him, regarding him now with a thoughtful gaze.

"That's true," she admitted. "You did. I never understood it. Why did you?"

"I saw what it was that made it so important to you. It was the need to avenge your father's death. The drive to fulfill a duty that had been given you. I understood that."

"How?" she asked with greater interest, staring intently into the face that was so earnest now as he tried to explain to her.

"It was something I had to do myself when my father died. I was given a duty much like yours to carry out. I had my chance to see it to its end. I couldn't deny you your own."

Her eyes met his forthright gaze for a long moment, probingly, and then she nodded.

"I believe you," she told him, for the first time in a gentler tone. "And I thank you for that."

"But do you trust me?" he asked hopefully.

"I don't know," she said with caution, considering. "Perhaps. If you proved that you trusted me by telling me the whole truth."

"What do you mean?"

"I'm not a fool, Finn MacCumhal. I listened to what your grandfather said, and I saw the place where he lived. There is something very strange going on, and it can't be explained away as just magic."

He looked at her thoughtfully for a time. Then he nodded.

"All right. I said we were together in this. You should know. But you must promise that it will remain a secret with you."

"I promise," she said with great sincerity.

He moved closer to her, his face very near to hers, his voice dropping to a conspiratorial whisper.

"That place we went to was a Sid—a hidden dwelling place of the Tuatha de Danaan. My grandfather is of that race of beings, as is my mother."

"They're of the Other!" Cuillen breathed in awe. "Of course!" Then, as the full understanding dawned, she looked with new interest at Finn. "But . . . then, that means you . . ."

"I am half of the de Danaan blood," he finished. "My father, Cumhal MacTredhorn, was a mortal man."

"Still, to be of their blood . . ." she said in wondering tones, eyes bright with the exciting thought. "I've heard of the Others only in tales of my childhood. I thought they were beings of smoke and mist—not real."

"They're real enough, and of flesh and blood, as you can see yourself," he said, smiling. "Once, they were a mortal race, cousins to the Firbolgs, living openly upon the earth. It was the defeat of them by the Milesians, your own people, that drove most to hide in the Sids, protected by magic."

"What is it like, to be of Them?" she asked, all her barrier of reserve gone in her curiosity."

"It's . . . like nothing," he said simply. "I've none of their powers, and outside the Sids there is no immortality. My mother gave up that life when she left her people to marry my father. She and I are ordinary people, nothing more."

"But the Others—do they really have the fabulous powers of the tales?" She moved even closer to him.

"Oh, yes," he assured her. "Great knowledge of magic was given to them by the gods Danu and Manannan MacLir. They can raise storms, heal wounds, change shapes."

"They can't," she said in disbelief. "Change shapes?"

"That they can," he said with conviction. He gestured toward Bran and Sceolan who lay beside the fire, watching them with large, black glowing eyes. "Why, the dogs are evidence of that."

At his words, even though whispered, the dogs perked up, raising their heads, lifting their sharp ears.

"The dogs?" repeated Cuillen. "How can that be?"

"They are the children of a human woman—the sister of my own mother."

"Now I know you're having a game with me. I'll grant the

animals have amazing intelligence"—here the dogs seemed to grin in pleasure at the compliment—"but children of a human?" She still sounded very skeptical, but there was a gleam of fascination in her eyes nonetheless.

"No, it's the truth I'm telling you," he insisted. "You see, nearly two years ago my mother came to Almhuin to visit. She had with her a sister named Tuiren. At the same time, Iollan Eachtach, a chieftan of the Ulster clans, was staying with me as well. And, as such things often happen, the two fell in love. Iollan asked for Tuiren in marriage and took her away to his house.

"But before he left, my mother had me make Iollan give his word that he would return her safely if I should ever ask for her. He did so gladly, and Caoilte and Goll swore to assure he'd keep the oath. Tuiren was given into his hand.

"The problem about it was that none of us knew Iollan already had a sweetheart of the Sidhe—that's a name for the de Danaan folk who live in the underground dwellings. Her name was Uchtdealb of the Fair Breast, and she was seized by a raging jealousy when she found he had taken a wife.

"In the disguise of a messenger she went to Tuiren and told her I had sent for her to come help me with a great feast. She recalled the oath of Iollan and came away at once. But once they were away from the house, the woman of the Sidhe took out her dark druid rod from her cloak and gave Tuiren a blow of it that changed her into a hound, the most beautiful that was ever seen. And then she went on, bringing the hound with her, to the house of Fergus Fionnliath, king of the harbor of Gallimh.

"This Fergus has been always the most unfriendly man in the world to dogs. He'd never even let one stop in the same house with him. But Uchtdealb said to him that I wished him good life and health and wished him to mind the dog till I could come for her. 'The animal is with young,' the woman told him, 'so do not let her go hunting when her time is near, or the wrath of Finn will be upon you surely.' And Fergus answered, 'A strange message that is, for Finn knows well enough my hatred for dogs. Still, for all that, it would be a foolish man who gave insult in such a thing.'

"So, he took the hound, and he tried her in the hunt, and she was the finest he ever saw. There was no wild creature she could not run down. So from that out, he took a great liking for hounds. He grew very careful of her, being sure that when her time was near she did not go hunting anymore, and he was by her when she gave birth to a fine pair of whelps.

"By this time, I had heard my mother's sister was not living with Iollan. I was angry and called him to fulfill the pledge he had given the Fianna. He asked me for time to go in search of her, promising that if he could not bring her back, he'd offer himself in satisfaction. To that I agreed, and he went off to his sweetheart, Uchtdealb, for he suspected that she'd played a part in this. He told her the way things were, and that his own life might be forfeit. 'If that is so,' said she, 'and if you pledge to keep me as your sweetheart all your life, I'll free you from the danger.'

"So, Iollan gave his promise, and she went away to the house of Fergus and brought Tuiren away—it nearly broke the heart of Fergus—and put her own shape upon her again. She came safely back to me after that, with her two whelps. But, as they had never been in the human form, they remained as hounds. I promised her to keep them always with me, as my two most valued prizes, and I gave them the names of Bran and Sceolan. They have been my close companions ever since."

It was obvious from her expression that the tale had enthralled Cuillen in spite of herself. Finn smiled at her in pleasure. But then, as if suddenly aware of her closeness, his expression grew more serious, more intent. He leaned toward her, clearly drawn in by that softly glowing face, those bright eyes, those lips parted almost expectantly.

His move broke the spell. With a start she drew back, looking flustered by what she had nearly allowed to happen.

"I am a practical woman," she said, putting on a stern tone in an apparent attempt to cover her lapse. "You can't beguile me with your fanciful tales."

"What?" he said, taken aback by this abrupt change of mood. "But . . . I wasn't! What do you mean, 'beguile'?"

"I told you that I had heard much about you," she said. "And I have heard much of the romantic exploits of Finn MacCumhal. They're quite the talk of all the girls in court. Such things excite them. But not me. You won't use your charming ways to win me over." She jerked her cloak more tightly around her in a defensive gesture.

"I'm doing nothing like that!" Finn protested, so sharply it startled the others from their sleep. "I was only trying to talk to you. You asked me—"

"You just keep your distance from now on," she interrupted, climbing to her feet. "And keep to our mission!"

With that she stamped away to the hut's far side and plopped down in a dry spot, her back to him.

He stared after her in shock and frustration. Then, aware he was being watched, his gaze moved around. The dogs and his three human companions were all staring at him with great interest.

"Sorry to wake you," he said in a somewhat-embarrassed way.

Conan grumbled something unintelligible but almost certainly coarse under his breath and rolled to his other side. Caoilte shook his head pityingly and settled himself again within his cloak.

"She is a girl of very independent spirit," Labran said in a commiserating tone.

"Just go back to sleep," said Finn tersely, clearly not in the mood for sympathy. Labran complied swiftly, and the young captain's eyes went to the dogs. "I can tell you two are laughing," he accused. "I'd surely love to know what you were thinking now. Ah well, you go to sleep too."

Obediently the animals lay down and closed their eyes, though the grins lingered on. Finn rolled himself in his cloak and settled by the fire. He tried to sleep, but his eyes strayed often to the figure huddled alone across the hut.

With a final sigh that blended anger, resignation, and regret, he rolled himself onto his other side, away from the sight of her, forcing his eyes closed.

From the leaking roof, a chill trickle of rain began to drip on his face.

Far away in the storm and darkness, a dragon boat fought its way in through enormous breakers skillfully, finally grounding on a strip of beach.

Dark figures climbed over its bulwarks, dropping into the boiling surf and making their way quickly onto shore. They formed into a tight group, one figure moving out to stand before them. Its hand moved behind the small shield that it bore. The jewel set at the shield's center glowed brightly, casting an eerie blue glare upon the scene, lighting the sinister face of Caisel.

"We have no time to waste," he shouted to the others over the roar of sea and wind. "We must head inland at once if we hope to intercept our enemies." He raised his free hand, revealing a cylindrical leather case. "I have the chart of Donn. Stay close to me and I will lead the way. No man is to act or even think without my order!" he warned darkly. "Nothing must go wrong. In two days' time, we will have a prize for our great king: the head of Finn MacCumhal!"

CHAPTER ELEVEN

PITFALL

It had at last ceased to rain, but a thick fog had dropped upon the land like a gray blanket of heavy wool. Finn's tiny company had now pulled up on the verge of a strange, new landscape and were peering intently ahead at a ghostly scene.

The ground was very flat, spreading away to be soon lost behind the solid-looking curtain of the fog. The earth was very dark and barren save for the black trunks of scattered trees, grotesque shadows in the gray, thrusting up bare, spiderlike limbs.

"The boglands," Labran announced. "A very treacherous place. We must walk the horses here."

"Why?" asked Cuillen.

"These bogs are soft, filled with holes that cannot be seen," he explained. "They'll suck a man in and hold him, drag him down in moments. The horses could stumble into one as could we ourselves if we don't move carefully."

"I once saw a man who had died in the bogs," put in Caoilte. "Found him when I was a boy, cutting the turf for our fires. His feet were sticking from the cut, and we dug him out. Very old he must have been, though he looked freshly dead, except that the peat had turned him quite black. Poor fella. From his look, he'd not died pleasantly."

He spoke conversationally, but kept an eye upon Cuillen, as if to gauge her reaction. He was not disappointed. She grimaced at the tale and cast a more-apprehensive gaze across the bogs.

"Couldn't we go around?" she asked Labran.

"It would take us a full day," he said. "Perhaps two. They extend for a great way."

"We must go through," said Finn determinedly, climbing from his horse.

The others dismounted as well, save for Cuillen. Seeing her hesitation, Finn addressed her brusquely:

"Well, what's wrong? It's for your high king, isn't it? We don't want anything delaying us!"

She shot him a hate-filled look and angrily climbed down. With all of the group gathered closely, following the cautious lead of Finn and Caoilte, they began to feel their way across the desolate boglands.

They pressed forward for a short time with fair speed, but the fog seemed to close in ever thicker as they progressed. Soon every yard became a greater struggle, the horses growing more reluctant, needing more constant and more violent urging.

At one piont the horse of Cuillen, straying to one side despite her efforts, stepped into a hole and nearly fell, yanking her forward. Had Finn not caught her, she would have splashed facedown into a slime-topped pool.

"Sorry," he said, quickly releasing her. "I didn't mean to come so close."

He stepped back as she scowled at him and then began the task of getting her horse free of the clinging mud.

"Shouldn't we help her?" the eager-to-please Labran asked Finn.

"Not her," Finn answered. "She means to do everything herself. Let her!"

So they watched as she strained and pushed and hauled at the animal, finally helping it to step up to firmer ground.

"About time," Finn commented, and turned from the outraged girl to lead them on again.

The fog had by now closed down so heavily around them that they could see less than a spear's throw.

"I don't like this fog," he said, eyeing it unhappily.

"I like the smell of it even less," remarked Caoilte, wrinkling his nose at the heavy odor of decay filling the air.

"Well, the quicker on, the quicker through!" Labran said in a cheering, optimistic way.

Caoilte and Finn exchanged a glance of amusement over the affable young man. Conan only gave Labran a hostile glare.

They traveled on uneventfully for some way further, and

then came upon a little copse of dead trees. Their trunks had been petrified to an ironlike hardness by the action of the oily sod. They stood now like a gathering of skeletons engaged in some solemn death rite.

The party moved through them with even greater caution, forced to climb over or skirt large logs half-buried in the ooze. The spectral figures of the trees looming about them in the fog clearly made them all uneasy. They glanced around continually as they slogged ahead.

Finn's eyes slipped across one bent, gnarled tree corpse and past a smaller shadow beside it. Then he froze, his attention fixing upon the second form. It was that of a human being!

He swung his gaze around. Other figures had suddenly appeared from the cover of the surrounding trees. He grabbed his sword's hilt and opened his mouth to shout a warning. But as he did, a blue stream of light erupted from the figure ahead and shot straight toward him.

Finn threw himself violently to one side. The beam sizzled past him and struck one of the trees, vaporizing its upper half in a spectacular blossom of crackling light.

The other figures about Finn's band charged forward, the faint light gleaming on their iron helmets and raised weapons. Finn sprang to his feet, his own sword already set. Caoilte and Conan drew, as well, quickly forming a triangle to face the enemy.

"Get behind us!" Caoilte snapped at Labran and the girl.

"I can help!" she said protestingly.

Caoilte parried an ax blow from one attacker, driving him back with a return blow.

"You can get killed, you mean!" he growled, grabbing the girl's arm and yanking her behind him.

He, Conan, Finn, and the two dogs now found themselves hotly engaged with a score of mailed warriors. But though Donn's men had great fighting skills, they were no match for the Fianna champions. All three demonstrated their abilities, each taking on several opponents at a time. Even the rotund Conan showed amazing speed and dexterity, using his bulk to slam attackers away and his strength to smash through their defenses. The dogs also did their part, leaping fearlessly upon the enemy, dragging men to the ground in the grip of their tearing fangs. In moments several of the ambushing group were down.

Still, the others continued to press bravely in, forming a close-packed mass. Then it was a most-eerie battle they fought in the dense fog. The damp, clinging, gray cloak of it muffled the sounds of the fight: the clashing of arms, the grunts of effort, and the cries of pain. It blurred the figures of those crowded together into one form, like that of some bizarre creature convulsing in the throes of death agony, thrashing out wildly with its many limbs.

Around this knot of contending warriors slunk the lean, serpentine figure of Caisel. His shield was up before him as he sought an angle to take another clear shot at Finn or one of his comrades without risking himself.

Then his chance came. Finn drove his sword through an opponent and the man fell back, leaving the young captain exposed to Caisel's view. Donn's henchman rose up with a grin of triumph, thrusting the shield forward to point at Finn. The blue stone glowed with building energy. The stream of light shot out.

But Caoilte had seen Caisel's move and realized his target. With a warning shout he threw himself before Finn, lifting his own shield in defense.

The dark warrior succeeded, but not totally. His shield deflected most of the deadly beam. It crackled across the surface, fragmenting into a spiderweb of lines and dissipating. But one edge of it skimmed past the iron rim and slipped along his side.

Even this seemingly minor touch of the weapon's power had a startling effect. Caoilte was knocked back as if a lightning bolt had struck him, crashing to the ground in a heap some distance away.

Finn looked in shock at his fallen comrade, and then back to Caisel. The weasel-faced man was pointing his shield for another shot. But heedless of the danger in his need for revenge, Finn leapt straight toward him with a cry of rage.

Caisel, seemingly flustered by this direct assault, fired too quickly and his shot went wide. The beam of energy whizzed off harmlessly into the fog. The young Fian captain reached his foe and swung out at him with his sword. The agile Caisel leaped backward to avoid the blow. He saved himself, but misjudged his landing place: his heels struck on the crumbling margin of an oily pool, and it gave way. Yelping in surprise, he fell back into the black sludge and disappeared beneath its surface.

Now other of the warriors attacked Finn from two sides and he was forced to back away to defend himself. Conan and the dogs were also heavily engaged, while Caoilte was now struggling, unsuccessfully, to get to his feet.

The dark warrior struggled halfway up, then his strength failed and he fell back, panting for breath. A mailed enemy, noting that he still lived, turned from Conan and started toward him. Finn saw the man advancing on his friend, but could do nothing to reach him. Through clouding vision, Caoilte watched the warrior stride up, a massive broadsword lifting in one hand.

But as the weapon started down for its death blow, another, smaller figure appeared suddenly beside the warrior, swinging up a spear to knock away the blade. Amazement filled Caoilte's face as he watched. For Cuillen, having seized a fallen weapon, had now joined the fight.

For all her slenderness of form, she fought with a great power and ferocity, descending like a whirlwind upon the mailed warrior. She used the spear like a staff, striking him with a swift series of blows to arm, face, and stomach, the last doubling him forward. Then she swung around him in a graceful move, sweeping the spear-haft against the back of his knee, taking out his leg. The man toppled onto the spongy sod and lay stunned.

A second warrior now charged in behind her, lifting his war ax. Caoilte tried weakly to call a warning, but there was no need. Some marvelous battle-instinct of the girl seemed to alert her, and she wheeled around as he neared. She struck out with precise timing—when his own weapon had risen above his head and left his body exposed—ramming the spearhead into his chest. His forward momentum drove the point on through his heart, and he collapsed, dead before he struck the ground.

The girl stepped over the fallen man, no pity showing in her grim young face as she looked down at him. With a jerk of her arm she pulled the spearhead free and went on guard, eyes sweeping the area for other foes.

"By Danu!" Caoilte breathed in awe.

Finn, Conan, and the dogs, meanwhile, were holding their own well against the remainder of the attackers. However, unseen by Finn, Caisel was now slowly rising again from the oily pool, looking like some swamp wraith in his dripping coat of black murk. Teeth bared in rage, he pointed his shield of power toward the warrior, hand clenching on the firing handle in a gesture of finality.

"Now, MacCumhal," he snarled, "you will die!"

Then his expression froze in shock that quickly turned to puzzlement. Nothing had happened. He tilted the shield upward and looked down at its face. The jewel was covered with a thick layer of the greasy mud. He tried to wipe it off. He shook the shield in frustration. He pressed the firing lever with increasing violence. Still nothing.

Desperation in his face now, he looked back to the fight. Half his men were down, the others hard-pressed to hold off Finn's little band.

With no further hesitation, he hauled himself from the sticky clutches of the pool, clambering onto hard ground on the side farthest from the fight. Then, with his own safe retreat assured, he called out to his men:

"Withdraw! Withdraw!"

Seeing that their leader had already begun this process, the warriors did not hesitate to obey. The elite troops of Daire Donn turned and bolted away, one shaking off the tearing jaws of Bran and sacrificing half his breeches in the process. In moments they had vanished into the fog.

The defenders, left so abruptly alone, stood looking about them in surprise for a moment. Then Finn and Cuillen rushed to Caoilte's side.

He was lying limply now, eyes closed, and Finn lifted him gently in his arms.

"Caoilte, my friend," he said urgently, "you can't be dead!"

The dark warrior stirred, his eyes opening. He gave Finn a weak smile.

"No, Finn, but it feels close. Very close."

Finn noted a wide, scorched mark across Caoilte's tunic. He carefully pulled the rent linen aside, revealing the flesh beneath.

He nearly grimaced at what he saw. The beam had torn a jagged wound along the warrior's side. The strange energy of the beam had made it seem already festered, swollen and black, while the skin on either side was puckered and white, as if withering away. This condition seemed to spread outward from the wound even as Finn watched.

Finn's eyes rose to Cuillen's. She too was stone-faced, but her own alarm at the awful wound was in her eyes.

Caoilte's gaze went from one face to the other.

"It is bad, isn't it?" he asked. "You can't hide it. I'm too old a warrior."

"It . . . it's not really so bad," Finn answered, smiling, his voice level. "We'll get you set right soon enough."

"It's always been impossible for you to lie, my friend," said Caoilte. With a great effort he strained to raise himself but fell back, wincing from the pain. "See there—I can barely move. If a warrior can't move, it's his end surely."

"Just rest easy," Finn said. "We'll get help."

Caoilte gave a short, sharp laugh at that.

"And what kind of help will you be getting me out here? No, Finn. You can't be wasting time. I'm through. The only service I can give you now is to make you leave me." He was fading, his voice growing weaker. But he seemed to pool the remainder of his strength for a final, earnest plea: "So go ahead, will you, now? Please, go ahead!"

This expended his energy and he fell into unconsciousness.

Finn eased him back to the ground and looked up. Conan, Labran, and the two dogs were now about them, gazing down at the stricken man. The two dogs looked anxious. Labran seemed quite distressed, but Conan's expression was more one of indifference.

"He's right, you know," the stout warrior growled in a frank, practical way. "He's finished. We'd be best to leave him."

"Oh, shut up, Conan!" Finn shot back angrily.

"Well, I was just saying the truth," Conan said defensively. "He's a warrior. He knows it well enough. So do you."

"Maybe," said Finn, "but I won't leave him."

"And what about our quest?"

"Not to save all Ireland will I let Caoilte die here," Finn answered fiercely. "He has saved me too many times." He gave Cuillen a challenging look. "But I suppose that's not to your liking either. You'd agree with Conan. Leave Caoilte here and be on with the high king's work!"

"No!" she protested quickly, clearly stung by the cruelty in his words. "I would never ask you to leave your friend."

His expression softened at that. He smiled at her.

"I thank you," he said. "And, once he is brought to some help, I promise you we will go on."

"But how long will it take to bring him to this help?" asked Conan, gazing around him at the barren landscape.

"Perhaps I can be of some assistance in that," came the voice of Labran, but in a tone a great deal more shrill than normal.

His companions turned about to look toward him. For a moment they looked puzzled, for it seemed at first glance that the man had vanished. But then Finn noticed a small, rodentlike creature with a coat of bushy yellow fur and a tremendous bulblike nose. The nose was twitching nervously.

"Labran?" he inquired in amazement. "Is that you?"

"Oh!" said the creature in a disconcerted way. "I forgot."

The nose began a more-violent twitching that shook the tiny body. Then the creature began to swell, shooting up into the lean form of the son of Tadg.

"What happened to you?" Cuillen asked him.

He seemed quite embarrassed, looking down at the ground and flushing.

"I . . . well, I meant to create the illusion of a monster about myself again and frighten them off. It—it didn't work quite as I expected."

"That's no great surprise to me," Conan said scornfully. "I knew you were useless from the start!"

This criticism seemed to devastate the young man. A look of anguish filled his expression.

"I know," he agreed, sounding ashamed. "I know I'm no good to you as a warrior, and I'm a coward on top of it. I was so frightened, I couldn't get the magic to work properly."

"It's all right, Labran," Cuillen told him consolingly, moving to his side. She took his hand and patted it gently, like a mother soothing a hurt child. "You meant well, and not all men must prove themselves by being fighters. Your only part in this was to lead us, and you've done that very well." She shot an angry look at Conan, her voice growing sharp. "And you, you great lout, stop bullying him!"

Conan muttered a dark curse and turned away.

"Now, Labran," she said coaxingly, "please tell us how you think we can help Caoilte."

"There is a place not far away," he said with some of his spirits restored to him. He pointed toward the northwest. "It's just beyond the boglands, over that way. It's a small Sid, and I know the ones who live there. They might be able to take care of Caoilte."

"Then, let's waste no more time in getting him there," Finn said briskly. "Conan, help me with Caoilte. Cuillen, get the horses."

While Cuillen rounded up their mounts, the stout warrior moved reluctantly to Caoilte's side. At Finn's direction, he and the young captain crouched down, slipped their arms beneath the limp form.

"Are you certain Caoilte will be welcome at this Sid?" Finn asked Labran as they prepared to lift. "There are many de Danaans hostile to the mortals of Ireland."

"Oh, he'll be welcome!" Labran said with an odd, little smile as they raised Caoilte gently from the ground. "He's a man, isn't he?"

CHAPTER TWELVE
THE SID OF WOMEN

Conan and Finn eased Caoilte back on the soft bed and moved away. As they did, their places were taken by three women who peered down at the wounded man's face with great interest.

"Oh, he is a fine-looking one, isn't he?" one said in a voice tinged with excitement.

"Yes! Yes, he is!" agreed a second. "And it's been so long!"

"He is only a man," said a third in a reprimanding way. "And a mortal as well. Kindly remember that."

Finn and Conan had now joined the rest of their little band. They stood in a tight group close outside the entrance to the small sleeping chamber where they had just laid Caoilte. The room that opened behind them was a cavern, like the Sid of Tadg. This was clear from the rocky walls that arched upward to form a vaulted ceiling. But beyond that, there was very little similarity. This Sid was much smaller, its atmosphere dry, comfortable, and very intimate.

This coziness of feeling was somewhat the result of a cheerful fire burning in a neat central hearth of stone. But it was even more the result of a pleasant decor. Large tapestries with country scenes in soothing colors hung upon the lower portion of the rough walls, while thick, braided rugs covered the chill stone floor. Countless delicate ornaments in bronze, gold, silver, glass, and porcelain softly reflected and multiplied the warm light of the flames. So did the highly polished oak of the finely wrought furniture, though little of these surfaces could actually be seen: for the tables were overspread with tatting in intricate, openwork designs, and each of the seats was covered with overstuffed, richly embroidered cushions. The total effect of all this, while a bit fussy and overcrowded, was a most homey one.

Around the base of the main chambers were visible many other small sleeping chambers like the one in which Caoilte now rested. Each one was appointed with equal care and comfort, but with touches of individual taste in colors and styles of decoration. Some of the occupants of these chambers were at work upon many domestic tasks about the Sid, cleaning, sewing, tending the cauldrons and spits upon the central fire. But most were gathered in an attentive crowd about the door of Caoilte's chamber, silent except for the faint, fluttering sound of excited whispering.

Conan MacMorna, looking all the stouter and quite out of place amidst the delicate objects, glared about him at the Sid and the women with an expression of enormous discomfort. His companions paid little heed to their surroundings, all their attention fixed on the three women around the stricken Caoilte.

"Well, Bebind, do you think that you can save him?" Labran called through the doorway.

The woman who had spoken third turned toward him. She was tall, lean, large-boned, and carried herself with tremendous dignity. Her features were handsome but austere: her face was long and straight of jaw; her nose sharp, thin, and emphatic; her mouth a tight-lipped line. This severity of look was reinforced by a manner both brisk and domineering.

"You have never been patient enough, young Labran," she told him in the tone of a teacher reprimanding a troublesome pupil. "I have barely begun my examination."

She turned back to the other women.

"Flann, removed his tunic," she ordered.

The woman she addressed fell obediently to this task. She was as plump in form as Bebind was lean, with a round, red-cheeked face and a cheery, helpful disposition. Skillfully and gently she pulled the tunic off Caoilte, leaving the warrior's broad chest exposed.

"My!" said the first woman with a sharp intake of breath. "He surely does have . . . the look of great strength."

Bebind shot her a disapproving glance.

"Remember yourself, Uaine," she said sharply.

The first woman was small and willowy of form. She had clearly once been a great beauty, but now faded, like a flower past its brief moment of full bloom. The clean lines of the finely sculpted features were blurred by the wear of years. At the words of Bebind, she blushed, dropping large, deep-blue eyes to the ground in embarrassment.

Meanwhile, the tall woman was getting on with a thorough examination of the hurt man. She ran her hands lightly across his chest.

"He is well formed, I will agree," she said. She touched several lines of old scar tissue. "Clearly a warrior who has survived much fighting. Good. His strength and courage are in his favor." She turned her attention to the gaping wound. "But this . . . this is against him. The wound itself should not be so serious."

She bent close to stare intently at the festering cut, then moved her gaze to the withering skin about it. The strange blistering had now spread more than a handsbreadth about the wound. She put out a finger and touched the infected flesh very gently. Still, Caoilte shifted, giving a moan of pain.

"What's wrong?" Finn asked in alarm, moving into the doorway. "Is he all right?"

"No, young man," Bebind said frankly, rising and turning to him, "he is not all right. He is dying. The energy of this weapon you spoke of has somehow poisoned him. It will spread slowly through his system, sucking the juices, the vitality, from his tissues."

"But can you stop it?" Finn asked urgently. "Labran said there was a chance that you could heal him."

"A chance . . . perhaps," the woman answered cautiously. Then, in a voice tinged with doubt, she added, "Though, I'm not certain we should be helping him. He is mortal, after all."

"But, sister," protested Flann, "he does seem to be such a fine young man, and a brave one as well, from what Labran has said. We can't turn him away."

"She is right," chimed in Uaine most imploringly. "Please let us help him. It has been such a very long time."

The tall woman listened, then dropped her gaze to Caoilte's young face, so pale and drawn with pain.

"Very well," she said. "Against my better judgment, I will consent." She looked around to Finn. "But I can promise you nothing, Finn MacCumhal. Do you understand? This poison is unknown to me. It may be greater than our healing arts can counter."

"I understand. All I ask is that you try."

Caoilte moaned again. His eyelids fluttered open and he looked about him in a startled way, his body tensing. Finn moved quickly to his side.

"It's all right, my friend," he said soothingly. "I'm here."

"Finn!" Caoilte said in relief. "But where am I?"

"We've found a place where you can rest and be healed."

"A place?" he repeated, looking quizzically at the chamber and the three women. "What sort of place?"

"It is a Sid. Labran knew of it. The de Danaans here have agreed to help you."

"You have done too much," the dark warrior said. "You must not delay more. Leave me now. Get on with the quest."

"Not yet," Finn argued. "I've got to be certain that you will survive."

With a tremendous effort, Caoilte lifted a hand to clasp Finn's shoulder in a fierce grip.

"No!" he said through clenched teeth. "My life or death now will change nothing, but your delay will destroy Ireland. If you are truly my friend, you'll not make me responsible for that! You've done all that you needed to. More! Don't be losing another moment. Go now, or our friendship's at an end!"

Finn hesitated, as if prepared to argue on. But then he sighed and nodded.

"It is the truth you're speaking, Caoilte," he reluctantly agreed. "I must be thinking of the rest of our comrades now." He smiled and put a hand upon his friend's. "You rest easy. We will go on. But we'll come back for you. Give me your oath that you'll be well by then."

"I'll do what I can, if you'll promise in return that you'll put me from your mind now. Think only of getting those weapons!"

"You have my word," Finn assured him.

Cuillen and Labran had come into the doorway behind Finn and were watching this. Caoilte's gaze fell upon the girl and he gestured her forward.

"Please, come closer," he said very weakly, for the effort to convince Finn had drained most of his strength.

She stepped over to the bedside next to Finn and bent down over him. Her face openly revealed her concern for him.

"You," he said, his voice barely above a whisper, "—I wanted you to know that I regret the differences we've had. I was wrong about you. It's truly a woman of great courage that you are, and a grand fighter as well. And you'll have need of both these things, for the task you've taken on is all the larger now. I'm charging you to look after Finn for me." He managed a smile. "Take care of him well. He's forever after getting himself into troubles."

"I will," she promised, giving him a smile in return. But then she quickly turned away to hide the tears that welled into her eyes.

This last speech had used the remainder of Caoilte's energy. He suddenly relaxed, his head rolling to one side, his eyes falling closed. Finn looked to Bebind in alarm.

"He has only fallen asleep," she assured him. "Quite natural with that wound. But leave him now to rest."

Finn and Cuillen went out of the chamber, followed by the three women. Out in the main cavern they found the crowd still gathered. Two rather buxom women of middle age had moved up close on either side of Conan and were running bold and wanton gazes up and down his considerable amount of form. He was clearly aware of their attention, but was trying to ignore it, staring ahead, his body rigid, his face quite red.

"Caoilte will be taken care of," Finn announced, unable to suppress a grin at the stout warrior's discomfort. "We will be going on at once."

"By all the gods my family swears by, that's good news," Conan said with great relief, stepping toward Finn and away from the women. "The sooner out of this place, the better."

"A great pity it is that you must leave us, Finn MacCumhal," said Uaine, moving up close before him, placing a hand lightly upon his chest. She was still a very beautiful woman, and her large eyes were of a deep blue-violet whose gaze was clearly captivating to young Finn.

"I am sorry too," he said politely. "But we really must be leaving."

"Too bad," she said, giving him a sultry smile and lifting the hand to softly stroke his chin. "I've seen few men as handsome as yourself."

Finn, still staring down into those eyes, seemed to become suddenly aware of the sensual invitation they contained. He lifted his gaze sharply and, over Uaine's shoulder, saw Cuillen watching him with an irritated glare.

"Well . . . I—I thank you," he told Uaine awkwardly. "We'll be returning. I will see you then, perhaps."

"Oh, I do hope so," she breathed.

"Uaine, behave yourself now," Bebind said impatiently. "Let the man go." She looked around at the crowd of other women with some annoyance. "And the rest of you, haven't you other tasks to occupy you?"

"We only wish to know if the dark man will be staying, Sister Bebind," one of them asked boldly.

"Yes, he will," she snapped. "But he is very sick and he will need much rest! Now, get about your work, all of you."

The group broke up, but with a buzz of most excited talk. The one who had spoken to Bebind could be heard remarking to a friend with great anticipation:

"He can't stay sick forever!"

Finn and his companions were escorted from the cavern by Bebind, along a passage much like that in Tadg's Sid, out through a similarly hidden doorway. The setting for the Sid of the women was different, however. It was surrounded by a green and pleasant glade, bright now with the sun that had finally reappeared. And the mound itself was no barren pile of rock but a soft, gentle swell of grass-covered earth.

They found their horses where they had left them tethered, guarded by the two dogs.

"Farewell, and good fortune in your quest," Bebind told them. "Now I must return and see to the healing of your friend."

She left them, and the four went to the horses, untethering them and preparing to mount. As they did so, Finn noted that Labran was grinning widely.

"And what is it that's amused you so?" he asked.

"It's a warm welcome you'll receive there if you ever decide to stay," Labran said, giving Finn a broad wink. "Of that I'm certain!"

"Just another conquest for the mighty Finn," Cuillen said scornfully. She climbed onto her horse and spurred it angrily away.

Finn stared after her, taken at a loss by her odd behavior.

"Now what do you suppose is wrong with her?" he asked Labran.

Labran shook his head, his expression one of pity for the young warrior.

"And my father thinks that *I'm* a fool!" he said.

As Labran spurred his rickety horse after Cuillen's, Finn noted Conan holding back, his expression even glummer than usual.

"And just what is it that you're concerned with?" he asked.

"Have you asked yourself who those warriors were?" said Conan, "and how it was they came to ambush us?"

"They had to be of Donn's army," Finn replied. "They wore the dress of his fighting men, and that one with the shield had to be the same as plagued us on the strand."

"And how did they reach the boglands before us?"

"I've no idea. Maybe they followed us from Corca Dhuibhne and slipped ahead of us last night."

"Followed us? On foot?" Conan said skeptically.

"Then what do you think?"

"I think someone may have sent them here to wait for us. Someone who knew what our route had to be."

"Like my grandfather, you mean," said Finn. "I did think of him. But I can't believe he'd risk himself and all Ireland just to destroy me. Even he isn't so depraved."

"Maybe not," Conan said darkly, "but I'm trusting no one in this from here out!"

With that they urged their horses ahead, to follow the other two. Neither man was aware that a mailed warrior was observing them from the cover of the nearby trees. He waited until they were safely out of sight, then moved quickly off through the underbrush, soon reaching a small clearing nearby.

Here the survivors of Caisel's war party rested. The warriors lay about in attitudes of exhaustion. Several were in the process of binding wounds received in the recent battle. Caisel sat apart, meticulously cleaning the muck coating from his shield.

The scout approached him, but Caisel seemed unaware, so absorbed was he in his work, his face knotted in a scowl of concentration.

"My captain?" the warrior ventured. "I have a report."

"Quiet!" the other barked. "Let me just finish!"

He wiped a last bit of black mud from the recesses of the firing mechanism. He lifted the shield on his arm and pointed it toward a tree. The warrior moved well back out of the line of fire as Caisel pressed the trigger.

Nothing happened. The blue stone remained dark.

"Curse this thing!" Caisel raged, casting the shield violently to the ground. He turned upon the warrior angrily. "Well? And what news do you have? Quickly!"

"They have left the wounded one near here, my captain," the man said.

"Near here?" Caisel repeated in disbelief. "Where?"

"Within a . . . a mound of earth," said the other, clearly aware how peculiar his tale sounded. "In some way I couldn't see, they just vanished into the thing. And now they've reappeared, but without him. They are riding on toward the north."

"We could have attacked them when they stopped," another warrior commented.

"Attacked?" said Caisel, voice heavy with sarcasm. "A brilliant notion. Then I could see my brave fighting men run like frightened does again!"

"There are only four of them now," the man said defensively.

"Yes, and there were only five before!" Caisel retorted nastily, "yet with twice your number you couldn't defeat them. You call yourself warriors. *Phaugh!*" He spat on the ground before the man, then pointed to the shield. "Until that is working again, we won't attack them. I must be certain they don't escape next time."

"We could send to Donn for more warriors," another suggested.

"No!" Caisel said quickly. "Don't be a fool. If Donn found out how miserably we had failed, our own lives would be forfeit. We must succeed."

"Then, what should we do?" asked the scout.

"We follow until I can repair my shield of power. Then we will strike." He turned to glare off in the direction Finn's party had gone. "And it will be my pleasure to burn this Finn MacCumhal to a smoldering lump of flesh, bit by tiny bit!"

CHAPTER THIRTEEN
THE HIGH KING'S SON

The troop of horsemen made a colorful sight as they crossed the hills of Corca Dhuibhne.

The riders atop the tall, proud steeds were of a similarly noble bearing. All were quite youthful of look, mostly slim, long-featured, and very fair. The hair of every one of them was dressed most carefully, as if each man was trying to outdo his fellows. Some wore the long hair flamboyantly curled. Others had it stiffened by lime into a great bush or braided into one or two or sometimes even dozens of neat plaits. Often these plaits were hung with balls of gold, entwined with silver chains, or had beads of glass and metal threaded upon them.

In dress the riders also seemed to be competing for most grand. Rich brocades, finely textured wools and linens, sumptuous embroidery, and golden fringing abounded. Much jewelry also adorned the elegant young men: bracelets on their arms; fine torcs of twisted gold thread at their necks; large, round, cloak-pins whose intricate spiraling designs were colored in brightly glowing enamels. So thick were the ornaments upon them that some glittered like the sky on a clear winter's night.

Altogether, the group looked more suited to a fine court than to a battlefield. Yet all wore harness and sheathed swords, carried shields freshly painted in clan colors and spears whose new-honed points flashed in the sun.

This resplendent troop rode steadily on across the hills until, topping a final crest, they reined their horses to a stop. Below them could be seen the crescent beach of the White Strand.

Along the edge of the embankment above the beach there was now a crude wall, of a man's height and formed of piled rock, some wooden stakes, upturned wagons, and wicker panels made of woven sticks. Against this defensive barrier the army of Daire Donn was furiously engaged in dashing itself. The men swarmed upward from the beach, using simple ladders of rope or wood to help them negotiate the rocky bank. Looking from the distance like ants upon a carcass, they made a solid, seething wave upon the beach and up the slope.

Here they piled up against the wall as they tried desperately to scale or breach it, smashing at its face with rams, trying to scramble over its top, even working under cover of fellows to dig a way through with bare hands. And while they struggled to break through, a line of Fianna warriors behind and atop the wall did their best to frustrate the efforts of their foes.

They threw spears and rocks at those climbing up from below. They kicked away ladders thrown up against the outer face. They engaged in hand-to-hand struggles with any who did manage to scale the rampart. No warrior of Donn succeeded in planting feet upon the sod behind the Fianna line. But that line had grown quite painfully thin in its valiant struggles.

The battle shouts and the clashing of arms drifted up clearly to the bright troop watching from the hill. The young man at its head—son of the high king of Ireland—listened and looked upon the chaos, and shook his head in dismay.

"Fergus True-Lips gave no lie to us when he spoke of the size of this invader's force," he remarked to the other youths close about him.

"He surely did not," one of them agreed. "Nor of the plight of the Fianna. If anything, their clans seem even weaker than he said they were."

"Then all the greater glory for us in riding to aide them!" declared the high king's son grandly. "Come on, my lads!"

With an enthusiastic cheer they urged their mounts on down the slope.

Below, Goll MacMorna was with his clansmen, fighting at the center of the line, when one of his warriors called his attention to the approaching company. Raising an eyebrow to register his tremendous astonishment, he left the wall, moving back out of the confusion of the embattled army to meet them.

Upon seeing this stolid warrior waiting, his body splattered with blood, the sword still in his hand, the troop of horsemen pulled up before him.

"So, it is Art MacConn," Goll stated, and if the appearance of the high king's son was a surprise, neither the face nor the voice of the impassive man betrayed it.

The young leader peered down curiously at him. Then his face lit with recognition.

"Ah, it's Goll MacMorna, isn't it! I know your colors, but I barely recognize you beneath that coat of blood."

"It's a somewhat poor time you've chosen for a visit to us," Goll remarked dryly and gestured toward the battle with his sword. "We're a bit . . . involved just now. We would sooner see you coming at a time when there would be musicians and singers and poets to make pleasure for you."

"It's not for playing I've come here," said MacConn, "but to give you my service in battle. I have brought a thousand and twenty good men," he waved a hand back over his troop proudly, "all sons of Ireland's highest noblemen. And each has a thirst he means to slake in his enemy's hot blood!"

"Is that so," Goll said, clearly unmoved by this bold talk. "But wasn't it your own father who said he'd be sending no one to help us?"

"He is old and spiteful," Art said disdainfully. "He has lost the courage to fight. But he'll not deny me the chance to prove myself." He struck a heroic pose.

"It is our task to defend Ireland," Goll reminded him, with just a hint of reprimand in his tone. "In allowing you to join us, we violate our oath to obey Conn, and we endanger you as well."

"Your task is to serve *all* the nobility of Ireland," MacConn returned with towering arrogance. "Your pay comes from the houses of all those with me, not just from my father. You have no right to stop us!"

"You are all untried," Goll said bluntly.

"We will show you," retorted Art. "We will prove that the so-mighty Fianna are not the only warriors in Ireland."

"So you believe. But I have never brought a lad new to the work into the breast of a battle. A lad coming into it like that often finds his death, and I'll not have you falling through me."

"Have no fear of that, MacMorna," Art assured him. "There'll be no blame put upon yourself. I give my word that I'll do battle on my own account if I may not do it on yours."

Goll considered the headstrong young man for a long moment, then he nodded.

"Very well. If you are so determined, you may fight." He turned, pointing with his sword toward an area of the wall. "See there? Our force is very weak there. Donn's men are striking hard to break through. Take your warriors and reinforce our clans. Drive back the enemy, if you can."

"If we can!" Art said with a sneer. "Watch us, old man!"

He gestured to his fellows and they dismounted. After taking some time to carefully arrange shields, draw swords, and get just the right grip on spears, they charged downward to the wall, whooping like children entering a hurley game.

Goll followed them down, his stony face not hinting at any emotion he might have felt. But Cael, seeing this force go by, moved to Goll's side with astonishment clear in his open, young face.

"Is it mad you are to let those children fight?" he demanded. "You're sending them against the red battalions of Cepda! They're some of the most savage of Donn's men!"

"Art would not be denied," Goll said calmly. "It was not reasonable to keep them from the fight when our men need so much help. And Art may learn greater respect for the skills of the fighting men of the Fians. He will be King one day."

"If he survives," added Cael.

Goll shrugged.

"Whatever his fate, it's his own choosing," he said. "No man may be denied that!"

Art and his warriors had by now reached the wall. Like a torrent they poured onto it, crashing against the red-clad enemy climbing up from the other side. The force of this unexpected and savage assault by a new, fresh contingent of men initially sent the attackers reeling back. They jumped from the wall, sliding and tumbling down the steep bank in retreat.

"After them. Keep at them!" cried Art, flushed by the ease of this first victory.

Shouting their triumph, his comrades obeyed, the eager, bright-faced youths springing from the wall, rushing down the slopes in pursuit.

They fell upon the men of Cepda, wreaking great slaughter for a time. But soon the tide began to turn. On the level beach now, the enemy regrouped. They turned to face their foes again and found themselves confronting a company of . . . boys! The proud, battle-hardened veterans of the red battalions struck back ferociously, clearly lusting to avenge themselves for the awful indignity of having run from such whelps.

Suddenly the young nobles of Tara found themselves hemmed in by a snarling pack, plunged into a real fight for the first time. They were pushed back against the base of the steep bank, battling for their lives. Their resistance was valiant, but their fighting skills were no match for those of their opponents.

One burly warrior with flowing black mustaches pushed from the mass of red-battalion men and swaggered toward Art's band. His bull-bellow of a voice reached above the din of the fight.

"I am Sligech, King of the Men of Cepda. Who of you has the courage to challenge me?"

Art pressed forward, his face still reflecting an arrogance that the hard fight had not yet beaten from him.

"I am Art, son of Conn of the Hundred Battles, King of all Ireland," he boldly answered. "I will challenge you, Sligech."

The others on both sides moved back, giving the leaders room for this single combat. As Art prepared, one of his comrades moved close and whispered urgently:

"Take a good heart now into the fight, for the Fianna will be no better pleased if it goes well with you than if it goes well for the foreigner."

Art nodded. He adjusted his shield, gripped his sword, and moved boldly forward.

Sligech met him with a sword of twice the weight. He slammed at Art with hard, broad, powerful strokes, battering the youth back. But, though strong, the man of Cepda was slow. Art's speed saved him, allowing him to duck the deadly blows as he feinted for position to strike in return.

Then a sweeping stroke of Sligech's blade made the youth leap back, and he thudded against the rocky embankment with a force that all but knocked the breath from him. A second blow he barely managed to turn upon his shield, but its impact swept him from his feet. He fell heavily forward, his face driving into the beach.

Weakly he lifted his face, spitting out a mouthful of sand. As his gaze rose, it took in the Cepda king, smiling gloatingly down. And then, above him, Art saw a figure standing on the wall. It was Goll MacMorna, his face impassive, his one eye glinting with cold light as he watched the humiliation of the high king's son.

The face of Art first grew flushed with anger, then hardened with determination.

"No, curse you, MacMorna!" he growled. And then, with a renewed energy, he gathered himself as the burly king charged in, diving aside as the man swung a great downward cut at him.

The blade sliced deep into the soft beach. Art rolled up onto his knees. With a bellow of rage, Sligech yanked his sword free and wheeled to strike again. As his weapon lifted, Art made a desperate, lightning move, striking in and up with all his power. The weapon went home, driving into the Cepda man's stomach, angling up into his chest.

He grunted with pain, looking down at the weapon in surprise. Art stared at the embedded blade too, clearly aghast at the gushing blood. Then Sligech shuddered, dropped his weapon, and collapsed backward to the sand, landing with the impact of a felled bull. He did not move again.

Stunned by their leader's death, the red battalions stood for the moment immobilized. Art, quickly recovering from his own shock, wasted no time in taking prudent advantage of this.

"Quickly, my friends, back up the slope!" he commanded.

The other young noblemen did not hesitate to obey. Much bloodied and much humbled by their experience, they lifted their dead and wounded comrades and began scrambling up the hillside toward the safety of the wall.

But they had nothing to fear from the men of Cepda, who made no attempt to follow. Indeed, they now gave over the fight altogether. Raising a great keening sound, they moved in to surround their fallen king. Several men lifted him tenderly and bore him back out of the battle, while the rest of the red battalions followed.

Art MacConn was free to direct his own troop in a safe retreat, himself staying at the base of the slope until the last had started up.

As he finally began the climb, he looked up to see Goll MacMorna still staring down and met the one, bright eye with a defiant gaze. When he did, it seemed that just for an instant, the faintest smile flickered across the graven features of that Fian chief.

Meantime, elsewhere in the battle scene, Daire Donn was raging over the retreat of the men of Cepda. One of his officers was trying to calm the leader with an explanation, having little success.

"I'll have the head of every man!" stormed Donn. "They are cowards! They betray me!"

"No, my king," said the officer. "It is their custom that makes them leave the fight. Until their king has been mourned and his body burned, they will raise no weapons."

"But they have thrown all our force into confusion! Look there! Now other units are retreating! Ah!" he cried in disgust, clenching a mailed fist. "The whole army is beginning to fall back! We've lost the day again. They are all cowards! Using any excuse to break off the fight."

"They are weary men, my king," the officer reasoned. "They have fought for many days, with great bravery. And now, with new forces joining the Fianna . . ."

"What, that handful of boys?" Donn said scornfully. "You saw them. They had the fighting skills of babes. They should never have been able to drive the red battalions back!"

"My king, it is as we have said: our men need rest, a chance to bind their wounds, to eat warm food, to become fresh again."

"No, Finnachta," Donn shot back. "The very opposite is true. If new men are coming to join the Fianna, then we must make all the greater effort to break through as soon as possible. And if not, we must not give our enemy a chance to rest. The attacks will continue."

"It would help us if Caisel would return victoriously," Finnachta said. "We had all hoped he would have returned by now."

"I know he will succeed," Donn said with confidence. "Soon he will be sailing back into this bay, and with the head of Finn MacCumhal dangling from the bow of his dragon boat!"

At this moment, the head of Finn MacCumhal was still very much attached to its shoulders. It was busily engaged in turning left and right as Finn scanned the countryside now before his little band.

"This is it?" he asked incredulously, looking around at Labran.

"It is," the other assured him. "The entrance to the Country of the Fair Men."

Finn and the others looked over the landscape again.

There was little to be seen but a wide, smooth meadow of grass over which floated a faint, gray-white mist.

"It's nothing but a flat, empty field!" Conan barked. He gave the son of Tadg a suspicious look. "What kind of trickery are you playing, you wretched dung heap!" He gripped his sword's hilt in a threatening gesture.

"Wait, Conan," Finn told him sharply. "There's no reason to be abusing Labran. I'm certain he wouldn't trick us."

"Ah, all these cursed Sid folk hate us," Conan growled. "I never have trusted him. And even if he is trying to help, he's likely made a mess of it and gotten us lost. He's a useless one, I'm telling you."

"I assure you I can be trusted," Labran said, sounding much offended. "And this *is* the entrance to the land that we're seeking. But, like all the places where the Tuatha de Danaan dwell, it is hidden away, protected from discovery by mortals."

"What do you mean, 'protected'?" Conan demanded.

"Well, when your race came to Ireland, defeated the de Danaan chieftains, and seized all for themselves, my people had no wish to leave the country they loved. So Manannan MacLir, the great god of the sea who has always been our protector, created the Sids for us to dwell in, safe beneath the earth. And he created barriers to surround them. They're not visible to mortals, but they keep all outsiders from finding their way into a Sid unless its inhabitants wish it."

Conan took this news with increasing gloominess, but it seemed to quite delight Cuillen.

"Like being led 'Astray,'" she said.

"That's right," Labran replied, smiling at her. "But another of the Sidhe can always find the way."

"Then, this Country of the Fair Men is another Sid?" asked Finn.

"In a manner of speaking," Labran said vaguely. "But on a bit grander scale. I can't explain it now. You'll have to see it yourself to understand."

"I've no liking at all for entering a stronghold of the Other," muttered Conan. "They'll have too great a power over us there. Who knows what sorcery they'll try?"

"There's little choice if we mean to gain those weapons," Finn said, "and it may take all of us to succeed."

"One man or a thousand—it'll all be the same," Conan said stubbornly. "Let this spindle of a man you trust so much get the weapons, if he means to help."

Finn eyed the balding warrior thoughtfully. It was obvious, despite his bluster, that Conan was fearful of entering the realm of these strange and mystical beings. He tried another tack.

"Very well, Conan," he said resignedly. "I don't want to be forcing you to do something against your will. If you'd feel safer staying outside again . . ."

"Safer!" bellowed the man, like a bull stung by a bee. "There's no safer about it!" He drew himself up with great dignity. "There's no man of the Baiscne clan ever lived in Ireland who can match one of the Morna clan in courage. You lead on, Finn MacCumhal, and I'll follow, into the lair of the Morrigan herself!"

"I thought it might be so," Finn said with a smile. He turned to the son of Tadg. "All right then, Labran, we're ready. Lead us into this Sid."

"Very well," said Labran. "But we must leave the horses here."

All dismounted, and the horses were staked on long tethers so they might graze without wandering too far.

"Now, stay very close to me," Labran told them in a lecturing tone. "Once we're inside the mist, I don't want to risk losing any of you. Not even Conan."

Conan muttered something under his breath and glared with irritation at the slender young man, but he made no reply.

They crossed the flat, harmless-seeming meadow slowly, heading toward the floating patch of gray. As they entered, its drifting tendrils softly enveloped them, whisking them with a cool, damp spray.

Though it had seemed a very small and very thin cloud of mist as they approached, it became ever thicker as they plunged into its depths. Finn kept his gaze constantly upon the forms of the dogs and his other comrades close about him as they became rapidly more obscure, fading to little more than vague shadows drifting in the white.

And then, abruptly, he came to a halt, his hand dropping to his sword hilt.

"What's happening?" he said with some alarm.

For the figures of his companions had suddenly and completely disappeared!

CHAPTER FOURTEEN

THE COUNTRY OF
THE FAIR MEN

"Don't be concerned," came the assuring voice of Labran from somewhere ahead in the mist. "Just keep moving on. We are nearly through."

"We had better be," came the unhappy growl of Conan.

Finn started walking on again. Soon it became evident that Labran was right. The mist grew thinner, fluttering away like shreds of finest gauze, finally leaving their view clear.

But it was not that empty meadow they looked upon now. It was another land, a far different land than any they had so far traversed in Ireland.

Above, the sky was a deep and brilliant blue. Oval, compact puffs of white cloud, evenly spaced, sailed slowly, serenely, across it like small ships on a calm sea. And all of them somehow seemed to avoid passing before a radiant sun whose beams lit every corner of the landscape with an intense illumination that gave all a startling, almost sharp edged clarity.

The smooth ground, swelling softly upward and away from the travelers, was covered with a carpet of flowers of many hues, growing in neatly separated groups to create enormous patterns across the field. Clearly not the work of nature, it looked more like a finely wrought piece of enameled jewelry.

Scattered trees with spreading bows dropped blossoms of crimson, purple, yellow, blue, and sparkling white. Strange birds with vivid plumage fluttered amongst their boughs, filling the air with their fine, sweet songs. A stream added its own rippling note as it flowed neatly down the slope in smooth, regular curves. Along its banks grazed peaceful herds, but somewhat peculiar ones. One was of sheeplike creatures, the animals as large as cows, with thick, bushy fleeces of a royal blue. The other was of horses, but with coats of shiny yellow-gold and burnished copper.

The whole land, in fact, seemed like some ornament fashioned by a craftsman's hand. And the set piece of this elaborate creation crowned the high point of the hillside right ahead of Finn's little band.

Here sat a great dun whose outer wall appeared to be formed of a single sheet of polished, gleaming bronze. Within its circle sat a house that shone even more brightly, for the walls that formed its precise octagon were vast plates of silver.

Finn, Cuillen, and even Conan stared at these wonders in open awe, both motionless and speechless for a time. The young captain, first to recover himself, finally spoke.

"This . . . all of this . . . it's within a Sid?"

"It is!" announced Labran, beaming proudly like a child showing a parent some bright toy. "It is quite something, isn't it? I told you you wouldn't understand without seeing it."

"I still don't understand," said Cuillen in a puzzled way. "The other Sids were like caverns. This is outside! There's a sky! Clouds! A sun!"

"This kind of hidden place is very special," Labran told her. "It's not exactly underground."

"Then where is it?" Finn asked. "I've never seen any place in Ireland like this."

"Well, it's not exactly in Ireland either," Labran answered carefully, clearly finding this extremely awkward. "But, in a way, it is. It doesn't actually exist anywhere. It's a place of its own, separate from anything you know, but part of it as well. It's a realm of fancy, really, shaped by the minds of its inhabitants, sustained by an energy that comes from the most powerful sources of the de Danaan magic."

"You mean, this isn't real?" asked Cuillen.

"In a way it is, but . . . in a way it's not," Labran said, making a face of frustration. "I'm afraid it's very difficult to explain."

"It would be, for the likes of you," said Conan, snorting in a scornful way.

"Quiet, Conan," Finn snapped at him. Then, to Labran:

"But the weapons—they are real, aren't they? They do exist somewhere?"

"Oh yes," said Labran. "In the protection of the king."

"And is he real too?" asked Cuillen.

"Quite real," he assured her. "His home is in that palace up the hill."

"Then let's be wasting no more time in getting there," Finn said briskly. "Labran, lead on!"

They started ahead, across the multihued carpet of flowers and up the slopes toward the gleaming palace. Conan, scowling around him at the bright landscape with obvious distaste, brought up the rear reluctantly, muttering all the while.

"No place for a fighting man," he kept repeating. "No. No place for a fighting man at all!"

"What do you mean, 'They're gone'?" demanded Caisel.

"They . . . just disappeared, my chieftain," the warrior explained tremulously.

Caisel jumped up from the boulder where he was seated and stalked toward the man across the rocky hillside where he and the remainder of his band were sheltered. His face was drawn tight with his rage.

"You idiot!" he shrieked. "You lost them! You lost them just when I'd managed to make my shield work again!" He lifted the metal circle on his arm, pointing the blue stone toward the hapless man. "I should test it on you for that!"

"No! No, my chieftain!" the warrior cried, cowering back and throwing up a hand to shield his face. "I didn't lose them. I swear to that. They were always in my sight. They just went out onto that plain beyond the hill . . . and then they vanished. It was as if the earth swallowed them."

"That's what happened to them before, my chieftain," put in the warrior who had followed Finn and his companions on their visit to the Sid of women.

"So, it's another of those magic places, is it?" Caisel said thoughtfully. He turned away and lowered his shield, much to the evident relief of his intended victim.

"What can we do now, my chieftain?" asked another of the men.

"Nothing but stay here and watch the place where they disappeared," he answered. "If they have entered some kind of hidden place, we can only hope they will come out again."

He considered, and then his long face lit with a sly smile. "And if this place is the one Tadg spoke of, we may have extra prizes for Daire Donn. Ones that will make him forgive all our bungling."

"What do you mean?"

"I mean," he said with rising excitement, "that if I'm right, we'll take back not only MacCumhal's head, but the magic shield and sword as well!" He looked around at them, his dark eyes glinting with a greedy light. "Then, my warriors . . . then *we* will have the power!"

Two fair-haired boys clad in white satin robes ushered Finn and his companions through enormous silver doors into a great hall.

In design it was much like the halls of Finn's own dun, but, like its outside, its inner walls seemed made of silver plates, while the slender columns supporting its high roof looked like solid gold. It all gleamed with a nearly blinding light from a central fire that blazed in a circle of polished black marble.

The room appeared quite empty, but as they entered, a high voice addressed them:

"Welcome, my friends. Please, come forward. And don't be worried. You've nothing to fear."

The voice came from beyond the fire, but the visitors' view of that side of the room was obscured by the glow of the flames. With Labran in the lead, they began to move slowly around the room, all peering anxiously ahead for a first view of the speaker. All, that is, except Conan. Despite the assurance from the voice, the stout warrior looked constantly about him, on his guard, his fist clenched tightly around his sword hilt.

Finally there came into view a high mound of cushions of white silk all edged in gold. And, perched upon them, appearing at first sight rather like an egg set in a cup, was a most odd looking being swathed in a flowing gown of bright silver.

As they moved closer, the nature of this being became more clear. In size he was closest to that of a boy of ten or twelve, but his form was more like that of a babe delivered prematurely. The head was the most pronounced feature, disproportionately large for the body. That is, the cranium itself was very high and rounded and smooth. It was almost devoid of hair, save for a faint, fair, whispy covering that caught the reflected silver light and created a halo about the head, as if the brain within that massive dome was radiating some energy of its own.

The face below this skull and a broad span of forehead was tiny. Its features were childlike, smooth and very delicate, and had an effeminate quality as well. Long lashes curled up from eyes of a gray so pale and bright they too seemed made of silver. The mouth was a small, neat bow with full, red lips.

The body of the man was also tiny. The shoulders were narrow, the shape of the torso lost in the full billows of the gown. The arms that poked from the gown's large, loose sleeves were spindly, with elbow and wrist joints that seemed unnaturally enlarged. And the long, bony fingers ended in wide pads, as if something had flattened the tips.

As Finn's party moved up to the base of the pillow mound, the enormous head turned slowly toward them. This was done with a great effort, the head wobbling slightly on the stalk of neck, as if the frail body could scarcely support so great a weight. The luminous eyes fixed upon the visitors benignly. The small mouth smiled sweetly. Then, in a voice as high, thin, and melodious as a piping bird, he spoke:

"I am very pleased to see visitors in my country," he said with obvious elation. "I enjoy them so much, yet I have so few here. Sit down. Join me." He raised his voice to call out: "Stewards, some refreshment for our guests."

At his command, several more boys also clad in white robes appeared around the band, bearing salvers and pitchers of wrought gold. They appeared so suddenly that they might have materialized from thin air. This quite alarmed both Conan, who dropped into fighting position, and the two dogs, who crouched down snarling. Finn and Cuillen, less startled, still looked around with some concern. But Labran moved close to them, murmuring in an assuring way:

"Be calm, please. It's all right. He's offering his hospitality. We must accept it. Just sit down. Sit down, all of you. And smile!"

They did as he requested, though Conan refused to smile. They settled into huge, soft cushions around the base of the mound. The boys, all with flowing golden hair and beautiful faces, gave them elaborately worked goblets that were filled with a liquid of warm, honey coloring.

"Drink of our fine mead and be refreshed," the strange being said. "I hope you find my servants as pleasing as I do.

They are some comfort to me, but one gets so easily bored. That is why I welcome such diversions as yourself." He looked upon the son of Tadg. "Well now, Labran, I know you, though it's been a great while since I've seen you. But your companions I do not know. Why don't you tell me who they are."

"Of course, my king," he said obediently. "This young man is Finn MacCumhal, captain of the Fianna of Ireland, son to Muirne, grandson to Tadg, and my own nephew!"

"Ah, yes!" the king said, fixing his gaze on the captain with great interest. "Even here I have heard much of your virtues. You are leader, seer, poet, and druid all in one, I understand. There has never been a better fighting man to stick his hand into that of an Irish king, so the tales go. It's said of your justice that were an enemy and your own son to come before you for judgment, you would make a fair one between them. That you are so generous as to never deny a man, so loyal as to never forsake a comrade, and so true that you would never promise at night what you would not fulfill on the morrow. A most impressive list that is! I've long hoped I'd meet you to see if such a fabulous being could truly exist."

Cuillen, stifling a sardonic smile at this, dropped her head and murmured for just Finn to hear:

"By the gods, I hope the poor man's not too disappointed."

Firing her a sideways glare of indignation, Finn hastened to reply to the strange man.

"You've made too much of me, my good king," he said in a properly self-effacing voice. "I'm no better than I ought to be and a great deal worse than they say I am. In short, my king, I'm just a simple fighting man of Ireland, seeking to serve her as best I can."

"Modest as well?" the king said with wide eyes. "My, I *am* impressed! But, seeing you, I can well believe that the tales are true. You have a most magnificent physique!"

His eyes flicked over Finn's body with an openly covetous look that clearly made the young warrior very uncomfortable. He shifted uneasily, his face growing flushed.

"And I knew you had the de Danaan blood when I first saw you," the king went on. "I could sense the aura of it about you." His gaze shifted from Finn to the two dogs. "I can sense a kind of aura about your hounds as well. Are they the ones I've been told are the offspring of your aunt?"

"They are," Finn said. "Bran and Sceolan."

The animals sat up, heads proudly lifted, and gave the king what appeared to be a bow of acknowledgment. Cuillen listened and watched in obvious amazement at this confirmation of Finn's bizarre tale.

"Most fascinating," the king said with delight, then turned his attention to the others. "Now, what about the rest of your companions?"

"This surly fellow is Conan MacMorna, brother to the chieftain of the great Morna clan," offered Labran. "Do not be offended by his attitude, my king. He is always this way."

Conan scowled at him, but said nothing.

"And I am Cuillen, Daughter to MacDremen, Emissary to the High King of all Ireland!" she grandly announced, independently asserting her own position there.

"Really?" said the king. "Well then, it is a most prestigious company I have here, indeed! Please, have more mead and tell me why it is you've come so far to see me."

"We've come to ask for something in your care," Finn said.

The being seemed surprised by this.

"Is it the Storm Shield and the Son of the Waves you're speaking about?" he asked.

"It is," said Finn. "It was my own grandfather who told us of them. He said that you might grant their use by me."

"Did he?" the king said, sounding yet more amazed. "And why would he say such a thing?"

"Because he knew that we have great need of them," Finn explained. "An army of fighting men gathered from all about the world has invaded Ireland and means to conquer it."

"I don't see why another war between mortals should concern me," was the king's puzzled response. "Those of the Tuatha de Danaan will not be disturbed. All are safe within their hidden places."

"Still, Ireland is the home of the de Danaans as well as the mortals," Finn reasoned. "The outerworld was once their own. We thought you would wish to help keep it from ruthless invaders who are seeking to ravage it."

The being gave a trilling laugh of great amusement at that.

"What an absurd notion," he said. "My dear Finn, it was *your* mortals who ravaged *our* Ireland. They came and wrenched it from our grasp, and quite brutally too." He still spoke in a most gentle tone that contrasted sharply with the harshness of his words. "They forced us to withdraw from the outer world and live a hidden life. So, you see, if another rapacious band of your mortals comes along and does the same thing to them, you can hardly expect that we'll be anxious to come to the rescue, can you?"

"But you must!" Cuillen put in. "These men will destroy everything! If you don't care about us, you must care about the land."

"My poor, pretty one," the king said, giving her a smile of pity at her innocence. "Don't you see? There is little they can do to harm the land. And in a thousand years their presence will have meant nothing at all. Violence is Ireland's destiny. It is in the very stones of her."

"But we're not asking you or your people to risk themselves," Finn explained. "All we need is your weapons to help us destroy this threat. I mean to challenge Daire Donn myself."

"Daire Donn?" the being repeated, clearly intrigued. "And who is that?"

"He is the leader of this army. He calls himself the King of the Great World, and means to make his title a true one. A special armor protects him, making both himself and his warriors invincible. Only weapons such as you have can give us any chance of defeating him."

"I quite understand your plight," said the king, "but these weapons were not intended for your use. Tadg had no right even to tell you of their existence."

"He felt he did," said Finn. "—Because he believed that you and the de Danaan people would want this Daire Donn beaten as much as the mortals of Ireland do. The man is a Fomor, a descendant of their pure, ruling blood. Many of his warriors are of the Fomor race as well. My king, he means to make Ireland a subject of their rule again. He means to recreate the ancient Fomor power!"

"How wonderfully exciting!" sang the being, apparently quite delighted at the dreadful possibility. Then a cautious note entered his voice. "Still, even if this is true, it was not meant for one of mortal blood to make use of our weapons. Only a great champion of the de Danaan race can wield the sword and shield."

"I am of de Danaan blood," Finn reminded him.

"True enough," agreed the king, fixing a thoughtful gaze upon the warrior. "Not wholly, of course, but then that was never said to be a necessity. And though we hold no love for the mortals you seek to help, we have less yet for our ancient enemies, the vile Fomor who so long and so brutally enslaved us."

"Does that mean you will allow me to take the weapons?" Finn asked hopefully.

"It means, my handsome young captain, that I will consent to let you try to earn that right. That is all."

"Earn it? What do you mean?"

"It will not be easy," the being cautioned. "The man who would be our champion must prove his worthiness. He must be tested in many ways. They are difficult and they are dangerous. Not one of my own people who have come here to try and win the weapons has ever survived them."

"It makes no difference," Finn said boldly. "Whatever must be done, I'll do."

"Ah, that is gratifying. Most gratifying!" the odd little man gushed, beaming ecstatically. "I had so hoped you would. No one has made the attempt in . . . oh . . . three hundred years now! With you, I just know it will be a most exciting diversion, no matter what the outcome."

"What have I to do?" Finn demanded, his face registering a certain dismay at his host's macabre glee. "We've got to begin at once. Time is precious to us."

"Of course, of course!" the being said, slowly nodding his great head. "The way to the weapon lies through seven gates, which must be opened with seven keys."

"Gates?" said Finn, looking around him. "Here? Within this palace?"

"No, Finn. All of this Country of the Fair Men is my palace, my dwelling place, my life. It is like no other you will ever see. So it is with the gateways. They may take any shape, as may the keys that open them. Discover the keys, and you may pass safely through. It is the peak of the mountain that marks the center of my domain that you must reach. There you will find what it is you're seeking. Win your way to the Son of the Waves and the Storm Shield. Clasp them in your hands, and they are yours."

"What about the rest of us?" asked Labran. "May we accompany Finn?"

"I will allow it," the king said carelessly. "Your presence will add interest to the game. But, mark this: It is Finn alone who may claim these weapons, and Finn alone who must unlock the doors."

Cuillen, who had listened to all this with growing impatience, now broke in forcefully.

"You cannot make us go through all of this foolishness," she told the king. "We must have those weapons, and we must have them quickly. I speak for the high king of all Ireland here. I demand that you give the sword and shield to us at once!"

The being tittered merrily at the girl's arrogant demand.

"Oh, very good! Most amusing, child. But your mortal king's authority is useless here. It is only I who say what is and what is not, as you will see. The leaders of all the Tuatha de Danaan gave that power to me, as they gave me the care of the sword and shield. They knew that I, better than any other, could see to their protecting. It must be clear to you that I'm suited to little else. I have none of your king's strength nor his thousands of warriors. I am barely able to move myself about. I have only one attribute available to me." He lifted a hand, touching the spatulate tip of one finger lightly to the immense swell of skull. "It lies here. And within the boundaries of my country, it gives me a freedom and a power that your king can never have or begin to understand. And it serves only the good of my own people."

"A power," Conan said, snorting derisively. "I'll wager it's no match for the touch of cold iron!"

"Conan, keep out of this," Finn told him warningly.

"That I will not!" the stout warrior blustered. "I've listened to your foolish talk too long. You've wasted enough of our time with this simpering frog!"

"Careful, Conan," Labran said nervously. "You don't know what you're doing."

"Quiet, you cringing fool!" boomed Conan. "No warrior of the Morna clan lets a creature like this one tell him what to do. I say, make him give the weapons to us—now!"

And in a swift move, he charged forward, drawing out his sword.

Before anyone could stop him, he was clambering up the pillow mound, his free hand reaching out to grasp the little king. That being, far from being frightened or trying to escape, seemed thrilled, clapping his hands and crying rapturously:

"An attack! Oh, what enormous fun! This will be even more entertaining than I had hoped!"

Then, as the thick fist of Conan began to close upon his scrawny neck, he giggled, waved, and promptly disappeared!

CHAPTER FIFTEEN
THE RED CLOWNS

Like a puff of smoke dissipated by a sudden gust, the odd being simply and quite totally vanished from the sight of his guests, leaving Conan's hand to close upon empty air.

Only the giggle remained. The high, rippling sound of it echoed within the walls of the huge silver room. Then it faded, to be replaced by the king's voice.

"Good fortune to you, Finn MacCumhal," it called, still full of amusement, "for you will surely have need of it. Your strength and your great fighting skills alone will not win this contest for you. You will have need of all those virtues that make a man a true leader. We will see if you possess them as the tales say you do. If you truly have them, you may just possibly succeed. So, farewell to you. The game has now begun!"

And with these parting words, the palace, the boyish servants, and the mound of cushions began to fade away.

Conan, alarmed by this disappearance of his support, quickly slid from the mound before it lost its solidity. The others looked around them in wonder as the shining walls grew thinner, thinner, first translucent, then transparent, revealing the bright country outside. In moments the palace was completely gone.

Recovering himself, Finn turned on Conan, his expression stern.

"Well, it was a great help you were in that, MacMorna," he said severely. "Your bullying ways will be getting us killed one time!"

Conan, however, was paying no heed to this rebuke. He

was still gazing about in open-mouthed amazement at the
landscape, the trees, the sky, the carpet of flowers, that had
appeared beneath his very feet. The top of the smooth hill was
now as empty and unmarked as if no palace had ever stood
there.

"How . . . how did he do that?" the stout warrior asked.

"This is a country of illusion," Labran explained, "created
by de Danaan magic, controlled by the mind of its king. You
must be careful here. We have entered a realm where only he
knows what is real and what is not. We must play out this game
according to his rules."

"This game?" repeated Cuillen, shaking her head in
puzzlement. "I don't see how he can make something that can
save or destroy Ireland into a game!"

"Over the centuries, it must have become so to him,"
explained Labran. "He's met many challenges from de Danaans grown arrogant with their own power who have come to
claim the weapons."

"Well, if we'll be having to depend upon the virtues of
Finn MacCumhal to win them for us, it's great trouble we'll be
in," Cuillen said sarcastically.

Finn only glared at her and then turned toward Labran.

"All right, then. The contest is begun. What do we do?"

"We go ahead. We find the first gate," the son of Tadg
responded simply.

"But, which way?" asked Finn.

All of them looked around at the countryside. The point
where they had entered the hidden land could no longer be
identified. From the hilltop on which they stood, smooth,
flower-covered, gently rolling meadows spread away in all
directions, looking much the same one way as another.

Then Labran pointed, crying out excitedly:

"Look! Look there! The mountain!"

Far away, in a direction that the sun told them was west, a
gray, blunted cone of rock thrust up starkly from the softly
rounded bosom of the land.

"That must be the goal the king said we would have to
reach!" Labran said. "That is the way we must go!"

"But it wasn't there before," said Conan, staring at it
suspiciously.

"It's there for certain now," Finn replied. "Let's be starting
for it."

They headed out across the countryside without delay.

The way was level, the ground dry and firm. The day was pleasantly warm. They traveled with good speed, the hill they had left fading quickly into the distance behind them. So easy was it that Conan's apprehension seemed to fade. He began to swing his bulk along with a decided swagger.

"Well, there's surely nothing to this!" he confidently declared. "You see, Labran?" he added, giving the slender man a slap that nearly knocked him down. "I told you that wretched bug you call a king hadn't the power to hinder a Fian man."

"Is that so?" said Labran, recovering his balance and gesturing ahead. "Then, what do you think of that?"

For, even as Conan had spoken, a strange feature had come into view before them: a line that cut straight across their path from side to side.

Conan's look of self-assurance slipped into one of dismay as he stared at it, for as they drew closer, it became clear that what lay before them was a wall of bronze, smooth, seamless, and unscalable, rising up to three times their height and running unbroken from horizon to horizon.

Conan approached it slowly. He looked up its shining height. He put out a hand to feel its polished surface. He laid his palm against the surface and threw his weight against it. The wall did not budge.

"Is it solid enough for you?" Labran asked with some sarcasm.

"All right, then," Conan admitted grudgingly. "So it's stopped us."

"The question is, What do we do now?" said Finn.

"If this wall lies between us and the mountain, then we have to get through it," Labran said thoughtfully. "That means a gate. Likely it'll be the first of the king's seven."

"Which way do we find it?" asked Cuillen.

"If we're meant to, as I think we are," answered Labran, "then likely either one."

So Finn started off toward the left, the others falling in behind. They moved along the wall only a short way before Labran's belief was proven right. They came upon a narrow opening.

"No great test here!" crowed Conan. "There's not even a door blocking it!"

He was right. The doorway had no barrier of any kind. Beyond it more open country could be seen.

"Let's go through, then," Finn said briskly. "Quick, now, before something happens!"

They rushed toward the opening, Labran frowning and shaking his head.

"It can't be so simple," he was muttering. "I know that it can't be."

Again, the son of Tadg was right. As the party neared the door, three figures appeared, moving swiftly to stand in line before it, barring the way.

Finn and his companions pulled to a halt, staring at these figures in some surprise. There was good reason for this, for the trio was a very strange one indeed.

They were enough alike to clearly be brothers, if not triplets. Each was round faced, ruddy of complexion, with a bald head surrounded by a fringe of bright red hair. They were clad in the baggy cloaks of clowns, striped in pink and red. All held spears in one hand and horns of red-gold in the other. Their clothes seemed covered by a fine coating of red dust that puffed around them in clouds when they moved.

"Good day to you," Finn greeted them in a friendly way. "It's important that we get through this doorway. Will you let us pass?"

"That we will not," they answered, their shrill, angry voices coming in unison. "We have waited here for your coming, Finn MacCumhal."

"So, you know us," Finn said thoughtfully. "Well, then, would you tell us who you are and why you're stopping us?"

"It is the three sons of Uar that we are," they squawked together. "Aincel and Digbail and Espaid—Ill-wishing and Harm and Want are our names. We're asking you to pay a blood fine to us. Do so, and your company may pass safely on."

"A blood fine?" Finn repeated in some puzzlement. "And what would it be?"

"The life of Conan MacMorna."

The young captain's gaze jerked around to the stout warrior. He found that the man's face had grown ashen.

"Conan? What do you know about this?" he demanded.

"Their father was Indast of the de Danaan," Conan replied darkly. "I killed him in a battle long ago, on Slieve nan Ean."

"No man has ever given a blood fine for one killed in battle," Finn told the three. "It's revenge you're seeking."

"Call it whatever you wish," they responded. "We will have Conan."

"Why are you reasoning with them?" Cuillen demanded in an exasperated way. "There are only these three, ragged vagabonds against us, and very poorly armed as well."

"They are much more," Labran warned. "They are three of the most deadly beings amongst the de Danaans. It is a poison dust that covers them, and coats their spearheads, and fills the horns they bear. Whoever it touches, it will kill!"

"He is right!" the trio shrieked in chorus. "No man of this world that we have gone against has escaped. So stay back and you will not be harmed. It is only Conan we want."

They started toward the balding warrior. But as they did, Finn leaped before his companion.

"I will not leave any man of the Fianna," he told the three.

"Then you will die with him," they replied, and quickly spread out to come against the pair from three sides.

Finn and Conan drew swords and moved back to back. Cuillen lifted her own spear and started toward them.

"I'll help you," she cried.

"No!" shouted Finn. "Bran! Sceolan! Keep her well back!"

The two enormous dogs moved into her way, forcing her back with their bodies, snarling threateningly when she tried to push past.

Meanwhile, the three red clowns closed upon Finn and Conan. They had only to touch the pair, with hand or foot or spear, to cause their deaths. But they quickly found that this was not an easy task.

The sons of Uar moved with an incredible agility and speed, more like sea birds diving suddenly for the kill than human beings. Their red-clad bodies were little more than crimson blurs as they feinted, whirled, bounded, and lunged in a furious, deadly jig about the pair of warriors, seeking even the slightest opening to dart in and plant their wasting dust.

Conan and Finn were forced to pivot around constantly, managing to keep back their adversaries with broad sweeps of their swords. But, while Finn's assistance was serving to keep Conan alive, this condition was clearly temporary. It was only a matter of time before one of the clowns succeeded in making some contact, no matter how slight. Then the remaining warrior would be alone, with no chance left at all.

The Fian men made several ever more desperate attempts to counterattack. But these efforts were always frustrated by the speed of the dodging, leaping clowns, which required the pair to be always closely defending one another's backs. The lunges and swings of the warriors had to be very short, and their blades were easily avoided by the capering trio.

Some distance away, Cuillen watched with a look of frustration from behind the barrier of hounds. Beside her, Labran, apparently in the throes of some emotional upheaval, was kneeling on the ground, crying out something unintelligible to the skies, his clasped hands uplifted as if in supplication to some god.

A lance thrust from one clown slipped by Finn's side, nearly grazing him. Another clown slipped in close enough to shake his golden horn at Conan, sending a puff of red dust flying toward him. He just managed to escape it by sweeping out his shield to fan it away.

"It's getting a bit serious," Conan growled.

"If we can't reach them, we've got to strike them from a distance," Finn replied.

"How?" asked the stout warrior, knocking away a thrusting spearhead.

"We can throw our swords. Can you hit them that way?"

"If a Baiscne can, then so can a MacMorna," he answered boastingly. "But it'll leave us unarmed, and with one left to kill us."

"No, it won't," Finn assured him. "Be ready." He lifted his voice to shout: "Cuillen! Use your spear! Dogs, let her free!"

Cuillen understood at once. As the dogs pulled back, she took three long strides toward the embattled group, set her lithe body, and in a swift move drew back and fired her spear.

Finn's faith in the girl's throwing ability proved justified. Though the clowns had realized the intent in Finn's shout and now moved to dodge the throw, her intended target proved too slow. The iron head struck him, tearing through his throat. Gargling on his own blood, the red clown staggered and went down.

Finn wasted no time in charging toward a second clown whose shocked gaze went from his fallen brother to the attacking warrior. He stood unmoving as Finn swept his sword up and flung it. The blade spun in the air, making a shining wheel as it flew to its mark. The point slammed home in the center of the unprotected breast. The force of the blow knocked the clown backward and he crashed to the ground.

The third of the crimson trio, galvanized to action by the

fate of his brothers, turned and ran. But Conan leapt after him, casting his own sword forward in a powerful throw. It spun through the air to the running target, not jabbing home, but descending edge first upon the hapless man's head, splitting his skull. Dead in mid-stride, the clown tripped and tumbled forward, rolling into a ragged bundle.

"Was that necessary?" Finn asked Conan harshly.

"They began it," the MacMorna warrior responded tersely. "Now it's ended."

"Look there!" cried Cuillen in amazement.

The three bodies lay motionless in what seemed to be crimson clouds of dust raised from their falling. But as Finn and his companions watched, these clouds grew thicker, darker, covering the dead clowns. They seemed to consume the forms of the three sons of Uar. First their flesh darkened, wrinkled, crumbled away. The ragged clothes shredded, falling from the bodies, revealing the white bones. Then these too seemed to rapidly decay, falling apart, disintegrating into fine dust that blended with the deadly red powder. In moments there was nothing left of the three but scarlet stains upon the ground.

"In death, without their magic to sustain them, they were consumed by their own poison," said Labran, getting to his feet.

Finn glanced around at Labran, then looked again, eyes widening in astonishment. Close over the de Danaan's head there floated a small, dark, obese puff of cloud now heartily engaged in raining solely upon him. Though extremely localized, the downpour was still heavy. He was already quite soaked.

"Labran, what are you doing?" Finn inquired, clearly trying not to laugh at the ridiculous sight.

"Doing?" Labran repeated, as if he didn't understand. Then he glanced upward at the cloud—getting an eyeful of rain in the process. "Oh, you mean that?" he said with an attempt at nonchalance, as if clouds followed him about quite regularly. "It's nothing. Just ignore it. It'll go away in a moment."

But when it didn't vanish, he grew redfaced, lifting his hands to wave it off, crying out in an angry and embarrassed way:

"Please, be off now, you cursed little cloud! Stop making a fool of me!"

"It seems that you can do that well enough alone," Conan put in.

Still, Labran's desperate plea seemed to work. The cloud broke up, its scraps fluttering away. And as the rain ended, Cuillen moved forward, taking up the hem of her cloak to wipe the water from the poor man's face. He seemed ready to cry.

"What happened, Labran?" she asked him gently.

"I only meant to raise a shower," he said dismally. "I thought it might wash away the poison and make them harmless. But I just couldn't make my magic work!"

"That makes the second time," Conan gloatingly reminded him.

"He tried," Cuillen told the stout warrior sharply. She gave Labran a smile and a reassuring pat on the arm. "I know you tried, and that's the important thing." Then, in an abrupt shifting of moods, she rounded angrily on Finn. "But you, you arrogant . . . stupid . . . *male!*" She seemed unable to come up with a more despicable epithet than this last. "How dare you keep me from the fight! How dare you sic your hounds on me!"

"I was trying to protect you," Finn argued in a reasoning tone. "I didn't see why we should be risking you or Labran or the hounds in this."

"Why not?" she fired back. "So you could get yourself killed playing the great hero? When will you understand that I want none of your 'protecting'? I'm here to see that you succeed, not to stand by and watch you fail. If you had let me join you from the start, that fight would have been over long ago."

"You're right, then!" Finn shouted in aggravation. "From this time on, I will not lift one finger to keep you safe. I am sorry that I tried to keep you safe this time. You don't *know* how sorry I am."

"And you can just keep your sarcasm to yourself as well, MacCumhal," she added curtly.

He sighed, drooping in resignation.

"All right," he said wearily. "Now, if you're finished with me, could we be getting on? Let's get our weapons, shall we?"

"Careful," Labran warned as Finn, Cuillen, and Conan moved to retrieve their weapons from the three stained spots. "Don't touch the blades until you've wiped them thoroughly."

Looking at what the poison dust had done to the red clowns, the three took Labran's warning most seriously. They carefully wiped blades and spearpoint upon the ground, rubbed them in the earth, and cleaned them with a scrap of cloth the son of Tadg eagerly supplied from the hem of his robe.

Once finished with this task, the party was ready to move on. The two dogs took the lead, followed by Labran and Conan. Finn and Cuillen, walking for a moment side by side, brought up the rear.

As Conan passed through the narrow opening in the wall, he glanced back, his expression again a smug one.

"Well, that one was easy enough," he commented, then went on, moving with that rolling, arrogant stride.

Cuillen looked after him in amazement, shaking her head.

"I cannot believe that man," she said to Finn. "You could have abandoned him instead of risking your life for him. He might at least have thanked you."

"There was no need. And despite his rude manner, I know he would have come to my side just as quickly." He looked at her and added earnestly, "You see, no matter what you believe, those of the Fianna do keep their oaths of loyalty."

With that, he picked up his pace to move ahead of her, leaving her staring after him in a thoughtful way.

Beyond the wall, the little band found a country that was in sharp contrast to the one they left. The pleasant, colorful land of flowers and trees and rolling hills was abruptly gone. Ahead of them now lay a vista as stark and flat as a weathered plank tabletop. The ground was a yellow-gray sea of sand that stretched away unmarked, save for the faint, wavy patterns of ripples created by the winds. There were no trees, no streams, no grassy hills. The only feature to break the monotony of the empty land was their mountain, thrusting above the distant line of the horizon.

Even the neat puffs of drifting cloud had disappeared, leaving a vacant sky where the round disk of the sun now seemed more swollen, burning with a great intensity.

"This is a land where nothing lives," said Cuillen.

"I have seen more welcoming places," Finn agreed.

"Ah, we'll be across it in a half-day's walk," Conan confidently declared, and started ahead, not waiting for the rest.

His companions, including the two dogs, exchanged a look that eloquently bespoke their joint amazement at the man's continued brashness. Then all fell in behind him.

They gamely pursued the horizon, but without success. The wasteland continued on and on. And the way grew steadily more difficult as they proceeded. The faint ripples swelled to become great waves. The surface became softer, forcing them to struggle at each step, their legs sinking deep into sand that seemed to suck at them, as if to pull them beneath the surface. They fought their way up the yielding slope of each dune only to view another beyond with ever more despairing looks.

The sun had an even more devastating effect on them. The blazing circle seemed to become larger, brighter, hotter, with every step. For Finn's company—used to an Irish climate where even the brightest days were seldom warm—it soon became a torture. Its heat radiated upward in shimmering waves from the sand beneath their feet. Its light beat upon their fair and unprotected brows. Sweat soaked their clothing, and this loss of their vital fluids seemed to drain their vitality as well. Each dune was climbed with a bit less vigor.

Finally, after clambering up yet another of the yielding mounds, the band halted for a moment, gazing ahead.

"Well, I'd say we've had your half-day's walk, at least," Labran said to Conan dryly.

"I don't understand," said Conan, peering toward the horizon. "That cursed mountain never seems to get any closer!"

"Well, what's behind us has certainly gotten farther away," put in Cuillen. "The wall we came through is out of sight."

The others looked. The wall had indeed vanished. Now they were surrounded by the treacherous dunes of the wasteland.

"This can't be!" Conan complained.

"Never mind," Finn said. "This is doing nothing to help us. Only our feet can do that, so let's move them along. Think about nothing but reaching that mountain."

"I'll think of finding myself some shade, if you don't mind," grumbled Conan, scowling up at the sun.

The fiery disk was now suspended directly over their heads. Indeed, it seemed to have become fixed there, its torrent of scorching rays cascading upon them unrelentingly.

CHAPTER SIXTEEN
THE PURGING

The sun seemed to expand, to fill the sky with light. The figures of the little band upon the dune were swallowed up, consumed by its blinding glare—

With a gasp of terror, Caoilte sat upright, eyes staring, face glistening with sweat.

The afterimage of the bright glow faded, the interior of the small chamber in the rock becoming slowly visible. He stared around at this in confusion, then started as a hand reached out to touch his arm. His gaze jerked around to the pleasant, round face of the woman called Flann as she learned toward him, speaking soothingly.

"Be easy now. Be calm. You are all right."

"My friends!" he said with great anxiety. "I've seen them. They're in danger!"

"Please, try to relax," she said, trying to ease him back. "You've only had a bad dream."

"No!" he persisted, resisting her pressure. "They need my help! I have to go!"

He struggled to rise as she tried, gently but firmly, to hold him down. For the small woman to so restrain the warrior would not normally have been possible, but so weakened was he by his injury that their contest was an almost even one.

"Sisters!" Flann called over her shoulder. "Come quickly. I need assistance here."

The response was immediate. The tall, imposing figure of Bebind sailed through the doorway, followed by the fluttery woman called Uaine.

Bebind moved directly to the bed and took a grip on the

146

young warrior's shoulders. Though lean, the woman had a sinewy strength and was easily able to hold him fast.

"Now, you listen to me!" she told him sternly. "This foolishness will do no good for you at all. So you just lie back there at once!"

So commanding was her tone that even such a one as Caoilte dared not defy her. He gave up his struggles, allowing the two women to lower him back onto the bed. He looked quite pale from his exertion, and grimaced with pain. Uaine, who stood by watching anxiously, revealed her empathy with him in a face that echoed his look of distress.

"There, now, you see?" Bebind said in a superior way. "You've only hurt yourself."

"Look here, I must go to my friends," he said desperately. "You promised that you would heal me. When will it be?"

"You were near death when you were brought to us," she pointed out. "Even after these several days of rest you are still very weak. The healing process is difficult and will put a tremendous strain on you. Before we begin it, we must help you to regain all the strength you can."

"I can survive it," he told her determinedly. "I feel strong enough now. Please, begin!"

Bebind exchanged a look with Flann.

"It may be he could get through it now," the plump woman said.

"I would advise against it," Bebind said stubbornly.

"But the poor lad is so very upset," put in Uaine most sympathetically. She moved up close to the bed and laid a soft hand caressingly upon his brow. "We can't leave him to suffer so."

"It is his life, Bebind," added Flann.

The tall, stately woman drew herself stiffly up to her full height, gazing at the other two indignantly, as if they were children challenging parental authority.

"Well, I thank you very much for your support. I can see that my opinion holds no weight here." She dropped her chill gaze to the face of Caoilte. "Very well, young man. If it is your wish, we will begin the healing," she told him in a crisp tone. "But, mark me well: this is against my own advice, and I will take no responsibility for the consequences. Do you understand?"

"I do," Caoilte said, and then managed a smile. "But it's all right. I promise not to die."

"That is a matter of complete indifference to me," she said. "I only promise to do my best." Her voice lifted in command. "Flann, fetch some of the other sisters. We must move him into the central chamber. Uaine, we will need the music."

"Other sisters?" Caoilte said curiosity. "There are more of you here?"

"A few," Uaine said with a coy smile as she and Flann went out.

"I didn't realize," said Caoilte. "I thought there were only the three of you."

"You have been unconscious nearly all these past days," Bebind pointed out. "We have kept the others away."

Now a number of women entered the chamber. They were of widely varied ages and types, but were all alike in their flushes of shyness upon entering the presence of the warrior. As they moved around him, there were also some titters of excitement.

"Now, sisters," Bebind said brusquely, "don't stand there gawking at the man. Get about the pallet. Lift it. Gently, now! Gently. All right. Now carry it out slowly. Slowly. Watch the door!"

At her direction, the women managed to maneuver Caoilte's bed out through the door and into the cavern. They carried it across the floor and set it down with great care close beside the fire, which blazed splendidly, giving out a pleasant warmth.

Here the rest of the women of the Sid were gathered, their expressions revealing an interest as avid as that of the others. They formed a half-circle close around the bed, jostling each other for better positions to see the dark warrior and exchanging murmurs of excitement.

Caoilte looked around him at the wall of them, at the many faces—young and old, pretty and plain, coarse and fine, round and lean, in wonderfully varied combinations—all gazing down at him with that same warmth coloring their cheeks, and that same light of arousal glinting in their eyes.

Under their stares, Caoilte himself colored. Clearly, for this young warrior, the situation was a discomforting one.

"Get back, women! Get back!" Bebind ordered impatiently. "We must have room to work, and he to breathe. Get on about your own activities!"

Reluctantly but obediently they complied, moving off to

take up various tasks, but looking back constantly toward Caoilte.

"How many of you are there here?" he asked Bebind.

"Three times fifty women dwell with me," she tersely replied.

"But, without men at all?" he said in puzzlement. "Why?"

"Even the world of the de Danaans is not without its sorrow," she said. "For many reasons—for love, for punishment, for penance, even for hate—these women have chosen to withdraw from the world of our people and abide apart."

"How long?" he asked. "How long have you been here?"

"Some of us for many centuries," Uaine said, a hint of sadness in her voice. "And it is often that we feel the loneliness."

"Centuries . . ." Caoilte repeated in amazement, looking about at them again, "without any men at all."

"Enough, Uaine," Bebind warned. "He has already been told more than a mortal—and a man—needs to know. So, young warrior, just rest yourself. We will soon begin!"

Flann now moved up on one side of the bed carrying a towel and a large, golden bowl filled with steaming liquid. One the other side of Caoilte appeared Uaine and eight other women, each carrying a delicate and exquisitely carved harp of red yew, mounted with silver and set with precious stones.

Caoilte watched all of them with a searching and somewhat suspicious eye.

"You may wash him now, Flann," Bebind ordered.

The plump woman set down her towel and bowl beside the bed. She reached out to take hold of the hem of Caoilte's tunic, but found her hands suddenly enveloped in the grip of Caoilte. She looked up to see him fixing her with an imploring gaze.

"Do you have to do that now?" he asked. "Here?"

"Young man," snapped Bebind, "if you wish this healing so badly, kindly do not interfere!"

Caoilte meekly submitted, but with obvious uneasiness, squeezing closed his eyes.

Flann slowly, tenderly, carefully, pulled up the tunic to expose his wound, along with a great deal more.

A chorus of soft gasps of appreciation fluttered up from around the room as the women of the Sid—most of whom had paused in their work at this point to sneak a glance—expressed their opinion of the splendid physique now bared. Caoilte's face, as well as other areas, grew quite flushed with embarrassment at this sound, while his eyes closed all the tighter.

"Enough, sisters!" Bebind called irritably. "This is not some entertainment. Where is your shame?"

The majority quickly turned away again, although a few, apparently not caring where their shame was, continued to stare on in defiance of the tall woman.

Flann now took up her towel, dampened it in the warm liquid in the bowl, and began gently to wash the wound and the flesh about it. This treatment had clearly been successful in halting the effect of Caisel's energy beam. Very little more of the flesh about the wound showed signs of the strange withering than when he had first arrived.

As Flann worked, Bebind went to a nearby cupboard of polished oak. From its recesses she produced a collection of vials and jars, which she lined up with great precision on a table by the fire. She returned to the cupboard to fetch a goblet of hammered silver, and filled it with liquid from a cauldron hanging upon the flames. Then, with brisk and practiced movements, the tall woman began to select from her rank of ingredients, adding into the cup a touch of this, a dollop of that, a sprinkle of another. With this process completed, she swirled the contents with a silver spoon, sniffed at the concoction, and nodded in satisfaction. Bearing the cup in one hand and a small crystal jar in the other, she returned to the bedside.

The plump woman had by now finished her washing and recovered Caoilte's body, much to his evident relief. She put aside her bowl and towel and turned to face Bebind. The tall woman handed the goblet to her and then proceeded to remove the stopper from the crystal jar.

Caoilte, his eyes once more open, watched with close interest as Bebind lifted the jar and poured its contents—a thick, mucous-textured substance of a vile yellow-green—into the mixture.

At once a feverish bubbling began within the cup. A cloud of brown smoke puffed up from the surface of the liquid, and with it a distinctly nasty odor wafted out.

Bebind waited for several moments until the churning of the concoction had slowed and the burnt-orange foam that had formed on the surface and receded somewhat from the rim. Then she nodded toward Uaine and her group of harpists.

"Begin the music," she ordered.

They began a slow, eerie, and soulful tune, the combined sound of the instruments like an autumn wind keening softly through a forest of bare limbs. As they played, Bebind knelt with great dignity beside the bed and, taking the cup from Flann, held it out toward the mouth of Caoilte.

"Drink," she told him gravely.

He looked down at the thick, dark, evil-looking brew just beneath his eyes. His nose wrinkling in defense against the smell, he raised his gaze to her face.

"I'm not so certain I should be taking this," he said cautiously. "What is it, anyway?"

"You have a great deal of poison in your body," she told him brusquely. "If you expect to be cured, it must be purged from you. You must drink."

"It's really awful looking stuff," he said, still hesitating. She sighed in exasperation.

"No more delays!" she snapped. "You must have it if you are to heal. It's you who are so anxious to go help your friends! Now drink!"

"There are dangers I would much rather face," he told her. Then, reluctantly, he lifted up his head, parted his lips, and let her pour a dose into his mouth.

He swallowed with great difficulty, his face tight with strain. Then, slowly, his face relaxed. He seemed surprised. A smile gradually appeared.

"Well, there was nothing to that after all!" he announced with pleasure. "I guess it's not—"

Then, suddenly, his face contorted. His body convulsed and he began to gag.

"Get the vat, Flann!" Bebind commanded as the young warrior heaved himself upright.

Flann quickly took up a large vat of copper and thrust it beneath the chin of Caoilte. She was just in time, for from deep within his shuddering body, he vomited forth a putrid, viscous mass.

He fell back heavily, gasping for breath, his energy much drained with the purging of the bile.

"By the Dagda!" he finally managed to get out, eyes wide in shock. "What was that?"

"I told you, the poison must be gotten from your body," Bebind reminded him curtly. She held the cup out. "Now you must take some more."

"What?" he cried, pulling himself up again to stare at her in complete astonishment.

"I also told you that it would not be easy," she snapped. "Come along now, great warrior. Show your courage."

Caoilte shot her an indignant look at the snide tone of this remark, but it had its effect. He actually seized the cup from her, and with bravado, downed a hearty swig.

He met her eyes triumphantly across the rim, as if to say he had shown her who was the courageous one. But this expression lasted only a moment, swiftly replaced by one of distress as he felt his gorge rising again.

"The vat, Flann!" he coughed out, thrusting the cup back into Bebind's hands and bending forward, retching violently.

Five times more the tall, stern woman forced the terrible purgative on him. Five times more he was seized by the wracking convulsion of his stomach. But finally, though it seemed he must be casting up his own insides with the muscle-tearing heaves, nothing more came forth. He fell back totally exhausted by his labors, panting heavily for breath, unable to move again.

"Now, Flann," said Bebind, "let him rest for a while. Then you may fetch warm new milk and give some to him." She looked toward the harpists. "Uaine, you and the sisters may give over playing now."

The mourning tune died away. The women put aside their instruments. Uaine moved to the bedside to look down at the young warrior in concern.

"Will he be all right?" she asked with great concern. "Poor boy. He looks so wan."

She put out a hand to caress his brow, but Bebind pulled it sharply back.

"Do try to keep your hands off him, Uaine," she scolded. "He needs rest. He will be quite well, in my opinion, although only time will tell us that for certain."

With an effort powered by his tremendous will, Caoilte managed to speak in a faint, croaking voice:

"This . . . this weakness," he said, obviously much alarmed by it, "I've never felt anything like it. And . . . my head . . . is swimming!"

"You may recall my also warning you that it would take all your strength to survive this," she said without the slightest hint of sympathy in her tone. "Rest, and you'll be feeling better soon."

"But . . . how long?" he gasped out. "How long will it take?"

"It will be three days and nights at least before the weakness has left you."

"Three days?" he said in despair. "In three days Finn and the others might all be dead!"

The band of tiny, bedraggled figures dragged themselves wearily over the crest of another sweeping dune. As they started down the slope, Cuillen's legs seemed to collapse. She fell forward, rolling down the hillside, spraying sand about her, unable to stop her tumbling.

Finn ran after her, slogging with difficulty through the knee-deep sand, plowing his way along. But he had no chance to catch her, and she rolled to the foot of the dune, fetching up in a heap there.

He reached the side of the girl as she began to struggle up, and tried to help her. Angrily, clearly embarrassed by her fall, she pushed him away.

"I can do it myself!" she snapped, but it was clearly with difficulty that she arose, her movements proclaiming immense weariness. She spat sand from lips split by dehydration, brushed back loose hair from a face baked red by the incessant sun.

Finn was in little better condition himself. His own lips were dry and cracked, his fair skin all but glowing with a painful-looking burn, his face streaming with sweat. He breathed the nearly stifling air in a labored way, his body sagging with fatigue after his last little run.

The others now reached the bottom of the dune and joined them. They too were clearly suffering dreadfully from the effects of the heat. Conan carried his ponderous bulk like a burden of lead. The dogs nearly crawled along, their great tongues hanging from their mouths. Labran, the least physically strong of the little band, seemed near the limit of his endurance, barely able to drag himself foreward, his thin body drooping, his pale skin painfully blistered.

"That cursed sun!" Conan said, glowering up at the blazing orb. "Why doesn't the thing move? Even night would give us some release."

"We must at least find water very soon," Finn said. "It seems as if we've been without it for days now."

"Aye. Water would help," Conan agreed. He gave the son

of Tadg a scornful look. "Too bad our magician here couldn't get his botched rain trick to work now, when it would be of use to us! De Danaan, ha! It's nothing but a fraud he is."

"Look, I've tried it a score of times already," Labran said dismally, clearly anguished at his continued failure. "I can't make it work, and I'm sorry. But there's nothing I can do."

"Being sorry won't save us," Conan said harshly, "and we can't keep on much longer without some relief. We'll be finished soon."

"The great MacMorna fighting man," Cuillen said derisively. "Where is your boasting now? We can't simply give up. We must keep on! This has to be another of the king's barriers. Somewhere, there is a second gate to pass, and another key to get us through it. He promised them to us."

"Then, where are they?" Finn demanded angrily. He lifted his voice and shouted to the blazing sun: "Are you watching us, King of the Country of the Fair Men? Can you hear us? If you only mean to torture us here, we'll play your game no longer. If it's truly a fair man you are, show us the key!"

As if in answer to this challenge, the dogs grew suddenly alert, ears rising, heads turning toward the next dune-top eagerly. They seemed to listen intently for a moment, lifted their noses to sniff the air, and then they were off, loping up the slope of sand.

"What are they about?" Conan growled. "Have they gone mad with the heat?"

"Hush!" said Cuillen sharply. "Listen! Can't you hear?"

They all listened. A musical, tinkling sound was drifting, faint but clear, in the still air.

"That's running water!" Labran cried happily.

"Follow the hounds!" said Finn.

With a renewed vigor, they fell in behind the animals, nearly bounding up the dune in their eagerness. At the top, they found an oasis, a tiny island of green floating upon the rolling sea of sand. A precise, round patch of lush grass, barely a dozen paces across, was shaded by the broad leaves of strange, tall trees evenly spaced around its perimeter. In the exact center of this circle sat a smooth, flat rock whose upper surface formed a shallow basin so symmetrical it seemed the hand of man must have shaped it. Up from the middle of it there spouted a thin geyser of water. Sunlight danced merrily within the life-giving liquid as it rose and then fell back into the basin, its splashing like the bright, rippling laughter of a child.

Bran and Sceolan had already reached the basin. But the loyal dogs, though clearly tortured by thirst, stoically took no drink, only taking up positions on either side of the rock as if to guard the precious water for the rest. Finn and the others moved up around the basin, staring down at the sparkling geyser with expressions of desire and caution mixed. At first none ventured even to touch the stone, as if afraid that this glorious vision might vanish.

"We may as well try it," Finn said at last. "Conan, you go first."

"Oh, no, MacCumhal," the man protested. "If this is more trickery by that devious runt of a king, there's no saying what he may have done to it."

"I'll go first," Labran volunteered affably.

"And what good would that be?" Conan snapped. "You're one of the Others too. You may be in this with him."

"Don't be such a fool," Cuillen said impatiently. She pushed past the men, leaned down, and took a mouthful of the liquid. She straightened and gave them a triumphant look. "There. It's only water. Fresh and clear and cold."

"Enough for you, Conan?" asked Labran.

The stout man grumbled something, then leaned down and took his own long draught.

"Don't be drinking all of it, MacMorna," Finn said.

Conan raised up, water dripping from his mustache, and shot Finn a nasty look. Then he moved back as Labran took his turn at the font.

"My, that is refreshing," said the slender de Danaan, when he had finished. "It makes me feel quite strong again." He smiled self-effacingly, adding, "Or, as strong as I ever get."

"Now your turn, Finn," Cuillen said.

"No. I'll have none till all of you have drunk. Conan, give me your shield."

The burly warrior passed over his large, concave circle of iron-rimmed leather. Finn held it out beneath the spout of water, letting the liquid pool in the hollow. This he then set down upon the ground.

"Bran, Sceolan——" he said to them——"you drink now. You have waited long enough."

"Wait, Finn!" Cuillen said with alarm. "The water! Look!"

He wheeled back toward the fountain. The thin stream was sinking as its volume shrank. Before he could even move to it, it had ceased flowing altogether. Its last, glittering drops fell to the basin where they dried instantly upon the stone.

CHAPTER SEVENTEEN
THE KING OF ULSTER'S SON

"It's stopped!" said Labran in distress.

"But it can't!" roared Conan, charging in and slamming a thick fist against the stone.

"There's no good in doing that," Finn said in a voice of reason. Still, he cast a look of both anger and disappointment at the treacherous font.

"At least you have what's in the shield," Cuillen said.

"That we do," he agreed. He looked at it. The two dogs, aware of what had occurred, were standing by it, watching him. Neither had even lowered a muzzle toward the now-priceless water within it.

An expression of intense yearning, of nearly overwhelming desire, came nakedly into his sun-scorched face for a moment. His squinting eyes fixed on the glinting pool tempting him from the hollow of the shield. His swollen tongue slipped slowly, achingly, across his parched and crusted lips.

Then his gaze went to the two loyal hounds, standing calmly by, eyeing him approvingly, prepared to sacrifice without hesitation. His desire faded from his face as it tightened with renewed conviction. He drew himself up into a determined stance.

"Go on, then," he told Bran and Sceolan firmly. "Drink!"

"What?" Conan cried in disbelief. "You mean to give it to them? What about yourself?"

"I'll drink no drop of it. There's hardly enough for two such hounds."

"You can't mean to sacrifice yourself for the sake of

animals!" the stout warrior argued. "Why, man, you're nearly perished from the thirst."

"The dogs are my sworn comrades as much as you are, Conan MacMorna," Finn told him stolidly. "And even if they were strangers to me, their need would come before mine. I'll give up no honor nor openhandedness to win this king's game. So long as I have something I can give and the will to give it, I'll do so gladly."

He turned again to the two dogs. They still had not touched the water, staring at him with expressions that could only be called stubborn.

"I know what it is you're saying, lads," Finn told them, "but I'll not let you defy me in this. I am your master, and you'll obey my commands. Drink!"

With great reluctance, the hounds obediently lowered their great heads and began to lap the water. There was little more than two cups within the shallow hollow of the shield, and it was gone in moments.

"I don't know whether to praise you or call you a fool for that, Finn MacCumhal," said Cuillen, looking curiously at him. "It may be your own life you've just given away."

"I don't think so," said Labran excitedly, pointing. "Look there! Look there!"

Ahead of them now, within the heat haze rising from the sandy waste, something else was shimmering into view.

As they watched, a new landscape formed, almost seemed to rise into view, like something submerged floating to the surface of the sea. It appeared where there surely had been nothing before, as the wall had. And, as with the wall, it crossed the whole landscape from horizon to horizon. But the barrier that now lay revealed to the wondering gaze of the travelers was otherwise of a quite different type: a ribbon of what seemed spun silver, glittering sharply in the hard sunlight.

"A river!" said Cuillen, echoing Labran's delight.

"A river!" growled Conan, shaking his head in bewilderment. "The way things come and go here is madness—just madness!"

"Not madness," said Labran. "This fountain must have been the king's second test; his second gateway, if you will. Finn's generosity found the key for us, and now we're through."

"But it can't be!" persisted Conan. "No magic can control the countryside."

"Perhaps it didn't," the de Danaan said. "Perhaps the river was there all the time. Perhaps we've just been made to wander in circles here. Or perhaps the river, the sand, and the sun don't exist at all outside the mind of the king. It's as I've been trying to explain to you. When we entered this country, in a way we entered his mind. Anything may be an illusion here, although to us it seems real enough."

"I don't understand," Conan muttered darkly, shaking his head again.

"I was afraid you wouldn't," said Labran, voice tinged with his frustration.

"Watch your tone, fool!" the stout warrior threatened. "I'll take no insults from the likes of you!"

Conan's reaction clearly distressed the affable and well-meaning young man.

"I'm sorry," he said quickly. "I didn't mean—"

"Could you leave over the arguing?" Finn said, breaking in impatiently. "I think we should test the reality of this stream as soon as possible, by having a long drink of it!"

This proposal was quickly accepted, and the little band started off, down the slope of their last dune and toward the river.

Had any of them bothered to glance back, they might have seen the strange figure that faded into view beside the font they had just left. It stood on spindly legs, great head wobbling on the skinny neck, looking much like a pumpkin set upon a stake. Tiny eyes sparkled with an excited light, and a tiny mouth stretched in a gleeful smile as he looked after the departing group.

"It's the most stimulating game you've given me so far, Finn MacCumhal," he said to himself. "But it's just begun. Oh, yes. It's just begun!"

The mother of Finn MacCumhal walked from the doorway of Mogh Nuadat's black tower and paused to look around her at the scene.

The courtyard before her was now a place of woeful sights and sounds. Hundreds of wounded Fianna warriors lay upon rude pallets of straw. Bindings of cloth about heads, limbs, and bodies gave grim evidence of many terrible wounds, with their wide stains of blood. Some men were mercifully unconscious or asleep, others awake but silent, concentrating, as if to will the pain away. But still others filled the air with a doleful chorus of gasps and screams and moans, stark proof that even the stoic Fianna men could not always defy the agony of such damage as ax or sword could cause.

About the wounded men, scores of people bent upon aiding them moved constantly. The healers and the druids of the clans used all their medical skills in treating wounds and administering potions to heal or at least ease pain. The rest, largely wives of the warriors who had accompanied the army, did whatever they could: bringing hot water from the several fires that burned about the yard, cleansing and binding wounds, comforting the distressed, helping to carry out the dead and make way for more wounded, who were always coming in.

Muirne looked around at all of this, her expression for a moment openly revealing both her repugnance and great sorrow at the dreadful spectacle. Then she put on a more determined look and moved forward, winding her way through the pallets to the outer wall.

Here she found the newly married Credhe, busily rubbing an ointment into a young warrior's gaping shoulder wound.

"Do you need any help here?" asked the mother of Finn.

"No, thank you," Credhe replied. "I'm nearly finished."

Muirne watched with great interest as the young woman tenderly worked the last of her ointment into the cut. It seemed to have a nearly miraculous effect, staunching the heavy flow of blood and pulling together the ragged edges of the flesh. The ointment gone, Credhe gently but tightly bound the wound with strips of cloth.

"Rest easy now," she told her youthful patient soothingly, stroking his brow. "Rest and sleep."

He obeyed at once, his eyes dropping closed, his pain-racked body relaxing as he drifted off.

"At least there's one who may survive," she said, climbing to her feet with a certain weariness and looking around. "Ah, but there are so many who won't."

"It's you who've saved the greatest number here," said Muirne. "But, my dear girl, you must be nearing exhaustion! It's three days and nights you've worked now without resting."

"And what of yourself?" Credhe returned. "You've been at

this for as long as I, and you've given over your fortress, even your own rooms, for hospital."

"Small things to do," Muirne told her modestly. "When I look at these suffering boys, I can only see my own son's face in each one of theirs."

"I know," said the younger woman. "It's Cael I see in them. Every day, I wait for him to be carried through the gates."

"Come with me," Muirne gently urged the girl. "At least have a bit of warm broth before you go on. Without some rest, you'll be collapsing soon."

Credhe nodded, and they moved to the closest fire, where a large pot of steaming broth was hung. Muirne procured small cups of it for them both and they sipped, but kept a watchful eye about them for emergencies.

"I've been noticing the healing skills you use," Muirne remarked in a quite casual way.

Credhe met the older woman's probing gaze thoughtfully for a moment, and then she smiled.

"I knew I'd not be keeping that secret from you long. You're right, Muirne. My mother was of the Sidhe. It's from her family that my arts in healing come." A look of some anxiety then appeared. "But you won't tell anyone else, will you? I don't want Cael ever to find out. It would make things so . . . well . . . difficult."

"My dear, no one would understand better than I what you mean by that!" Muirne assured her. "I've kept my own blood a secret from the mortal world long enough. I've loved two mortal men, but they don't really understand."

"I just want to live out a normal life with him," the girl said wistfully. "Simple and wonderful"—she cast a look about her at the chaos of the yard—"and peaceful."

A call from a watchman on the wall atop the gates interrupted their talk then.

"Warriors are coming in!" he said. "Horsemen and carts!"

"Can it be the end of the fighting for today?" Muirne remarked in surprise. She glanced toward the sun, only midway in its afternoon fall toward the sea. "It's very early."

"Pray to Danu that it is the end," Credhe said earnestly. "Maybe then the carnage will be less this time."

They stood watching as the gates were thrown open and the train of warriors and gates moved into the yard. Goll MacMorna himself led the train, Cael and Art MacConn at either hand. When Cael saw his wife, he pointed her out to Goll. At once the three men rode over to her and dismounted.

"Your husband tells me that you are the best healer here," Goll said in his brisk way. "We need your help at once."

He led the way to the first cart in the train. While the others were overloaded with wounded men, this one had only a single occupant, lying upon a heap of cloaks. The two women peered over the cart's wicker side at him.

He was a slender, fair-haired youth, beardless, fine-complexioned and most comely of feature. His body was marked by scores of minor wounds, while a great patch of blood soaking the chest of his tunic indicated a serious one.

"Who is he?" asked Muirne.

"The son of the king of Ulster," Goll replied. "He is badly wounded. Can you do anything for him?"

"I'll see," Credhe told him.

She climbed into the back of the cart and knelt beside him. Gently she tore open his already-rent tunic and laid bare his narrow chest. From a deep puncture wound close beside his heart there spouted a pulsing flow of deep-red blood.

"It is very bad," Credhe said darkly, shaking her head. Then she went immediately to work, trying to stop the torrent.

"Why was he even in the fight?" Muirne asked the men accusingly. "He's just a child!"

"He is only two years younger than myself!" countered Cael in a defensive way.

"The decision to enter the fight was his own," Goll responded tersely.

"And you couldn't stop him?" Muirne demanded in an angry tone. "Is that your excuse for letting this boy be harmed?"

Goll did not reply, and it was obvious from his stony expression that the stolid chieftain would say no more to defend his actions. This left it for the other warriors to come to his support.

"It wasn't the fault of Goll," Cael said. "We tried to stop him."

"What happened?" asked Muirne.

"He came to join us just today," explained Art MacConn. "Like myself, he had heard word of the battle here and wanted to come, but his father refused to let him go, telling him he was neither old enough nor strong enough." He gave a grim laugh at that. "Well, I surely can tell you how he felt then! He meant to defy his father as I did and prove himself. He convinced his twelve foster brothers to go with him, stole weapons from his fathers armory in the dead of night, and started for Corca Dhuibhne on foot."

"When he arrived, he went straight to Goll to demand service," Cael said. "Goll told him that he was no grown man, and not fit to face any fighting man at all. The boy would not listen. He argued that he feared no warrior, and that he meant to show Goll and his own father the truth of his words.

"But while he argued, his foster brothers—reckless young men seeking glory for themselves—went down to the battle line, saying no word, unknown to all of us. A champion of Donn's army was fighting there, taking on any who would come against him."

"Aye," put in Art. "I knew him. Dolar Durba, son of the king of the Sea of Icht he was. His father and brothers were all killed in the fighting yesterday. He meant to have revenge for them, and he fought his way onto our wall.

"He had killed many a Fian warrior already and was making loud, boastful challenge. It was then these twelve lads arrived and, seeing this lone man, thought to win quick renown by putting him down." He shook his head sadly. "Before anyone could stop them, they had moved against him."

Now Cael took up the tale again:

"We knew nothing of it until a warrior brought word to us where we were still holding the king's son back. 'Dolar Durba is just after killing your twelve comrades,' he said. 'You can hear the shouting of him now for more men to come against him.' The boy stared at him as if he would not believe such a tale. Then a great anger came upon him. He took hold of his arms, and no one could hold him or hinder him. He rushed down toward the wall where Dolar Durba was."

"All the warriors of Donn's army there gave a great shout of laughter when they saw him come upon the wall," said Art. "I think they believed the Fianna had been made an end of, to send such a young lad as that against one of their best champions.

"But when the boy heard that, he became all the angrier, and that anger fired him with a courage and a strength like that of a champion. He fell like a blasting winter wind upon Dolar Durba, and gave the man a dozen wounds before he knew he was attacked at all! Then the two fought hard together, reeling back and forth across the wall, giving and taking strokes with such a great savagery that finally their shields and swords broke apart from it.

"Even that did not slow the boy's attack. He grappled with Durba, and they wrestled on the edge of the wall, above the steep embankment to the beach. The boy's hands were on Durba's throat, and the bigger man could do nothing to shake him off. Finally, in desperation, Durba managed to wrench a dagger from his belt and plunge it into the boy's chest. The boy rolled aside, but kept his hold upon the other's throat.

"Locked together, the two tumbled from the wall, sliding and bouncing down the rocky bank, crashing onto the beach where both lay still."

"We thought they were both dead then," put in Cael. "But when the battle ended, we went down under the truce to collect our fallen and found the boy still lived. We brought him here."

"Dolar Durba was dead beneath him," Art added with a grim smile of satisfaction. "So it was the boy who got his victory."

"His victory," Muirne said scornfully. "Is it a victory for a child to lose his life through some foolish need to prove he is a man?"

"It was for much more than that," Art countered. "It was for his honor that he had to revenge his comrades."

"Honor?" repeated Muirne. "An even more foolish reason for a life to be wasted. It was honor that almost destroyed my own son's life."

"It also led him to take his rightful place as leader of the Fianna," Cael reminded her.

"This boy acted of his own will in this," Art MacConn added with force. "To do so, and to accept whatever fate it may bring with courage, is what makes a man and a true warrior." He glanced toward Goll. "That much I have learned since I joined you here."

There came a loud, rattling cough of pain from the cart. The figure of the boy had gone rigid, shuddering with the tension of his limbs, straining, arching the back high as if he meant to leap up. Credhe worked more frantically. With one hand she pressed the blood-soaked pad firmly down upon the wound. With the other she scattered a silvery powder across his chest, all the while chanting some unintelligible healing incantation under her breath.

Suddenly the boy's body went limp. With a great sigh whose tone seemed to blend surrender with relief, his narrow chest sank down. The ragged breathing did not begin again.

Credhe looked up toward the others, her face a mask of agony.

"He's gone," she said simply.

Goll MacMorna, who had said no word nor given any sign of emotion through any of this, showed no more reaction at the boy's passing. As stone-faced as always, he simply turned upon his heel and marched back toward his horse.

But Muirne pursued him, grabbing his arm, swinging him back toward her with a strength powered by her anger.

"How can you just walk away from him?" she asked in outrage. "Haven't you any sorrow at all for this child? What are you?"

"I am a chieftain of the Fianna," he responded coldly. "It is my task to keep the invaders upon the strand. To do so, I must send scores of my warriors, my clansmen, and my comrades to die every day. I can't be affording sorrow for every warrior who dies winning a hard fight, and I can't be sparing mourning time for each man who is lost. Now, if you'll allow it, I must return to the strand. The regrouping of our clans for tomorrow's fight must be seen to."

With that he strode purposefully to his horse, mounted, and rode out through the gates, giving them not even a backward glance. He left Muirne staring after him in disbelief.

"How could any man be so unfeeling?" she asked.

"It may be he has no other choice," remarked Art. "It's little more than his will that's holding the Fianna together now." He looked toward the still form in the cart. "But I'll keen for him," he went on most earnestly. "I feel a kinship with this boy who had so great a thing to prove to himself and his father. I'll see that he is buried, with his twelve friends. I'll have a flag-stone raised upon his grave, and I'll mourn there myself."

Cael, meanwhile, was helping Credhe to climb from the cart. She seemed weak, as if her labors had drained both strength and spirit from her. After she reached the ground, she continued to cling to him, pressing her face to his shoulder.

"Are you all right?" he asked in concern.

She lifted her face to him. Her eyes were filled with tears.

"He was so young, Cael. So very young."

"I know," he told her in a sympathetic way. "It was hard to see him die."

"Why must so many of them die!" she said in anguish. She glanced around her at the scores of wounded, and at the scores more being unloaded from the other carts. "Oh, Cael, I have seen so many. So many have died beneath my hands! And still, every day, more of them come. I don't know how long I can bear it—watching them die, waiting for it to be your own torn body that the carts bring through those gates."

He pulled her close to him again, hugged her tightly, as if he could pass his own strength to her.

"My love, have courage," he said in a determined and fortifying tone. "What we do is for all of Ireland. We must not be thinking of ourselves now, but of her, of the thousands of our people we are fighting to protect, as we have sworn to do."

"But what about ourselves, Cael?" she asked him in despair. "When will there be time for us?"

"Soon, my dear wife. Soon," he assured her, his youthful optimism untouched even in the midst of the chaos that surrounded them.

They stood together a moment longer then, savoring a too-brief taste of warmth and peace in each other amidst the horrors and death that filled the crowded yard.

CHAPTER EIGHTEEN
THE RIVER GUARDIAN

The river was a brutal force. It seemed to have used the power of its rushing waters to plow its way across the land, gouging out a crude, rocky channel along which it surged angrily. It crashed and shattered against the many rough-edged stones in its bed as if trying to blast them from its way, creating a surface of white, boiling foam. The sound of its battle was its lion's roar, its storm's thunder, its fighting-man's war cry.

Along the rugged bank moved Finn's small company, their figures dwarfed by the broad and violent flow. All of them looked refreshed now, most of their former vigor returned, though they did still carry the marks of their recent hardships in cracked and sunburned skin, ragged and sweat-stained clothes.

They walked the water's edge in a searching way, stopping at various places to examine more critically the surging waves, gazing with a certain longing toward the distant shore. For here the river created a stark dividing line between the barren lands they had just crossed and a green, forested land that lay beyond its boundary.

"It's maddening!" said Cuillen, scooping up a loose rock and throwing it into the waves with an angry gesture. "We pass through one barrier only to be blocked by another!"

"But, another barrier does mean another gateway as well," Labran pointed out cheerfully.

"Maybe," she said more hopefully. "I'm going on a bit to check ahead."

She moved toward a jumble of large rocks that blocked the view upriver. Bran and Sceolan, at a sign from Finn, fell in

167

with her, flanking her on guard. But she stopped to shoo them back, calling out in irritation to the young captain:

"Keep back your hounds, MacCumhal. I need none of their protecting just to scout the way."

He sighed, rolled his eyes heavenward, then signed the animals to return. She lifted her head in a triumphant way and strode on.

"Quite a spirited young woman, that one," Labran remarked admiringly, looking after her.

"Hmmm," Finn responded noncommittally, and turned his own attention across the river. "At least we know we're still heading the right way. There's that cursed mountain, like a great ogham stone, still there, still waiting for us."

From the low ground by the river, little could really be seen of the spire of rock now, but enough of its gray peak thrust above the soft, green woolliness of the forest that it clearly marked their goal.

"Likely the thing is just another illusion," muttered a thoroughly gloomy Conan, "meant only to lure us to our doom."

"Oh, I'm certain it's real enough," Labran offered in his helpful way. "The king promised it to us, and he'd not lie."

"Would he not?" Conan responded sarcastically. "And why trust him—or you, for all of that? You've done nothing to help us along in this. You're just baggage that we've had to carry with us!"

"I've told you that it's no fault of mine," Labran said defensively, hurt once again by the stout warrior's insults. "I've tried everything I can to help us, but I've little control of my magic in this country."

"You had no control of it outside, as I recall," Conan said with scorn.

"Enough, Conan," Finn said sharply. "Labran may have no magic, but he has been a help to us in finding the gateways. And a great deal more help than you've been."

"Have I? Really?" the slender de Danaan said, brightening somewhat.

"You have. Now give over bickering and put your minds to finding a passage here. It's clear enough there's no chance for a swimmer in that current. Even a boat would have a time of it not to be smashed to splinters on the rocks."

"Aye," Conan agreed. "I've never seen a river that looked as much a killer as this one."

"Perhaps there is a ford," offered Labran optimistically. "But I just know there will be something. We've only got to keep looking for it!"

"Your eternal cheeriness is wearing very thin, you scrawny clown!" snarled Conan, unchastened by Finn's warning to him.

"I've found something!" came the excited voice of Cuillen, and the other turned to see her sprinting back from the mound of rocks, face flushed in elation.

"What is it?" asked Finn. "A ford?"

"A boat!" she said. "Come see it!"

She turned and started back. The men exchanged a dubious glance and followed with the dogs.

"Careful," she cautioned as they reached the rocks. "Don't frighten him away."

"Him?" asked Finn, but she had already gone on, leaving him nothing to do but follow, his expression one of enormous curiosity.

She skirted the screen of boulders with some care to make no noise, and they did the same, picking their way across the rugged ground until they reached one large stone where she finally paused. Here the sound of harp music—played very badly—was clearly audible, drifting to them from somewhere close ahead.

Holding one finger to her lips to signal silence, she gestured over the rock. Then, cautiously, she lifted up to peer over its top. The others did the same, including the hounds.

Beyond the stone, a stretch of the riverbank was visible. A tiny finger of rocks thrust out at one point, forming a bit of harbor. Here, protected from the swift current, floated an old curragh—a small craft made of a lath frame covered with hide. Nearby, perched upon a tall boulder at the water's edge, was a rather thin, quite small, and extremely old man, sitting crosslegged and playing away with great gusto upon a harp.

The first impression of the man was one of ears. His were of a truly stupendous size, seemingly intended by the gods to fit a man twice as large, but put upon him for some joke or curse. They were like great scallop shells, thrusting straight out from the sides of his head, and in a hard wind, the little man was likely in peril of being borne away.

Then came the hair. It was a mass of intensely orange-red color, and was so curly it formed an uncombed bush sitting atop his skull like some creature nesting there. Below it, the head was shaped like a thick wedge, the forehead very wide, the face tapering quickly down to a sharply pointed chin. Its features were cunning, almost foxlike, with a long, pointed nose, wide, mobile mouth, and tiny eyes of a glittering bright green, topped by bushy brows of the same color as his hair.

The man's great age was clearly evidenced by his wrinkles. A network of deep lines spread outward from the corners of his eyes. Ravines swept out from the sides of his nose to curve down around the mouth. Uncountable furrows gave the broad plain of his forehead the look of a plowed field.

His clothing was that of a simple herdsman: wool trousers, tunic, and leather jerkin, all quite well worn. But in his hands he held a harp whose exquisiteness belied his poverty. The instrument was skillfully crafted from polished red yew wood. The sinuous arch of its bridge was incised with a design of strange beasts and birds intertwining in a complex design. The graceful curve of bow was inset with bands of silver and gold, while glowing jewels of red and green were mounted in the spaces between.

It seemed incredible that an instrument so fine could produce such an awful cat-wail of noise, even considering how badly the little man was playing it. Still, although the sound was piercing enough to raise the dead, he seemed pleased enough with it, playing on with great abandon.

"What do you think, Labran?" Cuillen whispered to the de Danaan. "Will he help us?"

"There's no way to be certain. He's of the solitary folk of my race. They avoid company and like to be left alone."

"Considering his playing, I'm certain no one objects to that," muttered Conan, scowling in pain.

"Well, we'll never know if he'll help us without asking," Finn said in a practical way. "Besides that, he reminds me of someone I know well. Come on. Let's try speaking to him."

He led the way, and they moved around the rock into the man's view, advancing slowly, so as not to startle him.

When the man did see them, however, he was far from startled. He put down the harp and smiled as if he had expected to see some company. The lines of his face all drew upward, giving him a joyous look, and his voice was full of warm welcome:

"Ah, my friends, come closer. I'll not be scampering off!" He gave the little band a searching examination with his bright eyes. "It would seem, by the look of you, that you've come through a bit of trouble."

"We have, that," Finn admitted. "And now we're needing to get across this river. Can you help us?"

"Can I help you?" he said with a laugh. "And haven't I been waiting here to do that very thing? And haven't I been making my great caterwauling on this harp just to bring you here?"

"You knew we were coming?" asked Finn.

"Who in the Country of the Fair Men doesn't know that the great Finn MacCumhal is playing the King's Game? And the gateway past the barrier this ragin' torrent makes is the selfsame Ruan O'Cealaigh you see before you!"

"Do you mean that you're to take us across?" asked Cuillen.

"In my curragh," the man told her.

Conan looked at the bobbing craft and laughed derisively.

"What, in that little basket? It'd be smashed to bits in those rapids."

"There's no finer-made nor hardier craft afloat than my curragh," Ruan assured him proudly. "And with my skill in handling her, she'll take the lot of you across as dry and safe as if you were at your own hearthside!"

"Ach, he's raving!" Conan told Finn bluntly. "Let's look elsewhere."

"Search if you wish," the little man said, shrugging, "but you'll find no other way at all."

"If he's playing the king's gateway here, he's likely right," put in Labran. "Searching on would be a waste of time."

"I agree," said Finn. "All right, Ruan, we'll accept your offer to take us across."

"Well, now, it wasn't exactly an offer," the man said carefully, and then gave them a cunning smile that made him seem all the more foxlike. "I can take you across, all right, but first there's a bit of a task you'll have to do for me."

"A task, is it?" cried an outraged Conan. "Finn, why are we even talking with this old fool? Let's take his curragh for ourselves. What can he do?"

"You never learn, do you, Conan?" Cuillen said sharply. "The last time you said that, the king vanished right out of your hands. Will you make our one chance to cross this river vanish as well?"

"She's right," Finn put in. "And there'll be no more talk

from a Fian man about taking anything we've not fairly earned. If there's a task to be done, then we'll do it!"

"You are a man of justice and of honesty," Ruan told him with sincerity, giving a little bow. "But I give you warning: It's not an easy test the king's set for you this time."

"This time?" said Labran in dismay. "And he thinks that the other two were easy?"

"What is it?" Finn asked.

"You must find and destroy three wolves who are roaming the countryside nearby," the little man said.

"Three wolves?" said Conan, snorting in contempt. "And what's that? A MacMorna warrior could deal with their likes himself!"

"Could he indeed?" Ruan said, seemingly amused by the stout warrior's boasting. "Well, that may be, but these are like no wolves you've met before. They're the three daughters of Arretaich, the last of the People of Oppression. A fierce clan of Sid-folk they once were, all with the shape-shifting power. But the Milesians destroyed the rest of them in the great battle for Ireland. Now they have a hatred for all mortals. They roam in darkness, plaguing herds and killing anyone they meet. Men of the outerworld live in dread when they're stalkin' the night."

Conan was unimpressed.

"They still seem little enough threat to me," he said carelessly. "With the hounds and our own weapons against them, they'll have little chance."

"You've got to catch them first, my proud champion," the old man pointed out. "They can sense danger, and they can smell a man well beyond a spear's throw. They're fleet as deer, besides."

"Bran and Sceolan can run down the swiftest deer in Ireland," said Finn.

"I've no doubt of it. But if these three are truly threatened, they've only to shift their forms to those of hawks and flap away from you. No, lad, you'll never come near 'em."

"Isn't there any way at all to draw them close?" asked Cuillen. "There must be someone or something that they'll come near to."

"A clever girl!" Ruan told her with a grin. "Yes, it's said that the harper's tune can call them in—if the playing's sweet enough. It recalls their lost palace and the fine life that they once had. Oh, they'll come near to a good harper, right enough."

Finn had been gravely considering through this. Now he stepped closer to the little man.

"Ruan O'Cealaigh," he said solemnly, "will you give the use of your harp to me?"

"I thought you would be asking," the man said shrewdly. "Aye, young Finn, I will. The truth be told, I've brought it for no other reason than to give to you." He smiled. "It must be clear enough that I've no use for it myself!"

He held out the instrument. Finn took it gently, cradling it and looking with admiration on the fine workmanship.

"What are you thinking, Finn?" demanded the girl, stepping up beside him. "Have you some plan?"

"I may have," he replied. He lifted his gaze toward the sun. Now apparently having become unstuck from its position high overhead, it was sinking toward the horizon in a quite ordinary fashion. "It looks as if it'll be night soon," he said. "We'll find out then if I'm right."

When night fell upon the Country of the Fair Men, it did so with a vengeance. The sun's disappearance spread a cloak of profound blackness across the land, unrelieved by any white twinkling of stars or yellow glow of moon. In all the vast expanse of dark, there shone only a single, golden cone of light. It came from a campfire blazing like a beacon in the center of a precisely circular open area. The wavering light of it fell upon the large boulders hemming in the spot, creating shifting patterns of light and shadow that made them seem like living creatures moving together in a slow and fluid dance.

The light also fell upon a single figure, looking almost like a boulder too as it sat hunched beside the fire, tightly wrapped in the thick folds of a wool cloak. Only the head sticking above the cloak revealed it was a man, and the gold light threw into sharp definition the features of Finn MacCumhal. Close beside him sat the harp, its strings and its metal fittings glinting sharply with reflected light.

Beyond the range of the fire's glow, hidden in the deep shadows cast by the encircling rocks, crouched Ruan O'Cea-laigh and the rest of Finn's companions, peering out cautiously toward the solitary man.

Cuillen pulled back and looked toward the others with an expression of disgust.

"It's another foolish risk he's taking," she said irritably. "Once more he's managed to put himself in jeopardy alone. The man's arrogance will destroy him yet, and lose us the shield and sword!"

"He knows what he's doing," rumbled Conan in a rare show of support for his captain. "A Baiscne man he may be, but even I have to say he's more clever than any I've ever met. If he's made a plan, it will work."

"You mean, you think this foolish notion of charming the wolves with music is clever?" she asked in disbelief. "And I suppose he fancies himself a master of the harp along with these other great virtues he's supposed to have?"

"I don't really think it's fair of you to be always belittling the lad's talents," Labran said with an uncharacteristic heat that caused her to look at him in surprise. "I'm sorry to be saying that, Cuillen, but he is known to be a grand player."

"And why wouldn't he be?" put in Ruan. "Wasn't he taught by Cnu Dereoil—the Little Nut—himself?"

"Who is Cnu Dereoil?" asked Cuillen.

"A strange little man," said Conan. "A wandering harper who visits Finn's court at Almhuin and plays for their feasts."

"He is the finest harper in all Ireland, is what he is!" Ruan said proudly. "His playing can make the stones weep and the dead rise up to jig! He has the magic for it, and he's my own nephew, besides! I know that if anyone could give the skill to Finn, it would be the Little Nut."

"Well, I still think Finn is mad to try this," Cuillen said tersely, apparently unchastened by the scolding of the men. However, when she turned her gaze back to that figure, so alone and vulnerable in the center of that open space, a look of concern showed clearly in her face.

Finn had now taken up the harp. He gave its strings a preliminary strum, the bright notes shimmering into the night as the vibrating strings shimmered in the firelight. Then he began to play.

The tune was lilting and lyrical in quality. The high, sweet notes that drifted upward with the cheering firelight seemed to paint an image, against the black sky, of grand halls filled with bright, rejoicing companies. The circular open space itself even took on the appearance of a great king's palace, the surrounding boulders growing upward to form roof poles upholding the ceiling of the night, and Finn becoming a host of musicians regaling a lively crowd with harps and tiompans and pipes.

Cuillen stared fixedly, fascinatedly, at Finn now. She, like the others, had clearly been caught up by the wondrous vision Finn was creating with the magic of the harp's tune.

Suddenly the dogs lifted their heads and cocked their ears.

"Careful, everyone!" Ruan warned softly. "They're coming!"

Soon a sound became audible to all of them: a rhythmic *fwooping* sound, growing swiftly louder.

Then, down from the black canopy above, three forms swept. They were enormous hawks, each beating its broad expanse of wings to settle to a landing within the circular glow cast by the fire, forming a triangle about it and the seated man.

They folded their wings and stood for a time, motionless save for the darting movements of their heads as they swept the glittering gazes of their eyes about the area. Then, apparently satisfied that Finn was alone here, one gave a sharp caw that was echoed by the other two.

At once, the shapes of all three began to change. A silver aura formed around them, its shimmering light growing more intense, swallowing up the outlines of the birds. The vague shadows of the beings within this cloak of light seemed to writhe and bulge grotesquely, then to stretch both outward and upward. Their bodies grew long. Wings and talons were replaced by slender legs. The heads grew broad and flat and sleek, while the beaks shot out into pointed muzzles.

"By good Danu, I surely wish I could do that so easily," Labran said in a voice filled with both awe and wistfulness.

The transformations ended. The silver auras began to fade, revealing the new forms. And Finn MacCumhal found himself now surrounded by three wolves who crouched, ready to spring upon their lone prey.

CHAPTER NINETEEN
THE WOLF-WOMEN

"By the Dagda, the beasts are huge!" breathed Conan.

There was very good reason for the stout warrior to be awed. The wolves stood as tall at the shoulder as a pony, their heads high enough that they could meet a man of even Finn's height eye to eye. Their bodies were hard and lean and sinewy, the fangs revealed in their snarling mouths long enough to tear the throat from the largest bull.

"I told you they were like nothing you'd ever seen, didn't I, now?" whispered Ruan.

"They'll kill Finn," said Cuillen. She looked at the two dogs crouched beside her, bodies tensed, almost quivering in their eagerness to attack. "Let's send Bran and Sceolan against them," she suggested.

"No," Labran said. "They'd be no match against such creatures. They'd only be killed, and Finn with them. He knows they can't be defeated as they are. Leave this to him."

"Aye," Ruan agreed. "I don't think they mean to harm him. At least, not yet. They've come to hear the music of his harp. Look!"

And, indeed, it seemed that the odd little man was right. The spell of the music had apparently captured the wolves now too, for they had ceased to slink cautiously forward and had sat down to listen. Slowly their savage expressions were turning to looks of contentment.

Finn played on, but watched the creatures from the corners of his eyes, shifting his gaze constantly from one to the other. When he finally seemed assured that all had ceased their stalking and become an audience, he ceased to play.

"Play on!" came the command from one of the wolves. Though the voice was a snarling and bestial one, it was still clearly that of a woman.

Now Finn looked around at the three openly for the first time.

"Oh, you wish me to continue?" he asked in an amicable way. "Well, I'll do so for you most gladly, especially as it appears I've little other choice. But, I understand that it is only the shape of wolves upon you—that you are women. If you truly love the music of the harp, it should be as women that you listen to it, as it was for the ears and the spirits of people that the music was created."

The three wolves exchanged a look, and the longing shone clearly in their dark eyes. But then their gazes returned to him, narrowed in suspicion.

"Ah, it's only myself here," he said. "One man, alone, and you with the skill to shift back to your beast-shape in the winking of an eye. What could I do against the three of you?"

They stared searchingly at him, then around them at the circle of rocks. No attack coming from there could take them by surprise. They were well beyond spear range. No enemy could reach them before they'd transformed. And Finn did look a harmless-enough figure, sitting there wrapped in his cloak. The wolves exchanged another long look. Finally one nodded, to be answered by nods from the other two. Once more the silver aura of their transformation rose about them, and in moments the fading glow revealed the forms of three women.

They were as gaunt and hard and sinewy as the wolves, but the fine bone-structure of their lean faces indicated that once, many years of hatred and hardship in the past, the three had been women of incredible handsomeness.

"All right, harper," said one, her voice still filled with the menacing snarl of the wolf, "play for us now. And no mistakes, or it's your death."

"And don't try to escape us," said another, "for as you said yourself, it'll take only an instant for us to become wolves again."

"And an instant more to run you down," said the third.

"I've given no thought to running," Finn assured them, and quite truthfully. "I'll play as I promised. And I surely hope the sound of it is pleasing."

"I pray to Danu it's the last sound they'll ever hear!"

muttered Conan, his thick fist tightening on his already-drawn sword.

Finn played. This time it was a slow, keening tune of great sadness, a valediction of longing and regret for a golden time now gone, when the Tuatha de Danaan had lived upon the surface of Ireland. He watched the women closely, and it soon became clear that the enchantment spun by the silver threads of the harp's music was enveloping the women gently in its web. Their gazes were fixed upon distant visions. They were entranced.

"Thank you, my Little Nut," Finn murmured to himself with great feeling.

Up in the rocks, Labran was smiling with great glee.

"See there! See there!" he whispered to Ruan. "Oh, he does have the skill!"

"I don't believe it!" said Cuillen, staring. "He actually seems to have gotten some kind of hold on them with the music!"

"Careful, now," Conan told them warningly. "Their guard is almost down. Finn will move soon. But as soon as he does, the spell will be broken. He may still not be swift enough to deal with them all. He'll have only one chance and then, if we don't reach him, he'll be dead. So be ready, Cuillen, and you hounds as well!"

Finn watched the faces of the women intently now. They were continuing to relax, grow softer. As they did, some shadowy semblance of the beauty they had once possessed became visible. A look of sorrow crossed the features of the young warrior at that. He seemed to be feeling pangs of remorse at what he would have to do. Though they were now more savage beasts than women, they were still living beings.

But there was no time for hesitation now. The time had come. In one swift move, he tossed away the harp and threw back his cloak, revealing his sheathed sword. The movement instantly broke the music's spell.

"It's a trap, Sisters," howled one woman, and they all began to shimmer with the first light of transformation.

Finn jumped to his feet, drawing out his sword. He leapt toward one of the three, striking out ruthlessly with his blade before she was completely enveloped by the glow. The weapon pierced her heart. She shrieked in agony and fell back, the silver light fading from her for the last time.

Cuillen, Conan, and the two hounds had by now broken

from their cover and were charging across the open space to help. But, behind Finn, the other two women were alrady fully enwrapped by their shining cocoons and beginning the process of metamorphosis.

Finn dove toward a second of the sisters and struck out again, ramming his blade through the center of the glowing chrysalis. The mass collapsed, the light flickered and then died away, revealing a hideous creature caught between the shapes of woman and wolf. The grotesque body convulsed in its death throes, a bloody froth bubbling from the jaws of the half-formed muzzle.

Finn stared, for a moment frozen by the awful sight. In that moment, the third woman's transformation was completed. With a howl of rage, the enormous wolf leapt across the intervening space and dove upon the young warrior's back.

The weight of the creature bore him down. He twisted, trying to avoid the tearing fangs and bring his sword around to strike. But he was trapped beneath the heavy body, and looked up in helplessness as the opened jaws dropped down to snap at his head.

Then, suddenly, the wolf was gone from him. He sat up and realized that Bran and Sceolan had arrived and thrown themselves upon his attacker.

Each of the animals was much smaller than the wolf, but their combined weight was enough to slam the beast off Finn. It recovered, jumping to its feet to face the hounds who now began a wary circling, teeth bared, expressions as savage as that of their hereditary foe.

Conan and Cuillen now reached Finn.

"Are you all right?" she asked. Her voice was filled with an unusual amount of concern, so much so that Finn gave her a curious look.

"I think so," he said. "Thank you for asking."

"What about the dogs?" said Conan. "Shall we help them?"

"No," Finn said. "It's what they're meant for. Let them have the pleasure of this kill."

So, Conan, clearly yearning for a fight himself, had to stand by with Finn and Cuillen, watching in frustration as the hounds battled to the death against the wolf.

The struggle was short but violent. Moving quickly back and forth, the dogs soon confused the larger beast. Then, in a move the two had likely played out many scores of times, they drove in, seizing the wolf's throat on either side.

It roared in anger. It howled in pain. It threw its massive head back and forth to dislodge the dogs, and when that failed, it rolled upon the ground. But they hung on, their teeth tearing ever deeper into the creature's throat as it struggled, until blood spurted thickly from a severed artery. Not long thereafter, the wolf's struggles began to slow. As if feeling its life pouring from it, it made one more desperate move for freedom, summoning a last energy from somewhere, rising and throwing off the hounds.

They struck the ground heavily but were instantly up again, facing their adversary. But they had no need to drive in again. The great wolf—last of the fierce People of Oppression—gave a final defiant cry of hatred and collapsed, crashing to the ground.

Finn, Cuillen, and Conan approached it cautiously, the hounds on either side. Bran nuzzled the still form, then lifted his head to give his own howl of victory, which Sceolan joined. The animal was dead.

"Strange," said Cuillen, looking down at the enormous beast. "Wolf and wolfhounds—ancient enemies. Yet alike at the same time. Both with the blood of the Sidhe in them."

"It's from the mind and not the blood that true loyalty comes," Finn said pointedly.

Labran and Ruan joined them then, the little man gazing about in amazement at the bodies of the slain beings.

"By the great Danu, herself!" Ruan exclaimed. "If I hadn't looked upon it with my own eyes, I would never have believed that you could destroy them all."

"And have we earned your help in return, old man?" Finn asked.

Ruan looked from the somber-faced young man to the blood-coated hounds who flanked him. Then he nodded with tremendous enthusiasm.

"I'll take you across, so I will," he said. "And it's a trip you've well earned, Finn MacCumhal. You've proven yourself a man of cleverness and courage and great skill in the harp."

"All I am now," Finn said slowly and with a somewhat impatient tone in his voice, "is a man who wants to be off with no more delays!"

* * *

The little curragh floated across the boiling rapids as if they were a pond on a calm day. Though stuffed quite full with the lot of Finn's band, the craft showed no distress at the great weight, responding handily to the urgings of Ruan's oars. A rising sun saw it grounding safely upon the river's far shore.

The travelers climbed out onto the bank and made a last farewell to the little man. He waved, with both his hands and his ears, then sent the curragh back into the currents. In moments it had borne him downriver, out of sight.

Now Finn and his companions shifted their attention from the river and the arid land behind them to the country that lay ahead. They turned and stood looking toward the edge of the forest, which began just beyond the rocky margins of the river bank. The trees grew thickly, their foliage twining to produce a heavy canopy casting the area below into deep gloom.

From there the forest stretched away to the distance, its dark green cover unbroken save for the same, grim mountain thrusting up above the treetops.

"The Battle Raven curse that thing!" Conan muttered. "It still looks as far away as ever!"

"We still have to reach it," said Finn. "Mark the direction well. When we enter the woods, we'll be losing sight of it."

"We must be very careful here," Labran warned. "Remember that illusion could be part of anything we see. And that could be even more so in the darkness and mystery of the wildwood."

"Ah, man, give over your fearful talk," Conan told him impatiently. "Look there. There's even a path that points right to that bloody mountain."

He was right. A wide opening was visible just ahead of them, forming a corridor that seemed to run deep into the trees.

"That path might be the surest way to be deceived," Labran said. "It's a bit too handy, isn't it? And why didn't any of us note it when we first landed? It's wide enough to drive a cart along!"

"Haven't you realized yet that the illusions of this king of yours can't stop men of the Fianna?" Conan blustered. "We've overcome everything he's put against us. A few trees will be no obstacle!"

"Why don't you ever listen to Labran?" Cuillen told him. "It's purest luck that's brought us this far, not your skill!" She looked to Finn. "What about you? You must realize the dangers here."

"Of course I do," Finn answered tersely, clearly somewhat irritated by her continued criticism. "But this time I agree with Conan. The Fianna do have some useful skills, hard as it is for you to accept, and knowledge of the forest is one of the greatest. A Fianna warrior spends half his life learning the lore of the woods, hunting and living under the sky. I was raised up in the glens of Slieve Bladhma myself. There are no forests I can't make my way in, unlike a girl raised in the comforts of the high king's court! So if you think me such an idiot as it seems, why don't you just stay here! Conan and the dogs and I are going on! This way!"

With that he stalked off, a grinning Conan and the hounds close behind.

Cuillen looked after him, then shook her head and took Labran's arm.

"Come along, then," she said in an exasperated way. "It seems the mighty captain of the Fianna has to prove himself again."

They started after the others, entering the shadowed corridor into the woods. As they moved between the ranks of trees that towered on either side, Labran looked into the darkness between them with apprehension.

"I don't like this at all," he said to her. "This is no natural wood."

Cuillen cast a more searching gaze around her. It was obvious what the de Danaan meant. The trees were spaced exact distances apart, forming neat rows that ran away into the shadows. Each tree had a long, straight trunk, limbless until the very top, where a symmetrical umbrella of branches thrust out, intertwining just its tips with those of its neighbors, creating a solid canopy with a pattern that looked like that of lace.

"It's very carefully laid out," she said. "And the trees are all of a height. It's as if they were planted all together, like a crop."

"It's even more unnatural than that," he said. "Look closer at the trees. They're not just similar; they're exactly alike!"

"They can't be!", she said skeptically, but then she examined several as they passed with greater care. Her look changed to one of wonder. "Why, they are! Like one tree copied again and again." She looked around at the rows running away into the dark infinity. "How many thousands of copies, Labran? How could they be made?"

"Maybe there is only one tree," he said. "Maybe none at all. It surely must be some creation of the king's mind we've entered, and . . . something's going to happen. I feel it."

Labran's fears seemed at first to be groundless ones. They proceeded some distance into the forest without incident. The path continued wide and smooth, and they moved with good speed.

But once deep into the woods, the path began to narrow. The trees seemed almost to creep in while their branches grew thicker, finally creating a nearly solid vault above. The travelers found themselves plunged into a murky twilight, where all shapes lost clear definition, and the shadows seemed like some inky liquid, filling up the trees about and threatening to flood in and engulf them too.

Here another difference between this forest and that about Tadg's Sid became evident. For while that wood was alive with bizarre creatures of the shadows, this one was strangely silent, apparently empty of all life. Not even the wind keened through the branches or stirred the topmost leaves.

Cuillen and Labran, at this point totally engrossed in searching the darkness about them, were unaware that those ahead had abruptly stopped until they banged into the backs of Finn and Conan.

"Say!" she exclaimed indignantly. Then she realized the two Fian men were gazing about them in a rather vague way. "What's the matter?" she demanded.

"The path is gone," Finn said.

"Gone?" she said. "What do you mean?"

"It just ended," he told her. "See for yourself."

She and Labran moved about the two to look ahead. Indeed, the pathway had simply and abruptly ended. Only the close-set trees, like those on either side, now lay before them.

"Well, that should be no problem for the great forester," she remarked in a sarcastic tone. "All your lore should tell us which way to go."

"I . . . I'm not certain," he reluctantly admitted, not meeting her eye.

"Why not?" she prodded. "I thought you could find your way in any wood!"

"Well, this is no normal wood," he shot back defensively.

"I can't see the sun or sky. There are no signs of game, no wind. There's not even a bit of moss growing on these trees! There's nothing to tell me our direction at all. Conan, what about you?"

"I don't know," the stout warrior admitted flatly, his usual overconfidence having vanished with the path. He turned, looking around him in perplexity. "I thought . . . maybe that way?" He shook his head in defeat. "But . . . no—I've no idea."

"Well, we can at least find our way back," she said impatiently. "We'll just take the path—"

She stopped short as she turned around. For the pathway that had brought them to this spot had now vanished as well.

"How could that be?" she said in astonishment. "We were just on it!"

"I was afraid of something like this," Labran said despairingly. "The king has done it to us now."

"Do you understand what's happened to us here?" Finn asked him. "Tell us what it means!"

"It means," said Labran unhappily, "that we've been sent Astray!"

CHAPTER TWENTY
THE HEALING

As the warm, steaming water swooshed over the body of Caoilte, the young warrior gave a sigh of great contentment.

He lay in a large basin of smooth marble set close beside the central fire of the Sid of women. Although he was quite naked, he seemed quite relaxed, head back, eyes closed, his expression one of pleasure. One woman with a skin of smooth snow-white and rippling hair of raven-black shaved his swarthy face most tenderly with a well-honed blade. Uaine and two other sisters—comely young women with hair of golden hue—administered the bath, using soft cloths to wash his limbs and torso slowly, skillfully, and most caressingly. All four went about their work with tremendous enthusiasm and little smiles of satisfaction. Other sisters, working about them in the great cavern, stole frequent glances toward them, their looks openly envious.

Caoilte's eyes parted slightly and he peered out at his nurses' progress. One young woman was working her way up his legs. The other was moving down his chest to his stomach. Soon they would meet between. Uaine, who was massaging the hard muscles of his shoulder, noted his interest.

"Is this pleasing to you, my champion?" she cooed.

"Yes . . . yes . . ." he said dreamily. But then a cold reality struck home. "I mean, no! No!" he said with force, sitting up and shaking his head as if to clear it of this seductive fantasy.

"What's wrong, my champion?" Uaine said in dismay.

"It's all wrong!" he said, grabbing up a towel and wrapping it around his nakedness. "You're stealing away my will with

185

this luxury. I can't be letting it happen any longer. Your three days have passed, and more! I've recovered my strength. I'm ready for the final healing. Uaine, you must call Bebind here to me!"

While Uaine rushed away to find the austere leader of the sisterhood, Caoilte climbed from the basin and moved back to his bed. Though he had regained much strength since the purging, he still moved with great difficulty, clutching at his as-yet-unhealed wound.

Uaine soon reappeared, Flann and Bebind in tow. The tall woman advanced upon him with a disapproving look.

"What do you mean, thundering about and making violent demands, you coarse man? You've quite distressed poor Uaine."

"I'm sorry for that," Caoilte said, "but I'll not be bullied by you or beguiled by your ladies any longer. It's time I was healed, so please get on with it!"

She eyed him sternly and stubbornly for a long moment. Then her gaze shifted about her, across the faces of the other women of the Sid who had now stopped to watch this little drama with great concern. Bebind gave a deep sigh of resignation.

"Perhaps it would be best to do it at once," she said. "Your presence here has quite disrupted the order of my Sid. The women do little but vie for a chance to serve you, to touch you, even just to look at you. They've lost all discipline and they defy me at every turn. All because of one, mere, mortal man. Yes, it would be best to have you healed and away from here."

"No, Bebind!" protested Uaine, and her voice was echoed by those of many others in the Sid.

"There, you see?" Bebind said to Caoilte. "A perfect example. Uaine and many others are completely smitten by you. Uncontrollable."

"But it's not fair!" Uaine said, nearly in tears. "It was my turn to care for him today!"

"We cannot leave the poor man badly wounded forever just so you and the others can play the nurse to him, now can we?" Bebind asked in a severe tone.

This logic seemed to get through to the other woman. She flushed and dropped her eyes, mumbling regretfully:

"No. No, Bebind. I suppose that we cannot."

"Fine!" the tall woman said briskly. "Then, let us pre-pare."

All the women of the Sid now moved in from about the cavern, forming a closely packed ring around Caoilte's bed. Bebind knelt down at the bedside and moved the covering back to reveal the wound. The cut was still gaping, the flesh about its edges still white and puffy, but it had lost that gangrenous quality.

"All right, sisters!" she commanded loudly. "Begin the chant!"

The women began a song in unison. It rose and fell in high, eerie ululation, more like the sound of hooting owls than human voices. As it began to echo back from the cavern's high dome and fill all the room, Bebind leaned forward, dropping her face toward Caoilte's bare side.

A look of consternation filled the young man's face as the prim and austere matron fastened her lips directly upon his wound!

The sensation must have been a strange one, for his expression began to mirror a combination of tension, puzzlement, and revulsion. His back arched and his limbs grew rigid. The chant grew louder, more strident, more wavering. Bebind kept up her bizarre action, her mouth fixed upon the wound like some giant leech. Caoilte's body began to quiver with his strain. His eyeballs rolled back up into his head. He voiced a long, low moan.

Bebind seized the quaking man and held him in her strong grip, keeping her contact. The chanting rose to a single, sustained note that was almost a shriek.

With a great expulsion of breath, Bebind pulled her mouth suddenly from his wound, releasing him. The chant abruptly cut off, its last note reverberating in the room, then dying away. Caoilte lay motionless, once more drained of all strength, panting like a winded hound.

"By . . . the blessed . . . Danu!" he finally managed to gasp out. "I . . . I didn't know . . . it would be . . . so . . . so—"

"So personal?" she finished in a brusque way. "Well, have no fear, young man. It gives me no closer feeling for you."

"Is it over, then?" he asked.

"See for yourself," she said, rising and stepping back.

Flann and Uaine rushed in on either side to help the weakened man sit up. He looked down upon his side, eyes widening in amazement. Save for a thin, white line of scar tissue, there was no sign of where the awful wound had been!

"Amazing!" he said. He touched the spot gingerly, then probed with more force. He twisted his torso, gently, then with more vigor, beaming in pleasure. "It really is amazing! It's completely healed! There's no soreness at all!"

"Of course not," Bebind coldly replied.

He waved Uaine and Flann away and arose by himself. He moved about, twisting and bending with vigor, stretching his supple body with obvious delight at having full use of it again for the first time in days.

"My sisters," he said, grinning around at the circle of them, "you don't know how grateful I am." He picked up his tunic from the bed and, shedding the towel, slipped the garment over his head. "But now, I can lose no more time setting out after my friends. So, if you could just get me the rest of my clothing and my weapons . . ."

"But you won't be needing them, my champion," Uaine said softly, smiling in her coquettish way.

"What do you mean?" he asked, not immediately grasping her implication.

"Yes, Uaine," Bebind snapped impatiently. "What are you playing at? Get him his things and let him be off!"

"I'm sorry, Bebind," Uaine answered in a voice with an unusually sharp edge, "—but Caoilte will not be leaving us."

"Look, I know it's difficult," he said, still not understanding what was taking place, "and I really do regret having to leave such a fine lot of women as yourselves, but I can't stay any longer. My friends need help!"

Uaine gave a gay little laugh at that.

"Dear Caoilte," she said, "let me explain to you: You won't be leaving us *ever!*"

The warrrior was stunned by this. He stood speechless, looking around him at the circle of faces, all smiling, all eyeing him with naked covetousness. All, that is, but Bebind's. That woman, taut with outrage, now advanced upon the small, whispy Uaine threateningly.

"How dare you speak this way? Are you mad?"

"I speak for all the sisters, Bebind," Uaine said with a superior little smirk, looking up fearlessly at the woman towering over her. "You see, we've talked, and we've decided that we want him here. We've all been much too long without men."

The indignant matron looked from Uaine to the plump woman by her.

"Flann, is this true?" she demanded.

"It is, Bebind," Flann admitted with some hesitancy, clearly embarrassed. Then, in a rationalizing way, she added, "And, you must admit it would be very nice having a man about after so many years."

"But it was to escape men that you all came here!" Bebind said in disbelief. She gazed about at the others, lifting her voice to address them all. "Don't you remember the pain? The anger? The humiliations you've suffered?"

"It's been much too long ago for most of us," countered Uaine. "Too long to remember. Too long to be alone."

"Men have not changed, I can assure you," the tall woman said with force. "Look at this one! In just the few days since he came among us, you've forgotten your own work, your own pride, your own wills!"

Her reasoning had no apparent impact on the women of the Sid. They watched her silently, stonily, no one giving even a murmur of support.

"I'm afraid it's settled, Bebind," Flann said gently. "If you wish to remain the matron to us, you'll give over your disagreement."

Bebind looked around at the solid front of her sisters once more, then nodded in a resigned manner.

"Very well," she said stiffly. "If that is the will of you all, then I must bow to it."

"What about my will?" cried Caoilte, who had by now recovered from his shock. "You can't just keep me here."

"Of course we can!" Uaine told him. "We've saved you, and now some years out of your mortal life are ours, if we choose to have them in repayment."

"I could just leave," he said ominously. "There's little you could do to stop me."

"There is a great deal we could do," Flann answered. "But there's no need for that. You'd never find your weapons or your way out of the Sid without our help, and your own Fian code prevents you from harming women."

"Please, don't struggle against this," Uaine said soothingly. "Accept it!" She moved to him, placing a small hand against his chest, lifting her face toward his with a look of ardor. "Think, my champion, what it could be for you here. You will not age, nor feel pain or want. And your life will be most, most pleasant."

He looked down at her, his expression one of growing helplessness.

"But . . . how long?" he asked in agony.

"Our de Danaan law is specific about that," Bebind answered dryly. "The longest a mortal may remain within our Sid is a mere seven years.

What little sunlight had been filtering down through the thick canopy of trees was now fading with the coming of night. The deep shadows that filled up the forest floor began to grow all the blacker, all the more menacing.

Even the nightfall brought no sounds of life to the strange forest. There were no rustlings or cries of prowling animals, no cries of birds, and still no faintest keening of wind. The only noise that rippled the smooth ocean of black silence was a slow, rhythmic chinking.

It came from the falling sword of Finn MacCumhal as he carefully hacked a blaze in the oddly smooth bark of the trees. In the rapidly gathering darkness, even his polished blade only made a faint crescent of light as he swept it up and down. His own figure and those of the others following closely behind him were swiftly being reduced to little more than vague shadows themselves. Soon they would be drowned in the overwhelming flood of night.

Conan followed Finn, using his bulk to force wider the path Finn cut. Then came Labran and Cuillen, side by side, while the hounds brought up the rear. Labran glanced toward the girl often. The farther they pressed on, the more her expression revealed a growing apprehension. This brought a look of concern to the face of the solicitous young de Danaan.

"Frightened?" he inquired.

"No! No, of course not!" she answered quickly, setting her face in more determined lines and assuming a brusque tone. "I was only wondering how long we're going to continue aimlessly wandering about in these woods!"

At this Finn stopped, turning back toward her with an exasperated look.

"And just what do you mean by that?" he asked.

"I think it's clear enough. The wonderful skills of the faultless Finn MacCumhal have gotten us hopelessly lost!"

"Look here," he said testily, "I've admitted being the fool for my boast, even though it was your own nagging that drove me to it. I should have been more cautious, all right? Now, would you kindly stop stinging me with that same needle of it?"

"I will, when you admit that you still haven't the slightest idea where we're going," she retorted.

"More idea than you'd have!" he shot back.

"Now, please, both of you," said Labran in a compromising tone, "remember that what's happened isn't anyone's fault. If we have been led Astray, it's clearly the king's work. It's magic. That makes this wood another of his barriers, with another gateway for us to find."

"Well, we'll never find it going about in circles!" said Cuillen sharply, refusing to be pacified.

"Oh, so now we're going in circles, are we?" Finn said in outrage.

"Yes! Even a girl raised in the court can see that!"

"Fine! Then why don't *you* pick a way?"

"I will," she agreed. She looked about her gravely, searchingly, then pointed off in a direction at right angles to the one they had been following.

"There!" she announced with assurance.

Finn bowed low, lifting a hand to sign her forward.

"Then, please lead the way," he said. "But be on guard."

"Of course!" she returned sharply and started ahead, her spear up and ready. Finn gestured to the others to fall in behind her. Labran went first, followed by the two hounds. As Conan passed the young captain, he muttered:

"You can't really mean for her to lead us?"

"Why not!" said Finn. "She likely can't do any worse."

"Maybe you're right," Conan grudgingly agreed. "Let her play the chief for a little time. She'll weary of it."

But, once again, Conan's conviction proved wrong. Cuillen had no chance to become weary, for after only a few paces she suddenly broke through a final screen of growth into an open space.

"There!" she announced, turning to beam in triumph upon her companions as they joined her.

It was another cleared corridor running arrow-straight through the close-set trees, but much wider than the first one they had followed. The open sky showed above, and although it was as starless as before, it did glow with a gray light, like an overcast before a full moon. This imparted at least enough illumination to reveal the surroundings.

"So you've found another path," Finn said, obviously

trying to sound unimpressed. "And just what good is that to us?"

"What good?" she echoed in surprise. "Why, it's better than chasing our tails in the trees!"

"Is it?" he said scornfully. "It could just be another trick, you know. It could just fade away like the first one did. Besides, even if it's real, how do we know which way to go on it?"

The two dogs went suddenly on alert. A sound of crunching footsteps could be heard coming up the corridor swiftly from their right, and then a strange, guttural *snorking* sound.

"Shhh!" hissed Labran. "Someone's coming!"

The little band slipped back into the cover of the trees and peered out cautiously. In moments the source of the sounds came into view.

First came a giant man, half-again taller than Finn, and as broad through the shoulders as a great bull. He was dark of face, wild of hair, and rude of dress. Across one massive shoulder was an iron fork as thick as a man's wrist, and caught in the prongs of it was a wildly struggling, grunting pig. Just behind the giant and his load there moved a slender, beautiful young girl with dark gold hair. Her face was shining with an eager light and she was prodding the giant along with a stick as fearlessly as a child herds an old milk cow.

As soon as they had passed the hiding spot of Finn's band, Cuillen jumped up from cover.

"Well, they can surely give us directions," she announced. "Come on!"

She started after them, but Finn seized her shoulder, holding her back.

"Let go of me!" she protested.

"You must have learned by now that we don't just rush in!" Finn scolded.

"Especially not in such a place as this," added Labran.

"You are right," she reluctantly agreed. "I forgot myself."

"It happens to us all," Finn told her with a grin.

Together they all moved cautiously ahead, following the way the odd trio had gone. The dogs moved before them as scouts. Finn, Cuillen, and Conan carefully scanned the road and the forest, their weapons ready in their hands. Soon a small light appeared some way ahead. Even more carefully they approached it, watching it grow and resolve itself into a rectangle of glowing yellow. Advancing a bit nearer, the travelers saw that it was a tiny hut that lay before them, a column of smoke rising from the hole in its peaked roof and warm firelight streaming from its open door.

"That must be where they've gone," rumbled Conan.

"It's a cozy enough seeming place," remarked Cuillen.

"'Seeming' is the word we must beware," Labran warned.

"Labran is right," said Finn. "Everyone stay on guard."

They moved up to the door in a line, flanked by the hounds. There was a smooth square of lawn just before it, and, on either side of the door, a small well set in a circle of cut stones. At the side of one well sat a copper pitcher, while by the other was a crude cup of iron.

Just by the open door there stood a frail, white-haired old man with a pink, pleasantly smiling face. Beside him stood the comely young woman, beaming at the visitors as well.

"Welcome to you," the old man said brightly. "Please come to our house and be our guests, all of you. I give my word that no harm shall come to you."

"I say, we shouldn't trust them," Conan murmured to Finn.

"Remember, the de Danaan courtesy is like our own," Finn whispered back. "Once hospitality is given, the guests are safe. So, be quiet and be gracious, if you can!" Then, to the white-haired man, he said aloud, "We accept your invitation gladly, my friend. Thank you for it!"

In a pointed gesture of trust, he sheathed his sword. Reluctantly, Conan did the same. The man and girl stepped back, holding up hands to usher their guests through the doorway. In single file, Finn and his comrades entered the hut. They looked about them curiously, blinking against the brightness of a blazing central fire.

The interior was a single, circular room. As its details became clear, the expressions of the little band changed from curiosity to dismay. Beside the fire sat the giant man, roasting an entire pig upon his iron fork. Against the back wall sat an ancient hag in a tattered gown, stroking a ram that lay beside her upon the bare-earth floor. And just opposite the giant sat a being clad in the simple dress of a countryman and quite ordinary in look except for a single fact: Across his broad forehead, in two rows, twelve eyes stared at the visitors fixedly, like a dozen fiercely glowing coals.

CHAPTER TWENTY-ONE

HOSPITALITY

"Let great respect be shown to Finn, Son of Cumhal, and to his people," said the old man as he and the girl moved into the room behind their guests.

The old woman and the twelve-eyed man voiced hearty agreement. The giant merely grunted an acknowledgment.

Finn looked around at the old man.

"So, you do know us?" he said, his tone suspicious.

"And who in this country doesn't know that Finn is questing after the Storm Shield and the Son of the Waves?" he said jovially.

"So I have heard," said Finn.

"We've expected your coming," the other told him, grinning all the more broadly. "So come now and sit with us. Rest. Eat! We are honored to have you."

He directed them to the side of the warm fire, but there wasn't enough room for the band to sit down together between the giant and the twelve-eyed man.

"Move over, you great lout!" the gray-haired man told the giant sharply. "Where is your respect for Finn and his comrades?"

"It is the way I am," the giant rumbled gloomily, "to be giving always and getting nothing."

Still, he shifted his great bulk over nearer the twelve-eyed man, and the visitors sat themselves at the hearthside, exchanging glances that reflected their uncertainty over the bizarre situation here.

"Is that pig ready yet?" the old man demanded of the giant.

"It is," the giant retorted in a surly way. "And *I'll* be doing the dividing of it!"

The girl fetched a tremendous platter and carried it to him. He lifted the pig from the fire as easily as if he held but a single loin upon his fork. He pushed the crisp-skinned carcass from the tines onto the plate. Juice oozed from the puncture holes, forming a steaming pool about it. The fragrances of the roasted meat filled the little room. The visitors, having traveled so long without relief, fixed ravenous gazes upon the pork. The tongues of the two hounds hung from drooling mouths, as did Conan's. Indeed, the rotund warrior seemed hard-pressed to keep himself from leaping across the fire onto the roasted pig.

"And just how will the dividing be done?" the old man asked the giant.

"One hind quarter will go to Finn and to his hounds," the grumpy being declared. "The other goes to his comrades. One fore quarter goes to myself, and the other to you and the girl beside you. The chine and rump go to the hag and this man by the fire."

"From this giant's nature," Cuillen murmured to Conan in a teasing way, "I'd say you and he could be great friends!"

"I give my word," the gray-haired host said to the giant, "you have shared it well enough."

At this, the ram that had lain quietly beside the hag rose to his feet and came toward the fire. He was a curious-appearing animal, with a white belly and a black head, green feet, and dark blue horns. Even more curious about him was the fact that he now spoke:

"And I give my word," he said in a hoarse, bleating voice, "that it is a bad division for me, as you've forgotten my own share in it!"

With that, he made a darting move, grabbed a leg of the roasted carcass, and yanked the whole thing from the platter. Before the startled giant could make a move to stop him, he had dragged the pig back to the wall and there fell upon it with the savagery of a starving cat.

"This place is too strange," Cuillen murmured in alarm.

"I'll agree with that!" said Conan, putting hand to sword hilt.

"Steady," cautioned Labran. "We're still guests here."

"Sit quiet!" Finn ordered Conan. "Make no threatening move!"

Conan subsided reluctantly, and the band watched, silent and motionless, as the enraged giant got to his feet and lumbered across the room toward the ram.

He grabbed the forelegs of the pig to pull it back. The ram gave an angry snarl and gripped the hind legs with his teeth, crouching down and digging his feet in. Then began a tug-of-war over the carcass. For a time it was even, but then the giant, for all his enormous bulk, appeared to be growing weaker. He struggled on for a time, groaning with the strain, but failed to wrest the pig from the grip of the ram. He released the legs, falling back in exhaustion. Panting heavily, he returned to the fireside and dropped down to sulk. The ram returned to his solitary dining.

But now the twelve-eyed man, who had sat silently and unblinking through these events, arose and turned to the giant, giving a great sigh.

"On my word," he told the big man with disgust, "it is a pity for anyone having you for a comrade, and you letting a sheep bring away your food."

With these words, the strange being approached the ram himself. Though slightly built, he grabbed the beast, hauling it and the carcass it still clutched over his head. He rushed to the open door with the load and unceremoniously flung it out into the darkness.

This was too much for Conan. First staring in dismay at the twelve-eyed man's actions, he then turned angry, jumping to his feet.

"Well, I've had enough of this!" he boomed.

"No, Conan!" Finn warned. "Stay out of this!"

"I will not!" Conan hotly replied. "It's a lot of madmen we've come among! It's bad enough that they're acting in a way no man should tolerate, but they've thrown out our dinner on top of it!" He swept a threatening gaze over the inhabitants. "So, you lot—no more games! Just tell us how to get out of your bleeding forest, and tell us quick!"

While his glare was fixed on those close-by the fire, he took no notice of the hag. She quietly arose and rushed suddenly forward from her shadows at the back of the room, sweeping the ragged, gray cloak that she wore out and up. It spread into an immense fan over her head. And as she released it, it came fluttering down upon the visitors.

Seeing the movement of the cloak, Finn and his companions looked up. Labran and Cuillen sat unmoving, looking merely puzzled by the hag's action. Conan, motivated by a warrior's instincts, tried to move from beneath it, but was too late. The garment fell upon him, and then upon Labran and Cuillen seated beside him. The hounds were not included in the range of the cloak, nor was a startled Finn MacCumhal.

Finn now leapt up, drawing his sword. Bran and Sceolan moved to crouch on either side, tense for action and growling ominously.

"What's happening here!" he demanded. "You, old woman, get back!"

She just gave a toothless grin and moved closer. Finn looked at his companions, only lumps beneath the spread of gray cloth now, and apparently frozen as they had been before the cloak fell upon them.

"Conan, Labran, Cuillen!" Finn called with some alarm. "What's wrong? Get out from beneath that thing!"

"They can't!" said the hag, and gave a wild, cackling laugh. "See, young man. See!"

She grasped the edge of her cloak in a bony, twisted hand and, in one quick move, jerked it from the heads of the three. Finn stared in horror at what was now revealed.

The three had become incredibly old. Conan appeared deflated, his skin sagging in great winkles, his body stooped. Labran had wasted away to a pale gray wraith, while Cuillen was now a bony hag, more wretched than the creature who had just cast the awful spell upon her. All three were shaking in their weakness and their fear, unable to stir, looking up to Finn with terror in their red, rheumy eyes.

Finn advanced upon the old woman, lifting his sword.

"Restore them at once!" he commanded.

She only laughed again and moved back to her place by the wall. The gray-haired host stepped up before Finn.

"It is not for her to restore your friends," he said in a calm way. "It is for yourself, Finn MacCumhal—if you are wise enough!"

"What do you mean?" Finn asked suspiciously, lowering his sword.

"There are two wells just outside my door," the man said. "Did you see them?"

"I did."

"Good." The man looked toward the giant. "Bring me the draughts!" he ordered, gesturing at the door. "Quickly now!"

The giant muttered an oath, then slowly rose and moved

toward the door. The comely young woman moved after him, goading him to move faster with pokes of her stick.

Soon the giant returned, carrying the fine copper and crude iron goblets that had sat beside the wells. At the girl's prodding, he placed them upon a table near to Finn. Both vessels were now filled with what seemed to be water.

"There you are," the old man said. "You must choose. One of the draughts before you comes from the Well of Truth. It has the power to restore your comrades."

"And the other?" asked Finn.

"It is of the Well of Lies. It has only the power to destroy."

Finn lifted his sword again, holding the gleaming blade up before the eyes of the man.

"And why can't I use this to make you restore them safely?" he asked.

"Young Finn, it is no fool that you are," the other replied easily. "You know as well as I by now that it's the king of this country who controls our destinies. You've no power over us. There's little you can do but play out the game as he has set it."

"I know," Finn agreed. "I gave my oath to do that. But, if this is part of the king's game, then there must be more to it than the saving of my friends."

"There is," the old man admitted, "for you must also know by now that the passage through each barrier must be won by a test."

"And, if I fail this one?"

"Then not only will your friends remain as they are, but your quest will be ended. You'll all be left to wander, lost in an endless forest where every way looks the same!"

"I understand," said Finn. He sheathed his sword and moved closer to the table, peering down at the two cups. He stared at them thoughtfully, evaluating their contents. Then he shook his head and looked up at the old man.

"The water in each looks the same," he said. "May I have a taste of both before I decide?"

"The spell is not upon you," the old man said. "You may drink of each one safely. Then you must choose."

He lifted the finely wrought copper goblet to his lips first. He took a small swig, swishing it about in his mouth, then swallowing. A look of warmth and pleasure brought a glow to his face.

"That's a fine drink!" he said. "It's sweet and rich like the finest honey mead. A drink so good as this must have a restoring power."

But then his expression abruptly changed. The pleasure was replaced by a grimace of distaste.

"But, what is that coming upon me now?" he said. "Thin and sharp it is, like the taste of old iron across my tongue." He looked down at the drink again. "How could something so fine at first become so bitter after?"

"Try the other drink now," prompted the gray-haired man.

Finn nodded, putting down the copper goblet and lifting the plain, battered iron one. He put it to his lips, tentatively touched the liquid with just the tip of his tongue. With a gasp of shock he pulled the cup away and looked at it in revulsion.

"By all the gods!" he said, "that's the vilest stuff I've ever drunk. It has the taste of something rotten."

"You must drink of it to know truly," the man said.

Finn looked at the liquid with great reluctance. Then he looked to his friends. They were watching him fixedly, a plea for release clear in their eyes. His gaze was held most by that of Cuillen, whose youth and lively spirit and lissome frame had been so cruelly taken.' As he looked at her, his own eyes momentarily revealed the torment raging within him. If he chose wrongly, Ireland was lost, and he had condemned her and his other comrades to a horrible, living death.

Still, as before, he had no choice in this. And so he set himself in a determined way, brought the iron cup to his lips, and boldly took a swig.

His face twisted in disgust. He held the liquid in his mouth a moment, cheeks bulging, lips squeezed tight. Finally, with a great effort, he swallowed, forcing the stuff down as if it were a solid object.

Then, amazingly, his expression cleared. The look of distress passed into one of delight. His face relaxed and he gave the old man a wide grin.

"Why, it's not bad at all. Once down the throat, it becomes warm and smooth, and spreads a sort of satisfaction right down to my belly."

"All right, then," said the man. "You've tasted both. Make your choice now. Which one will restore your friends?"

Finn set down the goblet by the other. He looked from one to another for a moment in consideration. His comrades watched him anxiously, clearly in great agony at this suspense. Finally, Finn took up the iron cup again.

"This is the one," he said with assurance.

"If you believe so, let them drink of it," said the man.

Finn passed the cup to the shaking hand of Conan. The once-stout warrior looked down at it hesitantly, then up to Finn.

"Trust me," Finn told him.

Conan looked again at the cup, then turned and thrust it into the bony hands of Labran. But he, too, was reluctant to put Finn's judgment to the test. He held the cup, staring at the liquid in agony.

Impatiently, the wizened Cuillen grabbed the cup from him and with no hesitation drank deeply from it. Its effect was immediate. Like a winter-shriveled flower blooming under the spring sun, she regained her vitality, her youthful form, and her color.

Finn gave a deep and heartfelt sigh of relief. Cuillen passed the cup to Conan and Labran, now most eager to drink of its water.

"How did you know?" she asked Finn.

"Well, I didn't really," he admitted. "It was a guess."

"A guess?" she said in outrage. "You mean that you were playing with our lives? You weren't certain?"

"There was little choice. But it seemed to me that the water in the copper goblet was more likely that from the Well of Lies, for it's sweet at first to be telling people a lie, but it's bitter in the end—while the truth, though it may be bitter to take, is much sweeter once it's swallowed."

"You are a clever man, Finn MacCumhal," said the old man, clearly impressed by the young warrior's logic. "You've proven that you truly have the wisdom that the tales give you, and you've shown a gracious nature as well, honoring the hospitality of my house. Has there been wonder on you, Finn, at the ways here?"

"I have never wondered more at anything I've seen," Finn said to him most sincerely.

"Then I will tell you the meaning of them. It's Cuanna that I'm called, and it is the House of Wisdom that you've entered. The giant you first saw having the pig on the tines of his fork is called Sluggishness. This lovely girl who is beside me is Liveliness, for it's liveliness that must always prod sluggishness

along. That man beyond there with the twelve shining eyes
stands for the World. He is stronger than anything else, as he
proved by making nothing of that ram. And the ram itself
stands for the Desires of Men.

"What about the old woman?" asked Conan, now having
swelled back to his normal, robust size.

"Ah, well, I should think her nature would be most clear
to you," said Cuanna. "Our hag is Old Age, whose cloak
whithers all men in time."

"If we have passed your test," said Finn, "have we won
our passage through this barrier your forest has made for us?"

"You have that," Cuanna assured him. "Your own wisdom
was the key to our gateway. And you will know the way to the
great peak of the king tomorrow. But it is very late now. You
have traveled far and without food. Sit with us and eat, sleep
well, and in the morning you will know your way from the
forest."

To this the weary and famished band of travelers agreed.
They sat at the fire and ate well of food cooked by the giant,
this time without any complications. Then, overcome by an
enormous fatigue, they stretched themselves out about the fire
and were soon soundly asleep.

When the dawn sun shone upon their faces, they awoke.
All peered up groggily at the white streaks of light slanting
down through the branches of the trees. Then a look of
surprise dawned in each face as they realized that something
was wrong here. They were looking directly at the forest, no
walls or ceiling intervening. The hut and its occupants had
completely disappeared!

"I should have expected the like," said Finn, getting to his
feet. "I've had de Danaans play such a trick before."

"If they were ever even here," said Labran. "Remember,
such peculiar beings could have been created by the king just
for our sakes."

"It makes no difference," Conan said gruffly. "Have those
conniving children of a sow given over their word to guide us
out of here?"

"No," said Finn, looking away toward the west. "Cuanna
promised that we would know the way. I think that just may be
it."

The others turned to follow the direction of his gaze.
There could be no doubting the truth of his words. The

corridor in the trees had now opened up, like great portals swinging apart. Beyond, there lay revealed a flat, treeless countryside. And framed in the precise center of the wide opening, surprisingly close to them now, rose the blunt spire of rock that was their goal.

CHAPTER TWENTY-TWO
THE DRUID'S PLOY

Credhe tightly wrapped the bandage about the upper arm of Cael, covering the deep but not dangerous gash there.

"It should be all right very soon," she promised as she worked. "I've used the most powerful of my healing ointments upon it." She looked down at the nearly empty jar beside her. "I'm glad that I was still able to give you this much help. I've so little left."

"Then you should not have wasted it on me," the young warrior said stoically. "There are too many others in much greater need."

"I know it seems cruel," she said in a voice that blended practicality with sorrow, "but I must first help those who can still return to the fight. The rest can only be made more comfortable while they wait to die."

Both the young people turned their gazes to the area about them. The yard of Mogh Nuadat's fortress was now crammed tight with wounded, a rippling sea of human bodies from outer wall to the edge of the cliff. Yet scores more were still streaming in for help.

"The numbers are growing daily now," Cael said grimly. "As we become weaker, our casualties increase. One man must take the place of two or even three."

"Most of these men have been wounded once before," she said. "Some, several times. Still, if they can move, they take up their shields and spears and march bravely back to the strand."

"We've little other choice," Cael told her. "Of the seven

cathas of Fianna who came here, we've not enough whole men
left to make more than two. And still there is no sign of Finn."

"What can we do?" Credhe asked him despairingly, and
gripped his own hand in both of hers tightly. "Oh, Cael, is
there any hope left to us, or will you all have to die here, and
to no good end?"

"Have faith yet, my love," he told her in a comforting way.
"If there is any way to sustain the fight, Goll MacMorna will
discover it. He's called a meeting of all the leadership here to
talk about it." He nodded toward the gateway. "See, there.
He's coming now!"

Goll MacMorna and a band of his chieftains, including Art
MacConn, had just ridden in through the gates. They dismounted and made their way across the crowded yard toward
the black tower on foot. As they did, the squat figure of Mogh
Nuadat appeared at the tower's door, ready to give them
greeting.

As they passed near Cael and Credhe, Goll turned from
his path and stopped before the pair, leaving the others to go
on. The young warrior looked up at the one-eyed chieftain
with curiosity.

"Well, young Cael, are you ready to join us?" Goll asked.

"You want me in your council?" Cael asked in surprise.
"But, my chief, I'm a mere fledgling in the ranks of the
Fianna!"

"You are one of the finest fighting men we have," Goll
corrected. "More than that, as so many of your clan are dead or
wounded now, you have become the highest ranking of them.
You must represent the Baiscne. So, come along."

Cael flashed his wife a broad smile, his face bright with
pride and excitement at this recognition. He jumped to his
feet and fell in beside Goll, leaving Credhe to look after him,
her own expression clouded by her doubts.

"Great Danu," she murmured to herself. "I don't know
whether you should be praised or cursed for bringing such an
honor to my husband."

Cael and Goll followed the others into the tower and took
seats at the tables circling the central fire as they had before.
But a vast change had come over the company since their last
meeting here, before Finn's departure. A number of the clan
chieftains and champions who had attended then were now
missing. There were some new faces and many gaps in the ring
of men. And those warriors who were present showed the

effects of the long, brutal war being waged. Nearly all were marked by wounds, often more than one. Their cloaks and tunics were badly tattered, stained by sand and blood and rain. Their jewelry—torcs and bracelets and brooches—had been removed or showed the tarnish of neglect. They had become a lean, worn, somber lot indeed.

In contrast, the five druids and the five ollamhs in the group made a quite clean and colorful show. As noncombatants, the rigors of battle had, of course, made no effect on them. They looked fully as pristine, fresh, and sparkling as upon their first arrival at the White Strand.

As before, Mogh Nuadat and Muirne took the hosts' place at the tables. At the table to their right sat Goll MacMorna, with Cael and Art MacConn beside him. The atmosphere was a gloomy and tense one, the discussion focusing immediately upon the desperate nature of their situation.

"I say that Finn MacCumhal is dead!" forcefully declared a square-faced chieftain with a wild mop of curling red hair. "All we can do here now is be slaughtered."

"My son is not dead, Cairell Battle-Stricker," Muirne replied with a mother's confidence; that is, tinged with a certain wishfulness. "I feel the truth of it."

"I don't know how you can be so certain," the chieftain stubbornly returned. "If he's not dead, even you must admit he's surely run upon something that's delayed him. And we all know what a terrible force it would take to slow Finn MacCumhal!"

There were many nods and murmurs of assent at that. Muirne sat back, obviously unable to respond to his remark. Her always-solicitous husband patted her hand in a consoling way.

"Just how much strength is left to us now?" Goll asked. He turned to a young, dark-haired warrior with a long and neatly braided mustache. "Conn Crither, how do the numbers stand for our cathas?"

"It's very, very bad," the man said gloomily, shaking his head. "Of all our fighting men, there are perhaps two or three thousand left unwounded. Perhaps five thousand more have wounds minor enough to let them continue in the fight. But nearly two thirds of all our warriors are either dead or too badly hurt to be of any use to us for a great time to come."

"I thank you for your cheering appraisal," Goll told him dryly. He turned the probing gaze of his single eye upon the others. "And what do any of you know of our enemy's strength?"

"I've tried to come to some estimate, my chieftain," volunteered a sandy-headed young ollamh. "I've talked to many of our warriors to compile the facts of the war for a chronicle. There is a great deal of exaggeration, of course. But, taking that into account, I would say Donn's army has lost some twelve thousand men so far, with over double that number badly hurt."

"Their losses have been rising more swiftly of late," Cael pointed out in an optimistic way. "They seem to be growing weary of the long fight."

"Still, that cursed Daire Donn drives them into the battle day after day!" complained Cairell. "And now they've got at least five fighting men to every one of ours. When they realize that, their spirits will rise quick enough, I can tell you."

"They'll have to realize soon," said Conn Crither darkly. "We can't hide our weakness from them much longer. Only this morning Fidach took his clan against the men of that Lochlann chieftain Mongach. His warriors were monsters, with heads like hounds, and he carried a flail with seven iron balls studded with spikes as long as a hand!"

He held out his own long, lean hand in illustration. Then he went on:

"They smashed through the Fianna men, tearing them into strings. But Fidach challenged him, and managed to avoid a blow of the deadly flail. He made a quick leap to one side and swung out with his sword, cutting off the black dog's two hands at the joint." He chopped at one wrist with the other in a graphic gesture. Then he shook his head sadly. "Still, it was the comely Fidach who lay his measure out as well. For as Mongach toppled, an iron apple of the flail went into our valiant chieftain's mouth, its thorns striking up into his brain. The two men fell lip to lip and foot to foot.

"Of course, his warriors took a bloody revenge upon the rest of Mongach's curs, but it was nearly the whole clan of Fidach that died in the doing of it. So now there's another empty seat at our tables this night, and no one to be filling it again."

Following this grim little recitation, there was a long silence about the circle. Finally, young Cael, gamely still struggling to see the best in things, spoke up:

"But maybe Donn's army is more sick of this battle than

we believe. After all, they've not come out against us in full strength for some three days now. They've sent only token assaults against us and kept the rest of their force within their camp. Couldn't they be planning to give up the fight and leave Ireland?"

"No, Cael," came the hard, flat voice of Goll himself. "What Cairell and Conn Crither have said here is the truth. We can't go on hiding our weakness from Daire Donn any longer. In fact, I'm certain that he's realized for some time that out strength is almost gone."

"What do you mean?" the young champion asked.

"I mean that Donn and his army are far from quitting Ireland or this fight. I've been watching the activity in their camp. From what I've seen, I'm convinced that he's preparing his fighting men for one, massive, final assault. Their forges blaze day and night to repair and replace their arms. The bulk of his men eat, rest, patch their wounds, and restore themselves while a small portion of them keep us constantly occupied. When the time comes, Donn will be able to send a vast force of fresh warriors against our slender line of battered ones. The blow will be falling any day now. Of that I'm sure. That's why I've gathered you all here tonight. With our numbers, we've little chance of surviving, this time. What can we do?"

"I say that we withdraw before them," put in an older chieftain with a lean, leather-skinned face and a striking hawk-beak nose. "We can fight them all the way back along the peninsula; delay them any way we can."

"Delay them, Aelchinn?" said Goll. "And to what end?"

This appeared to stump the chieftain. He shook his head.

"We must find more fighting men to join us," said Art MacConn.

"That is still a violation of our honor and of the will of your own father," Goll reminded him sternly.

"And just what is your alternative?" MacConn stubbornly argued. "I gathered the lads I brought here. Let me gather more!"

"Even if you could, there would be too few and it would be too late," said Goll. "The assault upon us could be coming with the sunrise. What we decide to do must be done now."

"I say we abandon this fight and return to our own clan territories," said Cairell.

"And leave Ireland to these raiders?" Cael asked in shock.

"We've got to think of protecting our own homes and our families," reasoned the chieftain.

"Your first loyalty is to the lords we're sworn to and to Ireland," Goll told him sharply, fixing the man with his one, coldly glittering eye. "—And even more to the honor of the Fianna. We defend all of our land, or we defend none of it. To do anything else is treachery of the worst kind!"

The red-haired man sat back, clearly cowed by this uncompromising speech.

"There'll be no more talk of retreating," Goll said pointedly, sweeping his gaze over the rest. Then he looked toward Muirne. "Now, my good lady, tell me honestly: How much do you really believe that your son is still alive?"

"With all the spirit in me," she told him with great earnestness. "More than that, I know he will return safely to us."

He considered her thoughtfully for a moment. Then he nodded.

"Though there's no logic in it," he said, "I feel within myself that you are right. Finn is still our only chance in this. We must find a way to continue holding on here."

"But there is nothing left to do!" the chieftain called Aelchinn pointed out in a disgruntled tone. "Without men, the host of Donn cannot be kept on the strand."

"My chieftain," spoke up the elderly, silver-haired leader of the assembled druids, "we have been trying many things with our magic, desperately seeking something that might help. It may be that we have a possibility."

"Say it then, Cainnelsciath," Goll ordered brusquely. "Let me hear it."

"Well, if they do mean to attack us because they believe our numbers are too small, we might raise an illusion to make them think otherwise."

"I dislike the using of magic," Goll said. "No true warrior would use trickery against an opponent. It is unfair."

"But this isn't a way to defeat our enemies," the druid assured him. "It won't add to our strength or help us in the fight. It will have no real power at all, save to convince them not to attack us, at least for a while."

"And just how would this magic work?" Goll asked.

"Through our combined powers, we can create sights and sounds to make it seem we have a much larger force."

"Goll, if there is any chance that it can save the lives of

your warriors," Muirne said in an imploring voice, "if it might delay Donn's attack until Finn can return, you must try it!"

He was silent a moment, clearly considering the druid's proposal and the logic of Muirne's words. Finally, he nodded.

"Very well," he agreed. "For Ireland's salvation, our own honor must give way once again. Cainnelsciath, do what you can. But do it swiftly, my friend. Swiftly!"

A white-robed druid laid a slender yew log across the blazing fire and stepped back. He joined a circle of his fellows who stood about the fire, arms linked, heads back, chanting in soft voices to the sky.

They performed their ritual high above the strand, atop the flat hillcrest that gave a sweeping view of the beach and the sea stretching beyond. The sky above was covered by a heavy overcast that seemed to drop lower and grow more ominous by the moment, as if the incantation of the druids was calling the clouds to earth.

Cainnelsciath moved through the circle of druids and stepped close to the fire. He had now given over the simple, gold-embroidered white robe of the others for a more resplendent garment. A scarlet cloak was about his shoulders. Long earrings of interlocking golden spirals dangled from his ears. A headpiece sporting outspread wings of white-speckled bird's feathers covered his silver-gray hair. And in his hand he clutched a gnarled and knobbed druid's rod of polished blackthorn.

As he reached the side of the fire, he lifted his other hand, sprinkling a fine powder upon the flames, which flared and sparkled as the particles fell through them, giving out a sizzling sound.

"Powder of coral," he intoned, "ashes of oak and mistletoe and man, all blended here, give power to our fire and send our message to the gods of sea and sky."

A thin white plume of glowing smoke now floated up from the crimson heart of the blaze, rising toward the clouds. A sharp wind carrying the sea's chill tang rose suddenly from the west, booming across the hilltop, fluttering the long robes of the druids, violently rending the smoke column into whispy shreds.

"I hear your answer, and it is greatly pleased I am," said Cainnelsciath. He turned toward the sea, raising his druid rod, pointing its tip toward the horizon, toward the gray-to-gray joining of the realms of sea and sky.

"Give us good help, gracious Danu and terrible MacLir. Make druid armies about us from the stalks of grass and from the tops of watercresses. Cry out to our invaders with the voices of a multitude in so strong a battle cry that it will take their strength and make the arms fall from their shaking hands. Hide from them our weakness so that it will be their own ears and eyesight that hold them back."

At this, the sharp wind rose again and screamed about the circle of druids. It closed in, swirling around and around them, creating a great whirlwind. Then it constricted, tightening its coils of rushing air, drawing the writhing serpent of its blast within their charmed ring. It passed by Cainnelsciath, tugging at his cloak and flapping the wings upon his head as if to lift him up. Then it concentrated its full force upon the fire. It spun around it in ever smaller, ever more rapid circles, twisting the blaze into a spire of flame that flared golden and finally white-hot. The fire corkscrewed up, rising higher, until its jagged spearhead thrust into the black, sagging belly of the clouds.

As if it were a great waterskin the blade of fire had split, a rain came at once. Fine, chill droplets, more like ice than rain, fell straight down upon the flat hilltop around the druids so thickly that all view beyond was cut off.

But then, vague shadows could be seen within the screen of white. They seemed to grow up from the ground, like some fantastic, quickly growing weed. They shot up to man-height in an instant, at first long, spindly forms waving like marsh weeds, but rapidly filling out, inflating, taking on form and then color.

Soon the circle of druids was surrounded by a host of motionless beings with the stolid figures and glinting arms of Fianna fighting men. They might have looked quite real, save for a curious sameness of features and a certain hazy, wraithlike quality about their forms.

"I thank you," the chief druid told the sky.

In answer, the hard rain abruptly ceased. The column of flame collapsed downward upon its base with a great whoosh, extinguishing itself. All that remained to drift gently down like snowflakes upon the druid were a few, scattered, faintly glowing sparks.

* * *

Sparks flew out in a blizzard from every side as forges were bellowed to a blazing peak and scores of hammers beat at the incandescent iron.

In the midst of the vast armory of the invading force stood Daire Donn. He was in his suit of mail, but was helmetless. The fearsome headpiece was in the hands of an attendant who stood nearby, sweating profusely from the intense heat. But the temperature seemed to have no effect on the high king of the Great World himself. Indeed, he seemed instead to be quite soothed by the torrent of heat and light and din that washed about him. It was as if he was absorbing the energies that played upon him and made the gleaming mail blaze with reflected light. He basked in the glare, like a serpent basking in the sun, his head thrown back, a look of vast contentment on his swarthy face. His eyes, also glinting brightly from the fires, seemed fixed on distant visions of sweet victory.

But Donn's moment of recreation was rudely disturbed by the headlong approach of a most-distressed warrior.

"My king!" he gasped out breathlessly, sliding to a stop before Donn.

The flaring gaze, narrowing in irritation, dropped from its image of future glories to the hard reality of the anxious man.

"Well, what is it?" he snapped.

"My king, a new force has joined the Fianna warriors. There are many thousands more men now upon their walls!"

"What!" Donn roared. A massive, gauntleted hand shot out to grip the man's mail tunic in a fist. Donn jerked the hapless fellow up and off his feet, dangling him, pulling his face close.

"It's a foolish man who'd dare to tell me so," he grated. "If it's a lie you bring me, you'll hang by your tongue from the dragonhead of my ship until the seabirds strip your bones!"

"I . . . I speak the truth, my king," the man said chokingly. "Please come! See yourself!"

With a bellow of rage, Donn flung the man from him and stalked from the armory toward the upper edge of the camp. Once out of the noise created by the smiths, a tremendous uproar of voices could be heard rising all about. And hundreds of warriors were now visible rushing through the camp avenues, all moving in the same direction as their king.

At the camp's periphery a crowd of men had formed already. They were staring toward the embankment and the Fian wall, gesticulating and talking excitedly. Donn impatiently pushed through them toward the front. Seeing who it was, they quickly opened a wide passage for him.

He stopped a few paces beyond them, gazing toward the wall. There were indeed men visible upon it now, a great many men, lined along the uneven top so thickly that it seemed to bristle like a hedgehog's back.

The glitter of their weapons was visible even in the gray light of an overcast dawn. And there now arose from them a strident, ululating war cry. The eerie sound, a product of thousands of voices combined, came clearly to the watching army of Daire Donn. It seemed to disturb his warriors, causing a stir of uneasiness amongst them.

Other of Donn's senior officers, brought by the uproar, had by this time joined the crowd, and were now moving quickly to their king. Their expressions revealed all to be naturally aghast at this unexpected development.

"My king, there must be ten battalions there!" the one called Finnachta cried in a shocked voice.

"I have eyes, Finnachta," Donn responded brusquely.

"But you told us that they had only a thousand men left to them," another officer said in a boldly accusing way. "Now they seem as strong in numbers as when they first came upon the strand! Where did these others come from so quickly?"

"It makes no difference," Donn said fiercely. "It will not change my plan."

"It must!" the man persisted. "You gave our men new spirit for the fight by telling them the Fianna were too weak. You promised that one more attack would break them. Now look!"

He gestured toward the crowd of their warriors animatedly discussing this new circumstance with obvious dismay.

"Perhaps more Irish fighting men will come," said another, clearly apprehensive man. "Perhaps it is time we left this strand."

"That is a coward's talk, Madan," said Donn angrily, rounding upon the man. "More of it and you'll face my own wrath. We will not leave this strand unless they can come and cast us into the sea, and that they can never do. We still have twice their numbers. We are fresh. We will attack!"

"Three times their numbers was not enough before," the bold officer pointed out. "It will be difficult to convince our warriors to go against them now."

"Convince?" Donn repeated in towering outrage. "I am their king! They will do as I order or they will suffer for it."

"You can't force them this time," Finnachta told him in a reasoning tone. "If you try, you may only push them to rebellion. You must convince them. Use your great aura to give them new will. Revive their fighting spirit once again."

The other officers added their agreement and support to this idea, and the logic of it seemed to finally reach even the manic Donn. The look of frenzy faded from his expression.

"Very well," he agreed reluctantly. "I will convince them, if I must, no matter how long it takes." He turned his burning gaze back to the wall. "But I swear now, I will not be denied my heritage. We will take Ireland or the bodies of every man will roll bloody in the surf!"

CHAPTER TWENTY-THREE
THE THREE RAVENS

The cliff soared up and up above them, a spire of rock whose top seemed to scratch the bottom of the sky.

Finn and his companions stood at the base of it, heads back, gazing up the sheer face. Behind them now lay the thick forest. It stopped abruptly, its edge of closely set, evenly spaced trees like a palisade wall, curving out on either side to form a neat, symmetrical ring about the mountain. Between forest edge and mountain base was a wide area of open meadow, smooth and featureless.

The overall effect was of some kind of carefully constructed monument. And the mountain itself did much to add to this impression. At close examination, it appeared to be anything but natural. It was nearly a cone, its sides rising acutely to an oddly flat top that looked as if it had been lopped off. Save for a ring about its middle that seemed to be a ledge, its outer surface was quite smooth, without rocky outcroppings, fissures, or jagged edges of any kind. It was a distinctly eerie sight there, jutting up so starkly, so abruptly, from the flat terrain.

"It is the strangest mountain I've ever seen before," Conan muttered, eyeing it with great suspicion.

"Nothing in this country would surprise me now," said Finn.

"Even the stone of it is very odd," said Cuillen, moving in close to slide a hand up and down the surface of the cliff. The rock face was extremely even and of a uniform gray-white. There were no marks of strata, nor, even so close, any signs of cracks.

"It's like something sculpted from a single block of the purest granite," she said. "Like something shaped and polished by a craftsman."

"A craftsmen," said Conan derisively. "That's madness. To shape a whole mountain? Why that would be im—" He stopped abruptly as he caught sight of the amused expression on Labran's face. "All right, you wretch, I know what you're thinking."

"I'm very sorry," the other said apologetically, quickly wiping off the smile. "But this is clearly meant as another barrier for us. There are three left, remember, before we can reach our goal . . . up there." He pointed toward the heights.

"Then, there has to be a way up," Finn said. "And so, my friends, we may as well begin searching once again." He looked to Cuillen, smiling agreeably. "Since you seem to have chosen the right way for us last time, would you make the choice now?"

"Don't you be patronizing me, Finn MacCumhal!" she replied scathingly. "Even a fool could make a choice of only two directions that end in the same place. So let's just be getting on with it! You and your beast friends—that includes Conan—can follow us!"

With that, she seized the arm of a somewhat-abashed Labran and marched off haughtily. Finn stared after her, his face wearing that now-familiar nonplussed look once again.

"I was only trying to be accommodating," he said in frustration.

"I'm beginning to think you actually like that cat clawing at you," Conan said, shaking his head. "Look here, why don't you just let her go? We could turn about and slip off the other way."

Finn gave him a sharp look but did not respond in words. Instead, he simply turned his back on the stout warrior and headed off in Cuillen's wake, the hounds trotting along at either hand. Conan followed, plodding sulkily, grumbling all the way.

They moved around the spire, staying close to the smooth curve of its base. In comparison to the mountain towering above, they were tiny figures, crawling with what seemed an agonizing slowness. Painstakingly they examined the face of the cliff as they passed for some sign of a way they might climb.

But all their searching was in vain. Only the smooth, featureless stone met their gazes.

"We must have gone 'round the cursed thing at least once by now," Conan finally complained. "There's nothing here. Why are we going on?"

"Because we've no other choice," Finn told him. "If this cliff is another barrier, then there must be a way to climb it. Sooner or later it must be revealed to us."

"It's the king again," Labran said, "having a bit more sport with us. Making it difficult just to see us squirm."

"Aye, like a boar on a spearpoint," snarled Conan. "Your king and his bloody game! It doesn't seem to me he's being fair with it at all."

"He can't be blamed for that entirely," Labran replied in a defensive way. "If you were forced to live hidden away here through the centuries, barely above to move, protecting the de Danaan treasures, you'd likely be making a sport of it yourself."

"More likely I'd of slit my own scrawny throat by now," said Conan. "Better that than living such a life."

"Say, look over there," said Cuillen, pointing away from the mountain. "Who're they, now?"

Finn and Labran stopped to look as well. Some way out in the flat plain surrounding the odd peak, about halfway to the precise, curved palisade of trees, several figures could be seen. There were a score of them, all quite small, all busily engaged in rushing about waving long, curved sticks.

Finn took a pace or two toward them, eyes narrowing as he peered at them curiously.

"Why, it's a group of small boys," he announced. "The oldest one can't be more than ten. They're playing at hurley. A spirited game, too."

"What's that above them?" Labran said, indicating three objects lazily drifting in the sky over the players' heads, looking like floating scraps of black cloth at the distance.

"Those are ravens, I think," Finn said, after a moment's stare. "Interesting. We've come upon no other living creatures since that lot in the forest. Now, to see such normal-looking lads at such an ordinary game in this unnatural place seems odd."

"Will you forget those lads!" Conan called irritably. He had gone on and was now peering around the curve of the cliffside. "Come here! I've found . . . something!"

They moved on to where he stood. From there they could see a knoblike projection thrusting from the smooth face just ahead. It was the first variation in the monotonous stone surface they had seen, and they all rushed eagerly to it. In its center was set a polished black object with the luminescent quality of a pearl. They examined it closely.

"It looks rather like the opening stone for the portal of my own father's Sid," Labran said. He put out a hand and gingerly touched the surface of the black jewel.

At once there arose a rumbling, grating noise within the cliff-face. A vertical crack appeared beside the knob. Labran turned to beam at the others gleefully.

"It was!" he said. "It's a door!"

The crack parted rapidly, immense stone panels drawing back on either side to reveal a wide opening into the mountain. Within was visible a broad flight of neatly fashioned stone steps leading upward and back into the shadowy depths.

"Couldn't ask for easier than that," announced Labran.

"Maybe too easy," Finn said, eyeing the stairway suspiciously. "There could be some trickery in it."

As if in direct answer to his words, the rumbling sound began again, and the massive stone doors began to slide, very slowly, closed.

"Stop it! Can't you stop it?" Cuillen shouted at Labran.

He was already frantically jabbing at the black stone, but to no avail. He shook his head, crying in despair:

"I can't! The knob won't work now!"

"Be calm, my friends," Finn told them soothingly. "There's time. We can get through them easily before they close. Come on."

But as they started ahead, a wild cry of terror came to them. They stopped and turned to look out across the plain. There the hurley game had broken up. The boys were rushing madly about brandishing their sticks over their heads. The reason for this was obvious: the three birds that had been gliding harmlessly in the sky above were now swooping down at them, and as they neared the ground, their true nature became terrifyingly clear.

"Those ravens are enormous," gasped Cuillen.

"They are that," agreed Finn. "Larger than a man."

They were far from exaggerating. The three birds were indeed larger than Finn himself in body, while their great, flapping canopies of wings spanned several times a man's height.

"Those boys can't fight off creatures like that alone," Finn said, drawing his sword. "They need help."

"No, Finn!" Conan protested quickly, stepping forward. "We can't delay this time. The doors are half-closed already. Soon we'll not be able to pass through."

"This may be some other trick of the king to make us fail," reasoned Labran.

Across the plain, one of the great ravens had made its pass, skimming low over the heads of the panicking boys. More desperate, fear-filled cries could be clearly heard.

"It makes no difference," Finn said with resolve. "If there's any chance these children are truly in peril, we must help them."

"Even if we risk the fate of Ireland this time?" asked Cuillen. "Finn, we must go up!"

"You're right," the young captain briskly agreed. "We'll do both. I'll deal with this; you and the others go on. Find some way to get those doors open."

"And if we can't?" she demanded.

"Then I'll find another way," he countered with greater irritation.

"No, Finn," she protested, shaking her head. "You cannot go alone!"

Patience exhausted, he seized her arm in a tight grip and jerked her close. His intense gaze bored into hers. His voice was fierce with his determination:

"Listen, Cuillen, I'll have no arguments this time! Those lads could be dead in moments. Do as I say. I'm going now!"

With that he released her and started away, racing across the plain with the speed of a stag.

"That brash and stubborn man," Cuillen said with exasperation.

"In that trait, young lady, he is most like yourself," Labran commented in a pointed way.

"What should we do now?" she asked him, looking from Finn to the closing portals in some perplexity.

"I say, the Morrigan take Finn," Conan angrily declared. "That door'll be closed too far to squeeze through, in a moment. I'm going up." He started for the opening, brushing past the others.

"But if Finn dies, the game is lost," Labran said to him. "Remember, the king said that only *he* can win the weapons."

Conan swung back to face him, thrusting out a thick finger and jabbing at Labran's thin chest to punctuate his words.

"Listen, you wretch, I've told you before what I think of your king's words. They're an insult to me, and I've had enough of them. There's not a MacMorna born who can't do anything a Baiscne can." He drew himself up, puffing out his barrel chest and tapping it now with his finger. "I, Conan MacMorna himself, will be proving that very thing to you right now!" he declared in a blustering way. "If Finn's gone, then it's left to me to do the saving of Ireland. And that I will do!"

He wheeled around and swaggered toward the closing portals. He pushed between them, barely managing to shoulder his wide form through the narrowing space.

"That thick-skulled, bragging oaf hasn't any chance alone," said Cuillen, watching him start up the steps beyond. "Shall we go too? We can still squeeze through."

"I'd say no," Labran answered with a force unusual to him. "I've been considering: every gateway's key up to now Finn has had to win for us. This stairway may well be a false way, meant to mislead us."

"You're right!" cried Cuillen, brightening with a dawning understanding. "It's the children! The children are his test! Come on!"

They turned away from the mountain and started off at a run after the now-distant Finn. Behind them, the stone doors into the mountain's depths closed with a final slam.

With the doors closed, the main source of light for the stairway was cut off, plunging it into a deep gloom. Conan paused, looking back to the now-sealed entrance. A shadow of apprehension flickered across his wide face. Then his expression reset itself in lines of grim determination. He drew out his sword, gripped it tightly, and continued to mount the stairs into a darkness that increased at every step.

He climbed up and up, beginning to puff from carrying his considerable weight. Then the light above began to grow again. Elation came into his face, and he climbed faster.

He came out soon into a level space whose size was hidden by the blackness. But straight ahead of him, seeming to float in the void, were a great shield and a long sword, giving off an aura of white light.

"They are here!" he murmured triumphantly. "Now we will see who is Ireland's greatest champion!"

He stepped toward the weapons, but as he did, their glow suddenly rose in intensity, throwing a hard, white light about the space Conan had entered. He stopped abruptly, staring down, a look of shock replacing that of victory.

He stood precariously balanced on the brink of a wide, exactly circular pit whose vertical sides were so smooth they glowed like polished iron. Far below him, filling the bottom of the pit to what appeared a great depth, was a tangle of human skeletons. And atop this pool, as if floating upon the grotesque white waves of bones, a score of gleaming skulls formed a neat ring. They seemed to peer up with black sockets and wide grins in gruesome delight at the sight of Conan teetering above.

"By good Danu!" he cried, trying to throw himself back.

But he was too late. The edge of the pit crumbled suddenly from beneath his feet. He flailed out wildly, but fell forward, plunging down, landing with a dreadful clatter in the midst of the bones and sinking out of sight.

The light about the weapons at once flared and died, plunging the room, the pit, and its terrible contents into a profound and silent blackness.

Outside the mountain, meanwhile, the rest of the band was still in full gallop across the open plain.

Finn had maintained his initial lead over Cuillen and Labran, although the incredible speed of the two hounds had cut their distance from him in half. But the young captain was now drawing near to the embattled group of boys. Close above, the three black figures of the ravens soared and dipped, swooping toward the ground and then lifting back in a constant cycle of attack that seemed precisely choreographed. Seen at this range, their vast size and their sleek blue-black covering of feathers made these common birds into monstrous creatures— true embodiments of the death and violence they had long symbolized in Ireland.

When they rose they were silent, save for the rhythmic *whooping* of their powerfully beating wings. But when they darted toward the earth, wings pulled back, sharply taloned feet and pointed beaks thrust forward for attack, they voiced rasping caws of anger that split the air.

Below them, the children had formed a tight ring, facing outward, desperately waving the curved hurley sticks above their heads to keep away the diving birds. Finn was almost to them. With no slackening of pace, it was clear that he planned to just charge into the fray.

"There he goes again!" said Cuillen, and lifted her voice to shout out: "Finn, wait! Wait for our help!"

He heard and paused, glancing back toward them. Though Labran and Cuillen were still a good way off, the two hounds were only a few bounds from him. Then a sharp cry of pain from one of the children drew his attention back to them again. A raven had boldly dived into the midst of the group and seized a small boy, its talons gripping his shoulders. Despite his wild struggles and the thrashing from the hurley sticks of the rest, the bird was endeavoring to lift its victim from the ground. The other two ravens spiraled in closer now as well, clearly preparing to join in.

Finn could delay no longer. He leapt forward to attack.

"We've got to help him," Cuillen cried to Labran. "Come on!"

She put on a burst of speed, flying ahead. A winded Labran tried to keep up, but soon was forced to stop, totally exhausted.

"You go on!" he managed to call after her. "I'll become a great hawk and swoop at them from above!"

He dropped down upon his knees, lifting his hands in supplication.

Cuillen didn't look back, plunging ahead, her face taut with her concern, her eyes fixed upon Finn. He had now reached the group and was making a first move upon the bird, very cautiously.

There was good reason for caution. The bird was turning constantly, the boy still dangling from his claws, using its wings and its sharp beak to beat the others back. As Finn came in at it, the raven struck out at him in a lightning move, the point of the beak barely missing him.

Finn dropped to the ground and rolled beneath a flapping wing, coming up behind the raven. Before it could wheel around to strike at him again, he leapt upon it, throwing an arm about its neck and jerking it backward. It gave a shriek of surprise, releasing the child, who fell safely into the arms of the others. The bird began to fight madly, scrawking in anger as it tried to twist its neck far enough about to jab at Finn. He only pulled his hold tighter with one arm and thrust his sword into its body with the other.

The raven screamed out its agony and then went limp, crashing forward heavily. Finn was thrown off, tumbling head over heels and landing upon his back.

Before he could rise, a second raven was upon him. It swept low over him, claws out to tear at him as it passed. But it was not low enough. The rending points of its talons barely touched Finn. Even at that, they raked across his chest, shredding the linen tunic and drawing deep furrows of blood across the skin.

He rolled and started to climb to his feet, grimacing as he moved, clearly hampered by the pain of the wounds. He barely had time to set himself and raise his sword as the third raven dived in. He swung out at its head as it closed. The head ducked aside as the blade swept by, and then the beak darted in at Finn's throat. He jerked away, saving himself, but the beak closed on the end of his flying plait of hair. As the bird swooped on, it yanked the long plait taut. Finn's head snapped around and he was wrenched violently backward. But his weight was too much. The plait was pulled free. He thudded heavily down on his back, while the bird, freed of its burden, banked sharply away.

The raven glided on, still close above the ground, looking back toward the downed Finn as it began a turn that would take it around for another pass. It didn't see the two hounds racing in toward it until Bran leapt up from the ground and caught one of the claws in his powerful jaws.

Jerked suddenly sideways and down, the bird heeled over and slammed to the ground. Sceolan was upon it in an instant, his own jaws fastening on the raven's sleek throat before it could recover and strike out. It thrashed wildly to free itself, but the two hounds were more than a match for it. Its struggled soon weakened.

Finn, meanwhile, climbed stiffly to his feet once more and began scanning the skies for the third attacking bird. A swiftly growing sound of rushing air behind him was enough to warn the young warrior, and he spun around, ducking away as the raven swished past, its claws making a futile grab for his head.

Finn watched it soar away and up, climbing and then looping back to strike again. But then its attention was drawn elsewhere and it banked sharply away from Finn, sweeping down toward another figure rushing in: that of Cuillen.

The girl stopped as she saw the great bird shooting down toward her. It seemed as if she was frozen by fear of the thing.

"Cuillen, get down!" Finn shouted, and ran toward her, but it was clear he could not reach her in time.

She stood rooted, motionless, staring at the raven. It arrowed for her, claws ready to seize this slender prey, voicing a harsh scrawk of victory.

CHAPTER TWENTY-FOUR

THE BRIDGE

The bird was barely five paces from Cuillen when she came to life. Her arm whipped the spear up and fired it in a swift, smooth move. Then she dove away as bird and weapon flew together.

The power of her throw and the forward motion of the raven combined to drive the spearhead deep into its shining black breast. Its victory cry changed to a shriek of agony. Its head and right wing dropped, sending the bird smashing heavily down. The momentum of its flight caused it to tumble forward, end over end, coming to a halt in a jumbled pile of shattered bones and splayed feathers.

"A brave move," Finn told Cuillen sincerely as he reached her side.

"The only move," she corrected in a matter-of-fact way as she stepped to the dead bird and jerked her spear from the tangle.

Not far away, the battle of the hounds had also ended. They rose from the still form of their raven and trotted to join Finn.

"Good lads," he told them, patting the broad heads.

"Oh dear. I've failed you again," said a piping voice.

The four turned about to see a peculiar-looking creature waddling toward them. It was waist-high to Finn, with a juglike black body, tiny head, and enormous flippers for feet. Large, soulful eyes blinked above a small, sharp beak, and stumpy wings flapped on either side as it shuffled up to the watchers.

"Labran?" Cuillen ventured. "That is you, isn't it?"

Even through the coating of feathers he seemed to blush with shame.

"I'm afraid it is," he admitted defeatedly. "I'm not a great eagle, then, am I?"

"Not quite," she said, clearly trying to be diplomatic. "But, you have managed to become some kind of bird," she added in a consoling way. "At least, I think so. I've never really seen one like you."

"Then why can't I fly?" he asked, giving the stubby wings a vigorous flap. His round body was so stiff and his neck so short that he was unable to bend far enough to see them himself.

"They're not much good for flying," she had to say. "They look more like . . . well . . . flippers than wings."

"Well, that's just typical for me, isn't it," he said despondently. "Naturally, I can't even turn myself into a hawk. And that was my best transformation, too." He gave a heartrending sigh.

Cuillen moved closer and stroked his head in a consoling way. The odd bird put his head against her side in response, allowing her to cuddle him.

"Look here, there's no time for that," Finn said with a distinct note of annoyance. "Just why did you come after me, anyway?"

"To be certain you survived," she retorted. "Without our help, you'd be carrion for those birds now."

"That I would not!" he protested indignantly. "I could have dealt with three ravens alone quite well enough."

"Could you?" she asked skeptically, stepping toward him and running a finger lightly across the still-bleeding gashes striping his chest.

"Never mind," Finn said quickly, stepping back from her. "The point of it is, now that you're all here, we're—" He paused suddenly, looking around. "Wait. You're not all here, are you? Where's Conan?"

"The stupid bull went on," she said.

"Alone?" Finn said, clearly somewhat appalled by this idea. "But he'll be—"

"Quite useless without us?" Cuillen finished for him. "Yes, I thought the same myself. But it may not matter whether he can reopen the cliff for us. Labran thinks the stairway was only a blind."

"A blind?" Finn repeated. He looked toward the de

Danaan, who had by now completed the transformation to become himself again. "What do you mean, Labran?"

"Only that the stairs seemed too convenient," he replied. "Every other time we've passed a barrier, it was only after you had succeeded in some test. There was none for the door."

"A test!" Finn said thoughtfully. "Is it the ravens you mean?"

"Not the ravens," Labran corrected, pointing behind Finn. "Them."

Finn turned around to look. He'd paid little attention to the band of children since the fight, except to briefly note that all had seemed unharmed. Now he gave them his first close examination.

All were very young, ranging from five to ten years in age. In appearance they seemed quite normal children, most with pale blond or reddish hair, all with the requisite inventory of freckles, dimples, pug noses, and immense bright eyes that add up to the charming, innocent look of early childhood. Yet, they were unnaturally quiet, especially considering their recent ordeal. Totally recovered from their panic, they stood unmoving, watching their saviors with smiles of complete serenity. And in those huge, glowing eyes there was a look not of innocence, but of great, great age.

"Who are you?" Finn demanded, stepping toward them.

"We are the children of the Sidhe," said the one who seemed to be the oldest. His tone was a child's, but the delivery of his words was precise and had the assured quality of a well-bred adult. "Labran is right, Son of Cumhal. It was for us to play our hurley on this plain and endure the ravens' attack as part of the King's Game. It was meant as another test for you."

"A test of what?"

"Of your generosity. You have proven before your willingness to help your friends, but to sacrifice your own needs and risk yourself for strangers, that is a greater virtue indeed."

"And if I'd chosen not to come help you?" Finn asked.

"Why, the ravens would have carried us away," the boy replied simply.

"It seems this test might have been a bit hard on you, then."

"There is nothing to that," the boy said with a shrug. "The champions have often made it to this place before. They have seen the great ravens attacking us. None before you has ever come to save us."

"None?" Finn said in surprise. "Then, how many of you have been killed?"

"All of us," the boy answered most soberly. "But if you fail in the game, the next champion who comes will find us all here, and the ravens as well."

"How can it be?" asked Cuillen. "The king said the game had been going on for centuries."

"And for those centuries we have played out our everlasting hurley match upon this plain."

"That's horrible," she said in dismay. "You children are trapped here, eternally tormented, for this mad King's Game?"

"It is for the good of the de Danaan race and the protection of the weapons that we play our part here, my lady," the boy told her. "It is our duty and our honor to serve the king." He looked to Finn. "And it is now my task to give you what your generosity has won, my champion. Please, come with me."

He left his fellows and started off at a brisk pace back toward the peak. Finn and his comrades exchanged glances and shrugs of resignation, and then followed. The rest of the boys stayed in their huddle, still motionless, still smiling those serene little smiles.

When the boy reached the base of the steep cliff, he turned to follow it. As he reached the knob of stone with its black gem, Finn and the others paused. They looked surprised to see the boy stride past it without giving it a glance.

"Wait!" called Finn. "Aren't you going to open this way again?"

"No, not that," the boy said, walking on a few paces more and then stopping to gesture up at the cliff-face. "Here. Here is your gateway past the barrier of this cliff."

They moved to him and looked up. Now clearly visible in the blank, curving wall of stone was a groove, a smooth and shallow indentation of man-width, forming a sort of chimney that ran vertically up the mountain. And maring the length of this groove, spaced like ladder rungs, were small footholds, cut no deeper than the thickness of a hand.

Finn slowly ran his eye up its length to where perspective shrank it to a pinpoint high overhead. He sighed wearily.

"I knew it just couldn't be so easy," he said.

"The easy path is a treacherous one," the boy remarked. "Only the hard, straight one can lead you to your goals."

"Now you sound like Cuanna," Finn said with a smile. But then the smile vanished as a new thought came. He swung around to face the boy, voice filling with concern.

"But if this is the true way, then what about Conan?"

"I am sorry," the boy said regretfully, shaking his head. "If your comrade chose the easy way, led by egotism and foolhardiness, he will go nowhere."

"What does that mean?" Finn demanded. "What's happened to him?"

"All I can tell you is that he is gone, like so many others before him," the boy replied. "None has ever come back out of the mountain's depths."

"We have to get him out!" Finn said forcefully, stepping closer to the boy. "Tell us how we can help him!"

"The king would never allow it," the boy said, his serenity unruffled by Finn's threatening look. "Your comrade has chosen this move himself, and he has lost. If you're wishing to continue in the game yourself, you must go on. Please accept it, Finn MacCumhal. You cannot help him now."

"Listen to him, Finn," put in Labran. "You know well enough that the king controls us here."

"Yes, Finn," added Cuillen. "His own bluster took Conan up those stairs. The oaf deserves whatever fate he finds there."

"I will grieve for Conan," Finn told her harshly. "I can't be so cold of heart as you are. I know that beneath his crudeness and bragging there was a good fighting man."

She flushed at the rebuke and fell silent.

"If we've no other choice, we must accept this for now," Finn said grudgingly, then he turned to the boy again. "But, listen here: Lad, you tell your king—" Here he stopped abruptly. For the boy was no longer there.

Finn scanned the area about. The distant huddle of other children was gone as well, along with the lumps of the dead ravens.

"I suppose I shouldn't even be surprised at that," Finn said.

"No," agreed Labran. "It's my feeling they weren't real beings at all. They may have been totally creations of the king's magic, or the wraiths of beings enthralled to him, as the red clowns and the wolf-women may have been."

"And can we trust this gutter in the cliff?" Finn asked. "We'll surely be at the king's mercy once up there."

"Is there any other way left to us?" was the de Danaan's matter-of-fact reply.

A foot slipped down, landing on a hand trying to maintain a solid grip on one of the shallow grooves. It was the hand of Finn, and he grunted with pain, jerking it from underneath.

"Careful, Labran," he called testily to the slender man above him, whose other foot now rested on the young captain's muscular shoulder, already bruised from many such contacts.

"Oh, sorry! Sorry!" Labran hastily apologized.

Finn was well wedged into the narrow chimney, using the leverage of his entire sinewy body, as well as of his hands and feet, to move himself up. This total effort had shredded most of his already-torn tunic and cloak and had scraped raw most of the skin on his back and legs. Still, it was allowing him to give Labran the greatest assistance possible, and the unathletic de Danaan was clearly in need of it.

On the other hand, Cuillen, climbing above them, was moving upward with the speed and agility of a fly.

Finn reached his free arm up, managing to boost Labran another rung higher. He then paused for a breath, glancing down.

The base of the cliff was now very far below. The two hounds, faithfully waiting at the bottom of the chimney, were merely specks. But the act of looking down appeared to discomfort Finn. His face tightened, his eyes grew wide, and he gave a loud gulp, as if something had gotten stuck in his throat. Then, quite purposefully, he turned his gaze upward and climbed on again, moving with a greater caution this time.

Cuillen, who had scrambled far ahead, took note that the men had fallen behind. She stopped to wait, watching with growing exasperation as they crawled slowly up toward her.

"And just what is it that's wrong with you?" she asked. "Can't you climb any faster?"

"It's my fault, Cuillen," Labran said meekly. "I should have stayed behind. Conan was right. I'm only a burden to you."

"Quiet, Labran," Finn said. "It's not you. I just can't make myself move more quickly. I've a feeling I'll fall surely if I do."

"A feeling?" Cuillen repeated. "What do you mean?"

"I don't know. Suddenly the height's put a dizziness on me. I've never felt the like!"

"Marvelous!" Cuillen said in a vexed way. "This is a fine time to discover that you're afraid of heights."

"Well, I couldn't know it before now, could I?" he shot back. "I've never been more than twice my height above the ground in my whole life!"

"Well, can you keep going?" she asked, glancing ahead. "We've still some way to go."

"Just climb on," he told her through gritted teeth. "I'll make it up."

"I do certainly hope so!" Labran said fervently, clutching at the shallow rungs.

Cuillen hovered close above them, watching the two men, her face revealing her anxiety for them. Finn pressed gamely upward, climbing at a slow but steady rate, pushing Labran ahead of him. But his skin was now shining with his sweat, and every muscle of his body was strained taut, nearly vibrating, as he concentrated his full effort on forcing himself up.

Finally his torture ended. Cuillen gave a cry of triumph and scrambled over an edge. For a moment she vanished, then reappeared head downward, reaching out an arm to grasp one of Labran's hands.

With Finn shoving from below, they managed to get the de Danaan safely up. Then Finn hauled himself over the edge, crawling onto a wide ledge.

Here he lay for a moment, panting heavily, seemingly a victim of total exhaustion. Labran and Cuillen exchanged looks of wonderment at the sight. But soon Finn levered himself up and climbed to his feet. There he stood, still breathing loudly, white-faced and completely soaked in sweat.

"I never thought to see the perfect Fianna captain showing any fear," she said, a tinge of gloating in her voice. "So, you are human after all."

"I hope the knowledge gives some great satisfaction to you," he gasped out. He took a final deep breath, seeming to control his palpitations by an effort of will. His color returned, and he apparently relaxed, but he carefully kept his gaze averted from the precipice.

Before them now lay a broad, level space, completely circling the middle of the cone-shaped peak. It curved off to their left and right, disappearing around the steep cliff-face of the peak's upper half. This smooth pinnacle rose to the curved rim of the top, still high above them.

Directly ahead of them, a true staircase was neatly cut into the otherwise-featureless stone. It offered an avenue to their final goal that seemed quite easy in comparison to the climb they had just made. But there still remained the problem of reaching it. For between the three travelers and the stairway to their goal lay a yawning chasm.

Finn stepped up to the edge of it and then quickly stepped back. It dropped sheerly away into a total darkness far below. Cuillen, clearly undisturbed by the height, perched precariously on the edge, leaning out to examine the depths more clearly.

"Get back, please!" Finn told her rather sharply.

She took a look at his apprehensive expression and complied, but gave him a superior smile as she did so.

The chasm was a dozen paces wide. It appeared to circle the upper part of the peak, completely separating them from it. This made the outer portion, which they had just climbed, into a sort of collar around the taller, narrower blunt spike they still had to reach.

Only one possible way was visible to them to cross this gap. This consisted of a row of columns—straight and precise octagons of smooth stone—that rose up from the shadowy depths. There were five of them, spaced equally apart, creating a line of stepping-stones across the space. Each was a short stride in width, and each was just more than a long stride from the next, insuring that one would have to leap from stone to stone, with little margin for miscalculation.

"Well, there's our path," said Cuillen.

"Let's be certain there's no other," Finn said quickly. "Come along."

He led the way in a circuit of the peak, his eyes searching carefully, and somewhat desperately, for an alternative way to cross. But the search was fruitless, taking them back to the line of stones.

"No point in wasting more time," Cuillen said briskly. "Let's get on across. It's easy enough."

"Strange that there's been nothing to test Finn this time." Labran commented thoughtfully. "What virtue of his could be the key to this?"

"I'd say it's fearlessness," she said. "Look at Finn."

Labran looked to their young captain. He was staring

fixedly across the space, seemingly frozen, his face quite ashen and his brow beaded with sweat.

"What's wrong with him?" Labran asked. "He looks about to faint!"

"The heights have done it," she said. "I've heard of such things before." She moved toward Finn, addressing him with more force: "Finn, listen to me! You have got to cross. It's the only way!"

"I know," he said in a faltering way. "But I . . . I can't! I can't seem to make myself move forward. My head's reeling as it is!"

"You've just got to overcome it," she said in a stern, parental tone. "Look, I'll prove to you it's safe. You can watch me cross. This time I'll be the first."

"Wait!" cried Labran. "I don't think—"

But she wasn't listening. She ran to the edge and—while Finn squeezed his eyes tightly closed—leapt for the first stone.

She landed safely and leapt onto the second. Lightly, almost carelessly, she made her way to the third and middle one, stopping to turn back toward her companions.

"Look at me, Finn!" she called gaily, lifting her arms in a gesture of triumph.

He opened his eyes and looked, but his face was tight in apprehension as she did a little jig upon the small surface.

"You see?" she said. "You can do it. It's quite easy, really! There's no danger at—"

Her voice was cut off sharply as a rumbling began. Her look of victory changed abruptly to one of concern as a shudder ran up through the columns of stone.

"Cuillen!" shouted Labran in terror. "Quickly, come back!"

But she had no chance to move. A stronger tremor made the columns sway more violently. She staggered and dropped to her knees.

The columns were vibrating continuously now, their movement accompanied by a low rumbling sound. Fissure lines began to appear, running up the lengths of stone. Portions of the sharp-edged octagons began to crumbled and fall away.

"The columns are breaking apart!" Labran shouted to Cuillen. "You have to get off!"

She managed to regain her feet, but before she could leap on, the edge just behind her heels suddenly gave way. She slid down, scrabbling wildly at the broken edge, managing to grip it and stop her fall. But now her body dangled above the chasm, held up only by her arms, her feet unable to find a purchase on the smooth stone.

"Finn," Labran said to him, "you must go after her. I haven't the strength to pull her up."

Finn nodded. He moved, with what was clearly a great effort, to the brink of the chasm. But there he halted again, rooted to the spot, face white with terror, gaze fixed on the awful depths.

The column just before him split with a sharp cracking sound. A large facet of it abruptly slid away.

"Finn, you have no more time!" Labran cried urgently. "All the rocks are giving way! Finn, you must go now!"

Still Finn stood motionless, while the column to which Cuillen clung shuddered once again, and the edge to which she clung began to crumble beneath her hands.

CHAPTER TWENTY-FIVE

ESCAPE

Finn's eyes lifted from the chasm to the terrified face of Cuillen as she cast a look of supplication toward him. That seemed to break the spell of the fear. Taking a deep breath, he leapt forward, landing on the first pier.

His impact made its top crumble beneath his feet. Without hesitating, he leapt on, striking the next, leaping again as it tottered and slipped away, landing with a great thud upon his stomach, draped across the remains of the middle column.

The landing made the pier shiver violently. The side beneath Cuillen fragmented, sliding down. She scrambled desperately, clawing her way upward with torn nails and bloody fingertips. But she was sliding back.

Finn pulled himself into a crouch, turning, leaning down and out over the depths to grab her. He was too late. The edge she was fighting to grip fell away all at once, taking her along.

Finn lunged foward, his whole upper body hanging over the edge, arms swinging down.

His hand closed around her wrist. Her fall ended in a sudden jerk that nearly pulled him from his insecure perch. Now she hung above the depths, swinging slightly, a dead weight on the end of Finn's one arm.

The columns continued to quiver. More jagged pieces were slipping away all around their disintegrating pier. Finn's neck and arm muscles were drawn taut, the tendons bulging from the strain. His face tensed in concentration. He began slowly, slowly, to lift her.

He got up to his knees, bringing her torso up above the

edge. Wrapping his other arm about her waist, he pulled her close. She clung to him, taking a shuddering breath of relief. He rose to his feet, still holding her, and looked around. There was little of their column left. The two behind had already tumbled, and the two ahead were about to give way.

There was no time for contemplating the next move. Finn simply acted. He gathered himself and sprang for the next pier. His foot struck crumbling stone and he pushed off at once, vaulting on across the abyss to the fifth column. It was dissolving from beneath him even as he touched it, but there was enough firm surface left to allow him to propel himself on, hurtling them both toward the far ledge with the full power of his sinewy legs.

The last column collapsed as he left it, the shattered pieces dropping into the chasm with a reverberating clatter. He slammed against the ledge, stomach hitting the sharp edge, upper body atop it, and pitched Cuillen ahead of him. While he hung there, legs dangling, breath knocked from him by the impact, she rolled and got up, rushing to him.

Grabbing the neck of his cloak, she hauled back, using all her power and weight. With her help he pulled forward, getting a leg over the edge and using it to heave himself up.

He fell full length upon the ledge. Exhausted by her own efforts, she dropped back beside him and both of them lay there, panting for breath.

Finally he lifted his head and looked down at her.

"You just had to go ahead, didn't you?" he said, managing a smile.

"It got you across, didn't it?" she answered, smiling in return.

"Say, there!" came Labran's urgent call. "Hello! Are you all right?"

They sat upright and looked across to where the de Danaan stood, anxiously gazing toward them.

"We're all right," Finn called back. "But it looks as if you'll be stuck where you are."

"It doesn't matter," he said in his cheerful, self-effacing way. "You're better off without me, anyway. I wish you good fortune with the rest of your climb."

Cuillen and Finn looked at one another, then turned their gazes up at the steep stairway cut into the remainder of the peak. From this perspective, it seemed to reach up to the bottom of the skies. Finn looked back to her.

"Are you ready?" he asked.

"Are you certain that you are?" she countered. "It's very high."

"After this," he said, gesturing to the abyss and grinning, "it'll be like strolling on a plain."

Together the two started the last, long climb that would take them to the top of the strange peak and their final goal.

A hand touched the bare shoulder of Caoilte.

Instantly the warrior was upright in his bed, hands raised to guard himself. The figure that had been beside him started and moved back. There came a scolding whisper:

"Easy, young man! I've not come here to harm you!"

"Bebind," Caoilte said, now recognizing the tall, lean shape in the shadows of the sleeping chamber. "But it's the resting time, isn't it? Night in the outside world. Why are you here?"

"To help you, young man," she said in her brusque way. "I've come to see that you escape our Sid."

"You want me to escape?" he asked. "But why? I thought I was a prisoner in this place."

"That was not my idea," she reminded him. "Your presence here has taken my authority and ruined the discipline we had. Now all the sisters do is think of you and neglect their work. You've ruined years and years of effort by me to give them worth, to let them be themselves, to free them of the burdens your kind has put on them, to free them of the pains you men have caused them."

"I haven't done any of that!" he replied indignantly, his voice rising.

"Quiet!" she warned. "We can't let the others know. They would likely try to destroy us both. I must get you away from here secretly. So come along now. Put on your clothing and hurry up. We must act while everyone is asleep."

Caoilte needed no more urging. Quickly he donned his boots, tunic, and cloak. Then silently, cautiously, he followed Bebind out into the main room of the Sid.

It was very dim. The torches in the wall sconces and the tapers upon the tables were all out. The large central fire had burned down to a bed of glowing red coals. No one was about. As Bebind led the way around the cavern, past the doorways of the separate sleeping chambers, he glanced in, seeing the sisters slumbering in apparent peacefulness.

They reached a chamber nearly opposite the opening that marked the tunnel out of the Sid. Here Bebind leaned close to whisper to him:

"This is Uaine's room. Be very still now. I must go in. She's keeping your weapons to watch herself now."

She crept into the room. He watched her anxiously. The frail Uaine was sleeping with a small smile of contentment, her faded beauty much returned to her in the relaxation of sleep. Bebind carefully opened a cupboard beside the bed, removing his round shield and his sword with its sheath and harness. These she carried back and gave to him.

Uaine stirred. Both of them froze, watching. But the woman only gave a sigh of pleasure and rolled onto her side.

"Dreaming of you, no doubt," Bebind whispered sarcastically. "Come on, young man."

They moved softly to the middle of the room, away from the encircling sleeping chambers. There Bebind tersely whispered her directions.

"Here I must leave you," she said. "Go up the tunnel to the outer door. I've left it open for you, and your horse is waiting just outside. Ride away from here as fast as you can. Don't delay and don't look back. Believe me, if they discover you, you'll be in great peril."

"What about you?" he asked.

"I will be able to take them in hand easily enough once the arousing influence of yourself has been removed."

"You make me sound like another poison you have to purge," he said with a grin. "Still, I'm grateful to you for helping me."

"I am helping myself, young man," she told him haughtily. "Now go, quickly."

He belted on his sword and started off across the floor toward the opening. Bebind turned away and headed back to her own chamber, allowing herself a prim smile of satisfaction.

The Sid was still quiet. It seemed that Caoilte's escape was assured.

Neither of them realized that in the chamber of Uaine, the little woman had shivered, as if a chill draught had passed across her, then had rolled and jerked upright, eyes snapping open. For a long moment she had stared ahead, holding her breath, apparently trying to absorb some faint, disturbing impression. Now she came suddenly to life, ripping off her bedclothes, rushing to her cupboard, flinging wide its doors.

What she saw—or failed to see—there clearly confirmed her fears. Her pale face was suffused by a flush of dismay. She turned and ran from her room into the main cavern in time to see Caoilte reach the tunnel opening.

"Caoilte!" she cried out.

Startled by her voice, he paused to look back.

"You can't leave me!" she implored in a frail, fluttering voice. "Please, don't leave!"

"I'm sorry, Uaine," he called back, his tone one of real regret. "I have to go. Please understand. Forgive me, but—good-bye!"

With that, he turned and disappeared into the tunnel.

"Forgive!" the scorned little woman said in a voice that now turned hard with anger. "I will destroy you for this!" She filled her lungs and shouted: "Awake! Sisters, awake! He is escaping! Come quickly!"

Her shout echoed along the tunnel to Caoilte. Its threat seemed to prod the fleeing warrior to a great effort. He now flew up the inclined corridor toward the outer door.

Meanwhile, in the cavern, the women were astir, some of the more alert already out, listening in rising shock and ire to Uaine's heated words.

"He is going up the tunnel. We must stop him. Flann, take some of the sisters and be after him."

"But what if he gets out?" the round woman asked in distress. "I don't think we can stop him then."

"If he escapes us, then we will make him pay for what he's done to us," Uaine said savagely. "Get after him. Hurry!"

As Flann and a score of sisters headed for the tunnel, Bebind joined the group about Uaine. Her expression was a disapproving one.

"You are fools to take revenge on him," she said in a scolding tone, sweeping them with her gaze. "Sisters, can't you see what this has done to you? Let him go!"

"That's what you'd like, isn't it, Bebind!" Uaine retorted. "Well, this time a man will pay for his wrong. So stay well out of it! And you other sisters, come with me!"

As this group moved off with Uaine, those with Flann were rushing up the tunnel in pursuit of Caoilte. The sounds of their running feet reached him, but he was already at the outer door. It was ajar, as Bebind had promised. He shoved the stone portal further open and pressed through the crack.

A cool, damp night greeted him. The sky was clear and bright with stars. Night birds called softly. He paused just a moment, breathing deeply, as if savoring the first sensations of freedom. Then the swiftly growing sound of the approaching women spurred him to action again.

His saddled horse was tethered to a nearby tree. He untied it swiftly, mounted, and urged the animal away. He was well removed from the mound before the first of the women burst from the opening.

They stopped when they saw him galloping off, looking after him with expressions of great chagrin. Only Flann seemed to take his escape in a philosophical way.

"Oh well," she said, shrugging, "maybe it is for the best."

However, this sentiment was not shared by Uaine, who now appeared atop the mound with the other group of sisters. She seemed almost to explode in outrage as she saw the shadowy figure of the mounted man racing away across the starlit meadows.

"So, he thinks he has made it safely away," she said. "Well, if we can't have him, we'll show him what it means to make fools of us." She turned to the others. "Quickly, sisters, join the ring. We must combine our powers!"

They formed into a circle atop the mound, linking arms.

"Now, sisters, concentrate!" urged Uaine. "Will our energy to pool."

They all closed eyes. Their faces tightened, mouths frowning, brows drawn down, jaw muscles taut. Their bodies tensed also, almost vibrating from the strain of concentration.

Around each of them a vague aura of light began to form. It grew stronger, until each was enveloped in a golden glow. When all the lights had reached the same peak of intensity, they began to flow away, like a shining honey being poured, the streams oozing into the space within the ring.

There they joined, a single mass of light swelling up, looking much like a full, autumn moon rising above the curve of the earth. It grew quickly, absorbing all the energy from the women, lifting higher to become a complete sphere, suspended in the center of the circle of women. There it hung, pulsing with its power, casting a golden brightness across the whole hilltop.

Uaine glanced around toward the departing Caoilte. The dark form of man and horse were far away now, nearing a low hill.

"Hurry, sisters!" Uaine said. "Direct your thoughts to him. All together—send our energy to strike him. Ready? Now!"

Moving as one, the circle of women threw up their arms as if physically throwing an object away from them. The golden sphere rose upward suddenly, soaring high into the night sky, drawing a streak of light across the black as it formed a wide, graceful arch and then dropped back toward the earth, and toward the fleeing horseman.

The bright, extra glow growing so swiftly above him alerted Caoilte. He looked up, eyes widening in astonishment at the thing descending upon him. Then he leaned forward over the horse's head and spurred it to greater speed, heading for the crest of the hill just ahead.

It was a deadly race between himself and the globe of energy. He reached the hilltop but barely before the golden sphere. The horse galloped across the crest and started down the far side. Its body passed below the black curve of the ground, but the head and shoulders of Caoilte were still visible when the bright sphere struck the crest.

There was a soundless explosion of blinding light. The sphere swelled outward like an opening flower, spreading countless threads of golden light, expanding to a hundred times its original size. Then it died, the glowing tendrils burning out. A shower of sparks drifted downward, most flickering out before they struck the ground. Others floated upward, as if to join the company of the stars.

Of Caoilte there was now no sign. The black hilltop was empty.

Below the mound, a watching Flann closed her eyes in shock, saying with dismay:

"Oh my! That poor, poor lad!"

Atop the mound, the women with Uaine who had caused this stunning spectacle stared toward the blasted spot with looks of awe.

"Did we destroy him?" one asked in a hushed voice.

"If he was within the compass of that blossom of light, he is now with those floating sparks," Uaine said, smiling pitilessly. "He'll scorn no more women."

"Still," said another with a sigh of regret, "it does seem a shameful waste."

* * *

The gauntleted hand of Daire Donn slammed onto the planks of the tabletop.

"I will not tolerate this cowardly delaying any longer!" he roared. "If you cannot command the loyalty of your warriors, perhaps there are others who can!"

The giant man drew himself up. Helmetless but clad in the suit of mail, he made an imposing figure. It was night, and the light of the torches was reflected and multiplied by the gleaming silver links, making him seem to flicker with energy and appear all the more immense against the shadowy background.

He cast a dark, ominous gaze about him. The captains seated at the table in his tent exchanged uneasy looks at the bald threat. One of them hastened to reply.

"My high king, there's no question of loyalty here—either that of our warriors or ourselves. There's not a man of your army who'd think of leaving the strand so long as you're determined to stay. It's just that . . . well . . . they're not quite so anxious to attack that wall with so many warriors defending it now. I mean, it wasn't taking them more than a fifth our number to keep us back before."

"Aye, my good king," put in the boar-faced Finnachta. "Now, if they'd come down upon the strand, even with numbers equal to our own, why, your men would fight with all their spirit for you. They'd fight to the death, so they would!"

There were sounds of agreement from the others at that, but Donn seemed unplacated.

"It is not good enough!" he said. "We can't just sit here. We have to—"

The sentence went unfinished. A sudden blast of wind whipped through the camp, striking against the tent like a solid object. The walls shivered. The flaps were blown open and the gust entered the tent, fluttering the torches. It seemed to suck the light from the torch flames and they faded to faint, red glows, plunging the interior abruptly into deep gloom.

"What's happened?" Donn shouted. "Get the torches relit. Close the tent doors!"

But his commands were unnecessary. The wind died as suddenly as it had risen. The torch flames grew, regaining their former strength. Light filled the room again.

It revealed a new presence in their midst. A figure now sat at the end of the long table, opposite Donn. He was a slender, finely featured being in a silver robe. His small mouth was drawn in a severe line, and his bright, silver-blue eyes met the king's black iron ones boldly.

"Tadg!" breathed Donn in some astonishment.

CHAPTER TWENTY-SIX
THE FINAL TEST

"What are you doing here?" the king of the Great World demanded of his strange visitor.

"I have come to help you again, Donn," the deceptively gentle voice of the druid replied. "I have taken a risk in doing so. I am in much greater danger of discovery this time."

"What do you mean?" the king demanded suspiciously.

"I will just say that there are others now greatly interested in your little war," Tadg answered in an ambiguous way, "—others who must not know that I am helping you. So I have little time, and it is urgent that we talk. But, I think that we should be alone."

"Yes," agreed Donn. He swept the officers with a stern gaze, snapping, "Leave us now. Try to restore some backbone to your companies!"

The men, clearly relieved to be leaving his presence, lost no time in filing out. When the last one had departed, Donn strode the length of the table, stopping to lean over the druid.

"Now, speak to me," he said brusquely.

"Very well. The news has come to me that your Caisel has failed. Finn has reached the hidden place where the weapons are kept. He has managed to come very close to gaining those weapons. I warned you that he could not be taken too lightly. He has incredible skills and great fortune on his side. He might just succeed."

"Is this why you've risked yourself to come here?" Donn asked angrily. "To tell me this? That's of no help to me. It makes things worse. We sit here, waiting for him to return and challenge me."

"It was that very thing that brought me," Tadg said. "I was astounded when I heard that you had not already destroyed the Fianna. It must be done at once. If Finn returns, there can be none of his warriors left here to help him. He must face your host alone. No weapons can save him then."

"Do you think I don't know that?" raged Donn, this time slamming his massive fist to the planks in front of Tadg with a force that splintered the thick wood. He then wheeled away to pace the tent floor like a penned wolf, snarling: "Don't you think I would have finished these Irishmen long since if I could? But there is a new force upon their cursed wall. A strong force that has stolen the manhood of my warriors."

The little druid, clearly unperturbed by the man's violence, gave a knowing smile.

"And that is where I will give my help to you," he said softly, soothingly. "You see, Donn, there is no new force upon the wall."

"Are you a madman?" Donn cried, stopping and turning back to face the druid. "My own eyes tell me it's so."

"Eyes, my high king, even your own, may be deceived," Tadg said placidly. "What you see upon the wall is trickery. It is the magic of the Fian druids. There is no more than a single catha of whole men facing your host now."

"A single catha?" Donn repeated skeptically. "And how do you know such a thing?"

"Even with much of my powers taken from me, my own magic is still vast compared to that of the simple Fian druids. Look here, Donn. I will prove my words to you."

He stood at the table and swept one silver-draped, shimmering arm toward a shadowy side of the tent. Something immediately began to form there, wavery at first, like an image in a wind-ruffled pond. But it quickly grew steadier, the shape and colors growing clearer, stronger.

The eyes of Donn grew wide in amazement as he stared, and then he suddenly leapt back, grabbing up his ax. For a line of grim warriors in the garb of the Fianna clans now faced him across his tent.

"Be easy, High King," Tadg told him with amusement. "They are not real. Approach them. They'll not act against you."

Casting a doubting glance at Tadg, Donn approached the men very cautiously, ax up to strike, eyes examining them searchingly. None of them moved. They stood as silent and motionless as statues, staring ahead.

"They don't even seem alive," Donn commented, stopping close before one and staring at his face.

"Strike at them now," Tadg offered. "Just swing out with your ax."

Donn shrugged and complied, stepping back and launching a flat blow of his ax that should have severed the warrior at his waist. Instead, the weapon struck nothing palpable. It swished through the figure, the wind of its passing dissolving the warrior as a puff of air whirls away a cloud of smoke. As the one vanished, the rest of the line fluttered and faded away as well.

Donn, momentarily bewildered, looked to Tadg. The little druid laughed.

"You see?" he said. "They are creatures of mist. So are those upon the wall. They will vanish as these did when you attack them. The very breeze raised by your rushing upon them will sweep them away. Now, Donn, prove yourself a man of supernatural power to your men. Go first to the wall yourself and show them you can turn their enemies to air."

"Yes!" the high king said with a rising excitement. "Yes. I'll lead them, and they will follow, knowing it is a phantom host they face."

He rushed to the doorway of the tent, throwing back a flap, shouting into the night:

"Finnachta! Come at once!"

The officer appeared swiftly.

"Yes, my king?"

"Call all the officers to return. We must begin preparing the companies to attack."

"Attack, my king?" the man said in surprise.

"Yes, Finnachta. Soon I will show you all with my own hand that the host facing us is no threat. Now, go!"

Finnachta went, sprinting away into the darkness. Donn, smiling gloatingly, turned back into the tent.

"Well, it's a much greater service you've done me this time, Tadg," he began. "Is there anything else I can—"

He stopped abruptly. Tadg had already gone. But the soft voice of the druid floated back from some distant place to him:

"Just see that the Fianna are destroyed, High King. Destroyed!"

* * *

Finn and Cuillen mounted the final steps and came onto the edge of the mountaintop. There they paused for breath, looking over the scene that now lay before them.

The top of the curious peak was precisely circular, as smooth and as flat as a table of carefully dressed stone. In its center was a ring formed of a dozen standing stones, each a man's height in width and twice as tall. They were of a dull gray-black, like slate, only a handsbreadth in thickness, straight-edged and sharp-cornered. Spaced at equal and exact intervals, they surrounded three more stones—two short ones set upright and a third laid on top—forming an altar.

"I've seen ancient stone rings in Ireland like this," Finn remarked in a hushed voice.

"So have I," Cuillen softly replied. "But their stones were great, thick pieces, roughly hewn and badly weathered. Not like these. They're too perfect, and too exactly alike, as the trees in the forest were. More magical creations?"

"It doesn't matter anymore," Finn said with a certain weariness. "All that matters is the weapons. Come on."

They started toward the ring, heading toward the altar. It was now clear, from this height, that it sat at the very axis of this most peculiar land. From the peak, the countryside formed concentric circles: the forest's band of green; the shining line of the river, impossibly making a closed ring; the gray-yellow of the desert enclosed by the reddish gleam of the first barrier—the copper wall. And all of it seemed frozen, as silent as if it were a precious bauble sealed under a blue-glass dome that formed the sky.

They reached the ring of stones and paused again. From there they could see that objects lay upon the stone altar.

"Look!" Finn said. "That must be the weapons."

"Then, we have made it!" she said with relief.

With a renewed energy, they moved closer. As they approached, it became clear that weapons did, indeed, lay upon the flat stone. They stopped nearby to examine them carefully. One was an oval, undecorated shield that would protect a man from knees to shoulders. The other was a slender-bladed sword with a simple hilt. Both were of a softly glowing black metal.

"They don't seem much," Cuillen said frankly.

"It's what they can do that we care about," he said.

"Well, there's no one about," she said, scanning the

mountaintop. "Nothing to stop us. Get them, and let's start the journey out of this awful place!"

He nodded and stepped toward them, then stopped in surprise. For the figure of the odd king of this country—materialized in a twinkling from the empty air—now sat atop the altar before him.

"Greetings to you!" the man said exhuberantly. "I've been most anxiously awaiting your arrival here. You've played the game excellently. Excellently! I don't know when I've been more greatly entertained."

"Then, you have been watching us," Finn said.

"Much more than that," the man said with great delight. "Watch me!"

And before the astonished gazes of the pair, the infant-like form of the king altered, swiftly going through a series of transformations that included the impish Ruan O'Cealaigh, the gray-haired Cuanna, and the boy leader of the hurley players.

"You see?" he announced triumphantly, resuming his own form. "I've been close to you all along!"

"All right," Cuillen said somewhat impatiently. "We're most impressed. But Finn's passed all your tests. Give him the weapons and let us go now."

"Not so hasty, my fair Cuillen," the being said with a high trill of laughter. "Finn has passed six barriers only. Our young champion has one more test to prove his worthiness, and we mustn't disappoint all those others who are so eagerly following the game."

"Others?" Finn repeated. "Who do you mean?"

"Why, my beautiful Finn, your exploits here have roused the most avid interest of the de Danaans of all Ireland! None believed that you would be able to come so far. Naturally, many want you to fail. They'd like to see you mortals savage one another. But there are others who would like to see you win. Both sides are equally concerned in the outcome, of course. So the news of your progress is being carried by winds and clouds and creatures of the air to every Sid."

"I'm pleased to know we're providing such enjoyment to your people," Finn said with a note of sarcasm. "But, let's waste no more time. Tell me what I must do to finish this game of yours."

"First, I must tell you something," the king said more gravely. "Before you risk yourself again, know that it might not be to any purpose. Your Fianna are nearing the end of their strength. Even now, Daire Donn is preparing for a massive assault which could likely finish them."

"How do you know this?" Finn demanded.

"Our people have taken an interest in your battle as well. The black war-ravens of the Morrigan take great delight in soaring above that bloody strand."

"It is a cruel people the de Danaans are, to let this happen and then take pleasure in watching it," Finn told him bitterly. "Delay me no longer with your talk. I'm ready to go on."

"Oh, I had so hoped you would!" the little man cried ecstatically. He clapped his long-fingered hands so vigorously in demonstration of his joy that the enormous head bobbed upon the spindle of a neck.

"Just tell me what the last test is," Finn said sharply, his patience clearly exhausted.

"Why, can't you guess it?" the man said with a cunning grin. "It's me!"

And with that, he began suddenly to expand.

So rapidly did he grow, that Finn and Cuillen were forced to leap backward and avoid being crushed. As he swelled upward he also swiftly metamorphosized. In an instant an immense creature stood between them and the altar with its precious weapons.

The thing they now faced seemed to be a bizarre conglomeration of several creatures, in that way like the form that had been on Labran when Cuillen and Finn first met him. But while that creature's oddly mismatched parts had made it look absurd, the appearance of this one was far from comical.

The body of the thing was like that of an enormous cat, lithe, sinewy, and furred. But the beast's feet were scaled and taloned like a bird's, and vast, leathery wings stretched out from just behind the shoulders on either side. A long, thick, and reptilian-looking tail stretched out behind it, curling around the altar in a protective way, switching nervously. Its presence was most certainly needed to keep the thing balanced, for from its shoulders there grew three snakelike necks, each topped with a flat, serpentine head.

The long necks lifted the heads to twice the height of the standing stones. From this vantage point they looked down at Finn and Cuillen with slit-pupiled golden eyes. The forked ribbons of their tongues flicked constantly, rhythmically, from wide mouths equipped with long and sharply pointed fangs.

The three heads moved constantly as well, swinging gracefully on the sinuous necks, even entwining at times.

"Now," came a soft, sibilant voice from all three heads at once, "try to reach your prize."

Finn darted in, trying to swing around the beast and get to the altar. But the three heads swept down to strike with astonishing speed.

Two drove in at his front, hissing angrily. The third shot in from behind, mouth open, fangs ready to sink into his unprotected neck.

"Look out, Finn!" cried Cuillen, casting her spear at the third head.

It was a hard and accurate throw, hitting the creature just below the eye, but it didn't penetrate. The point rebounded as if the scales of its hide were metal plates, and the spear fell to the ground.

Still, the warning saved Finn. He turned and ducked away as the head struck, swinging a blow of his sword to its neck as it shot past. This also rebounded from the hard scales.

With no apparent way to harm the creature, Finn was no match for the three heads. As they darted in from all sides with a bewildering speed, Finn beat a judicious retreat. With Cuillen he backed swiftly away from it, swinging his sword to hold it off.

But the beast didn't follow. Once they had passed beyond the ring of stones, it stopped. Finn and Cuillen took shelter behind one of the slabs and peered around it to see the thing resume its position before the altar and stand watching them with its three sets of baleful eyes.

"It seems reluctant to leave the altar," commented Cuillen.

"Why should it?" asked Finn. "It only has to wait. I have to come to it. There's no way to sneak up behind it and no way to wound those heads."

"Well, what about your so-mighty virtues?" she said. "There must be one useful here. This is supposed to be another test."

"I don't know of one," he said, smiling. "I think I've used all my virtues up. That should be a great relief to you."

"This is no time to be amusing," she said sharply.

"You don't think a little tune might work this time, then?"

"No. And neither will your charm or your generosity. Think!"

"Well," he said more soberly, "there is one thing. I suppose you'd call it a talent. I've a gift of knowledge I acquired with the help of an old bard and an obliging salmon."

"What?" she said in a perplexed way.

"Never mind. I'll tell you about it later. But it will sometimes give me knowledge of how to act, though it'll only work in desperate situations."

"And what would you call this?" she inquired.

"You're right," he agreed. "You keep watch, then. I'll see what I can do."

He moved back behind the slab and leaned against it, closing his eyes and shifting his sword to his left hand. Cuillen caught his movements in the corner of her eye and her astonished gaze swiveled around to him. For Finn had just thrust his right thumb into his mouth.

"What are you doing?" she gasped, as if he had gone mad.

"Quiep," he said around the thumb. "I hab to confontrate."

She watched in a dumbfounded way as he continued to stand, eyes closed, sucking on the thumb in a contemplative way. Then, suddenly, his eyes flicked open. He pulled out the thumb and turned to her with a triumphant grin.

"I've got it!" he said excitedly. "That thing is another of the king's illusions. If I believe it isn't real, I can find a way to defeat it."

"And what if you can't believe that?" she asked, peering out toward it. "It looks real enough to me."

"The thumb will help me, at least enough to weaken the illusion so I can have a chance at it."

"The thumb?" she repeated. "Why the thumb?"

"I only get the knowledge when the thumb is in my mouth," he said. "I know it seems foolish, but that's how the magic works. Now, it's going to take the both of us for this. Are you ready to go along?"

"You mean, you'll actually trust me to help you this time?" she asked sarcastically.

"We're partners in this," he said with gravity. "After what we've been through together, I've no more question of your fighting skills or your loyalty."

She met his eye searchingly for a moment, then nodded.

"Nor I of yours," she said with a like seriousness. "I'm ready."

"Take this sword, then," he said, handing it to her. "You'll have to go first. Try to get the attention of all three heads on you, just for a moment. I have to have time to get your spear and then use my thumb to show me how to strike."

"Come along. Come along!" came the hissing voices of the creature, sounding a bit petulant now. "You're spoiling the game! Don't hide there. You must play! I'm getting quite bored with waiting."

"Shall we go play?" Finn said to Cuillen.

"Just don't get yourself killed, Finn MacCumhal," she told him urgently. "Not now. Not when . . ." she paused, looking flustered, then went on, ". . . when all Ireland is at stake."

"You take care, as well," he said, taking her free hand and giving it a squeeze. "Or who will I have then to tell me what to do?"

She managed a smile in return. Then, setting her young face in determined lines, she leapt from cover to charge at the beast.

She moved to one side within the ring of stones, sweeping widely as if she meant to come in behind the creature and try for the weapons. It shifted its body to follow her, the heads shooting forward to cut her off.

That was when Finn moved, running at his swiftest around the outside of the ring, then darting in toward the fallen spear.

He came in almost opposite to Cuillan. Still, one of the heads noted him, swinging away from her toward him. Finn made a grab for the weapon as the jaws snapped out, and jumped swiftly back as they clicked closed where his head had been. He retreated a few steps and stopped there.

The beast was now between Finn and Cuillan, watching both of them warily. One head kept its yellow gaze fixed on her. Another held on Finn. The third switched nervously this way and that, ready to join in parrying an attack from either side.

But Finn did not attack. Instead, he took the spear in his left hand and raised his right thumb to his mouth.

"Oh no, Finn MacCumhal!" the beast's three voices cried. "I know of your thumb's power. You'll not live to use it here!"

Ignoring Cuillen now, it swung all three heads toward Finn and started forward. Cuillen, in a desperate move to stop it, leapt upon its tail, hauling back on it. The creature snarled and switched the tail sharply, tossing her away.

But even this moment's delay was enough for Finn. The thumb was already doing its work. The image of the beast had grown hazy, translucent. Beneath it was visible a much smaller, darker form. And as the monster descended upon him, its three jaws open to tear at him, he cast the spear with his left hand.

It shot through the hazy beast-form, striking the smaller one. At once the beast stopped its attack. The heads lifted to voice trilling cries of pain. The necks writhed, winding together in the throes of agony. The massive body shuddered.

Then the beast's form started to dissolve, melting downward like a statue of ice set by a fire, losing form, collapsing into a shapeless mass that dwindled rapidly, as if soaking into the ground. Revealed now in the monster's place was the infantlike form of the king, his frail body transfixed by Finn's spear.

He staggered back against the altar. Using it for support, he managed to raise his wobbling head and fix his large eyes on Finn. And then, incredibly, he smiled.

"I . . . thank you . . . Finn MacCumhal," he gasped out. "You have won the game. And you have freed me from the duty that has kept me its slave for all these centuries. The weapons . . . are yours."

He slumped, sliding from the altar to the ground.

As he did, the mountain began a violent shuddering, as if in its own death throes. The sky grew instantly black. Winds whipped across the peak, tearing at Finn and Cuillen.

Finn rushed to the altar and seized the weapons. He went to Cuillen, pulling her to her feet. Together they started away, heading for the stairway in the cliff.

They didn't even make it out of the ring of stones. With a great roar, the whole mountain collapsed at once, pulling them down, burying them in the rubble of the shattered peak.

BOOK THREE
THE BATTLE ON THE STRAND

CHAPTER TWENTY-SEVEN

SURVIVORS

Finn MacCumhal groaned and opened his eyes.

He was staring up into a blue sky striped with fleecy tendrils of white cloud. His face registered a surprise that quickly changed to great bewilderment. He sat up.

His gaze first fleetingly took in the scene before him: not the rubble of the king's shattered mountain, but a wide, flat meadow, dark green with a covering of lush grass. From this his eyes dropped to the objects in his hands. He still grasped the sword called Son of the Waves and the massive iron oval of the Storm Shield.

There came a soft moan, and his gaze swept around toward the sound. He discovered the forms of his companions—Cuillan, Labran, Conan, and the two hounds—laid out in the grass beside him. Cuillen was the closest, and it was from her that the moan had come. He threw aside the weapons and moved quickly to kneel over her.

She moaned again and stirred. Her eyelids fluttered and then slowly opened. The brown eyes focused upon him, growing wider in astonishment.

"Finn," she breathed. "Aren't we dead?"

"It seems not," he said, helping her to sit up. "Though I'm not certain how."

She looked about her in a disoriented way.

"But, we should have been buried!" she said in amazement. "We should have been crushed beneath an avalanche of rock! Where are we?"

"Well, that looks like our horses over there," he said, pointing to a group of animals grazing some distance away. "I'd say we're back at the place where we first entered the Country of the Fair Men."

She began to get up, and he rose with her, supporting her. She was a bit unsteady, shaking her head as if to clear it of a lightheadedness. Around them the others were beginning to stir. Labran sat up, putting hands to head.

"Oh my!" he said giddily. "That was a most astonishing experience."

"Labran!" Cuillen said delightedly. "You're safe as well!"

"And all the rest," Finn added. "Even Conan."

The hounds were awake now, recovering quickly to leap up and rush to their master. He bent down to stroke the great heads affectionately.

"And you've even managed to bring the weapons out," said Cuillen, seeing them on the ground beside Finn. Her face lit with a tremendous grin. In a spontaneous show of enthusiasm, casting aside her normal restraint, she threw her arms about him in a great hug. "Oh, Finn, we've done it! We've won the game. We've actually won!"

Finn was not reluctant to return her hug with an ardor of his own, lifting the slender girl and swinging her about. But their moment of mutual enjoyment was interrupted by the gruff voice of the awakening Conan.

"By the Bloody Raven," he bellowed, sitting up and staring at them. "What's happened? Where are we? And have you two gone mad?"

"Of course not!" Finn said with a laugh, setting down a now flushed and breathless Cuillen. "We've won the weapons and escaped the king, my comrade. I'm glad to see you. We thought you were dead."

"I think I may have been," the stout warrior growled, shaking his head groggily. "I'm not certain what happened to me. Not even whole nights of drinking ale have left me feeling so bad as this!"

"But what has happened?" Cuillen asked. "How did we get here?" She looked at Finn more closely, then at herself. "And look, there's not even a sign of the hardships we've come through."

Finn looked down at himself. She was right. His clothing, which had been reduced to little more than tatters, was clean and intact once again. He pulled out the neck of his tunic and peered down at his bare chest. There was no sign of the ragged tears made by the raven's claws. He looked at the others and found their condition as unmarked.

"It's as if none of those things ever happened to us," he said.

"I . . . I'm not really certain that they did," said Labran. "Maybe the entire Country of the Fair Men was a land of fancy. A dream. Spun by magic within the king's own mind. When he died, it all died with him, crumbled away with him."

"The only important thing is that we've managed to escape from it alive and bring the weapons with us," Finn said. "Now we can't let anything more be delaying us. The king said there was little time left for our clansmen. We've got to start for the White Strand at once!"

Labran and Conan got to their feet, and the reunited band started toward the horses. Conan, who seemed now to have fully recovered his wits, had recovered his blustering manner as well.

"It looks as if we showed that king of yours after all," he crowed to Labran as he swaggered along. "We proved that even the great de Danaans can't stop men of the Fianna."

"Well, it's good to see that your experience hasn't made a humbler man of you," Finn said, exchanging a wry smile with Cuillen.

The horses had been tethered at the edge of a little copse of trees. They seemed none the worse for the time they had been left there.

"Now we've only got to ride back and see to Daire Donn," Conan boisterously went on as they neared the animals. "Once Finn's done for that one, the Fianna'll have no trouble casting the rest of his foul lot into the sea." He gave a triumphant laugh. "Ha! Why, the battle's nearly won now!"

From the shelter of a tree close beside the tethered horses, the figure of the chieftain named Caisel stepped suddenly into the open. With no hesitation the man raised the round shield, pointing its blue stone straight at Finn. A beam of the destructive light shot out toward the young chieftain.

Finn had no time to duck from the beam's path. All he could do was to throw the curved oval of the great Storm Shield before his body. The stream of light struck it squarely, crashing against its black surface like a water jet, bursting into strands that curled out around the edges of the shield and then dissipated, flickering out with a sharp crackling of expended energy.

The rest of Caisel's band of mailed warriors now rushed out from the trees to surround Finn and his comrades. Conan, Cuillen, and the hounds went on guard, preparing for a fight. Finn himself, unharmed by Caisel's beam, started toward the enemy chieftain, lifting the Son of the Waves to strike.

Though dismayed by his failure to incinerate the young Fian leader, Caisel did not lose his head. Quickly he turned the blue stone of his shield toward Cuillen, calling to Finn:

"Stop there, MacCumhal, or I will destroy your friends, beginning with this girl."

Finn stopped, his eyes flicking from Caisel to the girl and back.

"So, the weapons are as powerful as I was told," Caisel said. Greed flared in his small, dark eyes. "They will give their owner great power indeed. Great power."

"Harm her and I will kill you," Finn told him with great ferocity. "That I promise."

"I believe you," Caisel said. "But it would not save this one." He smiled cunningly. "Only your surrender can do that, my Finn MacCumhal. Give those weapons to me, and I promise that I will let you all go unharmed."

"Don't believe him, Finn," pleaded Cuillen. "He will kill us anyway. He likes to kill."

Finn met her anguished gaze. He hesitated. Then he shook his head.

"I can't do it," he told her. "I can't just let you die."

"You're a fool!" she shouted at him. "My father sacrificed himself to save me. I won't let you do the same!"

She charged forward, spear up to strike at Caisel. But two of his warriors darted in from either side and seized her arms, jerking her back. She struggled, but the burly warriors held her firmly.

"Now, MacCumhal, decide quickly!" Caisel warned, holding his power shield out toward the girl. "Will you give me the weapons?"

"I will," Finn said tightly.

A grin of victory curled the skinny lips of his foe.

"Good. Then bring them here. Strap them upon your horse. Carefully, now. Any sign of a trick and she will burn."

Finn walked slowly to his horse. With cautious moves he fastened the massive shield and the sword on the animal's back. Then he stepped away.

"You have my weapons," Finn said. "Now release us as you promised."

Caisel gave a short, harsh laugh at that. He moved the shield, bringing the glowing stone of it around to point at Finn.

"You should have listened to the girl, MacCumhal," he said, gloatingly, his eyes glinting with a light of anticipation. "She knows that there's none of your warrior's sense of honor in me! You will die now. And slowly, MacCumhal. Slowly."

His hand tightened upon the triggering mechanism. The blue-white stone flared brightly. Finn braced himself for the impact of the beam.

From a tree whose branches arched out over Caisel, a figure suddenly dropped. It slammed down with both feet directly onto the shoulders of Caisel, driving the man forward.

The shield angled down, its beam of energy slanting into the open meadow some distance away, exploding there and sending up a geyser of burning sod. Caisel thudded hard against the ground, the weight of his attacker atop him, and lay stunned. The attacker leapt from him, brandishing sword and shield, and flashed Finn a broad smile before charging to engage three of the mailed warriors.

"Caoilte!" Finn cried joyously at the sight of the familiar swarthy face. Then he quickly regained his battle senses, leaping upon one of the warriors holding Cuillen.

Caisel's men had been startled into temporary immobility by Caoilte's unexpected attack. This gave the unarmed Fian leader a chance to seize his foeman's sword and wrestle the man down. Freed of his clutch, Cuillen spun swiftly, parried a cut by the second man, and rammed her spearpoint home in his throat.

She turned to Finn, but he needed no help. He had already twisted the sword from his opponent's hand, and a short, accurate thrust of it ended that struggle. Then both moved to help their embattled friends.

Caoilte, Conan, and the two hounds were not doing badly as it was. The big warrior was whaling away with great gusto, smashing the enemy from his way as if he were cutting kindling. Caoilte was also fighting most enthusiastically, glowing with the battle-light, clearly releasing the fighting spirit that had been pent up so long. With the savage assistance of Bran and Sceolan, they were tearing apart the war band of Caisel.

That individual had by now recovered his wind and lifted his face from the earth to see his men being decimated by Finn's party. Typically for the shrewd but spineless ferret, he made no move to endanger himself by coming to the aid of his warriors. Looking around, his gaze fell upon Finn's horse, standing peacefully just over him, the coveted weapons still upon its back.

In the confusion of the melee, no one was paying any mind to him. He seized his opportunity at once. Taking up his shield, he crawled around behind the mount. Using its body to shelter him, he pulled himself into its saddle. Then, with a yell and a hard jab of his heels, he urged the horse away.

"Look!" cried Labran, pointing after him. "He's escaping with the weapons!"

Finn was the quickest to react. Swiftly dispatching his present opponent with a single, fierce blow, he ran to the horses, leaping upon the back of one, slashing its tether with his sword and spurring it off in Caisel's wake.

Once more abandoned by their treacherous leader, the few survivors of Caisel's band now gave up the losing fight and made their own retreat. Left suddenly alone, Finn's comrades looked after the departing young captain.

"Finn can't stop him that way," said Conan. "The man'll burn him with that magic shield if he comes too close."

"Well, he surely can't do anything without help!" Cuillen said. She ran to the horses, untethered her own, and climbed aboard, urging it away. Bran and Sceolan went too, trotting along on either side.

"I'll get my horse," Caoilte said, starting off at a run. "It's hidden beyond the trees."

"I'll take this spavined wreck, if it'll carry me," growled, Conan, heading for Labran's strange-looking mount.

"But that's my horse!" protested the de Danaan. "I want to go, as well!"

"You stay here," Conan said brusquely, pushing him back. "You'd be of no help anyay."

With that, the stout warrior heaved himself up into the saddle. The wretched nag, for all its apparent scrawniness, bore the great weight without sign of strain and took off at once under Conan's urging, quickly speeding to a gallop.

A crestfallen Labran watched him depart. Then he dropped to his knees, raising his hands in supplication. His voice was filled with pleading:

"Please, good Danu, don't deny me now. Please, let me help them this time. Just this time!"

As he finished, a shimmering aura of silver light appeared about Labran, and within this bright cocoon the hazy shadow of the de Danaan's slender form began to change.

Meanwhile, Finn was closing the gap between himself and the fleeing Caisel. Donn's henchman was having a difficult time with the unfamiliar mount, and it seemed reluctant to run. The man looked back to see his enemy drawing nearer. He twisted his body around in the saddle, bringing his power shield to bear, and fired the beam.

Finn saw him point the shield and tugged the reins, turning the horse sharply off its original course as the jet of energy flashed by to explode against the base of a tree in a ball of white fire. Then, doggedly, Finn resumed his course again, pushing the horse to make up the distance lost.

He was forced to zigzag constantly now as he tried to close with Caisel. Every time he drew within firing range of the man's strange weapon, it was fired. Most of the shots, made by a desperate man atop a running horse, went wide. But one sizzled by just above Finn, forcing him to duck forward. And another exploded against the ground just before the horse's front hooves.

This last shot, though a miss, caused the animal to shy. It neighed in fear and twisted to one side, nearly throwing Finn off. Clearly, if Finn continued trying to close, it was sure that he would eventually be hit.

Still, the stubborn warrior reined his horse into control and set off once again. This time Caisel watched him come, the shield ready, hand on the trigger, apparently planning to wait until he was near enough to make the next shot a certain one.

Then something whooshed close over the man's head, talons ripping a bloody gash across his nearly bald dome.

He winced in pain and cast his gaze upward to see a sleek, golden hawk soaring away, voicing what sounded like a triumphant cry.

It lifted upward on its widespread wings, then wheeled gracefully and swooped back to strike again. This time Caisel dodged aside as the bird screamed past. As it lifted, he brought his shield up and fired the ray of energy. The shot blazed past a wingtip closely enough to singe its feathers. But this did nothing to discourage the hawk. It turned at once, boldly diving in again at the Lochlanner.

Caisel tried to aim his shield, but wasn't quick enough. The hawk struck at him, its powerful beak darting in and tearing off the top of his ear as it sailed past.

His face streaming with his blood now, Caisel seemed to go mad from pain and frustration. He threw up the shield and triggered off burst after burst of energy, teeth bared in a snarl of animal rage. The hawk swooped agilely back and forth, avoiding the beams, but staying close enough to keep drawing Caisel's fire.

With Caisel's attention on the diving bird, Finn saw his own chance. He charged straight in, hoping to reach his enemy before he was noticed.

But as he drew near, Caisel took note of him. The man swiveled, bringing the blue stone down and around to point at him. At this move, the hawk swiftly acted, streaking down to strike directly at Caisel's back, sinking its talons deep into his long neck, batting at his head with its wings.

This Caisel was unable to endure. He swung back, sweeping the shield up, trying to swat the hawk off with his free hand. It released him, flapping away. But this time it had taken too great a risk. As it fought to gain height and distance, Caisel brought his shield to bear, triggering the power. The ray caught the hawk fully on one wing. The bird was enveloped by a burst of intense light. The wing afire, it spun helplessly, tumbling from the sky, crashing to the earth.

But its sacrifice had allowed Finn to close the final distance. Before Caisel could turn again to fire, he leapt from his moving horse upon his enemy.

His momentum carried them both off of Caisel's horse, and they thudded heavily to the ground. Caisel kicked Finn savagely away and rolled to his feet, bringing up the shield. Finn threw himself sideways as the beam shot out, missing him, bursting against the sod.

Caisel's horse reared, neighing in terror. Finn jumped for the plunging mount. Casting away the sword he held, he grasped the Storm Shield and the Son of the Waves, yanking them free. Desperately Caisel fired again. Finn caught the ray upon his great shield and the force of the beam was shattered, flaring away.

Finn charged at Caisel, lifting the massive, black-iron sword. Once more Caisel fired. The bolt of energy crashed against the Storm Shield like a sea wave against a marble cliff, bursting into a harmless spray of sparks. Finn brought his sword down in a hard stroke upon the edge of his foe's round shield. The blade sliced into the metal as if it were thin silver plate, cleaving it from the rim to the sapphire jewel glowing at its center.

The jewel blew apart, releasing all its energy at once. Tendrils of the blue-white lightning curled back, crawling across Caisel's body, ensnaring, wrapping, enveloping him with the terrible, searing energy. The horrified man opened his mouth to scream, but there was no sound save for the sizzling of his fiery shroud. He froze that way, jaw hanging, eyes wide, as his flesh withered and his body shriveled, crumpling down. The enormous power of the shield gave a final crackle and faded, extinguished forever. It left a formless lump of smoldering flesh that had been the right hand to Daire Donn.

Finn was still staring at these remains with an expression of fascination and revulsion when his comrades reached him.

"That was incredible, Finn," said Caoilte, grimacing as he looked at the smoking mound.

"But what happened to Labran?" Cuillen asked him anxiously.

"Labran!" Finn said, his face now mirroring her concern. "He was the hawk, then? He was struck by the beam. He fell just over there!"

He led the way across the field to where the bird had landed. But it was not the stricken hawk they found. It was the form of the frail de Danaan. He lay still in the grass, alive but breathing shallowly. One shoulder and his chest were badly damaged by the strange burning of the ray. And the withering effect had already spread to the area of his heart.

Cuillen knelt by him. The others gathered around, looking down, expressions grim. Labran stirred and opened his eyes, gazing up toward them. With an obvious effort he managed to speak:

"You're all unhurt," he gasped out. "And the weapons?"

"They're here, Labran," said Finn, holding them up. "You saved them."

"That you did, man," said Conan earnestly, bending down. "And you saved all Ireland, as well. The bards'll be singing of your courage through all the years for that, if I've got to see it done myself." He hesitated, looking truly abashed for the first time. "I owe you as much for all my hardness with you."

"Thank you for that," Labran said, giving that familiar, self-effacing smile, "but it's enough just to have been of some use, just one time. Now—" He stopped, wincing with pain, and then went on. "Now . . . maybe . . . even Father will be proud."

His slender body suddenly went limp, the eyes falling closed, a final breath fluttering from his lips.

"We're all proud, Labran," Cuillen said gently, leaning forward to lay a parting kiss upon the wide, pale brow.

Suddenly a strange wailing sound rose around them. A wind from nowhere swirled about them, ruffling the treetops and the grass, pulling at their cloaks. The keening sound grew louder, clearer; not the sound of wind, but of thousands of voices blending.

"It must be the Others," Cuillen said, looking around her. "They are mourning the death of one of their children."

"No," said Finn, gazing toward the treetops being tortured by the angry wind. "I think it's more than that. It sounds like a hosting of the Sidhe!"

CHAPTER TWENTY-EIGHT

THE HELP OF THE MEN OF DEA

At the White Strand, little notice was at first paid to the increasing roar that sounded like the rising of a great inland wind. Everyone there was far too involved with more pressing concerns.

The warriors of the Fianna were fighting a valiant but clearly final battle to hold back the rising flood of Donn's army. Already the wall atop the embankment had been breached in several places. The druid-created companies of phantoms had been dissipated like fog before a breeze by the first assault, just as Tadg had promised. Now Donn's men could no longer doubt that he had spoken the truth: the Irishmen's line was worn to a breaking point. And now the invaders were fighting with an enthusiasm that only the scent of imminent victory could inspire.

Beyond the wall, Goll MacMorna worked coolly, skillfully, and rapidly to repair the holes or bolster up weak points. But he was only serving to delay for just a bit longer what all had to know must be coming soon.

"We are going to die here, aren't we, Goll?" Cael asked the chieftain.

The two were, at the moment, fighting together atop the wall, alone holding a wide break against Donn's men, like a plug in a dike holding back the entire sea.

The chieftain turned the gaze of his single, glittering eye on the young warrior for an instant. Then, in a tone still quite matter-of-fact, he answered:

"We may well die here today, lad. But are there any better ways for a Fian man to find his end?"

These words seemed to act like an invigorating draught upon Cael. He pulled himself a little straighter, put on an expression of fierce determination, and struck out with all the greater power, using shield, sword, body, even legs, to knock attackers back out of the breach.

Here the Fianna held the wall. Elsewhere that struggle had been lost. At one point mailed warriors were now pouring through a collapsed section, the tide of them flowing over, drowning the few Fianna men still trying to drive them back.

There, atop the wall, stood Daire Donn himself, his giant mailed form agleam. He looked down at his warriors flooding through the breach, spreading to left and right, preparing to inundate the whole Fianna line. His dark eyes glittered with triumph.

"Leave none of them alive!" he exhorted in a thundering voice. "Destroy the Fianna utterly! Utterly! Then Ireland is ours!"

A booming sound came suddenly from the east, rolling down from the mountains of Corca Dhuibhne toward the sea. The sound brought with it a sharp gust of wind that blasted across the fighting men atop the embankment, raised a cloud of sand from the beach below, and shivered the surface of the water in the bay.

A strange silence fell upon the battle scene as Irishmen and invaders alike turned their startled gazes to the hills above, seeking the source of this phenomenon. And in the stillness, all now became aware of another sound: a deep, continuous, roaring sound that grew swiftly louder.

Then, over the crest above, the creator of this roar came into view. A single mass it seemed at first, but its nature resolved as it spread down the slope toward the White Strand. It was a vast army of men—tall, lean-bodied men clad in bright tunics and richly embroidered cloaks, carrying green-painted shields and slender spears and swords whose metal glinted like polished silver.

"Who are they?" asked Cael, staring up to them. "Are they enemies or men of Ireland? I have never seen their like."

"Neither have I," said Goll, "but I have long heard their like described." He turned to face the young warrior, his usually stolid face showing true astonishment for the first time. "They are of Ireland. Not of those who live upon its face, but of those who live in hidden places beneath its sod. Cael, they are the Tuatha de Danaan!"

Elsewhere upon the wall, Daire Donn was expressing a certain astonishment of his own.

"What is this force?" he cried. "Are these more Fianna men?"

"They are a great host," a nearby captain said in awe.

"They are not real," Donn said emphatically. "It is another trick! Another phantom army!" He wheeled toward his captain. "We will not yield. Pass the word to stand fast. This 'army' will likely vanish into the air before it reaches us!"

He was wrong.

The host of elegant warriors—golden hair streaming, bright weapons flashing, beautiful faces glowing with battle-light—swept through the ranks of the astounded Fian men and struck against the force of Daire Donn. And it was not as a gentle puff of summer breeze that they struck, but as a hammer of iron. The slender, fine-featured beings with the graceful weapons were savage in their attack. They tore into the foremost lines of Donn's men, sending them reeling back.

"What are they?" said another of Donn's officers. "They seem as wraiths and fight as wolves."

"It makes no difference," Donn said in a rage. "We hold the wall now. We'll not surrender it!"

"Too late, my king," the officer told him unhappily. "Our men are already falling back."

'Falling back' was a most charitable way to put it. The forces of Donn were now in headlong flight, white-faced and terror-stricken, scrambling from the wall, tumbling down the rocky embankment in a reckless desire to escape.

Finding himself suddenly almost alone upon the wall, facing a host of strange but ferocious warriors, even Donn was at last forced to make a somewhat-undignified retreat, scrambling down the slope to the beach.

But once there, he looked back up toward the Fian wall, his eyes narrowing in surprise.

"They aren't following!" he cried, grabbing the officer beside him and turning him back. "Look there! Why aren't they following?"

"It makes no difference," the man said in terror. "They have beaten us!"

"Coward!" barked Donn, smashing the man to the ground with a blow of his massive, gauntleted fist. "We are not beaten until they come down to the strand to finish us." He turned his burning gaze back up to where the slender warriors now lined the battlements. "There is something strange in all this. Very strange. And I will not let it force me to quit this fight."

Finn and his companions rode through the gate and into the yard of Mogh Nuadat's fortress. They looked about them in some dismay at the vast numbers of wounded crowding the enclosed space.

"The stink of death is strong in this place," Conan growled.

No one was aware of their arrival at first. The wounded were preoccupied with their pain, the healers and attendants busy at their tasks. Finn's company dismounted at the stables and started across the yard with no notice being taken.

But then Cael, who stood near the tower in intimate conversation with his young wife, glanced around and saw them. He stared for a moment as if doubting his own eyes, but this was quickly replaced by a widening grin.

"It's Finn," he said. He swept Credhe up and gave her a most enthusiastic hug. "It is Finn!" he said more emphatically. He lifted his voice to call out to all the yard: "Finn's come back! Finn's here!"

Others saw and quickly took up the joyous shout. Soon the yard echoed with the rising cheer. Even the wounded men, seemingly revitalized by the return of their captain, took part. Many ignored their pains to climb to their feet and join the crowd gathering about Finn and his band.

In moments Mogh Nuadat and his wife appeared at the tower's door to investigate the noise. On seeing Finn, they moved toward him at once, followed out by Goll MacMorna and the other Fian leaders.

The crowd made a passage for them, and Finn was quickly in his mother's welcoming arms.

"My son," she said with tears of happiness, hugging him tightly, "I never doubted that you would return." She looked around at the others. "I am glad to see you all safe," she told them, and smiled warmly upon Cuillen, "—especially you, my dear."

"We . . . we're not all safe, Mother," Finn said with a certain awkwardness. "Your brother . . ."

"It is all right, my son," she said, a shadow of pain crossing her face. "I know Labran is dead. I have done my mourning for him. His death gave meaning to his life."

"You know?" said Finn in bewilderment. "But how could you?"

"Come into the tower," she said. "Many things have happened. It will be easier to explain them there."

She and Mogh ushered the little band toward the tower. Goll MacMorna, who with his usual restraint had stood by through this greeting, now fell in beside Finn.

"So, you did succeed," he remarked flatly, eyeing the shield and sword that Finn bore. "Well, it's good to see you alive, my captain." He cast a brief look at his brother, adding tersely: "And you, too, Conan."

"Don't be overwhelming us with your show of joy, Brother," the stout warrior grumbled. "We've only defeated some of the most terrible forces in all Ireland to fetch these weapons here."

"That was your duty," Goll told him sternly, "as it was ours to hold the White Strand."

"It's a bloody, terrible time you must have had in doing that!" said Finn, looking around at the many wounded. "And it was a great amazement to us that you had succeeded. We expected to run upon the army of Daire Donn all the way back here. How did you do it? We were told some days ago that you were finished then!"

"We nearly were," Goll told him honestly. "It wasn't by our fighting skills alone that we've kept Donn on the strand. We've had some help."

"Help?" repeated Cuillen, having overheard this. "What, from the high king?"

"No, young woman," Goll answered coldly. "Never from that man. But I'll let you see its nature for yourself."

They had reached the tower now. Goll and the others stepped aside to allow Finn and his comrades to enter first. As they passed through the doorway into the main hall, they stopped, looking ahead in some wonderment.

There, at the ring of tables about the central fire, stood a score of men who were not of the Fianna. They were men of slender form and noble bearing, tall men with delicately handsome features, fair and flowing hair, glowing white skin, and glittering, nearly silver eyes. Their garb was rich beyond the dreams of even the high king himself. Their tunics were silk, embroidered about hem and neck in complex, interlaced designs of silver and gold thread. Their jewelry was of softly glowing beaten gold set with glinting stones. Their cloaks were of fine wool, dyed in brilliant shades, brocaded and fringed with gold.

One among them, whose elaborate torc of twisted gold strands marked him as of high rank, lifted a hand in greeting. His voice was soft, but clear and precise:

"We welcome you, Finn MacCumhal. It is our honor to meet one of whom we have heard so much."

"And who are you, welcoming me into my mother's house as if it were your own?"

"You are a man of pride, Finn MacCumhal," the other said with a smile. "It is the blood of Muirne speaking in you. I am called Bobd Derg."

"Bobd Derg?" Finn echoed, clearly stunned. "You are the high king of the Sidhe of all Ireland?"

"I am," the man answered simply. "Now, you and your companions, sit with us. Your way has been long and difficult, and you must be wishing a good meal." He gestured over the tables which were set for a feast, laden with steaming food and pitchers of drink. "As you see, we were expecting you."

Finn exchanged glances of amazement with his friends as they moved to take places at the tables. At Bobd Derg's direction, he and the others of this band sat opposite the chieftains of the Sidhe. The two hounds took places at either side of their master. The rest of the Fianna people filled in the remaining places at the ring of tables.

"Tell me now what has happened," Finn demanded. "What are you doing here?"

"We have come, with a host of the Tuatha de Danaan, to hold the White Strand until your return. It is our own warriors who now man your defensive wall."

Finn looked toward Goll.

"It is true, my captain," he confirmed. "They came three days ago, driving Donn's army back when it had nearly broken through. Without their help, we all should almost certainly be dead now."

"But, why?" Finn asked the de Danaan king. "We were told that you would never help us; that many of you would welcome our destruction."

"*Welcome* is a harsh word," Bobd Derg said with a little smile. "To say we were indifferent would be more fair. But, that has changed."

"And what changed it?" asked Finn.

"Several things," was the careful, reasoning reply. "Your own courage was one of them. You won the Son of the Waves and the Storm Shield despite the effort of our king to stop you. No man of the de Danaans has ever been able to do that. Clearly, it was meant for you to have them. It was meant that you stop this threat of Fomor resurgence, for us as well as for your mortals. Then, there was the death of Labran. We know now that the treachery of your own grandfather, Tadg, was in part responsible. He will suffer a punishment for it that his own hatred has helped to make. From this time, he will live forever trapped in his dismal cave, totally powerless and completely alone.

"But his son's death at the hands of Donn's cruel warriors convinced many of my people that we must wreak our own vengeance upon this invader. The Fomor, after all, are a far greater and far more ancient enemy than your people.

"So, following his death, it was decided that we would give help to you. Not to win your war for you, understand. We would never become so involved in interfering with the affairs of mortal men. No, our intent was only to redress the balance. So we stopped your battle, as a parent might step between two quarreling children. We kept Donn's army upon the strand until you could return with the sword and shield. Now you may face each other on equal terms, as it should be, and our part is ended. Tonight will be our last upon the wall. Tomorrow we will have vanished like fall leaves whisked off by a gust of winter wind."

"No!" Muirne put in sharply, drawing the surprised gaze of everyone to hear. "Your task cannot be ended yet, Bobd Derg. Not if you really mean to see things fairly done."

"Not ended?" the high king said with indignation in his tone. "Remember, Lady, that all we have done here has been from charity. We were in no way bound to help the men of Ireland out of this strait. Yet we have hosted. We have gathered from Bri Leith and Magh Suil, from the Sionnan and the Boinn, to fight at the White Strand."

"It is still not enough," she told him bluntly, clearly not the least bit awed by the imposing nature of the de Danaan leader. "You said you wished to redress the balance. That has not been done. Finn's return was delayed too long. The Fianna are very weak. The weapons alone are not enough to save them now."

Finn, somewhat taken aback by the ominous import of these words, turned to Goll MacMorna.

"Is that true?" he asked. "How weak have we become?"

"Since the last fight, we have only a single catha of men left to us," the chieftain answered frankly.

"Three thousand men," Finn said grimly. "And Daire Donn?"

"He has perhaps ten times that number of warriors left to him. And even with the coming of the Sidhe, he shows no sign of giving up the fight. So long as he leads them, they will never leave the strand. They will wait and watch and probe for a chance to break through. And when the Sidhe leave us, they will come upon us like a wolf pack on a crippled lamb."

Finn turned back to Bobd Derg, his look now very grave.

"If this is so, High King, then my mother is right. The sword and the shield alone will not save Ireland. Even if I manage to kill Donn, there won't be enough of the Fianna left to keep his army from leaving the strand. And their thirst for their own revenge will make their ravaging of our people and our homes all the more savage."

"You must give us more help," Muirne said with force. "I know what you feel about these mortals who wrested the land from you, but you are still of Ireland, and in that you are both one. If you don't do something that will give the Fianna at least a fighting chance against Donn's host, what you have done so far will mean nothing. Bobd Derg, you must help!"

The gaze of the de Danaan leader's luminous eyes rested thoughtfully upon her for a long moment. Then he smiled.

"The spirit of your grandfather, Nuada Silver-Hand, lives in you, I can see," he said graciously. "I regret that you have chosen to leave our world. Your strength and wisdom are still spoken of in the Sids of Ireland. I will respect your words."

He drew himself up proudly, cast his gaze about him at the circle of mortals who watched him expectantly, hopefully. His eyes came to rest on Finn.

"Very well, Son of Cumhal and Muirne. We will give more help to you, but it will be our last. We will make a well of healing for you. Its waters will cure every wound made in battle. After bathing in it you will be as whole and as sound as on the day of your birth. Heal all your wounded, Finn MacCumhal. Then you will have an army to face Daire Donn. Then your battle will be an equal one again."

"We will owe a great debt to you for that, High King," Finn told him gratefully.

"You will owe us nothing," Bobd Derg sternly replied. "Our host will stay upon the wall until your fighting men are all restored. Then we will be gone. Our obligation to you will be ended and we will once more retire from the surface of Ireland to our hidden places. From that time, Finn MacCumhal, the fate of Ireland will rest in your own two hands!"

CHAPTER TWENTY-NINE
PREPARATION

The courtyard of Nuadat's fortress, the scene of much misery not long before, was now bustling with renewed vigor. Attendants moved amongst the wounded, doling out cups of clear and sparkling water from pitchers. The miraculous water seemed to take immediate effect. Color returned to wan checks. Faces wasted by pain grew full again. Men staring and motionless, at the point of death, began to stir and look about in astonishment.

Already some of the less severely hurt were up and moving about. They examined with curiosity the white scars of completely mended wounds. They jigged and capered like boys before comrades to demonstrate their restored heartiness. Many had gone to work honing their weapons and strapping on their gear.

"It's a bloody marvel!" Conan MacMorna pronounced as he looked down from an upper window of the tower on the scene in the yard. "Two days, and they're nearly all healed! By tomorrow every man will be ready to fight again."

He turned about and strode across the room. There, in the private chambers of Mogh Nuadat, Finn and his most valued advisers were gathered to discuss the situation for their coming battle. Finn, Goll, and other of the chiefs were seated about a large table, perusing a chart of the strand and the camp of Donn. Cuillen, Muirne, and Mogh Nuadat were in attendance there as well.

"With all our wounded restored to health, we triple our strength," Finn said. "From your estimates, that will reduce the odds against us to little more than three to one."

"A fair enough difference," Goll said most seriously.

"So long as they don't have Daire Donn to drive them on," Finn corrected. "With his spirit goading them, they are a match for us, or worse. I must challenge him to single combat."

"It won't be easy," pointed out Cael. "He doesn't come into the forefront of battle unless his men need help. And if he knows about your weapons, he may avoid combat with you once he sees you have returned with them."

"Aye. The treacherous monster would send his warriors against us while he kept safe," added the lean, dour warrior called Conn Crither.

"Then, our warriors must face him to enter the battle," Finn said. "And I must not show myself to him until I can confront him and challenge him before his men. Then he will have to fight."

"I hope these weapons will give you a chance against him," Conan said doubtfully, examining the black shield and sword that stood propped against the wall. "They don't seem much." He turned to the others, giving an avaricious smile. "But, you know, if they really are as strong as the de Danaans say, then they would make Finn the most powerful man in Ireland! Why, he could challenge even the high king himself! He could truly make the Fianna the rulers, and pay old Conn for his wrongs to us."

At these words, Cuillen rose from the table, shock and fury drawing her young face taut.

"So!" she stormed, pointing an accusing finger at Finn. "I was right in mistrusting you, Finn MacCumhal. I was right to believe what I had heard about you. You, with your great virtues and your winning way—you had finally convinced me that you meant only to help Ireland. Well, it's the proper fool you've made of me, haven't you? Now I see that you've meant only to use the weapons for your own, selfish ends. You are a traitor to the high king, and I curse the sod you walk upon, for myself and for the spirit of my dead father!"

Finn, staring in dumbfounded silence through this savage speech, now tried to respond.

"Cuillen," he began, "I've never meant—"

But she paid no attention. Overcome by her outrage, she spun on her heel and stalked from the room. Finn turned a baleful gaze upon the stout warrior.

"I thank you, Conan, for that truly ill-considered remark.

Once more you've proven that you can speak without a single thought passing through your head!"

"Maybe you should go after her," suggested Caoilte.

"No," Muirne said quickly. "She'll not listen to you now, my son. Better to let her go until the rage burns out. It's much she's been through, and much she must work out herself."

Meanwhile, Cuillen's angry retreat had carried her down the stairs and out of the tower into the courtyard. Here Art MacConn was seeing to the healing of some of his comrades. He saw Cuillen burst from the doorway and charge blindly across the yard. He moved to cut her off, gripping an arm to stop her.

"Cuillen," he said, "what's wrong?"

She tried to pull away, but he held on firmly, forcing her around toward him. Now he could see that her eyes were brimming with tears.

"Cuillen, it's me, Art MacConn! Tell me, what's wrong?"

She looked at him for the first time, recognizing him, and her pent-up anguish burst from her.

"Oh, Art," she said, "you should know what's happening. It's Finn MacCumhal. He's plotting against your father. He means to use the weapons to gain power for himself. He's betrayed us."

"Cuillen, that's nonsense!" he told her in a surprised tone. "I don't know what's made you say it, but Finn would never do that."

"What?" she said, her look of anger changing to one of disbelief. "How can you say that?" You know the tales of the Fian greed and arrogance. You know what your own father has said of Finn's treachery."

"I know what my father has said out of his own jealousy and weakness and fear," he corrected. "Listen to me, Cuillen. Please. We grew up together in the court of Tara. We've been friends since childhood. Listen to me and believe me now."

"I will listen," she said, but reluctantly.

"Fair enough. I understand what you're feeling. I thought like yourself when I came here. The Fianna were our servants, to be treated with contempt, not to be trusted. But I've learned that all we were taught was lies. I've fought beside the men. I've seen their lives. I've heard them speak of Finn. There are no men in all Ireland so loyal to her. Why, look around you, Cuillen! These men have suffered here. They've fought on with wounds that would have left most unable to move with pain. They have faced odds of more than ten to one. Thousands have died. Do you really think they've made these sacrifices out of greed or arrogance? No! They've made them to save Ireland and to honor their oath to a high king who would rather see them destroyed."

"I won't believe that," she said stubbornly. "It can't be true."

"It's true, Cuillen," he insisted. "Father refused to send any help to the strand. He tried to keep me from coming here. He declared loudly before the assembled nobility of Tara that he hoped the Fianna would be defeated. It is Conn himself who is the traitor to Ireland."

"But the high king could have good reason to mistrust," she countered with a certain desperation. Clearly she was fighting off acceptance of Art's truths. "Finn's told me he has no love for your father. He wishes to gain more respect for the Fianna. He could wish to usurp your father's power."

"My father has done everything he could to keep the Fianna subservient to him," Art replied. "Now that I have heard the Fianna side of things, I've come to realize how treacherous my father has been. He even conspired with Tadg to kill Finn's father and keep Finn from winning his father's place! If Finn were to usurp Conn's throne, it would only be what the old man deserved. But Finn will never do that. He has never done anything that would violate his oath of service. So whatever respect he seeks for the Fianna is owed them, along with all the wealth and honors Ireland can heap upon them. Mark this, Cuillen. If I ever do become high king, things will change. The overfed and pompous lords of Ireland will no longer be treating these brave warriors as their hounds."

"This comes too fast," Cuillen said in a bewildered way. "I . . . I don't know what I should believe."

"Believe your heart and your eyes, Cuillen," Art implored her earnestly. "You have been with Finn. You have watched him, listened to him, battled at his side. Has he given you any reason to mistrust him, or to believe he's not truly a man of honor and loyalty?"

"No," she admitted, looking abashed. "No, he has not."

"I know you, Cuillen," he said more gently, smiling now. "I think it might be that the only thing you dislike about him is that his pride and will are as strong as your own. You can't dominate him, can you? And you hate admitting it to yourself.

Because it seems to me that your real feeling for him is very far from hatred . . ."

"You're not the first who's said those things to me," she told him thoughtfully.

She looked back to the tower, toward the upper window of that chamber where she had left Finn.

"Could they be true?" she said, now to herself. "Could they really be true?"

The yard of the black tower was quiet. The few warriors remaining there were rolled in their cloaks, sleeping beside the banked fires.

Only two figures moved. They seemed to glide through the deep shadows that filled the yard, carefully skirting the fires, climbing the stairs onto the inner wall. Here they strolled together, moving out toward the edge of the cliffs where they stopped, looking out across the sea. The soft, white glow of a near-full summer moon sparkled upon the gently rippling surface. The light also revealed the pale, young faces of the two who stood, arms linked, enraptured by the scene; Cael and Credhe.

Within the fortress' tower, all was quiet as well. Hosts and visitors had long since retired. Within his own room on the upper floor of the tower, Finn slept fitfully, shifting restlessly upon his pallet beside the central fire.

Some small sound brought him suddenly to sit up, fully alert. The warrior's instinct took his hand to the hilt of the Son of the Waves laid by his side. He peered across the glowing embers of the fire toward the doorway. A slender figure stood there, glowing with a soft, silver aura from the moonlight flooding through a window behind it.

"Who is it?" asked Finn.

The figure moved forward, silent on bare feet. It stopped at the hearthside opposite him. Light from the fire's embers revealed its identity.

"Cuillen!" Finn said with some surprise. Clad only in a long white gown, her unbound hair framing her pale face, she looked very young and very fragile.

"I'm sorry to wake you," she said, a certain shyness in her tone that was quite unusual for her. "But I had to talk to you. I . . . I couldn't sleep."

"Neither could I," he admitted, his look of surprise changing to one of curiosity.

She knelt down by the hearth. The ruddy glow of the hot coals tinged her gown, gave a flush to her fair cheeks, caused copper lights to glint in the torrent of her auburn hair. She did not look up at him at first, like an embarrassed child facing a parent. Finn waited, watching her closely, expectantly.

"I had to talk with you tonight," she said at last. "I thought . . . well, after tomorrow . . ."

"I might be dead?" he finished. He grinned, adding in a teasing way, "I see that your confidence in my abilities is as great as ever."

At this she lifted her head sharply, fixing him with a gaze that seemed to smolder from the reflected light. Her voice took on a warning edge:

"Do not be doing that now, Finn MacCumhal. Let's have no more quarreling between us. At least, not this night. Even with that great, foolish arrogance of yours, you can't truly tell me that you're certain to win."

"That I cannot," he admitted. "Even with the gods smiling upon me, they'll not make me more than equal to Donn. Yes, I very well could lose. And may Danu help Ireland if I do."

"Never mind Ireland," she said fiercely. "It's not her I'm thinking of now. It's yourself."

"Is it?" he said with some disbelief. "But why should you be concerned with me now? We've fetched the weapons. Tomorrow we'll be going out to save your high king's land. Unless you still believe I plan some treachery."

"I do not!" she said quickly. Then she hesitated before going awkwardly on. "It's for that reason I've come to you. I didn't want you going to the fight thinking I mistrusted you. I . . . I want to apologize." She shook her head impatiently. "It's just very difficult."

"Likely because you've had little practice," he said dryly.

Instead of growing angry this time, she grew more contrite.

"It may be that I deserve your scorn," she said unhappily. "I've certainly done nothing but deride and doubt you. You've good reason to show no kindness to me now."

She shivered suddenly, pulling her legs up close to her and wrapping her arms about them. She appeared very sad, lonely, and vulnerable. Finn's expression softened.

"It's very chill tonight," he said in a more solicitous way. "There's a sharp breeze off the sea. You're not dressed for it."

He moved around the fire to her side, holding out his covering to her. "Here," he said, "get under this. But we'll have to share it. I'm wearing only a tunic myself."

She made no objection and he wrapped the heavy blanket about both their shoulders, settling in close beside her.

"Now," he said gently, "I'll say nothing else of insult to you. I don't mean to be hurting you with my words. I know what all of this has meant to you and what you had to do. I understand your feelings. I don't hate you at all, you know. I'm grateful that you were with me. I'd not have won the weapons without your help."

"Is that the truth?" she asked him, fixing her glowing brown eyes urgently upon him.

"It is," he said with honesty, squarely meeting her gaze. "No warrior could have done more. Not even Caoilte. Your father would have been very proud, I'm certain."

"Thank you for that," she said gratefully. Then they were quiet, gazing musingly into the radiant red heart of the burned-down fire. For the moment they seemed at peace, content to sit together, each aware of the other's company.

"Tell me," she said at last, "—is it true that you had to win your father's place as leader of the Fianna?"

"It's true," he said. "What do you know of it?"

"Likely all of it. I asked Caoilte to tell me. I know how you had to fight to earn your father's place as captain of all the Fianna. I had never heard the tale before in Tara, as you can guess. I never realized what you had to go through. Now I understand why you said you'd had a task like my own to do. And I know as well that you have good cause to hate the high king. He's done much treachery against you and the Fianna. I'm sorry my own blindness to the truth set me against you."

"Don't think of it," he told her. "It was no fault of yours. You only meant to help Ireland. In that we were never at odds. And you've no need to make apology to me. It's enough for me to know I've helped you do what you had to do."

She lifted her face again to him, her eyes meeting his. She smiled warmly.

"You are truly a man of great virtue, Finn MacCumhal. I thank you for your kindness to me."

She leaned toward him, kissing him upon the lips.

Beneath the covering, his arm slid around her waist, holding her, prolonging the kiss. For a moment it grew more ardent for them both. Her head fell back, her eyes closed, her body yielded to him. Then her eyes shot open and she jerked her head back, breaking off the kiss.

Her look was one of surprise and bewilderment. Her face was suffused with a rosy glow. Her voice came breathlessly.

"No!" she gasped. "We can't do this!"

She jumped to her feet, cast the cover aside, and rushed away from him, stopping by the chamber's window. At first taken aback by her sudden retreat, he stared after her, his own breathing rather accelerated and his own face flushed. Then, in an abashed tone, he spoke:

"I'm sorry. I didn't mean to do that. I . . ." He paused, considering. "No," he went on more positively, "I can't truly say that. I did mean to do it. And I've meant to do it for a long time."

"And do you think I haven't?" she returned with some heat. "I've been running away from what I truly felt since I first met you. I know that now, and yet it still seems wrong to think of it, think of just ourselves, with all that's happening around us." She looked beseechingly to him. "Is it?" she demanded. "Is it wrong?"

Before he could reply, she shook her head angrily, making her hair ripple with red-gold light.

"I just don't know," she said in frustration. "I don't know what to think anymore."

She turned away from him to gaze searchingly out into the night, as if her answer might be found amongst the stars.

"Cuillen, I understand," Finn told her earnestly. "I was a fool for what I did. It wasn't fair to you. The way things have been for us, you can't be certain what your feelings really are. And so long as you still have your duty to Ireland and your father to see through, you can't be free to think about yourself. I know that well enough. Forget what's happened between us until this is finished. After tomorrow—then there will be enough time for us."

Her eye had now been caught by a movement below, and she dropped her gaze from the stars to the top of the outer wall. There the figures of Cael and Credhe stood, locked in a tight embrace.

She stared at them a moment, a look of firm resolution replacing the uncertainty in her face.

"No," she said with a sudden intensity, turning toward him again. "After tomorrow there may be no time for us at all. But we have now, and I'll not let it go."

She crossed the room, dropping down before him.

"We will have at least this one night for ourselves," she told him. "I want that."

"Are you certain?" he said in a cautious way. "It may be a—"

She put a finger up across his lips, silencing him.

"Quiet now, Finn MacCumhal," she said warningly. "Are you still trying to tell me what I should do?"

He smiled, taking her hand gently into his own.

"I've learned better," he said, looking into deep brown eyes that now smoldered with a fire other than anger. "I know when I'm lost."

"Then, no more arguments," she told him. "No more talk."

Her arms lifted to wrap about his neck and pull him to her. His own arms moved out, bringing the cover around to envelop them both.

Kennard C. Tirst

She crossed the room, drawing closer before him.

"You will have at least one of us with us," said Princess of Tirst Hall.

For his certain, perhaps on a good - I was. The king

CHAPTER THIRTY
THE GREAT FIGHT

Daire Donn pushed through the flaps of his pavilion and stopped to fix a challenging gaze upon the boar-faced man who waited there.

"Well?" he asked stormily. "Why are you disturbing my morning meal?"

"They are coming, my high king," said Finnachta of the Teeth, chief man to Donn since Caisel's departure. "The host of the Fianna is coming to the strand!"

"Stewards!" Donn called sharply over his shoulder, "follow me!"

He started forward at a quick stride, Finnachta falling in beside him, while two attendants appeared from the tent to follow. One carried the leader's massive gauntlets and his battle-ax, the other his fearsome, gleaming helmet.

They strode through the camp to its upper edge and stopped there, looking toward the embankment above the strand. From the battered wall atop it, men were pouring down, forming a dark, solid mass across the base of the slope.

Daire Donn eyed them with a look of satisfaction.

"So, they have finally chosen to come from behind their coward's barricade and fight us eye to eye!" he grated. "Good!"

"But they are too strong!" Finnachta said in alarm. "If they come to the strand, they will overwhelm us!"

"Use your eyes, Finnachta," Donn said impatiently. "Where are all those thousands who came upon us above? They have vanished. They were some trick, as I told you they were. The Fianna must have exhausted their magic now."

"You are right," said the chief man, a wide smile revealing

283

the yellow tusks that had clearly earned him his name. "They are barely a third our number now."

"Call the companies to form," Donn commanded. "Quickly now! They will be ready to move upon us in moments!"

Finnachta was off at once, and soon the horns were blaring through the camp, calling the army to assemble.

As warriors scampered to don mail and helmets, seize weapons, and join their companies, their officers hurriedly gathered around Daire Donn.

"This will be our final battle," he told them as he slipped on his gauntlets. "My power is your own. Do not doubt it. So long as the will is with you and your fighting men, we cannot lose. Give no quarter. There will be no retreat this time. We will break these Fianna, who have so long humiliated the Army of the Great World. We will have Ireland today!"

His forceful words seemed to infuse them with vitality. They roared their agreement energetically and then rushed off to take command of their companies.

Donn took his helmet from its attendant and settled it upon his head. He adjusted the sidepieces carefully about his jaws and dropped the grim-visaged mask down before his face. Completely enclosed in the bright armor now, he took us his ax and turned to fix his glittering black gaze upon the gathering Irishmen.

"Soon, my ancestors," he muttered to himself. "Soon!"

The army of Donn was quickly formed up in tight, neat companies above their camp. Facing them, the Fianna warriors had now finished their hosting, as well. The bright colors of their grouped clans made their force look like a patchwork quilt stretched across the sands below the embankment. For a long moment the two armies were still, thousands of men seeming to hold their breaths, staring intently toward their foes, weapons gripped tensely, faces taut in expectation of the coming clash.

Then, from the warriors of the Baiscne clan, Caoilte stepped out before the Fian host. He lifted the huge, gleaming horn called the Dord Fionn to his lips and gave a great blast upon it. At once its sound was echoed all up and down the line, the blaring horns joining in one ringing call to war.

From all the fighting men of Ireland there rose a battle cry and they began to move, spreading out as they surged down across the strand.

In the ranks of Donn's army, other horns replied. The

warriors of the invader started forward together, shimmering like a single coat of polished mail.

The two hosts met at the midpoint of the strand, running together like the tall trees of two thick forests meeting. There rose a terrible din of iron on iron, of weapons cracking through bone, of screaming men. The seabirds, wheeling above the bloody fray, answered the screams with their own shrill cries. Even the waves of the ocean seemed to mimic the sounds of battle as they crashed upon the shore, while the ground shook with the tramping feet of so many men.

Conan MacMorna was at the forefront of the battle, slashing his way into the enemy ranks with a savage power that appeared to astonish even his impassive brother. With his eyebrow raised, Goll called to him above the uproar:

"It's good work you are doing upon our enemies today, Conan. I've never seen such energy in you."

"I have much to be making up for," growled Conan, hacking an attacker from his path with a single, mighty sweep of his sword. "For the Clan na Morna, and for myself as well."

Elsewhere, Daire Donn paced impatiently behind his battle line, watching the surging mass of warriors with a sharply scrutinizing eye. Finnachta appeared from the ranks and approached him, his bristled snout wrinkled in concern.

"What's wrong?" Donn asked angrily. "Why can't we drive them back? Our men are fresh, their weapons new!"

"The Fianna fight as fresh warriors too, my king," the chief man explained, "and with great ferocity as well! They are forcing us back at many points. Our warriors must see you in the fight. It will give them the spirit to crush this tiny force."

"Is there any sign of this young captain of theirs among them?" Donn asked.

"The one called Finn? No, my king. He's not been seen among them."

"Then he cannot have returned," Donn said with a note of triumph in his voice. "Caisel must have succeeded after all. With their brave leader and his weapons lost to them, with their magic gone, these Fian warriors must be truly desperate men."

"Still, they fight stubbornly enough now," Finnachta pointed out. "Will you lead us to the victory yourself?"

"Yes. Yes, I will," Donn said. "It will be my pleasure to see to their final defeat. Show me where their attack is strongest."

Finnachta led the way, and Donn soon strode forward into the battle lines, his great ax swinging in one hand.

On the embankment above the fight, meanwhile, Finn MacCumhal paced back and forth behind the battered defensive wall, swinging the Son of the Waves about him in an irritated way.

As he came below one higher section of the wall, he stopped, looking up toward where a bushy head of flame-red hair was visible.

"Fergus, which way is the battle now?"

The head lifted and turned toward him, revealing the face of Finn's messenger, Fergus True-Lips.

"It's hard thing to tell you," the messenger replied. "The sand grains of the beach itself are no closer together than our armies are now. The bosses of their shields overlap like the links of tight-knit mail. Sparks shoot out from the edges of their swords, and blood rains like a fall shower. Locks of hair— black and brown and fair—cut off by the weapons, are blowing more thickly than the autumn leaves blown from a great forest. It is hart to tell one man from another now, save by the clan colors that flash at times."

"But can't you tell me anything?" Finn demanded. "Can't you see which way the battle is going?"

The messenger turned around to cast a searching gaze across the field of battle.

"We seem to be cutting deeply into them, my captain," Fergus called back to him.

"Who is best in the battle now?" Finn asked.

"It seems to be the clans of Cairell Battle-Striker and Aelchinn of Cruchan," Fergus replied. "They fight side by side and have pushed far into the enemy ranks. The Clan na Morna, on our right flank, is doing well too. Goll and Conan have forced the end of Donn's army to curl back upon itself."

"And what of Caoilte and the Clan na Baiscne?"

"They're pressing hard into the center, my captain. They're herding the invaders before them as if they were a flock of frightened sheep!"

"It's maddening to have to stay here while my warriors fight and die upon the strand," Finn said in frustration. "If I could only see the battle . . ."

"No, my captain! Not yet!" Fergus said quickly, spinning about to look down at Finn with an expression of alarm. "With that silver hair of yours you would be too quickly noticed. You must wait until you are certain Daire Donn himself is in the fight!"

"All right! All right, Fergus!" Finn said sharply. "Just look again and tell me what's happening. Who's first in battle now?"

Fergus looked out again, his gaze scanning the embattled warriors, then fixing on one spot. He stared at it fixedly for a time, and when he finally spoke, his voice was filled with excitement.

"By my oath, Finn, it is no friend of ours who is in it now. It's Daire Donn himself! He's rushing through our warriors like flames across a high hill thick with furze. He's making his way to the clans of Cairell and Aelchinn. Now those two chiefs are giving him challenge."

"No!" Finn cried in vain protest. "It's death to meet him. They know that!"

"Their own pride won't let them do anything else," Fergus replied. "Now they are falling upon the men with Donn. They are forcing them back. But Donn charges toward them. They strike out, but their blades have no effect. He brushes them away as he would brush pestering bees. He swings out with his ax. Ah! Aelchinn is down, split open at the throat. Still, Cairell Battle-Striker moves boldly in. He makes a terrible, great blow upon Donn's helmet. The sword is turned away with a great spray of fire! Donn swings back at Cairell, and his ax strikes our brave chieftain's shoulder, making two halves of him!"

"Tell me no more!" Finn cried in anguish. He took up the black Storm Shield and slipped it upon his arm. "I will hide no longer upon this hill. Now the battle fever is hot in me, and I will face this monster before another Fianna man dies waiting for me!"

With the shield on his left arm and the sword gripped in his right, Finn climbed upon the wall. He paused to glance upward to where the figures of his mother and Cuillen stood watching from the hilltop. Then he left the wall, starting down the embankment to the strand.

With their chieftains dead, the clansmen of Cairell and Aelchinn were now falling back before the advancing Donn. As he saw them retreating, opening up a hole in the Fianna host, the mailed giant turned to bellow orders to his own warriors.

"Charge in now!" he told them. "This is their end! Tear through and divide their forces. Then we will crush each half!"

None of them moved.

"What's wrong with you!" he cried in rage. "The way is clear. Cowards and fools! Move forward!"

But they stayed rooted, staring past Donn toward something beyond. The King of the Great World wheeled around to see.

Across the open space cleared by the Fian warriors stood Finn MacCumhal.

Donn's iron gaze flicked from the young captain's silver hair to the black shield and sword. For an instant the eyes widened in astonishment, and the faintest light of dread glinted there. But then the hot, white flame of his madness returned. He strode toward Finn calling out to him:

"So, Captain of the Fianna, you have managed to return from your quest after all."

"I have, Daire Donn," Finn answered. "The charred carcass of the one you sent to stop me lies on a lonely plain, unburied and unmourned."

"Caisel deserves no mourning if he failed me," Donn said harshly. "And are these the fabled weapons you sought? The Son of the Waves and the Storm Shield of the Sidhe?"

"They are."

Donn stopped only a few paces before his enemy. His words rang out slowly and heavily, like the tolling of a great bell:

"Then they are my own, for they are formed of the armor of my own ancestor, Balor One-Eye, leader of the Fomor!"

"They were won fairly from the Tuatha de Danaan, who destroyed your Balor," Finn replied. "And they are the weapons that will bring you your death."

"Those weapons alone will not defeat me, Finn MacCumhal. It is only great battle skills that can do that. And you haven't the power to best me. Go back now. Escape with your life."

Indeed, the massive figure in the gleaming mail did seem a being of great power, towering nearly a head above the leaner, unarmored form of Finn. But the young captain seemed undismayed by his imposing adversary.

"I have faced monsters greater than yourself before and won," he responded with a like bravado. "For the first time, you will be in an equal fight, Daire Donn. If that frightens you, take your Army of the Great World and leave the White Strand. For the men of Ireland will have no mercy on them once you are dead."

"No!" Donn thundered back. "I will never leave Ireland again. It is mine! Mine! Do you understand that? You took it from me, as you took the armor of Balor. It was stolen from my people and I will have it back. Nothing will stop me from that. All that is left is to sweep you from my way!"

With that, he drove forward suddenly, swinging his enormous battle-ax out in a powerful blow.

It was aimed to take off Finn's unprotected head, but the young warrior was too quick, lifting the Storm Shield. The ax struck upon the upper rim of the black iron oval and there was a loud, sharp clash, like the stroke of lightning. The blade was turned away, leaving no more than a faint nick upon the thick boss.

Finn struck swiftly in return, sweeping out around the shield with the Mac an Luin in a try for Donn's left leg.

The giant jerked back, only the tip of the sword slipping across his outer thigh. But this touch of the miraculous blade was enough to rend the metal links of the mail as if they were knitted wool, tearing a gash in the flesh beneath.

Donn backed away and looked down at his leg in shock. The red blood of his wound shone with a startling brightness against the silver mail.

"Donn is wounded!" came a horrified cry from one of his watching men. And the cry was taken up, passing like a sudden wind through the surrounding mass. "Donn is wounded! Donn is wounded!" It grew more strident, more filled with consternation, as it spread. The evidence of their leader's vulnerability seemed more unmanning than the attack of an overwhelming host.

Donn heard the voices of dismay, and they seemed to galvanize him. He roared in anger, charging upon Finn, delivering a swift series of hard blows. Clearly, he knew he now needed to destroy his opponent, and quickly, to restore his aura of invincibility.

Finn used sword and shield to parry the blows. He succeeded, but only in part. One blow slipped by his shoulder, laying it open. A second tore the skin from his right hip.

He countered, and the battle was on in earnest, the two men striking at one another with great force, the black shield booming and crashing when the ax of Donn struck it, raising a din like that of a fierce storm from the sea.

The fight took them down the strand, the warriors of both hosts parting before them. They passed below the lines of battle and fought their way along the avenues of Donn's camp, wreaking great havoc with blows of their weapons and their bodies as they heaved back and forth, often wrestling together like two stags who have locked antlers in a last death struggle.

Finally through the camp, they now took their conflict off the strand, into the surf. Here, knee-deep in the incoming waves, around and between a line of small boats, they battled on, churing the water to a white froth.

Both men were badly bloodied now from numerous small wounds. Finn's clothing hung in tatters; his white tunic and his pale arms and legs seemed striped with red. And Donn's armor seemed now more crimson than silver, with blood running from the many cuts in the gleaming links.

Both men were clearly wearying, their moves coming more slowly, their weapons swung with greater effort. Still they fought with no less savagery, giving and taking massive blows any one of which would have finished an ordinary man.

Finally Finn managed to strike one clean, straight blow to the top of Donn's helmet. The strange metal of the blade clove right through the gold serpent that served as a crest, cutting into the metal of the cap itself.

There was a flash of brilliant light at the point of contact. Power crackled along the black metal of the Mac an Luin and Finn jumped back as if stung. The helmet was sliced open, but it was still not enough. The black scalp of Donn, exposed in the open slit, was unmarked.

Both men stood apart, eyeing one another warily, catching their breaths in a moment of unspoken truce.

"You've been hurt, Donn," Finn said. "Your magic armor can't help you anymore. Your men have seen it. You've lost your hold on them already. Look!"

Donn cast a quick glance toward the shore. His army had indeed fallen apart. The companies had dissolved, ranks had fragmented, and a confused melee had now ensued. Many of Donn's warriors had abandoned the fight to run for the boats and the safety of the sea. Others fought desperately to hold back the Fianna, who now ripped through them.

"You've lost, Donn," Finn told him. "I don't need to kill you now. Give it up. Surrender and end the slaughter of your men. Take them, and leave the White Strand with your life."

"I will not bow to you, MacCumhal," Donn spat out, fixing Finn with a gaze that blazed now with his madness. "There is only one way for this to end. You've taken my dream.

For the spirits of my ancestors, I curse you. With my last power, I will see you dead."

He leaped suddenly toward Finn, using his broad shoulder as a ram against Finn's shield, slamming the warrior back. Finn had not noticed the small boat floating just behind him in the surf. Donn had. His move caused Finn to stagger against it, the backs of his calves striking the boat's bulwarks. He lost his balance and toppled back, crashing down into the hollow of the craft.

Donn splashed forward, sweeping up the ax in both hands and striking down. Finn rolled sideways, out from under the blow. It tore through the boat, crushing through the stout wood as if it were dry twigs, breaking the craft nearly in two. As Donn recovered and yanked his weapon free of the wreckage, Finn managed to lever himself up and dive out into the water. Donn aimed a sideways sweep at him as he moved. The edge of the wide blade caught Finn's side, slashing deeply into him. Badly wounded this time, Finn grunted with pain as he crashed down into the shallow water.

Donn lifted the ax again. Finn struggled to his knees. The water was up to his waist, the shield and sword both submerged. He shook his head to clear the water from his eyes, and looked up.

The giant figure of Donn loomed above him, aglow in the sunlight. The ax had already begun its downward swing toward the young captain's unprotected head.

CHAPTER THIRTY-ONE

HEROES

Finn desperately jerked the Storm Shield upward. It exploded from the water in a burst of spray, slanting up to stand vertically as Finn ducked down below the level of its rim.

The ax came down, falling upon the shield's upper edge with a great clang, stopped by the wonderful metal. Finn struck out around the side of the shield then, slashing at the closest vulnerable point: Donn's leg.

The sword struck home across the lower calf, just above the ankle. The magically honed black blade, backed by Finn's full power, sliced through the links of mail easily and cut on through flesh and bone, all but severing Donn's foot.

Donn screamed in agony and toppled like a felled tree, smashing down into the surf. The blood pulsing from his severed artery welled up, turning the white foam to rose.

Finn, his own lifeblood gushing from the deep wound in his side, managed with an effort to push himself up, using the Storm Shield as a cane. Donn pulled himself into a crouch, head thrust forward. Dropping the ax, he grasped the wounded leg with both gauntleted hands in an effort to stop the flow of blood.

Finn moved forward to stand over him. He let the Storm Shield fall and lifted the Mac an Luin in both hands.

Donn looked up to him. He met Finn's gaze squarely, defiantly.

"May Ireland destroy your people as it has my own, MacCumhal," he snarled.

With all his strength, Finn brought down the sword. The well-aimed blow caught the giant at the base of his helmet. It sliced through the flared skirt of metal protecting his neck, the keen edge of the weapon cleanly severing Donn's head.

It dropped into the waves. The mailed body jerked, then collapsed sideways and lay still.

Finn took up the black shield again and started away, heading for the shore. But his wound had clearly weakened him too much. He stumbled, dragging his feet through the clutching surf. He staggered, and dropped heavily to his knees again.

Before him, all was chaos. The Fianna were taking a ruthless revenge upon their cruel invaders. Men fought amidst the tents and stalls. But most of Donn's remaining warriors were running, scrambling for the boats, struggling for space, desperately trying to push them off from the shore. Scores of them were already pulling out, making for the larger dragon ships anchored in the bay.

Finn's comrades were fully caught up in the confusion of the fight. Goll was trying to regroup the clans and restore some order, while Conan, ignoring him, was working out his own revenge on his foes with a savage satisfaction. Even Caoilte, heavily engaged, was unable to free himself to come to Finn's aid this time.

But Cael, fighting nearby, was able to get clear of the tangle and rush to help the Fian leader. He tried to get Finn to his feet, but the captain was unable to rise. Cael was forced to drag Finn from the surf and up onto the shore, where he propped him gently against an upturned boat.

"Finn, how badly are you hurt?" Cael asked anxiously, for his captain seemed shockingly weak, his face pale.

"I . . . I don't know," said Finn. "I can't seem to move my legs!"

"I'll fetch you help," Cael earnestly promised.

Finn looked closely at the eager, boyish face. It was streaked with blood from a deep scalp wound. Cael's body, too, showed the marks of many wounds.

"Cael, you're badly hurt yourself!" said Finn. "You've done enough. See to your own wounds and just let me rest here. It's over now. It's all over."

He seemed about to drift into unconsciousness, but his eyes fell upon the body of Daire Donn and opened wider in shock. He lifted himself up on his arms to stare more intently.

Finnachta of the Teeth and two mailed warriors, unnoticed in the confusion, had pulled a small boat up beside

their fallen king. As Finn watched, they lifted the huge body
with an effort and wrestled it into the craft.

"Look!" Finn said. "They're taking Donn's body. I have to
stop them . . ."

He tried to rise but failed, falling back.

"You can't do it, Finn," said Cael. "You've no more
strength."

Finnachta had now found the helmeted head of Donn
and, in a somewhat-cavalier gesture, tossed it into the boat.
He signaled his two warriors to board.

"They'll get away!" Finn said desperately, looking up to
Cael. "They must be stopped. If these raiders make off with
that armor, one day Ireland will be facing another Daire
Donn!"

"Then, I'll stop them," Cael assured him with bold
determination. And before Finn could restrain him, he rose
and ran toward the water.

By now Finnachta and his men had boarded the craft and
had pushed off. The two warriors were rowing strongly out
toward the anchored dragon boat of the high king. Cael
splashed out into the surf after them, but they were into deep
water before he could reach them. Gamely, the young warrior
cast aside his sword and shield and dove in. Despite his
wounds, he stroked powerfully ahead, quickly closing the gap
with the laden boat.

His foes were only halfway to the dragon boat when he
caught them. He threw an arm up, seizing the low side. His
weight caused the small craft to heel over dangerously.

Finnachta turned and saw the young man's head lifting
above the side as he tried to pull himself up. The boar-faced
warrior seized a spear from one of his men. He stood up over
Cael and, with a cruel smile that revealed the yellow tusks, he
thrust downward.

The point drove deeply into Cael's shoulder, just beside
his neck. He grunted in pain, but did not release his hold.
Instead, he shot one arm forward, catching Finnachta's ankle
in a tight grip, and yanked back.

His foe was jerked off balance. He tried to recover, flailing
wildly, but he failed. He fell forward onto Cael, taking the boat
over with him. It capsized, throwing his warriors—and Donn's
head and body—into the waves.

The two warriors surfaced at once, splashing off toward

the dragon boats without a backward glance. But the remains of Donn, of Finnachta, and of Cael did not reappear.

On the strand, Finn had watched the struggle with a look of great anguish. Now his eyes scanned the surface carefully for some sign of the young warrior. But there was none. Finally, clearly far too weakened to fight off unconsciousness any longer, he fell back, his eyes dropping closed.

"Finn! Finn!" came the insistent voice through the darkness.

Finn opened his eyes. The face of Cuillen was above him.

"Was . . . wasn't this the other way 'round last time?" he said weakly.

"He's alive!" she called to someone, and a leather flask was passed to her. She looked back down to him, smiling in relief. "Thank all the gods," she told him. "I was certain you had finally gotten yourself killed. Here. Drink this."

She slipped an arm behind his head and gently lifted him, holding the flask to his lips. He took a sip, and then a deeper draught. At once color bloomed in his bloodless cheeks. He seemed to gain strength, pushing himself up to a sitting position and looking around. Then he saw that Muirne and Caoilte were standing beside Cuillen.

"Mother!" Finn said with surprise. "What are you doing here?"

"We've come to give the healing waters of the Sidhe to those still alive," she said.

"Aye, Finn," put in a much bloodied but beaming Caoilte. "The battle's ended. We've won, my old lad."

Finn turned his head, sweeping his gaze from the wreckage of small boats along the shore, across the shattered remains of the camp, and to the open beach above. There were bodies everywhere, strewn so thickly that there was not a grain of the white sands to be seen, while blood poured in rust-brown rivers down into the lapping surf. Fian men were putting to the torch the vile remnants of Donn's camp, and already several fires sent thick pillars of gray smoke up to the dark ceiling of an overcast sky. Very few fighting men of Ireland seemed to be standing amidst this awful landscape. Most were helping the healers and other women of the clans search through the tangled piles of bodies for those still alive.

"Only some few hundreds of Donn's great army managed

to escape," Caoilte said, pointing toward the bay. "They'll not be quick to invade Ireland again."

Finn looked to the sea. A mere score of dragon boats out of that vast fleet had lifted sails and were making for the mouth of the bay. He looked back to his comrade.

"What were our own losses?"

"Heavy," Caoilte said bluntly. "Even when they knew they were finished, many of the bloody marauders put up quite a fight. They were as tough a lot of warriors as I've ever met. I'll give that to them. Goll is organizing what's left of our clans, of course. But there's hardly a man of the Fianna left to stand. Still," he added with satisfaction, "we've won, and it was a good fight!"

"A good fight," Finn repeated tonelessly, looking across the thousands of fallen again.

"We'll save many with the healing waters," Muirne said in an encouraging way.

"Many," Finn said grimly, "but not all." This seemed to bring a new thought to him, for he suddenly looked about him more sharply. "Where's Credhe?" he asked. "Is she with you?"

"Yes," Cuillen told him. "She went to look for Cael."

"Then, I've got to find her," Finn said with urgency. "I've got to tell her. Help me up!"

His wound had already knitted itself to the point where he could rise with only a slight grimace of pain. With Cuillen supporting him, he started up the strand. Both searched across the seemingly endless field of bodies and litter for a sign of her. Then Cuillen stopped abruptly, staring up the shore.

"There she is," she said in a stricken way.

"Then, I'm too late," said Finn regretfully.

For the young woman now knelt in the blood-tinged surf. Her slender body was bent forward. Her head rested on the body of Cael, washed back upon the White Strand by the uncaring waves.

Tadg looked up in surprise from his tiny fire. A figure was crossing the floor of his dank and desolate cavern.

His look grew hostile as the figure came close enough to be recognized as that of Bobd Derg. This visitor stopped across the fire from the silver-haired druid and stood eyeing him sternly, silently.

"Well?" Tadg at last demanded in a haughty and defiant tone. "What is it that brings the great high king of the de

Danaans to my wretched hole? And what is this scowl you're fixing upon me?"

"You know well enough, Tadg," the other replied. "It was not difficult for us to discover that it was you who sent Finn on a quest that you felt certain would destroy him; or you who set the vicious wolves of Daire Donn upon him to make his death doubly sure. Those things were reprehensible enough. But to also send your own son to his death to achieve your ends—that is a crime the people of Danu can never forgive!"

"He was a fool to the end," Tadg said callously. "He did not have to die."

"He was a good and caring man," Bobd Derg replied. "Your hatred has taken you too far this time. Though we could condemn you to death, your own actions have helped to fix a punishment much more terrible for you: You will be stripped of the last of your powers. You will be imprisoned forever in this Sid." He gestured around him at the awful place. "And you will be totally alone here now, as well, Tadg," he went on coldly. "For you have yourself destroyed your only company, your son, Labran."

He turned and started away. But Tadg, a look of horror having erased his look of proud disdain, called after him in a wavering, desperate tone:

"Wait! You can't mean it! You can't mean to leave me buried here for eternity!"

Bobd Derg paused to look back. He smiled, but there was no humor in his words.

"Oh, there's no reprieve this time, Tadg. And while you sit here, moldering like the walls of your earthen cell, you will not have even your vengeance to comfort you. You've won nothing with your ruthlessness. Instead of Finn and the Fianna being destroyed, they have taken the name that was on the Army of the Great World. They have taken the ships and the spoils of Donn's host. From this time they will have charge of the whole of Ireland, and they will not lose that power until the time comes for them to fight their final battle. So, good-bye to you forever, Tadg. You'll have nothing but your failure to brood on in your loneliness."

With that he strode away, leaving the tiny, solitary figure nearly lost in the midst of that vast and dreary cave.

CHAPTER THIRTY-TWO

PARTINGS

The huge stone tipped slowly upright and slid down the pile of smaller, rounded stones, its base thudding into the deep hole. At once a team of workers began to tamp earth into the hole around it to fix it firmly in place. Others started to clear away the stone pile.

It was the third and the last such stone to be set standing in that place. The rough-hewn spires formed a triangle, each one a dozen paces from its mates, each one rising to more than twice man-height.

Goll MacMorna supervised the work about the last stone with his usual stolid efficiency. Finn and Caoilte, with the two hounds, stood nearby and watched the procedure with great interest.

"It will be a fine monument," Finn at last pronounced in a satisfied way. He turned slowly to gaze about at the surrounding scenery. "And this is a fitting place to commemorate our battle and bury our dead."

The Fianna truly had chosen an impressive site for their memorial. The three stones had been erected on the flat crest of the hill that overlooked the White Strand. To the east lay the rugged mountains and sweeping valleys of Corca Dhuibhne. To the west lay the curve of the bay and the bright sea beyond.

The workmen were soon finished. Under Goll's orders they packed up their tools and began to depart. The chieftain of the MacMorna clan left them and approached his two comrades.

"Everything is completed, my captain," he briskly reported to Finn. "The last of the Fianna are preparing to start the journeys back to their. homes. By your leave, I'll join my own clan now and see they're made ready to depart."

"Of course, Goll," Finn said. He put out a hand and the two men grasped one another's arms in a gesture of farewell. "It's your name that should be most honored in Ireland for this victory," he added warmly. "For it was you who did more to save us than myself."

"There is no need for praise, my captain," Goll told him, sounding almost perplexed that Finn should say such a thing. "What we did was only our duty to Ireland. Nothing more."

"Of course," Finn said with a hint of a smile. "Well, farewell to you, Goll MacMorna. We will be meeting again at the Festival of Samhain."

"It will be coming soon," Goll said, looking at the sky. "This battle has made the summer fly away. The scent of fall is already in the air. Farewell, my captain. May Danu ride with you."

With that he strode away to where three horses waited. He mounted one, riding off in the direction of the strand.

"We must go too," Finn told Caoilte. "Our own clansmen are anxious to go home. Let's ride to the fortress and I'll make my good-byes to my mother."

"What of Credhe?" the dark warrior asked as they started toward their horses. "Will she be going home with us?"

"She'll be staying here with Muirne for a time. She and my mother have a strange affinity. It's been a great comfort to the girl. When the time comes, my mother said that she would see to Credhe getting home to her own people."

"You know," Caoilte said thoughtfully, "when we get home, I may start looking for a wife myself. It might just be time."

Finn was clearly struck by both the musing tone and the unusual content of his friend's words. He gave Caoilte a most astonished look.

"You? Look for a wife? A woman, who is like a burden on a good warrior's back?"

"Every warrior should have someone to mourn for him," the other replied defensively. "It's not right that any man—or any woman—should be alone."

"Just what was it that happened to you in that Sid of women, Caoilte?" Finn asked with tremendous interest. "It's done something to you."

"Nothing happened," Caoilte said sharply. Then something beyond Finn caught his eye and he stopped, peering toward it. "Say, isn't that the company of Art MacConn?" he said, obviously relieved at being able to change subjects.

Finn turned to look. It was indeed the king's son and his companions riding up from the direction of Nuadat's tower. The bright company of hot-blooded young warriors who had come so arrogantly to the White Strand was much subdued now. Its elegant trappings were worn and stained. Its numbers were greatly reduced. But its survivors now rode with the greater confidence of seasoned fighting men.

They were headed north and east, toward the mountain and its high gap. But as they passed below the hilltop with its monument, one rider broke off, sending its horse galloping up the slope.

"Why, that's Cuillen!" Finn said as the rider drew near enough to be recognized.

His face lit with a warm smile of welcoming, but this faded as he saw the grave expression on her face. She rode up to them and dismounted. Her manner seemed unnaturally hesitant as she approached Finn.

"I . . . I haven't much time," she said, not meeting his eyes. "Conn is returning to Tara, and . . . and I'm going with him."

"Back to Tara?" Finn said in a tone of bewilderment and dismay. "But . . ."

"I have to go, Finn," she said more firmly, this time lifting a determined gaze to his. "But I had to speak to you again before I left."

"I think that I'll just walk over here," said Caoilte uncomfortably, clearly aware that he was unneeded. He walked away toward the far edge of the hill to look out upon the sea.

"Why must you go back to Tara?" Finn asked Cuillen.

"I've no choice," she told him in a decided way. "I'll be having to assume my father's place now. It'll be for me to see to the proper running of our tuath."

"But, I thought we had decided that, once this was ended . . . once you were free . . ."

"I'll never be free," she said, breaking in. She took one of his hands and gripped it tightly, her eyes holding his. "Don't you see that, Finn? I'll never be free and neither will you. It's our own duty, to ourselves and to Ireland, that binds us. There can't be room in our lives for anything else. I knew that when I saw Credhe keening over the body of Cael. I could never give myself that completely to you, and I could never ask you to give yourself to me. It's fate that needs both of us for something else."

He looked into those eyes that searched his own as if imploring him to understand. Finally he nodded.

"Yes," he said in a carefully emotionless way, "I do see. Strange, isn't it, that the same likeness in our spirits that draws us close also makes me understand why we're going to part. Though I could wish for it to be another way, I'll not argue with you." He managed a smile. "I told you, I'd not be doing that again."

She smiled in return, but a sadness shone in her eyes.

"Then, good-bye, Finn MacCumhal," she told him. "And may we meet one day in the Blessed Lands, when our duties in this world are ended and we have only ourselves."

She leaned down, one hand caressing the massive head of each of the hounds who, as usual, closely flanked their master.

"Farewell, my lads," she told them, and they rubbed their noses against her sides in a gesture that bespoke their own regret. "And a good-bye to you as well, Caoilte," she called to the dark warrior. "I give the care of this one into your hands again."

"I will try to do as well as you did," he called in reply, turning toward her.

She looked once more at Finn, and her control seemed to weaken. A look of intense longing filled her eyes. She began to lift a hand toward him. Then, abruptly, she wheeled about and rushed to her horse, mounting it and urging it away, galloping off to join Art's company. She did not look back again.

Finn stood staring after her, seeming for that moment a forlorn figure there on the open hilltop, flanked by his two hounds. Caoilte strode back to join him and stood silently, patiently, beside his friend for a while as the troop of riders dwindled to a formless moving patch of color.

"Come along, Finn," he said finally in a gently prodding voice. "Let's be going home ourselves. There are still some days of summer left to us. We can go hunting."

His comrade's words seemed to break the spell that held Finn. He turned his gaze from the distant company to Caoilte, looking a little surprised at his suggestion.

"Hunting?" he said. "Can't you ever be at rest, Caoilte? Wasn't this long, bloody fight enough even for you?"

"Fighting is what a Fian warrior's whole life is about," the dark warrior answered as he moved to his horse. "He can never have his fill of it."

He climbed onto his horse, but Finn hesitated a moment, looking down toward the golden curve of beach where so many thousands of warriors had met their end.

"Can't he?" the young captain of the Fianna said gravely. "I wonder, Caoilte. When I think of the good fighting men, the good comrades, we lost down there, I have to wonder just what it was all for."

Far below him, the rushing surf was foaming angrily about an object in its way. The waves boiled over the object and then receded, leaving it revealed.

It was the helmeted head of Daire Donn himself that the sea had cast back upon the shore. It sat upright, facing inland. The sun, dropping toward the horizon through a screen of clouds, cast a bright, ruddy swath across the shimmering waves that caused the still-shining helmet to flare with a blood-red light.

And from the holes in its fearsome mask, the iron-black eyes of Daire Donn, their gleam of madness now dulled by a film of sand, stared out on the White Strand.

GLOSSARY

Here are pronunciations of some of the more difficult words:

Aelchinn .... All-kin
Cael .... Kale
Cainnelsciath .... Kon-nel-ska
Cairell .... Kar-ell
Caoilte .... Kweel-ta
Conn Crither .... Konn Kri-her
Credhe .... Krae-a
Cuanna .... Ku-ana
Cuillen .... Kwill-en
Daire Donn .... Dary Don
Finnachta .... Finn-ata
Finn MacCumhal .... Finn Mac-Coo-al
Fionnliath .... Fi-on-lee-a
Gallimh .... Gol-yiv
Ruan O'Cealaigh .... Roan O-Kelly
Sceolan .... Sko-lawn
Sligech .... Slee
Uchtdealb .... Uk-dalv

The following are items about which the reader might appreciate having some further information:

Astray a magical force said to protect the dwelling places of the Others in Ireland. Such a force is still believed by some to exist around ancient stone circles and mounds, and there are modern accounts of those who have experienced its disorienting effects.

Almhuin (All-oon) the name of the home fortress of Finn MacCumhal. Now called the Hill of Allen, it is located near present-day Kildare in County Kildare.

Balor a one-eyed giant who ruled the Fomor, a race of piratical beings. He was destroyed by the champion Lugh Lamfada in the final battle between Fomor and de Danaan forces. Balor's single eye was said to have the power to destroy anything upon which it looked.

the Blessed Lands another name for Tir-na-nog, the mythical Land-of-the-Ever-Young. This island, connected with the origins of the Tuatha de Danaan, is located somewhere in the ocean west of Ireland. Unfortunately, modern tours seldom include a stop there.

Bobd Derg (Bov Derg) Son of the Dagda, a champion of the Tuatha de Danaan, he assumed the high kingship of the de Danaans after the death of Nuada Silver-Hand in the final battle with the Fomor.

Boinn now known as the Boyne River, it is located in County Meath. Along its banks are many sites linked to the Celtic and pre-Celtic eras, including Knowth and Newgrange, giant burial mounds.

brehon another of the distinguished learning classes of Ireland's Celtic society. The brehon was a justice, determining the application of law for the rulers. The vast and complex body of laws developed by them—called Brehon Laws—were in use until fairly recent times. They are much admired by modern scholars for their fairness and thoroughness in covering many types of social relationships.

catha (ka-ta) another name for the battalions that made up the Fianna. Traditionally, there were three cathas of Fian in time of peace, each with three thousand men. In time of war, seven cathas could be hosted from the provinces.

Clan na Baiscne (Bask-na) the clan of Finn MacCumhal, most powerful clan in the province of Munster and one of the most powerful in all Ireland at this time. Clans provided the basis for the structure of Irish political divisions. Each clan was in effect an extended family ruled over by its chieftain and identified by its own colors and symbols (much like the system that exists in Scotland to this day). Tradition holds that each of the Fian clans supplied three times nine soldiers to its battalions.

Clan na Morna the most powerful clan in the province of Connacht and second only to the Baiscne clan in all Ireland. Its most famous chieftain is Goll (meaning "one-eyed") MacMorna.

Cnu Dereoil (Nu Der-ee-oil) a harper of the Tuatha de Danaan who chose to leave his Sid and travel the mortal world, entertaining and enjoying the excitement of mortal life. He befriended a young Finn MacCumhal and helped him in the quest to regain this father's place as captain of the Fians.

Connacht (Kon-akt) the westernmost of the five provinces that comprised ancient Ireland, and home province of the MacMorna clan. Its area encompassed the present-day counties of Mayo, Galway, Sligo, Roscommon, and Leitrim.

Corca Dhuibhne (Corn-a-Gween-eh) this peninsula on the extreme southwest coast of Ireland is now called Dingle. It is near Tralee, and has become a modern tourist attraction for its scenic wonders and its many historic sites dating to both medieval and Celtic times.

curragh (kur-aa) a boat made of bent lath-strips covered by hide. A sturdy type of craft still produced in Ireland. St. Brendan is said to have used one to visit the New World long before Columbus, and a larger version of such a craft crossed the Atlantic in our own time.

Dagda the greatest champion of the Tuatha de Danaan, he became a sort of earth god/father god figure in Celtic mythology. He figures quite prominently in the story relating the de Danaan struggle against the Fomor.

Danu the powerful queen who gave the Sidhe their magical powers. They took the name Tuatha de Danaan (Children of Danu) in respect to her.

Dord Fionn a great horn used by Finn to call the men of the Fianna to a hosting. It is said that Finn and his heroes are not dead but sleeping in a hidden cave, and that one day, when Ireland is in peril, the Dord Fionn will sound three times. Then the Fianna will rise up as strong as they ever were and appear again on the earth.

druid one of the many learned classes of Irish society. Men of great knowledge and some magical powers, they served as religious leaders and as advisers to the rulers. Their power was so great that they were often considered as equals to the kings themselves.

Fianna an army of specially selected and trained warriors whose duty was to carry out the mandates of the high kings of Ireland during the late second century. During the warm half of the year, these warriors lived in the open, hunting when there were no battles to fight. During the winter they were given quarters with the ruling classes of Ireland.

Fomor a race of sea raiders said to have been deformed in various grotesque ways. Their home was in a glass tower on what is now Tory Island, off Ireland's north coast, but they also held sway over Ireland during the time when the Tuatha de Danaan lived upon the surface of the earth. For some years they exacted cruel tribute from the de Danaans, but the young champion Lugh Lamfada led his people in a revolt that eventually destroyed the Fomor power. In much of the Irish mythology, the Fomor are closely identified with a group of raiders called the Lochlanners, who were likely Norse.

Leinster another of the ancient provinces of Ireland, it was located in the southeastern quarter of Ireland.

Lochlanner an Irish name for the sea raiders who often visited Ireland throughout the centuries. The name may have originally applied to the Norse or Viking raiders who were so active throughout northern Europe. In some legends, the Lochlanners are linked to or seen as descendants of the Fomor, a much more ancient race of raiders. The legend of the Battle of the White Strand, from which this novel is derived, may have begun as a real battle between the Fianna and an army of Viking invaders.

Manannan MacLir known in Celtic religion as a powerful god of the sea. He made his home on the present-day Isle of Man, but often visited Ireland to involve himself in the affairs of its inhabitants. His primary function was as a kind of guardian figure to the de Danaans. He was instrumental in helping Lugh Lamfada to free the de Danaans from the Fomor yoke, and later supplied the de Danaans with the magical means to withdraw into their hidden places. Though a being of great power, afforded much reverence in the mythology, his personality seems that of an eccentric, fun-loving man. He often appeared to those of Ireland in disguise, most popularly that of a baggy, awkward clown.

Mogh Nuadat (Ma Nu-a-dat) a legendary ruler of Munster and notable opponent to Conn of the Hundred Battles. After freeing Munster from the cruel subjugation of the warlike Ernann tribe, he warred against and won concessions from the high king of Ireland. Conn was supported in these fights by the loyal Morna clan of the Fianna, led by the stolid Goll MacMorna, but not by Finn MacCumhal and the Baiscne clan.

Morrigan a woman champion of the Tuatha de Danaan, she is closely identified with the Irish raven, into which she can metamorphosize. In Celtic religion she becomes a symbol of death, as does the raven itself, hovering over battlefields, slaking her thirst in the blood of the slain.

Muirne (Mur-na) mother to Finn MacCumhal. Though daughter to Tadg and of the Tuatha de Danaan, her love for Cumhal MacTredhorn, Finn's father, led her to leave her people and marry him. When the treachery of her father and High King Conn caused her husband's death, she saw to it that her newly born son, Finn, was hidden safely away. When he had grown to manhood, she aided him in thwarting the plans of Conn and Tadg and in regaining Cumhal's place as captain of all the Fianna.

Munster another of the ancient provinces of Ireland, it is located in the southwest quarter of the country. It encompassed the present-day county of Kerry and the Dingle Peninsula.

Nuada Silver-Hand high king of the Tuatha de Danaan during their conflict with the Fomor. He lost a hand in an early battle and received a silver one in its place, thus gaining his name. Lugh Lamfada later restored his real hand to him and helped him to lead his people in defeating the Fomor. Nuada died in the final battle. Mythology established that he was the father of Tadg, grandfather to Muirne, and thus linked by blood to Finn.

ollamh (ol-laf) another of the learned classes holding high prestige in the Celtic society. The ollamh was a poet, responsible for learning and passing on the history of his people. He also composed new poems to chronicle events occurring during his time (as in the case of the young ollamh in this story who was researching the facts of the Battle of the White Strand for his own work).

Sid the name given to the hidden, underground dwelling places of the Tuatha de Danaan. Once the rulers of Ireland and living upon its surface, the de Danaans chose to retire to the Sids after their defeat by a race of mortals (called Milesians) who invaded Ireland. Manannan Mac-Lir, a being of great powers who acted as guardian of the de Danaans, created the Sids for them, protecting them from the mortals with magic. He also provided special food and drink that would prolong their lives indefinitely.

Sidhe (Shee) a name for the people who dwell in the Sids, also known as Tuatha de Danaan or the Other. Belief in these supernatural beings was strong in Ireland until quite recent times, the old forts and rings and mounds considered to be the dwellings of the Sidhe and therefore to be respected. Though the power and majesty of the Sidhe had degenerated with the gradual loss of belief in them, some forms of the Sidhe have survived into modern times. The most popularly known of these forms are the leprechaun and the banshee (*ban*, "woman"; *shee*, "sidhe").

Sionnan now known as the Shannon River, the largest river in Ireland. It flows through the heart of Ireland and empties into the Atlantic by the city of Limerick. This has also become a popular name in modern times, for both girls and boys, regardless of national origin.

Tadg (Teag) a powerful member of the Tuatha de Danaan, his own father was Nuada Silver-Hand, high king of the de Danaans during their struggle with the Fomor. With de Danaan permission, he left his people to become chief druid to Conn, the high king of Ireland, and to observe mortal affairs for the enlightenment of his fellows. But he abused his powers, conspiring with Conn to destroy his daughter's mortal husband, Cumhal MacTredhorn. For this he was stripped of much of his powers and banished to a lonely existence.

Tara seat of both sacred and political power in Celtic Ireland, the high kings of Ireland ruled from here until well into the Christian era. Located a short distance to the north and west of Dublin, it is a most scenic spot where the enormous mounds and earthen rings of the fortifications can still be seen. In modern times, of course, the name was repopularized by being given to Scarlett O'Hara's home in *Gone With the Wind*. Subsequently, thousands of small girls were given this name, many by parents who had no idea of its famous origin.

the Thumb of Knowledge a strange, magical feature of Finn MacCumhal. During his quest to gain his father's place, young Finn discovered that he must have the skills of a bard to become a leader of the Fianna. He found an old bard to train him, but only after catching a wondrous Salmon of Knowledge that the man had been seeking for seven years. In cooking the salmon, Finn inadvertently put his thumb into the hot fish. To cool it, he thrust the burned thumb into his mouth. This bestowed the gift of knowledge upon him. From that time out, when he was in desperate straits, he could call upon this knowledge by replacing his thumb in his mouth. Then all information pertaining to his situation would be granted to him.

torc (tork) a neck ornament made of either a tube or twisted strands of gold shaped in a stiff semicircle, with large knobs on the ends. One end was turnable, to allow the wearer to fit it about the neck, and the knobs then hung in the front, at the hollow of the throat. This was a popular form of decoration for the rather foppish Irish warriors. The elaborateness of the torc often indicated the rank of the wearer.

Tuatha de Danaan (Too-a-ha day Don-an) also known as the Sidhe, the Others, or the Men of Dea. This mystical race once held sway over Ireland, but chose to retreat to hidden places beneath its sod rather than battle a host of invading mortals. They afterward took little direct action in the affairs of men, but did continue to watch over them with interest and sometimes help or hinder them.

Ulster the northernmost of the ancient provinces of Ireland. It largely encompassed what is now known as Northern Ireland, and the ancient name is still quite often used when referring to this area. Its present troubles seem to continue a history of turbulence leading back far into the Celtic times.

the White Strand the site of the great battle between the Fianna and the Army of the Great World. This strand lies just to the west of the town of Ventry, on the extreme tip of the Dingle Peninsula. It is a quite scenic area, visited by many tourists. Above the harbor and strand is a hilltop on which Finn is said to have erected standing stones as a monument to the battle. These massive stones can still be seen there today, and one of them has remained standing.

ABOUT THE AUTHOR

KENNETH C. FLINT became interested in Celtic mythology in graduate school, where he saw a great source of material in this long neglected area of western literature. Since then he has spent much time researching (in the library and abroad in England and Ireland) those legends and incorporating them into works of fantasy that would interest modern readers. His novels to date include *A Storm Upon Ulster, Riders of the Sidhe, Champions of The Sidhe, Master of the Sidhe,* and *Challenge of the Clans.*

Mr. Flint is a graduate of the University of Nebraska with a Masters Degree in English Literature. For several years he taught in the Department of Humanities at the University of Nebraska at Omaha. Presently he is Chairman of English for the Plattsmouth Community Schools (a system in a suburban community of Omaha). In addition to teaching, he has worked as a freelance writer, producing articles, short stories, and screenplays for some Omaha-based film companies.

He currently lives in Omaha with his wife Judy (whose family has roots in Ireland) and his sons Devin and Gavin, and he is hard at work on his next novel.